The

BLUE MOON
EROTIC READER

The
BLUE MOON
EROTIC READER

Edited by

BARNEY ROSSET

BLUE MOON BOOKS
NEW YORK

Published by
Blue Moon Books
841 Broadway, Fourth Floor
New York, NY 10003

ISBN 1-56201-119-7

Library of Congress Catalog Card Number: 99–075439

Manufactured in the United States of America

The publisher would like to thank Richard Manton, who shepherded this project through its earliest stages, for his generous assistance and unfailing support.

CONTENTS

Foreword	ix
My Secret Life *by Walter*	1
Eveline *by Anonymous*	20
A Man with a Maid *by Anonymous*	24
"Frank" and I *by Anonymous*	99
Sadopaideia *by Anonymous*	103
Voluptuous Confessions from	
The Boudoir *by Anonymous*	112
Suburban Souls *by Anonymous*	172
Miss High Heels *by Anonymous*	191
Secret Talents *by Anonymous*	246
Gynecocracy *by Viscount Ladywood*	254
Beatrice *by Patrick Hendon*	262
Shades of Singapore *by Angus Balfour*	268
The Captive *by Anonymous*	275
The Prussian Girls *by P. N. Dedaux*	303
Spring Fevers *by Martin Pyx*	315
The Days at Florville *by Richard Manton*	334

Chrysanthemum, Rose, and the Samurai *by Akahige*
   Namban   346
Eros: the Meaning of My Life *by Edith Cadivec*   355
Our Scene *by Wilma Kauffen*   369
Ironwood *by Don Winslow*   376
The Correct Sadist *by Terence Sellers*   391
An Excess of Love *by Jac Lenders*   405
Adagio *by Daniel Vian*   423
Shadow Lane *by Eve Howard*   436
Sundancer *by Briony Shelton*   450
What Love *by Maria Madison*   461

FOREWORD

It is high time that Blue Moon Books produced this anthology.

Founded in 1987 by Barney Rosset, Blue Moon Books is an erotic press with more than 150 titles to its credit. Many of these works comprise the backbone of contemporary erotica. Rosset has also kept in print an extraordinary collection of Victorian erotica, including *My Secret Life*, *The Romance of Lust*, *Suburban Souls*, *The Boudoir*, and *A Man with a Maid*, all excerpted here. Those readers new to Victoriana are in for a treat, as these novels and memoirs record an extraordinary variety of sexual behavior. These works are frank and rich catalogues of the many ways in which humanity has taken its pleasure. Thanks to the Victorian era's reverence for attentive detail, these texts are also still surprisingly fresh records of the emotional vagaries of love, as each seduction, no matter how insignificant, is painstakingly recorded for posterity.

If Rosset founded Blue Moon upon the bedrock of Victoriana, he hardly stopped there. He has published many works by authors writing in the classical tradition of Victorian and Edwardian erotica, like Richard Manton and P. N. Dedaux, whose work is represented in this volume. Both writers favor dense, sophisticated narratives that explore male sadism, particularly as directed against deserving, "uppity" women, with the enthusiasm of Sade himself. Too often taboo in these politically correct times, the fantasies these novels record may well prove liberating in our "safe, sane, and consensual" age, when our most forbidden desires are regulated; in this case, by language.

The American publisher of *Story of O*, Rosset has also promoted the work of a number of women, including "uppity" ones. He has encouraged female sadists like Terence Sellers, whose treatise *The Correct Sadist* established her as one of the most important S&M theorists of the past two decades. He also unearthed and commissioned a translation of Edith Cadivec's *Eros, the Meaning of My Life*, an early apologia for corporal punishment by a Viennese schoolteacher who was imprisoned for her beliefs in the 1920s. Documents by women dating to this period are rare, making *Eros* an extremely significant find.

Rosset has almost single-handedly helped foster a space where a self-determined female masochism has been articulated and theorized. Perhaps most remarkable are Maria Madison, a fine novelist who explores masochism from a feminist perspective, and Eve Howard, a spanking aficionado whose Shadow Lane series chronicles a group of characters as they enjoy this practice without reservation.

Those readers interested in the fiction of male masochism have not been neglected, either, for Rosset has published work depicting these fantasies as well. Examples excerpted in this volume include cross-dressing classics like *Miss High Heels* and *Gynecocracy*, as well as Jac Lenders' remarkable contemporary novel, *An Excess of Love*.

A testimonial to to the publication of quality erotica, *The Blue Moon Reader* presents more than twenty-five romantic and exciting excerpts. These selections vary by period and theme. Good taste—and passion—are the watchwords here, making for a union of sex and sensibility available, one might say, only once in a Blue Moon.

—Marti Hohmann

My Secret Life
by Walter

This chronicle of a Victorian gentleman's sexual adventures, first published in the last decade of the nineteenth century, is remarkable for its candor. Begun in the 1840s, when the author was about twenty-five years old, it is his attempt at a faithful record of his entire sexual history. The first excerpt included here relates young Walter's sexual initiation with Charlotte, a domestic in his household; the second his voyeuristic pleasure at, and remarkably nonjudgmental attitude towards, the spectacle of two women making love.

1.

She was a little over eighteen years old, had ruddy lips, beautiful teeth, darkish hair, hazel eyes, and a slightly turned-up nose, large shoulders and breasts, was plump, generally of fair height, and looked at least nineteen; her name was Charlotte.

I soon spoke to her kindly, by degrees became free in manner, at length chucked her under her chin, pinched her arm, and used the familiarities that nature teaches a man to use towards a woman. It was her business to open the door, and help me off with my coat and boots if needful; one day as she did so, her bum projecting upset me so that as she rose from stooping I caught and pinched her. All this was done with risk, for my mother then was nearly always at home, and the house being small, a noise was easily heard.

I was soon kissing her constantly. In a few days I got a kiss in return, that drove me wild, her cunt came constantly into my mind, all sorts of wants, notions, and vague possibilities came across me; girls do let fellows feel them, I said to myself, I had already succeeded in that. What if I tell that I have seen it outside? Will she tell my mother? Will she let me feel her? What madness! Yet girls do let men, girls like it, so all my friends say. Wild with hopes and anticipations, coming indoors one day, I caught her tightly in my arms, pulled her belly close to mine, rubbed up against her, saying, "Charlotte, what would I give, if you would . . ." It was all I dared to say. Then I heard my mother's bedroom door open, and I stopped.

Hugging and kissing a woman never stopped there; I told her I loved her, which she said was nonsense. We now used regularly to kiss each other when we got the chance; little by little I grasped her closer to me, put my hands round her waist, then cunningly came round to her bum, then my prick used to stand and I was mad to say more to her, but had not the courage. I knew not how to set to work, indeed scarce knew what my desires led me to hope, and think at that time, putting my hand onto her cunt, and seeing it, was perhaps the utmost; fucking her seemed a hopelessly mad idea, if I had the expectation of doing so at all very clearly.

I told a friend one or two years older than myself how matters stood, carefully avoiding telling him who the girl was. His advice was short. Tell her you have seen her cunt, and make a snatch up her petticoats when no one is near; keep at it, and you will be sure to get a feel, and some day, pull out your prick, say straight you want to fuck her, girls like to see a prick, she will look, even if she turns her head away. This advice he dinned into my ears continually, but for a long time I was not bold enough to put his advice into practice.

One day, my mother was out, the cook upstairs dressing, we

had kissed in the garden parlor, I put my hand round her bum, and sliding my face over her shoulder half-ashamed, said, "I wish my prick was against your naked belly, instead of outside your clothes." She, with an effort, disengaged herself, stood amazed, and said, "I never will speak to you again."

I had committed myself, but went on, though in fear, prompted by love or lust. My friend's advice was in my ears. "I saw your cunt as you got down from your father's cart," said I. "Look at my prick"—pulling it out—"how stiff it is, it's longing to go into you, 'cock and cunt will come together.' " It was part of a smutty chorus the fellows sang at my college. She stared, turned round, went out of the room, through the garden, and down to the kitchen by the garden stairs, without uttering a word.

The cook was at the top of the house. I went into the kitchen, reckless, and repeated all I had said. She threatened to call the cook. "She must have seen your cunt, as well as me," said I; then she began to cry. Just as I was begging pardon, my friend's advice again rang in my ears, I stooped and swiftly ran both hands up her clothes, got one full on to her bum, the other on her motte; she gave a loud scream, and I dashed off upstairs in a fright.

The cook did not hear her, being up three flights of stairs; down I went again, and found Charlotte crying; I told her again all I had seen in the courtyard, which made her cry more. She would ask the cook, and would tell my mother; then hearing the cook coming downstairs, I cut off through the passage up into the garden.

The ice was quite broken now, she could not avoid me. I promised not to repeat what I had said and done, was forgiven, we kissed, and the same day I broke my promise. This went on day after day, making promises and breaking them, talking smuttily as well as I knew how, getting a slap on my head, but no further, my chances were few. My friend, whom I made a confidant of, was always taunting me with my want of success and boasting of what he would have done had he had my opportunities.

My mother just at that time began to resume her former habits, leaving the house frequently for walks and visits. One afternoon, she being out for the remainder of the day, I went home unexpectedly; the cook was going out, I was to fetch my mother home in the evening; Charlotte laid the dinner for me; we had the usual kissing, I was unusually bold and smutty. Charlotte, finding me not to be going out, seemed anxious. All the dinner things had been taken away, when out went the cook, and there were Charlotte, my little brother, and I, alone. It was her business to sit with him in the garden parlor when mother was out, so as to be able to open the street-door readily, as well as go into the garden if the weather was fine. It was a fine day of autumn, she went into the parlor and was sitting on the huge old sofa, Tom playing on the floor, when I sat myself down by her side; we kissed and toyed, and then with heart beating, I began my talk and waited my opportunity.

The cook would be back in a few minutes, said she. I knew better, having heard mother tell cook she need not be home until eight o'clock. Although I knew this, I was fearful, but at length mustered courage to sing my cock-and-cunt song. She was angry, but it was made up. She went on to give something to Tom, and stepping back, put her foot on the lace of one boot, which was loose, sat down on the sofa and put up one leg over the other, to re-lace it. I undertook to do it for her, saw her neat ankle, and a bit of a white stocking. "Snatch at her cunt," rang in my ears. I had never attempted it since the afternoon in the kitchen.

Lacing the boot, I managed to push up the clothes so as to see more of the leg. Resting as the foot did on one knee, the clothes tightly between, a snatch was useless, but lust made me cunning. I praised the foot (though I knew not at that time how vain some women are of their feet). "What a nice ankle," I said, putting my hand further on. She was off her guard; with my left arm, I pushed her violently back onto the large sofa; her foot came off her knee, at the same moment, my right hand went up between her thighs, on to her cunt; I felt the slit, the hair, and moisture.

She got up to a sitting posture, crying, "You wretch, you beast, you blackguard," but still I kept my fingers on the cunt; she closed her legs so as to shut my hand between her thighs and keep it motionless, and tried to push me off, but I clung round her. "Take your hand away," said she, "or I will scream." "I shan't!" I cried. Then followed two or three very loud screams. "No one can hear," said I, which brought her to supplication. My friend's advice came again to me: pushing my right hand still between her thighs, with my left hand I pulled out my prick, as stiff as a poker. She could not do otherwise than see it; and then I drew my left hand round her neck, pulled her head to me, and covered it with kisses.

She tried to get up and nearly dislodged my right hand, but I pushed her back and got my hand still further onto the cunt. I never thought of pressing under towards the bum, was in fact too ignorant of female anatomy to do it, but managed to get one of the lips with the hair between my fingers and pinch it; then dropped on to my knees in front of her and remained kneeling, preventing her getting back further on the sofa, as well as I could by holding her waist, or her clothes.

There was a pause from our struggles, then more entreaties, then more attempts to get my right hand away; suddenly she put out one hand, seized me by the hair of my head, and pushed me backwards by it. I thought my skull was coming off, but kept my hold and pinched or pulled the cunt lip till she screamed and called me a brute. I told her I would hurt her as much as I could, if she hurt me; so that game she gave up; the pain of pulling my hair made me savage, and more determined and brutal, than before.

We went on struggling at intervals, I kneeling with prick out, she crying, begging me to desist; I entreating her to let me see and feel her cunt, using all the persuasion and all the bawdy talk I could, little Tom sitting on the floor playing contentedly. I must have been half an hour on my knees, which became so painful that I could scarcely bear it; we were both panting, I was sweating. An experienced man would perhaps have had her then, but I was a boy inexperienced, and without her consent almost in words would not have thought of attempting it; the novelty, the voluptuousness of my game was perhaps sufficient delight to me. At last I became conscious that my fingers on her cunt were getting wet; telling her so, she became furious and burst into such a flood of tears that it alarmed me. It was impossible to remain on my knees longer; in rising, I knew I should be obliged to take my hand from her cunt, so withdrawing my left hand from her waist, I put it also suddenly up her clothes, and round her bum, and lifted them up, showing both her thighs, whilst I attempted to rise. She got up at the same instant, pushing down her clothes, I fell over on one side—my knees were so stiff and painful—and she rushed out of the room upstairs.

It was getting dusk; I sat on the sofa in a state of pleasure, smelling my fingers. Tom began to howl; she came down and took him up to pacify him. I followed her down to the kitchen; she called me an insolent boy (an awful taunt to me then); threatened to tell my mother, to give notice and leave; and left the kitchen, followed by me about the house; talking bawdily, telling her how I liked the smell of my fingers, attempting to put my hand up her clothes, sometimes succeeding, pulling out my ballocks, and never ceasing till the cook came home, having been at this game for hours. In a sudden funk, I begged Charlotte to tell my mother that I had only come home just before the cook, and had gone to bed unwell; she replying that she would tell my mother the truth, and nothing else. I was in my bedroom before cook was let in.

Mother came home later; I was in a fright, having lain in bed cooling down and thinking of possible consequences; heard the street-door knocker; got out of bed; and in my nightshirt went halfway downstairs listening. To my relief, I heard Charlotte, in answer to my mother's inquiry, say that I had come home about an hour before and had gone to bed unwell. My mother came to my room, saying how sorry she was.

For a few days I was in fear, but it gradually wore off, as I found she had not told; our kissing recommenced, my boldness increased, my talk ran now freely on her legs, her bum, and her cunt, she ceased to notice it, beyond saying she hated such talk, and at length she smiled spite of herself. Our kissing grew more fervid, she resisted improper action of my hand, but we used to stand with our lips close together for minutes at a time when we got the chance, I holding her to me as close as wax. One day cook was upstairs, mother in her bedroom, I pushed Charlotte up against the wall in the kitchen, and pulled up her clothes, scarcely with resistance; just then my mother rang, I skipped up into the garden and got into the parlor that way, soon heard my mother calling to me to fetch water, Charlotte was in hysterics at the foot of the stairs—after that, she frequently had hysterics, till a certain event occurred.

My chances were chiefly on Saturdays, a day I did not go to college; soon I was going to cease going there and was to prepare for the army.

I came home one day, when I knew Charlotte would be alone—the cook was upstairs—I got her onto the sofa in the garden parlor, knelt and put my hands between her thighs, with less resistance than before, she struggled slightly, but made no noise. She kissed me as she asked me to take away my hand; I could move it more easily on her quim, which I did not fail to do; she was wonderfully quiet. Suddenly I became conscious that she was looking me full in the face, with a peculiar expression, her eyes very wide open, then shutting them. "Oho—oho," she said with a prolonged sigh. "Do—oh, take away—oh—your hand, Walter dear—oh, I shall be ill—oho—oho." Then her head dropped down over my shoulder as I knelt in front of her; at the same moment, her thighs seemed to open slightly, then shut, then open with a quivering, shuddering motion, as it then seemed to me, and then she was quite quiet.

I pushed my hand further in, or rather on, for although I thought I had it up the cunt, I really was only between the lips—I know that now. With a sudden start, she rose, pushed me off, snatched up Tom from the floor, and rushed upstairs. My fingers were quite wet. For two or three days afterwards, she avoided my eyes and looked bashful, I could not make it out, and it was only months afterwards that I knew that the movements of my fingers on her clitoris had made her spend. Without knowing indeed that such a thing was possible, I had frigged her.

Although for about three months I had thus been deliciously amusing myself, anxious to feel and see her cunt, and though I had at last asked her to let me fuck her, I really don't think I had any definite expectation of doing it to her. I guessed now at its mutual pleasures, and so forth, yet my doing it to her appeared beyond me; but urged on by my love for the girl—for I did love her—as well as by sexual instinct, I determined to try. I also was quickened by my college friend, who had seen Charlotte at our house and now knowing it was the girl I had spoken to him about, said to me, "What a nice girl that maid of yours is, I mean to get over her, I shall wait for her after church next Sunday, she sits in your pew, I know." I asked him some questions—his opinion was that most girls would let a young fellow fuck them, if pressed, and that she would (this youth was but about eighteen years old), and I left him fearing what he said was true, hating and jealous of him to excess. He set me thinking why should not I do it if he could, and if what he said about girls was true? So I determined to try it on, and by luck did so earlier than I expected.

About one hour's walk from us was the town house of an aunt, the richest of our family and one of my mother's sisters. She alone now supplied me with what money I had; my mother gave me next to nothing. I went to see my aunt, who asked me to tell my mother to go and spend a day with her the next week, and named the day. I forgot this until three days afterwards, when hearing my mother tell the cook she could go out for a whole holiday; I said that my aunt particularly wished to see mother on that day. My mother scolded me for not having told her sooner, but wrote and arranged to go, forgetting the cook's holiday. To my intense joy, on that day she took brother Tom with her, saying to Charlotte, "You will have nothing to think of, but the house, shut it up early, and do not be frightened." I was as usual to fetch my mother home.

In what an agitated state I passed that morning at school, and in the afternoon went home, trembling at my own intentions. Charlotte's eyes opened with astonishment at seeing me. Was I not going to fetch my mother? I was not going till night. There was no food in the house, and I had better go to my aunt's for dinner. I knew there was cold meat, and made her lay the cloth in the kitchen. To make sure, I asked if the cook was out—yes, she was, but would be home soon. I knew that she stopped out till ten o'clock on her holidays. The girl was agitated with some undefined idea of what might take place;

we kissed and hugged, but she did like even that, I saw.

I restrained myself whilst eating, she sat quietly besides me; when I had finished, she began to remove the things. The food gave me courage, her moving about stimulated me, I began to feel her breasts, then got my hands on to her thighs, we had the usual struggles, but it seems to me as I now think of it that her resistance was less and that she prayed me to desist more lovingly than was usual. We had toyed for an hour, she had let a dish fall and smashed it, the baker rang, and she took in the bread, and declared she would not shut the door unless I promised to leave off. I promised, and as soon as she had closed it, pulled her into the garden parlor, having been thinking when in the kitchen how I could get her upstairs. Down tumbled the bread on the floor; on the sofa, I pushed her, and after a struggle she was sitting down, I kissing her, one arm round her waist, one hand between her thighs, close up to her cunt. Then I told her I wanted to fuck her, said all in favor of it I knew, half-ashamed, half-frightened, as I said it. She said she did not know what I meant, resisted less and less as I tried to pull her back on the sofa, when another ring came: It was the milkman.

I was obliged to let her go, and she ran downstairs with the milk. I followed, she went out, and slammed the door, which led to the garden, in my face; for the instant, I thought she was going to the privy, but opened and followed on; she ran up the steps, into the garden, through the garden parlor, and upstairs to her bedroom just opposite to mine, closed and locked the door in my face, I begged her to let me in.

She said she would not come out till she heard the knocker or bell ring; there was no one called usually after the milkman, so my game was up, but nothing makes man or woman so crafty as lust. In half an hour or so, in anger, I said I should go to my aunt's, went downstairs, moved noisily about, opened and slammed the street-door violently, as if I had gone out, then pulled off my boots, and crept quietly up to my bedroom.

There I sat expectantly a long time, had almost given up hope, began to think about the consequences if she told my mother, when I heard the door softly open and she came to the edge of the stairs. "Wattie!" she said loudly. "Wattie!" Then much louder, "He has . . ." said she in a subdued tone to herself, as much as to say that her worries were over. I opened my door, she gave a loud shriek and retreated to her room, I close to her; in a few minutes more, hugging, kissing, begging, threatening, I know not how; she was partly on the bed, her clothes in a heap, I on her with my prick in my hand. I saw the hair, I felt the slit, and not knowing then where the hole was or much about it, excepting that it was between her legs, shoved my prick there with all my might. "Oh! You hurt, I shall be ill," said she, "pray don't." Had she said she was dying I should not have stopped. The next instant a delirium of the senses came, my prick throbbing as if hot lead was jetting from it at each throb; pleasure mingled with light pain in it, and my whole frame quivering with emotion; my sperm left me for a virgin cunt, but fell outside it, though onto it.

How long I was quiet I don't know; probably but a short time; for a first pleasure does not tranquilize at that age; I became conscious that she was pushing me off of her, and rose up, she with me, to a half-sitting posture; she began to laugh, then to cry, and fell back in hysterics, as I had seen her before.

I had seen my mother attend to her in those fits, but little did I then know that sexual excitement causes them in women and that probably in her I had been the cause. I got brandy and water and made her drink a lot, helping myself at the same time, for I was frightened, and made her lay on the bed. Then, ill as she was, frightened as I was, I yet took the opportunity her partial insensibility gave me, lifted her clothes quietly, and saw her cunt and my spunk on it. Roused by that, she pushed her clothes half down feebly and got to the side of the bed. I loving, begging pardon, kissing her, told her of my pleasure, and asked about hers, all in snatches, for I thought I had done her. Not a word could I get, but she looked me in the face beseechingly, begging me to go. I had no such intention, my prick was again stiffening, I pulled it out, the sight of her cunt had stimulated me, she looked with languid eyes at me, her cap was off, her hair hanging about her head, her dress torn near her breast. More so than she had ever looked was she beautiful to me, success made me bold, on I went insisting, she seemed too weak to withstand me. "Don't, oh pray, don't," was all she said as, pushing her well on the bed, I threw myself on her and again put my doodle onto the slit now wet with my sperm. I was, though cooler, stiff as a poker, but my sperm was not so ready to flow, as it was in after days, at a second poke, for I was very young; but nature did all for me; my prick went to the proper channel, there stopped by something it battered furiously. "Oh, you hurt, oh!" she cried aloud. The next instant something seemed to tighten round its knob, another furious thrust—another—a sharp cry of pain (resistance was gone), and my prick was buried up her, I felt that it was done, and that before I had spent outside her. I looked at her, she was quiet, her cunt seemed to close on my prick, I put my hand down, and felt round. What rapture to find my machine buried! Nothing but the balls to be touched, and her cunt hair wetted with my sperm, mingling and clinging to mine; in another minute, nature urged a crisis, and I spent in a virgin cunt, my prick virgin also. Thus ended my first fuck.

My prick was still up her when we heard a loud knock; both started up in terror, I was speechless. "My God, it is your mamma!" Another loud knock. What a relief, it was the postman. To rush downstairs and open the door was the work of a minute. "I thought you were all out," said he angrily. "I have knocked three times." I said, "We were in the garden." He looked queerly at me and said, "With your boots off?" and went grinning away. I went up again, found her sitting on the side of the bed, and there we sat together. I told her what the post-man had said; she was sure he would tell her mistress. For a short time, there never was a couple who had just fucked in more of a foolish funk than we were; I have often thought of our not hearing the thundering knocks of a postman whilst we were fucking, though the bedroom door was wide open; what engrossing work it is so to deafen people. Then after unsuc-cessfully struggling to see her cunt, and kissing, and feeling each other's genitals, and talking of our doings and our sen-sations for an hour, we fucked again.

It was getting dark, which brought us to reason. We both helped remake the bed, went downstairs, shut the shutters, lighted the fire, which was out, and got lights. I then, having nothing to do, began thinking of my doodle, which was sticking to my shirt, and pulling it out to see its condition, found my shirt covered with sperm smears, and spots of blood; my prick was dreadfully sore. I said to her that she had been bleeding, she begged me to go out of the kitchen for a minute; I did, and almost directly she came out and passed me, saying she must change her things before the cook came home. She would not let me stay in the room whilst she did it, nor did I see her chemise, though I had followed her upstairs; then the idea flashed across me that I had taken a virginity; that had never occurred to me before. She got hot water to wash herself. I did not know what to do with my shirt; we arranged I should wash it before I went to bed. We thought it best to say I had not been home at all, and that I should go and fetch my mother. After much kissing, hugging, and tears on her part, off I went, hatching an excuse for not having fetched my mother earlier, and we came home with Tom in my aunt's carriage, I recollect.

2.

Sarah, whom I am sure had then lost her man, and was more and more impecunious, used to come home early, often ill-tempered and low-spirited. Unasked, she then would get into bed with us. She was kind—to an extraordinary degree—to Lizzie, would kiss her when lying by her side. Sarah's fingers were always on the little one's cunt. She laughed when I found them there, and then used to push her hand over Lizzie and catch hold of me. Sometimes Sarah used to feel Lizzie whilst I was fucking her, and frig herself at the same time. She made no secret about it now. "I must do something. I don't often spend with a man, and I like frigging while you are doing Liz."

Previously I had somehow formed the opinion that Sarah liked feeling the cunts of young ones, but thought nothing much about it. One day she was slightly tipsy, and got into bed just as I got out to piddle, then pulling every thing up and showing all her parts, she said, "I'm getting stout, Doctor, aren't I?" I felt her bum and belly and just opened her cunt lips. "I want a fuck, so give me one."

"I'll try after I have had Liz again." Sarah turned 'round and, clutching Liz, lifted her on her belly, began to kiss her passionately, twisted her limbs over her, and wriggling her belly up to her so that their cunts were close together, moved as if fucking. Liz tried to get away. "Don't, now, don't," she said. After a few heaves Sarah let her go, laughing, and then turned her rump towards us and frigged herself.

I thought of this a good deal, and it increased my desire for knowledge. This form of sexual voluptuousness amongst women now haunted me. I questioned Liz about Sarah's behavior in bed with her, for she always now slept with her, and no man was ever there. It was not as formerly when Sarah said, "You mustn't come for three days," and so on. I found that

Sarah had a letch for frigging herself, and that her taste for the man was perhaps diminishing. She had done this almost from the first day Liz came to London. Then I guessed that Sarah did something more. I asked questions and threatened not to see Liz any more if she did not tell me the truth. She disclosed that Sarah pulled the girl on the top of her, and pressing clitoris to clitoris, rubbed them together, till Sarah at least had the full enjoyment of that voluptuous friction. It was flat fucking, tribadism, the amusement of girls at boarding schools and convents, and perhaps harems (and often, as I know since, of some harlots).

"Don't tell her," said Liz. "She has made me promise not, and says you'd hate me if you knew of it—you won't hate me will you? I don't like her thinging me—I don't like her wet thing in mine."

"Is it not nice?"

"It be a little nice sometimes, but I don't like thinging like that." I promised to keep Lizzie's secret.

"You call it 'thinging.' Why?"

"Because her thing be 'gainst my thing," said the girl laughing. "It be like two snails." I roared with laughter at such an illustrative remark, and never heard flat fucking called "thinging" before or since. (I have since heard a funny term for it, though.)

Then I began to think about flat fucking, and recollected what in my youth Fred had said, and what I had been told by Camille of women rubbing their cunts together, and that I had seen two French women doing it (for my amusement, as I thought, and simply to show me how by placing themselves like a man and woman in copulation, they could close their cunts on each other). One woman I recollected had a strongly developed clitoris, and I had not liked it. But I did not believe in women having pleasure that way, and the bawdy sight had passed from my mind. Nor had any clear idea of the truth even arisen in my mind, when I saw two servants on each other in the bathroom at my cousin's school, or Gabrielle on Violette.

I had heard since of women flat fucking, and suddenly recollected a row at a brothel, in which the amusement had been referred to.

When I spent my first fortune, I took after a longish period of continence to visiting harlots who let me have them for five shillings, and would let a man do almost anything. One night I went to see a woman and arrived just as she was having a row with a woman who was about forty-five years old. My girl came into the room with me, but was unable to contain herself and left me. I opened the door and heard her and another lodger bullying the woman for getting quite a young girl into her bed. "You old cat, you dirty, slimy-cunted old bitch—I'll tell them all." She came back into the room with me and slammed the door. She was slightly screwed and noisy. "The old bitch gets Mary into bed with her. It's the little servant here—and pulls her about—Polly caught her at it, and the girl said she did."

"Why does the girl let her?"

"Oh, she's a dirty little bitch, too."

"Well, I pull you about and you me."

"Oh, that is quite different." Perhaps the woman was jealous, or was it whores' morality? I told her I saw no harm in two women doing what they liked to do.

I had never given the subject much thought, but now began to think of the ways women could bring their organs together for mutual pleasure, and of various tricks that way which I had seen women perform, but the subject never interested me fully till now. Then I got some medical books and some French books, and under "Lesbos," "tribade," etc. and some other words, got the key to the full mysteries of Sappho and the Lesbians, which added a mite more to my knowledge and admiration of the wonders of the article called cunt.

I kept my promise of secrecy, but often looked at Sarah and longed to question her on this subject. I began to talk about quim-to-quim friction—flat fucking—and explained the word "tribadism," a word Sarah had never heard—I let her know that I thought there was no harm in women rubbing their cunts together, or gamahuching each other; and Sarah at once, I thought, got more free in her manifestations towards the girl.

Sarah was much more often drunk now than previously, just as if she were in trouble. One night she came in when we were in bed, for she did not now always stop in for me, and lay down beside us. "Get on the top of her Liz," said I, just to see how far I could go in that direction. "I like to see you on top of her like a man fucking her."

Liz refused. Sarah gave her a kiss and laughed, put one leg out and her arms 'round her, and rolling on to her back, pulled Liz right on to the top of her, kissing all the time.

"She looks as if she were fucking you," said I. "Put your cunts together, pull off your chemises, let's see you both naked." I assisted in pulling them off. Liz resisted slightly. But Sarah heaved up her thighs 'round the girl and grasped her little arse. "Be quiet Liz," said I, "and do it with her."

Sarah suddenly seemed quite excited, her eyes looked wild with lust, she held tight on to the girl—heaved up her legs, and put her heels 'round Lizzie's calves. I threw myself on the bed.

Widening open Lizzie's thighs a little, I could see Sarah's black-haired cunt below, meeting the mossy cunt of the damsel. I put my fingers there; begged Lizzie, who was restive, to be quiet; incited Sarah to get her cunt as close to the girl's as she could; and they were soon so close that I got two fingers up Sarah's cunt, and the thumb of the same hand, and with difficulty, touched Lizzie's.

Then bawdiness reigned supreme. I was delighted. "Rub your cunts together," said I after a minute's fingering.

"We can't."

"Try. Rub your cunts together and I will give you a sovereign."

"What do you mean?" She was still holding the girl in her arms.

"Oh! How modest. You know all—did you never have pleasure with a woman by flat fucking her? Rub away at Liz, hold her quite tight—squeeze your quim up to hers, teach her, she'd like to know everything, and a man can't teach her that," said I, now wild with lust.

Sarah kissed Lizzie without ceasing—it was one long unbroken sound of osculation—and began heaving her buttocks and wriggling, but I saw she was shamming. "I am not going to give you a sovereign to be humbugged," said I and, putting my hand down between both their thighs, I pushed two of my fingers into Sarah's cunt again.

My fingers seemed to stir Sarah's lewdness. Wriggling and kissing Lizzie passionately, she said, "Never mind him, let me darling—do." The girl, told by me to let Sarah do what she liked, lay quiet. The little one's legs were held by Sarah's big legs, and she wriggled and fucked while I kept my fingers at work in her cunt as well as I could. There lay the big woman clinging to Liz, twisting and writhing, wriggling and sighing, kissing the girl with passion, thrusting out her tongue, and almost burying her fingers between the girl's buttocks. It was a very long embrace, and neither of them took heed of me now. Liz was obedient, and Sarah's eyes were closed except at intervals. Instinctively, at last, Lizzie grasped Sarah's haunches. With a sigh, Sarah said, "Oh—do it—darling—ah—ah—aha." Sarah relaxed her hold and was quiet. I knew well from the look of her face, from that changing of color when she spent, that she had spent now.

The lasciviousness of the scene, the intense enjoyment of Sarah, urged me on: I now lusted for Sarah. "Get off, Liz—is your cunt wet? Is Sarah's wet? I'll fuck you, Sally."

Sarah opened her eyes and looked at me, remarking, "That bugger knows everything." Then, lifting her thighs, she again began squeezing Lizzie and rubbing against her. "I'll fuck you, Sally." She took no notice, but writhed as hard as she could, embracing the girl. "I've only begun," said she. "She's a darling."

Randy to madness I pulled Lizzie off, and the next instant was up Sarah's cunt. Lizzie laid by the side—my fingers went into her little cunt, feeling, groping the little moist slippery article, until I emitted what sperm was left in me up Sarah's vagina. Then Sarah, with my libation in her, clutched Liz like a fury, and got her between her thighs. In vain she struggled; the big woman held her fast, their cunts met, and Sarah had her Sapphic delight, screeching out, so that the lodgers below would have heard enough had they been listening. But Sarah in her maddening pleasure forgot all about them then.

After that night, I talked with Sarah about her liking for the girl, and about flat fucking. Sarah avoided the subject, said she had only done it for a lark and had not wanted anything of the sort, preferred a prick to any other kind of solace for her cunt. On other occasions, I told Sarah all I had read and knew—that I thought no worse of a woman for having a woman than I did of a man for frigging a man. "Your cunt's your own, and if two cunts agree to frictionize each other, it is a perfectly legitimate pleasure." Little by little she admitted much—but considering that I had spent in and on her in every way possible for nearly four years, I had difficulty in getting her to admit her liking for flat fucking Liz. She never did quite admit it. She had done it once or twice she said, when drunk, but had no taste for it. She liked a good, thick, stiff prick up her.

EVELINE

by Anonymous

First published in four volumes in 1904, Eveline *is a prostitute's fictional autobiography in the tradition of* Fanny Hill
and Moll Flanders. *Almost picaresque in its relation of her
sexual adventures, the novel is democratic in its representation of sexual experience, its players ranging from the most-
to least-privileged members of Edwardian society. In the following excerpt, Eveline, pretending to be broke and adopting
a sham Cockney accent, is picked up by an unsavory photographer in search of a model.*

As I approached the Pimlico distract, the houses became a
little better. Steps had been cleaned and doorknockers polished. A carriage stood outside one, from which a man of about
thirty-five descended. Paying the cabman, he stared at me and
then walked quickly across my path.

"Pardon me, but you are exceedingly pretty. Allow me to
introduce myself. I am Edwin Pickles, photographer."

"Indeed? And how would that interest me?"

I placed a nasal Cockney twang in my voice, but my vocabulary evidently puzzled him. He was of neat attire and wore a
sporting jacket and modishly tight trousers with black silk
bands running down the sides. His shirt was open. Like the
corset designer, he wore a cravat.

"I seek models. You would make a perfect one. I would pay
you, of course."

"Oh! Ain't you a lark! Naked, I suppose?"

"Would you like to talk about it? I pay a guinea for first poses—more later."

I sniffed. I was remembering the manners and speech of some of the maids we had had. To imitate them amused me. "As you like."

We mounted the steps of the house. The hallway was clean within. I was led into a sitting room, as it is called in such dwellings. Scarce had I sat down than a woman appeared.

She was much of the man's age and had a slightly common but attractive face. He introduced her as his sister, Edwina. Her eyes cast up and down me.

"This one will do, yes. A pretty one."

I affected to look pleased, pretended a bit of sharpness, and tried to bargain for thirty shillings, but they would not have it. A glass of cheap sherry apparently assuaged me. I was led up two flights to the studio, which had a large roof light. Couches, armchairs, and drapes of various shades lay about. On the floor were cushions. A painted cloth backdrop showed a rural scene. There was even a Penny Farthing propped in one corner. In the center of the room stood a large brassbound camera of mahogany on a sturdy tripod. The back of it was covered with a black cloth. A big brass lens gleamed at the front.

"Take your clothes off, and I will pose you."

I had little enough to take off. My dress followed my bonnet. I stood naked in my stockings and boots.

"What a beauty! I swear you are the loveliest girl I have had here!"

"Then you should pay me more, eh? How about it?"

He was close upon me. Poor girls did not struggle very much, I imagined, if there were money in the offing. He made bold to caress my naked bottom. I wriggled it a little and cast my eyes down.

"Will you pay me more if I do?"

His erection was evident already. He pressed it to me, raised my face, and kissed me. His hand sought my breasts. It was two days since I had been mounted, and I still had visions of Emma in her transports.

"Another guinea, by God, you shall have it!"

"Promise? You got to promise? Oh my gawd, what a whopper, what a big one!"

We were on the cushions. Their purpose was obviously twofold. A shaft of impressive size quivered in my grasp. His mouth smothered mine. I absorbed his tongue. Breeches sliding down, he prepared himself for the assault. I would have preferred some preliminaries, but my lust was as great as his. I panted. I guided the knob to the orifice. It sank within. A gasp of pleasure escaped us both.

"My, you're lovely! What breasts, what a bottom—it's as round as a peach! Put your legs up over mine!"

I obeyed. It would not do to be too forward with my skills. His cock sank in me to the root. I squeezed.

"Oh! You're hurting me with it! Don't go too fast!"

"There, there, you'll like it in a minute. Hold it in. Can you feel it throb? No one ever brought it up so quick, I swear. What a perfect fuck you are!"

"Suck my tits, then—I like that."

He began to thresh. His piston moved in my spongy clasp. I closed my eyes and felt a complete delirium. There are occasions when I can be mounted three times in a day and then feel that the fourth is the first I have had for weeks. It was so now. I bucked my bottom to encourage him.

"Do it fast—I like it! Make me come!"

"You beauty! Oh, what heaven!"

His knob seemed to be thrusting up almost into my womb. His balls made a fine smacking sound. Beneath the cushions the floorboards squeaked. I was wet already with my spendings. The perfect, simple glory of the act overcame me. Those who scorn such "wanton pleasures" know nothing of the richness of experience such as only the truly initiated can enjoy. My pleasure was twice and thrice his own, had he but known it. Lithe in his movements, he pumped it back and forth, his cock well oiled by my juices.

"Don't come in me! Suppose I'as a child?"

Too far gone, he did not care. I pretended of a sudden the same abandon. I heaved to his heavings. Our pubic hairs rubbed together. My nipples were stark against his chest.

"You like it? Have I got a big one? Is it nice?"

"Oh, I love it! Do it more!"

A MAN WITH A MAID

by Anonymous

Of unknown authorship, A Man with a Maid relates the story of a gentleman named Jack who, because he has been jilted by Alice, the maiden, "vows to make her voluptuous person recompense him for his disappointment." Setting up residence in the "Snuggery," once been the "mad" room of an insane asylum, replete with iron rings and rope pulleys, he lures her there and gradually introduces her to the joys of sexuality. Perhaps the best-known erotic novel of its era, A Man With a Maid is remarkable for Jack's steadfast "violation" of Alice, a fantasy he scrambles to reinvent each time she experiences pleasure; indeed, consents.

1.

I, the Man, will not take up the time of my readers by detailing the circumstances under which Alice, the Maid, roused in me the desire for vengeance which resulted in the tale I am about to relate. Suffice it to say that Alice cruelly and unjustifiably jilted me! In my bitterness of spirit, I swore that if I ever had an opportunity to get hold of her, I would make her voluptuous person recompense me for my disappointment and that I would snatch from her by force the bridegroom's privileges that I so ardently coveted. But I dissemble! Alice and I had many mutual friends to whom this rupture was unknown; we were therefore constantly meeting each other, and if I gave her the slightest hint of my intentions towards her it would have been fatal to the very doubtful chances of success that I had! Indeed, so successfully did I conceal my real feelings under a cloak of genuine acceptance of her action that she had not the faintest idea (as she afterwards admitted to me) that I was playing a part.

But, as the proverb says, everything comes to the man who waits. For some considerable time, it seemed as if it would be wise on my part to abandon my desire for vengeance, as the circumstances of our daily lives were such as did not promise the remotest chance of my getting possession of Alice under conditions of either place or time suitable for the accomplishment of my purpose. Nevertheless, I controlled my patience and hoped for the best, enduring as well as I could the torture of unsatisfied desire and increasing lust.

It then happened that I had occasion to change my residence, and in my search for fresh quarters, I came across a modest suite consisting of a sitting room and two bedrooms, which would by themselves have suited me excellently; but with them the landlord desired to let what he termed a box or lumber room. I demurred to this addition, but as he remained firm, I asked to see the room. It was most peculiar both as regards access and appearance. The former was by a short passage from the landing and furnished with remarkably well-fitting doors at each end. The room was nearly square, of a good size and lofty, but the walls were unbroken, save by the one entrance, light and air being derived from a skylight, or rather lantern, which occupied the greater part of the roof and was supported by four strong and stout wooden pillars. Further, the walls were thickly padded, while iron rings were let into them at regular distances all 'round in two rows, one close to the door and the other at a height of about eight feet. From the roof beams, rope pulleys dangled in pairs between the pillars, while the two recesses on the entrance side, caused by the projection of the passage into the room, looked as if they had at one time been separated from the rest of the room by bars, almost as if they were cells. So strange indeed was the appearance of the whole room that I asked its history and was informed that the house had been built as a private lunatic asylum at the time that the now unfashionable square in which it stood was one of the centers of fashion, and that this was the old "mad room" in which violent patients were confined, the bolts, rings, and pulleys being used to restrain them when they were very violent, while the padding and the double doors made the room absolutely soundproof and prevented the ravings of the inmates from annoying the neighbors. The landlord added that the soundproof quality was no fiction, as the room had frequently been tested by incredulous visitors.

Like lightning the thought flashed through my brain. Was not this room the very place for the consummation of my scheme of revenge? If I succeeded in luring Alice into it, she would be completely at my mercy—her screams for help would not be heard and would only increase my pleasure, while the bolts, rings, pulleys, etc., supplemented with a little suitable furniture, would enable me to secure her in any way I wished and to hold her fixed while I amused myself with her. Delighted with the idea, I agreed to include the room in my suite. Quietly, but with deep forethought and planning, I commissioned certain furniture made which, while in outward appearance most innocent, as well as most comfortable, was in truth full of hidden mechanisms planned for the special discomfiture of any woman or girl that I might wish to hold in physical control. I had the floor covered with thick Persian carpets and rugs, and the two alcoves converted into nominal photographic laboratories, but in a way that made them suitable for lavatories and dressing rooms.

When completed, the "Snuggery" (as I christened it) was really in appearance a distinctly pretty and comfortable room, while in reality it was nothing more or less than a disguised Torture Chamber!

And now came the difficult part of my scheme.

How to entrap Alice? Unfortunately she was not residing in London but a little way out. She lived with a married sister, and never seemed to come to town except in her sister's company. My difficulty, therefore, was how to get Alice by herself for a sufficiently long time to accomplish my designs. Sorely I cudgeled my brains over this problem!

The sister frequently visited town at irregular intervals as dictated by the contingencies of social duties or shopping. True to my policy of *l'entente cordiale*, I had welcomed them to my rooms for rest and refreshment and had encouraged them to use my quarters; and partly because of the propinquity of the rooms to Regent Street, partly because of the very dainty meals I invariably placed before them, but mainly because of the soothing restfulness induced by the absolute quiet of the Snuggery after the roar and turmoil of the streets, it soon became their regular practice to honor me with their company for luncheon or tea whenever they came to town and had no special engagement. I need hardly add that secretly I hoped these visits might bring me an opportunity of executing my revenge, but for some months I seemed doomed to disappointment: I used to suffer the tortures of Tantalus when I saw Alice unsuspectingly braving me in the very room I had prepared for her violation, in very touch of me and of the hidden machinery that would place her at my disposal once I set it working. Alas, I was unable to do so because of her sister's presence! In fact, so keenly did I feel the position that I began to plan the capture of both sisters together, to include Marion in the punishment designed for Alice, and the idea in itself was not unpleasing, as

Marion was a fine specimen of female flesh and blood of a larger and more stately type than Alice (who was "petite"). One could do much worse than to have her at one's disposal for an hour or two to feel and fuck! So seriously did I entertain this project that I got an armchair made in such a way that the releasing of a secret catch would set free a mechanism that would be actuated by the weight of the occupant and would cause the arms to fold inwards and firmly imprison the sitter. Furnished with luxurious upholstery and the catch fixed, it made the most inviting of chairs, and, from its first appearance, Alice took possession of it, in happy ignorance that it was intended to hold her firmly imprisoned while I tackled and secured Marion!

Before, however, I resorted to this desperate measure, my patience was rewarded! And this is how it happened.

One evening, the familiar note came to say the sisters were travelling to town on the next day and would come for lunch. A little before the appointed hour Alice, to my surprise, appeared alone! She said that, after the note had been posted, Marion became ill and had been resting poorly all night and so could not come to town. The shopping engagement was one of considerable importance to Alice, and therefore she had come up alone. She had not come for lunch, she said, but had merely called to explain matters to me. She would get a cup of tea and a bun somewhere else.

Against this desertion of me, I vigorously protested, but I doubt if I would have induced her to stay had not a smart shower of rain come on. This made her hesitate about going out into it since the dress she was wearing would be ruined. Finally she consented to have lunch and leave immediately afterwards.

While she was away in the spare bedroom used by the sisters on their visits, I was in a veritable turmoil of excitement! Alice in my rooms by herself! It seemed too good to be true! But I remembered I yet had to get her into the Snuggery; she was absolutely safe from my designs everywhere but there! It was imperative that she should be in no way alarmed, and so, with a strong effort, I controlled my panting excitement and by the time Alice rejoined me in the dining room I was my usual self.

Lunch was quickly served. At first, Alice seemed a little nervous and constrained, but by tactful conversation, I soon set her at ease and she then chatted away naturally and merrily. I had craftily placed her with her back to the window so that she should not note that a bad storm was evidently brewing: and soon, with satisfaction, I saw that the weather was getting worse and worse! But it might at any moment begin to clear away, and so the sooner I could get her into my Snuggery, the better for me—and the worse for her! So by every means in my power, I hurried on the procedure of lunch.

Alice was leisurely finishing her coffee when a rattle of rain against the windowpanes, followed by an ominous growl of thunder, made her start from her chair and go to the casement. "Oh! Just look at the rain!" she exclaimed in dismay. "How very unfortunate!"

I joined her at the window: "By Jove, it is bad!" I replied, then added, "and it looks like it's lasting. I hope that you have no important engagement for the afternoon that will keep you much in the open." As I spoke, there came a vivid flash of lightning closely followed by a peal of thunder, which sent Alice staggering backwards with a scared face.

"Oh!" she exclaimed, evidently frightened; then, after a pause, she said: "I am a horrid little coward in a thunderstorm: It just terrifies me!"

"Won't you then take refuge in the Snuggery?" I asked with a host's look of concern. "I don't think you will see the lightning there and you certainly won't hear the thunder, as the room is soundproof. Shall we go there?" I opened the door invitingly.

Alice hesitated. Was her guardian angel trying to give her a premonitory hint of what her fate would be if she accepted my seemingly innocent suggestion? But at that moment came another flash of lightning, blinding in its intensity, and almost simultaneously a roar of thunder. This settled the question in my favor. "Yes, yes!" she exclaimed, then ran out, I closely followed her, my heart beating exultingly! Quickly she passed through the double doors into the Snuggery, the trap I had so carefully set for her was about to snap shut! Noiselessly I bolted the outer door, then closed the inner one. Alice was now mine! Mine!! At last I had trapped her! Now my vengeance was about to be consummated! Now her chaste virgin self was to be submitted to my lust and compelled to satisfy my erotic desires! She was utterly at my mercy, and promptly I proceeded to work my will on her!

2.

The soothing stillness of the room after the roar of the storm seemed most gratifying to Alice. She drew a deep breath of relief and turning to me she exclaimed: "What a wonderful room it really is, Jack! Just look how the rain is pelting down on the skylight, and yet we do not hear a sound!"

"Yes! There is no doubt about it," I replied, "it is absolutely soundproof. I do not suppose that there is a better room in London for my special purpose!"

"What might that be, Jack?" she asked interestedly.

"Your violation, my dear!" I replied quietly, looking her straight in the face, "the surrender to me of your maidenhead!"

She started as if she had been struck. She colored hotly. She stared at me as if she doubted her hearing. I stood still and calmly watched her. Then indignation and a sense of outrage seized her.

"You must be mad to speak like that!" she said in a voice that trembled with concentrated anger. "You forget yourself. Be good enough to consider our friendship as suspended till you have recovered your senses and have suitably apologized for this intolerable insult. Meanwhile I will trouble you only to call a cab so that I may remove myself from your hateful presence!" And her eyes flashed in wrathful indignation.

I quietly laughed aloud: "Do you really think I would have taken this step without calculating the consequences, Alice?" I rejoined coolly. "Do you really think I have lost my senses? Is there not a little account to be settled between us for what you did to me not very long ago? The day of reckoning has come, my dear; you have had your inning at my cost, now I am going to have mine at yours! You amused yourself with my heart, I am going to amuse myself with your body."

Alice stared at me, silent with surprise and horror! My quiet determined manner staggered her. She paled when I referred to the past, and she flushed painfully as I indicated what her immediate future would be. After a slight pause I spoke again: "I have deliberately planned this revenge! I took these rooms solely because they would lend themselves so admirably to this end. I have prepared them for every contingency, even to having to subjugate you by force! Look!" And I proceeded to reveal to her astonished eyes the mechanism concealed in the furniture, etc. "You know you cannot get out of this room till I choose to let you go; you know that your screams and cries for help will not be heard. You now must decide what you will do. I give you two alternatives, and two only: You must choose one of them. Will you submit yourself quietly to me, or do you prefer to be forced?"

Alice stamped her little foot in her rage. "How dare you speak to me in this way?" she demanded furiously. "Do you think I am a child? Let me go at once!" She moved in her most stately manner to the door.

"You are no child," I replied with a cruel smile. "You are a lusciously lovely girl possessing everything that I desire and able to satisfy my desires. But I am not going to let you waste time. The whole afternoon will hardly be long enough for the satisfaction of my whims, caprices, and lust. Once more, will you submit or will you be forced? Understand that if by the time the clock strikes the half-hour, you do not consent to submit, I shall, without further delay, proceed to take by force what I want from you! Now make the most of the three minutes you have left." And turning from her, I proceeded to get the room ready, as if I anticipated that I would have to use force.

Overcome by her feelings and emotions, Alice sank into an armchair, burying her face in her trembling hand. She evidently recognized her dreadful position! How could she yield herself up to me? And yet if she did not, she knew she would have to undergo violation! And possibly horrible indignities as well!! I left her absolutely alone, and when I had finished my preparation, I quietly seated myself and watched her.

Presently the clock chimed the half-hour. Immediately I rose. Alice quickly sprang to her feet and rushed to the far side of the large divan-couch on which I hoped before long to see her extended naked! It was evident that she was going to resist and fight me. You should know that I welcomed her decision, as now she would give me ample justification for the fullest exercising of my lascivious desires!

"Well, Alice, what is it to be? Will you submit quietly?"

A sudden passion seemed to possess her. She looked me squarely in the eyes for the first time, hers blazing with rage and indignation: "No! No!" she exclaimed vehemently. "I defy you! Do your worst. Do you think you will frighten me into satisfying your lust? Once and for all I give you my answer: No!

No! No! Oh, you cowardly brute and beast!" And she laughed shrilly as she turned herself away contemptuously.

"As you please," I replied quietly and calmly, "let those laugh who win! I venture to say that within half an hour, you will not only be offering yourself to me absolutely and unconditionally, but will be begging me to accept your surrender! Let us see!"

Alice laughed incredulously and defiantly. "Yes, let us see! Let us see!" she retorted contemptuously.

Forthwith I sprang towards her to seize her, but she darted away, I in hot pursuit. For a short time she succeeded in eluding me, dodging in and out of the furniture like a butterfly, but soon I maneuvered her into a corner, and, pouncing on her, gripped her firmly, then half dragged and half carried her to where a pair of electrically worked rope-pulleys hung between two of the pillars. She struggled desperately and screamed for help. In spite of her determined resistance, I soon made the ropes fast to her wrists, then touched the button; the ropes tightened, and slowly but irresistibly, Alice's arms were drawn upwards till her hands were well above her head and she was forced to stand erect by the tension on her arms. She was now utterly helpless and unable to defend her person from the hands that were itching to invade and explore the sweet mysteries of her garments; but what with her exertions and the violence of her emotions, she was in such a state of agitation that I deemed it wise to leave her to herself for a few minutes, till she became more mistress of herself, when she would be better able to appreciate the indignities that she would now be compelled to suffer!

Here I think I had better explain the mechanical means I had at my disposal for the discomfiture and subjugation of Alice.

Between each two of the pillars that supported the lantern-skylight hung a pair of strong rope-pulleys working on a roller mechanism concealed in the beams and actuated by electricity. Should I want Alice upright, I had simply to attach the ropes to her wrists, and her arms would be pulled straight up and well over her head, thus forcing her to stand erect, and at the same time rendering her body defenseless and at my mercy. The pillars themselves I could utilize as whipping posts, being provided with rings to which Alice could be fastened in such a way that she could not move!

Close by the pillars was a huge divan-couch upholstered in dark leather that admirably enhanced the pearly loveliness of a naked girl. It stood on eight massive legs (four on each long side), behind each of which lay, coiled for use, a stout leather strap worked by rollers hidden in the upholstery and actuated by electricity. On it were piled a lot of cushions of various sorts and consistencies, with which Alice and Marion used to make nests for themselves, little dreaming that the real object of the "Turkish Divan" (as they had christened it) was to be the altar on which Alice's virginity was sacrificed to the Goddess of Love, the mission of the straps being to hold her in position while she was violated, should she not surrender herself quietly to her fate!

By the keyboard of the grand piano stood a duet-stool, also upholstered in leather and with the usual mechanical power of adjustment for height, only to a much greater extent than usual. But the feature of the stool was its unusual length, a full six feet, and I one day had to satisfy Alice's curiosity by telling her that this was for the purpose of providing a comfortable seat to anyone who might be turning pages for the pianist! The real reason was that the stool was, for all practical purposes, a rack actuated by hidden machinery and fitted with a most ingenious arrangement of steps, the efficacy of which I looked forward to testing on Alice's tender self!

The treacherous armchair I have already explained. My read-

ers can now perhaps understand that I could fix Alice in practically any position or attitude and keep her so fixed while I
worked my sweet will on her helpless self!

All the ropes and straps were fitted with swivel snap-hooks.
To attach them to Alice's limbs, I used an endless band of the
longest and softest silk rope that I could find. It was an easy
matter to slip a double length of the band 'round her wrist or
ankle, pass one end through the other and draw tight then snap
the free end into the swivel hook. No amount of plunging or
struggling would loosen this attachment, and the softness of
the silk prevented Alice's delicate flesh from being rubbed or
even marked.

3.

During the ten-minute grace period I mentally allowed Alice to
recover from the violence of her struggles, I quietly studied her
as she stood helpless, almost supporting herself by resting her
weight on her wrists. She was to me an exhilarating spectacle,
her bosom fluttering, rising and falling as she caught her breath,
her cheeks still flushing, her large hat somewhat disarranged,
while her dainty well-fitting dress displayed her figure to its
fullest advantage.

She regained command of herself wonderfully quickly, and
then it was evident that she was stealthily watching me in horrible apprehension. I did not leave her long in suspense, but
after going slowly 'round her and inspecting her, I placed a
chair right in front of her, so close to her that its edge almost
touched her knees, then slipped myself into it, keeping my legs
apart, so that she stood between them, the front of her dress
pressing against the fly of my trousers. Her head was now above
mine so that I could peer directly into her downcast face.

As I took up this position, Alice trembled nervously and tried to draw herself away from me, but found herself compelled to stand as I had placed her. Noticing the action, I drew my legs closer to each other so as to loosely hold her between them, smiling cruelly at the uncontrollable shudder that passed through her when she felt the pressure of my knees against hers! Then I extended my arms, clasped her gently 'round the waist, and drew her against me, at the same time tightening the clutch of my legs, till soon she was fairly in my embrace, my face pressing against her throbbing bosom. For a moment she struggled wildly, then resigned herself to the unavoidable as she recognized her helplessness.

Except when dancing with her, I had never held Alice in my arms, and the embrace permitted by the waltz was nothing to the comprehensive clasping between arms and legs in which she now found herself. She trembled fearfully, her tremors giving me exquisite pleasure as I felt them shoot through her, then she murmured: "Please don't, Jack!"

I looked up into her flushed face as I amorously pressed my cheek against the swell of her bosom: "Don't you like it, Alice?" I said maliciously as I squeezed her still more closely against me. "I think you're just delicious, dear, and I am trying to imagine what it will feel like when your clothes have been taken off!"

"No! No! Jack!" she moaned, agonizingly, twisting herself in her distress. "Let me go, Jack . . . don't . . . don't . . ." she began again, and her voice failed her.

For an answer, I held her against me with my left arm around her waist, then with my right hand I began to stroke and press her hips and bottom.

"Oh . . . ! Don't, Jack! Don't!" Alice shrieked, squirming in distress and futilely endeavoring to avoid my marauding hand. I paid no attention to her pleading and cries, but continued my stroking and caressing over her full posterior and thighs down to her knees, then back to her buttocks and haunches, she all the while quivering in a delicious way. Then I freed my left hand, and holding her tightly imprisoned between my legs, I proceeded with both hands to study, through her clothes, the configuration of her backside and hips and thighs, handling her buttocks with a freedom that seemed to stagger her, as she pressed herself against me in an effort to escape from the liberties that my hands were taking with her charms.

After toying delightfully with her in this way for some time, I ceased and withdrew my hands from her hips, but only to pass them up and down over her bosom, which I began lovingly to stroke and caress to her dismay. Her color rose as she swayed uneasily on her legs. But her stays prevented any direct attack on her bosom, so I decided to open her clothes sufficiently to obtain a peep at her virgin breasts. I set to work unbuttoning her blouse.

"Jack, no! No!!" shrieked Alice, struggling vainly to get loose. But I only smiled and continued to undo her blouse till I got it completely open and threw it back onto her shoulders, only to be balked as a fairly high bodice covered her bosom. I set to work opening this, my fingers reveling in the touch of Alice's dainty linen. Soon it also was open and thrown back—and then, right before my eager eyes, lay the snowy expanse of Alice's bosom, her breasts being visible nearly as far as their nipples!

"Oh! Oh!" she moaned in her distress, flushing painfully at this cruel exposure. But I was too excited to take any notice; my eyes were riveted on the lovely swell of her breasts, exhibiting the valley between the twin globes, now heaving and fluttering under her agitated emotions. Unable to restrain myself, I threw my arms 'round Alice's waist, drew her closely to me, and pressed my lips on her palpitating flesh, which I kissed furiously.

"Don't, Jack," cried Alice, as she tugged frantically at her fastenings in her wild endeavors to escape from my passionate lips; but instead of stopping me, my mouth wandered all over her heaving delicious breasts, punctuating its progress with hot kisses that seemed to drive her mad, to such a pitch, in fact, that I thought it best to desist.

"Oh! My God!" she moaned as I relaxed my clasp and leaned back in my chair to enjoy the sight of her shame and distress. There was not the least doubt that she felt most keenly my indecent assault, and so I determined to worry her with lascivious liberties a little longer.

When she had become calmer, I passed my arms around her waist and again began to play with her posterior; then, stooping down, I got my hands under her clothes and commenced to pull them up. Flushing violently, Alice shrieked to me to desist, but in vain! In a trice, I turned her petticoats up, held them thus with my left hand while with my right I proceeded to attack her bottom, now protected only by her dainty thin drawers!

The sensation was delirious! My hand delightedly roved over the fat plump cheeks of her arse, stroking, caressing, and pinching them, reveling in the firmness and elasticity of her flesh under its thin covering, Alice all the time wriggling and squirming in horrible shame, imploring me almost incoherently to desist, and finally getting so hysterical that I was compelled to suspend my exquisite game. So, to her great relief, I dropped her skirts, pushed my chair back, and rose.

I had in the room a large plate glass mirror nearly eight feet high that reflected one at full length. While Alice was recovering from her last ordeal, I pushed this mirror close in front of her, placing it so that she could see herself in its center. She started uneasily as she caught sight of herself, for I had left her bosom uncovered, and the reflection of herself in such shameful dishabille in conjunction with her large hat (which she still retained) seemed vividly to impress on her the horror of her position!

Having arranged the mirror to my satisfaction, I picked up the chair and placed it just behind Alice, sat down in it, and worked myself forward on it till Alice again stood between my legs, but this time with her back to me. The mirror faithfully reflected my movements, and her feminine intuition warned her that the front of her person was now about to become the object of my indecent assault.

But I did not give her time to think. Quickly I encircled her waist again with my arms, drew her to me till her bottom pressed against my chest, then, while my left arm held her firmly, my right hand began to wander over the junction of her stomach and legs, pressing inquisitively her groin and thighs, and intently watching her in the mirror.

Her color rose, her breath came unevenly, she quivered and trembled as she pressed her thighs closely together. She was horribly perturbed, but I do not think she anticipated what then happened.

Quietly dropping my hands, I slipped them under her clothes, caught hold of her ankles, and then proceeded to climb up her legs over her stockings.

"No! No! For God's sake, don't, Jack!" Alice yelled, now scarlet with shame and wild with alarm at this invasion of her most secret parts. Frantically she dragged at her fastenings, her hands clenched, her head thrown back, her eyes dilated with horror. Throwing the whole of her weight on her wrists, she strove to free her legs from my attacking hands by kicking out desperately, but to no avail. The sight in the mirror of her struggles only stimulated me into a refinement of cruelty, for with one hand I raised her clothes waist high, exposing her in her dainty drawers and black silk stockings, while with the other I vigorously attacked her thighs over her drawers, forcing a way between them and finally working up so close to her cunt that Alice practically collapsed in an agony of apprehension and would have fallen had it not been for the sustaining ropes that were all that supported her, as she hung in a semi-hysterical faint.

Quickly rising and dropping her clothes, I placed an armchair behind her and loosened the pulleys till she rested comfortably in it, then left her to recover herself, feeling pretty confident that she was now not far from surrendering herself to me, rather than continue a resistance which she could not help but see was utterly useless. This was what I wanted to effect. I did not propose to let her off any single one of the indignities I had in store for her, but I wanted to make her suffering the more keen, through the feeling that she was, to some extent, a consenting party to actions that inexpressibly shocked and revolted her. The first of these I intended to be the removal of her clothes, and, as soon as Alice became more mistress of herself, I set the pulleys working and soon had her standing erect with her arms stretched above her head.

She glanced fearfully at me as if trying to learn what was now going to happen to her. I deemed it as well to tell her, and to afford her an opportunity of yielding herself to me, if she should be willing to do so. I also wanted to save her clothes from being damaged, as she was really beautifully dressed, and I was not at all confident that I could get her garments off her without using a scissors on some of them.

"I see you want to know what is going to happen to you, Alice," I said. "I'll tell you. You are to be stripped naked, utterly and absolutely naked; not a stitch of any sort is to be left on you!"

A flood of crimson swept over her face, invading both neck and bosom, which remained bare; her head fell forward as she moaned: "No! . . . No! . . . Oh! Jack . . . Jack . . . How can you . . ." She swayed uneasily on her feet.

"That is to be the next item in the program, my dear!" I said, enjoying her distress. "There is only one detail that remains to be settled first and that is, will you undress yourself quietly if I set you loose, or must I drag your clothes off you? I don't wish to influence your decision, and I know what queer ideals girls have about taking off their clothes in the presence of a man; I will leave the decision to you, only saying that I do not see what you have to gain by further resistance, and some of your garments may be ruined—which would be a pity. Now, which is it to be?"

She looked at me imploringly for a moment, trembling in every limb, then averting her eyes, but remaining silent, evidently torn by conflicting emotions.

"Come, Alice," I said presently. "I must have your decision or I shall proceed to take your clothes off you as best as I can."

Alice was now in a terrible state of distress! Her eyes wandered all over the room without seeming to see anything, incoherent murmurs escaped from her lips, as if she was trying to speak but could not, her breath came and went, her bosom rose and fell agitatedly. She was evidently endeavoring to form some decision, but found herself unable to do so.

I remained still for a brief space as if awaiting her answer; then, as she did not speak, I quietly went to a drawer, took out a pair of scissors and went back to her. At the sight of the scissors, she shivered, then with an effort said, in a voice broken with emotion: "Don't . . . undress me, Jack! If you must . . . have me, let it be as I am . . . I will . . . submit quietly . . . oh! My God!!" she wailed.

"That won't do, dear," I replied, not unkindly but still firmly, "you must be naked, Alice; now, will you or will you not undress yourself?"

Alice shuddered, cast another imploring glance at me, but seeing no answering gleam of pity in my eyes, but stern determination instead, she stammered out: "Oh! Jack! I can't! Have some pity on me, Jack, and . . . have me as I am! I promise I'll be . . . quiet!"

I shook my head, I saw there was only one thing for me to do, namely, to undress her without any further delay; and I set to work to do so, Alice crying piteously: "Don't, Jack; don't! . . . don't!"

I had left behind her the armchair in which I had allowed her to rest, and her blouse and bodice were still hanging open and thrown back on her shoulders. So I got on the chair and worked them along her arms and over her clenched hands onto the ropes; then gripping her wrists in turn one at a time, I released the noose, slipped the garments down and off it and refastened the noose. And as I had been quick to notice that Alice's chemise and vest had shoulder-strap fastenings and had merely to be unhooked, the anticipated difficulty of undressing her forcibly was now at an end! The rest of her garments would drop off her as each became released, and therefore it was in my power to reduce her to absolute nudity! My heart thrilled with fierce exultation, and without further pause, I went on with the delicious work of undressing her.

Alice quickly divined her helplessness and in an agony of apprehension and shame cried to me for mercy! But I was deaf to her pitiful pleadings! I was wild to see her naked!

Quickly I unhooked her dress and petticoats and pulled them down to her feet, thus exhibiting her in her stays, drawers, and stockings—a bewitching sight! Her cheeks were suffused with shamefaced blushes, she huddled herself together as much as she could, seemingly supported entirely by her arms; her eyes were downcast and she seemed dazed both by the rapidity of my motions and their horrible success!

Alice now had on only a dainty Parisian corset that allowed the laces of her chemise to be visible, just hiding the nipples of her maiden breasts, and a pair of exquisitely provoking drawers, cut wide especially at her knees and trimmed with a sea of frilly lace, from below which emerged her shapely legs, encased in black silk stockings and terminated in neat little shoes. She was the daintiest sight a man could well imagine, and, to me, the daintiness was enhanced by her shamefaced consciousness, for she could see herself reflected in the mirror in all her dreadful dishabille!

After a minute of gloating admiration, I proceeded to untie the tapes of her drawers so as to take them off her. At this she seemed to wake to the full sense of the humiliation in store for her; wild at the idea of being deprived of this most intimate of garments to a girl, she screamed in her distress, tugging frantically at her fastenings in her desperation! But the knot gave way, and her drawers, being now unsupported, slipped down to below her knees, where they hung for a brief moment, maintained only by the despairing pressure of her legs against each other. A tug or two from me, and they lay in snowy loads 'round her ankles and rested on her shoes!

Oh, that I had the pen of a ready writer, so that I could describe Alice at this stage of the terrible ordeal of being forcibly undressed, her mental and physical anguish, her frantic cries and impassioned pleadings, her frenzied struggles, the agony in her face, as garment after garment was removed from her and she was being hurried nearer and nearer to the appalling goal of absolute nudity! The accidental but unavoidable contact of my hands with her person as I undressed her seemed to upset her so terribly that I wondered how she would endure my handling and playing with the most secret and sensitive parts of herself when she was naked! But acute as was her distress while being deprived of her upper garment, it was noth-

ing to her shame and anguish when she felt her drawers forced
down her legs and the last defense to her cunt thus removed.
Straining wildly at the ropes with cheeks aflame, eyes dilated
with terror, and convulsively heaving bosom, she uttered inarticulate cries, half-choked by her emotions and panting under
her exertions.

I gloated over her sufferings and I would have liked to have
watched them—but I was now mad with desire for her naked
charms and also feared that a prolongation of her agony might
result in a faint, when I would lose the anticipated pleasure of
witnessing Alice's misery when her last garment was removed
and she was forced to stand naked in front of me. So, unheeding
her imploring cries, I undid her corset and took it off her,
dragged off her shoes and stockings and with them her fallen
drawers. During this process I intently watched her struggles
in the hope of getting a glimpse of her Holy of Holies, but
vainly, then slipped behind her; unbuttoning the shoulder-
fastenings of her chemise and vest, I held these up for a moment, then watching Alice closely in the mirror, I let go! Down
they slid with a rush, right to her feet! I saw Alice flash one
rapid stolen half-reluctant glance at the mirror, as she felt the
cold air on her now naked skin. I saw her reflection stark naked,
a lovely gleaming pearly vision; then instinctively she squeezed
her legs together, as closely as she could, huddled herself cow-
ering as much as the ropes permitted—her head fell back in
the first intensity of her shame, then fell forward suffused with
blushes that extended right down to her breasts, her eyes closed
as she moaned in heartbroken accents: "Oh! Oh! Oh!" She was
naked!!

Half-delirious with excitement and the joy of conquest, I
watched Alice's naked reflection in the mirror. Rapidly and tu-
multuously, my eager eyes roved over her shrinking, trembling
form, gleaming white, save for her blushing face and the dark

triangular mossy-looking patch at the junction of her belly and thighs. But I felt that, in this moment of triumph, I was not sufficiently master of myself to fully enjoy the spectacle of her naked maiden charms now so fully exposed; besides which, her chemise and vest still lay on her feet. So I knelt down behind these garments, noting, as I did so, the glorious curves of her bottom and hips. Throwing these garments onto the rest of her clothes, I pushed the armchair in front of her, and then settled myself down to a systematic and critical inspection of Alice's naked self!

As I did so, Alice colored deeply over her face and bosom and moved herself uneasily. The bitterness of death (so to speak) was past, her clothes had been forced off her and she was naked; but she was evidently conscious that much indignity and humiliation was yet in store for her, and she was horribly aware that my eyes were now taking in every detail of her naked self! Forced to stand erect by the tension of the ropes on her arms, she could do nothing to conceal any part of herself, and, in an agony of shame, she endured the awful ordeal of having her naked person closely inspected and examined!

I had always greatly admired her trim little figure, and in the happy days before our rupture, I used to note with proud satisfaction how Alice held her own, whether at garden parties, at afternoon teas, or in the theatre or ballroom. And after she had jilted me and I was sore in spirit, the sight of her invariably added fuel to the flames of my desire, and I often caught myself wondering how she looked in her bath! One evening, she wore at dinner a low-cut evening dress and she nearly upset my self-control by leaning forward over the card table by which I was standing, and unconsciously revealing to me the greater portion of her breasts! But my imagination never pictured anything as glorious as the reality now being so reluctantly exhibited to me!

Alice was simply a beautiful girl, and her lines were deliciously voluptuous. No statue, no model, but glorious flesh and blood allied to superb femininity! Her well-shaped head was set on a beautifully modeled neck and bosom from which sprang a pair of exquisitely lovely breasts (if anything too full), firm, upstanding, saucy, and inviting. She had fine rounded arms with small well-shaped hands, a dainty but not too small waist, swelling grandly downwards and outwards and melting into magnificent curves over her hips and haunches. Her thighs were plump and round, and tapered to the neatest of calves and ankles and tiny feet, her legs being the least trifle too short for her, but adding by this very defect to the indescribable fascination of her figure. She had a graciously swelling belly with a deep navel, and, framed by the lines of her groin, was her Mount of Venus, full, fat, fleshy, prominent, covered by a wealth of fine silky dark curly hairs through which I could just make out the lips of her cunt. Such was Alice as she stood naked before me, horribly conscious of my devouring eyes, quivering and trembling with suppressed emotion, tingling with shame, flushing red and white, knowing full well her own loveliness and what its effect on me must be; and in dumb silence I gazed and gazed again at her glorious naked self till my lust began to run riot and insist on the gratification of senses other than that of sight!

I did not, however, consider that Alice was ready to properly appreciate the mortification of being felt. She seemed to be still absorbed in the horrible consciousness of one all-pervading fact, namely, that she was utterly naked, that her chaste body was the prey of my lascivious eyes, that she could do nothing to hide or even screen any part of herself, even her cunt, from me! Every now and then, her downcast eyes would glance at the reflection of herself in the faithful mirror only to be hastily withdrawn with an excess of color to her already shame-suffused cheeks at these fresh reminders of the spectacle she was offering to me!

Therefore, with a strong effort, I succeeded in overcoming the temptation to feel and handle Alice's luscious body there and then, and being desirous of first studying her naked self from all points of view, I rose and took her in strict profile, noting with delight the arch of her bosom, the proudly projecting breasts, the glorious curve of her belly, the conspicuous way in which the hairs on the Mount of Venus stood out, indicating that her cunt would be found both fat and fleshy, the magnificent swell of her bottom! Then I went behind her, and for a minute or two, reveled in silent admiration of the swelling lines of her hips and haunches, her quivering buttocks, her well-shaped legs! Without moving, I could command the most perfect exhibition of her naked loveliness, for I had her back view in full sight while her front was reflected in the mirror!

Presently I completed my circuit, then standing close to her, I had a good look at her palpitating breasts, noting their delicious fullness and ripeness, their ivory skin, and the tiny virgin nipples pointing outward so prettily, Alice coloring and flushing and swaying uneasily under my close inspection. Then I peered into the round cleft of her navel while she became uneasier than ever, seeing the downward trend of my inspection. Then I dropped on my knees in front of her and from this vantage point I commenced to investigate with eager eyes the mysterious region of her cunt so deliciously covered with a wealth of close curling hairs, clustering so thickly 'round and over the coral lips as almost to render them invisible! As I did so, Alice desperately squeezed her thighs together as closely as she could, at the same time drawing in her stomach in the vain hope of defeating my purpose and of preventing me from inspecting the citadel wherein reposed her virginity!

As a matter of fact, she did to a certain extent thwart me, but as I intended before long to put her on her back and tie her down, with her legs wide apart, I did not grudge her partial success, but brought my face close to her belly. "Don't! Oh, don't!" she cried, as if she could feel my eyes as they searched this most secret part of herself; but disregarding her pleadings, I closely scanned the seat of my approaching pleasure, noting delightedly that her Mount Venus was exquisitely plump and fleshy and would afford my itching fingers the most delicious pleasure when I allowed them to wander over its delicate contours and hide themselves in the forest of hairs that so sweetly covered it!

At last I rose. Without a word, I slipped behind the mirror and quickly divested myself of my clothes, retaining only my shoes and socks. Then, suddenly, I emerged and stood right in front of Alice. "Oh," she ejaculated, horribly shocked by the unexpected apparition of my naked self, turning rosy red and hastily averting her eyes—but not before they had caught sight of my prick in glorious erection! I watched her closely. The sight seemed to fascinate her in spite of her alarmed modesty, she flashed rapid glances at me through half-closed eyes, her color coming and going. She seemed forced, in spite of herself, to regard the instrument of her approaching violation, as if to assess its size and her capacity!

"Won't you have a good look at me, Alice?" I presently remarked maliciously. "I believe I can claim to possess a good specimen of what is so dear to the heart of a girl!" (She quivered painfully.) After a moment I continued: "Must I then assume by your apparent indifference that you have, in your time, seen so many naked men that the sight no longer appeals to you?" She colored deeply, but kept her eyes averted.

"Are you not even curious to estimate whether my prick will fit in your cunt?" I added, determined, if I possibly could, to break down the barrier of silence she was endeavoring to protect herself with.

I succeeded! Alice tugged frantically at the ropes which kept her upright, then broke into a piteous cry: "No, no . . . my God, no!" she supplicated, throwing her head back but still keeping her eyes shut as if to exclude the sight she dreaded, "Oh! You don't really mean to . . . to . . ." she broke down, utterly unable to clothe in words the overwhelming fear that she was now to be violated!

I stepped up to her, passed my left arm 'round her waist and drew her trembling figure to me, thrilling at the exquisite sensation caused by the touch of our naked bodies against each other. We were now both facing the mirror, both reflected in it.

"D-don't touch me!" she shrieked as she felt my arm encircle her, but holding her closely against me with my left arm, I gently placed my right forefinger on her navel, to force her to open her eyes and watch my movements in the mirror, which meant that she would also have to look at my naked self, and gently I tickled her.

She screamed in terror, opening her eyes, squirming deliciously. "Don't! Oh, don't!" she cried agitatedly.

"Then use your chaste eyes properly and have a good look at the reflection of the pair of us in the mirror," I said somewhat sternly: "Look me over slowly and thoroughly from head to foot, then answer the questions I shall presently put to you. May I call your attention to that whip hanging on that wall and to the inviting defenselessness of your bottom? Understand that I shall not hesitate to apply one to the other if you don't do as you are told! Now have a good look at me!"

Alice shuddered, then reluctantly raised her eyes and shamefacedly regarded my reflection in the mirror, her color coming and going. I watched her intently (she being also reflected, my arm was still 'round her waist holding her against me) and I noted with cruel satisfaction how she trembled with shame and fright when her eyes dwelt on my prick, now stiff and erect!

"We make a fine pair, Alice, eh?" I whispered maliciously. She colored furiously, but remained silent.

"Now answer my questions: I want to know something about you before going further. How old are you?"

"Twenty-five," she whispered.

"In your prime, then! Good! Now, are you a virgin!"

Alice flushed hotly and painfully, then whispered again: "Yes!"

Oh, my exultation! I was not too late! The prize of her maidenhead was to be mine! My prick showed my joy! I continued my catechism.

"Absolutely virgin?" I asked. "A pure virgin? Has no hand wandered over those lovely charms, has no eye but mine seen them?"

Alice shook her head, blushing rosy red at the idea suggested by my words. I looked rather doubtingly at her.

"I include female eyes and hands as well as male in my query, Alice," I continued. "You know that you have a most attractive lot of girl and woman friends and that you are constantly with them. Am I to understand that you and they have never compared your charms, have never, when occupying the same bed . . ." But she broke in with a cry of distress. "No, no, not I, not I, oh! How can you talk to me like this, Jack?"

"My dear, I only wanted to find out how much you already knew so that I might know what to teach you now! Well, shall we begin your lessons?" And I drew her against me, more closely than ever, and again began to tickle her navel.

"Jack, don't!" she screamed. "Oh, don't touch me! I can't stand it! Really, I can't!"

"Let me see if that is really so," I replied, as I removed my arm from her waist and slipped behind her, taking up a position from which I could command the reflection of our naked figures in the mirror, and thus watch her carefully and noted the effect on her of my tender mercy.

4.

I commenced to feel Alice by placing my hands one on each side of her waist, noting with cruel satisfaction the shiver that ran through her at their contact with her naked skin. After a few caresses, I passed them gently but inquisitively over her full hips, which I stroked, pressed, and patted lovingly, then bringing my hands downward behind her, I roved over her plump bottom, the fleshy cheeks of which I gripped and squeezed to my heart's content, Alice the while arching herself outwards in a vain attempt to escape my hands. Then I descended to the underneath portion of her soft round thighs and finally worked my way back to her waist, running my hands up and down over her loins and finally arriving at her armpits.

Here I paused, and to try the effect on Alice, I gently tickled these sensitive spots. "Don't!" she exclaimed, wriggling and twisting herself uneasily. "Don't, I am dreadfully ticklish, I can't stand it at all!" At once I ceased, but my blood went on fire, as through my brain flashed the idea of the licentiously lovely spectacle Alice would afford, if she was tied down with her legs fastened widely apart, and a pointed feather-tip cleverly applied to the most sensitive part of her—her cunt—sufficient slack being allowed in her fastenings to permit of her wriggling and writhing freely while being thus tickled, and I promised to give myself presently this treat together with the pleasure of trying on her this interesting experiment!

After a short pause, I again placed my hands on her waist played for a moment over her swelling hips, then slipped onto her stomach, my right hand taking the region below her waist while my left devoted itself to her bosom, but carefully avoiding her breasts for the moment.

Oh! What pleasure I tasted in thus touching her pure sweet flesh, so smooth, so warm, so essentially female! My delighted hands wandered all over her body, while the poor girl stood quivering and trembling, unable to guess whether her breast or cunt was next to be attacked.

I did not keep her long in suspense. After circling a few times over her rounded belly, my right hand paused on her navel again, and while my forefinger gently tickled her, my left hand slid quietly onto her right breast, which it then gently seized.

She gave a great cry of dismay! Meanwhile my right hand had in turn slipped up to her left breast, and another involuntary shriek from Alice announced that both of her virgin bubbies had become the prey of my cruel hands!

Oh, how she begged me to release them, the while tossing herself from side to side in almost uncontrollable agitation as my fingers played with her delicious breasts, now squeezing, now stroking, now pressing them against each other, now rolling them upwards and downwards, now gently irritating and exciting their tiny nipples! Such delicious morsels of flesh I had never handled: so firm and yet so springing, so ripe and yet so maidenly, palpitating under the hitherto unknown sensations communicated by the touch of masculine hands on their virgin surfaces. Meanwhile Alice's telltale face reflected in the mirror clearly indicated to me the mental shame and anguish she was feeling at this terrible outrage; her flushed cheeks, dilated nostrils, half-closed eyes, her panting, heaving bosom all revealing her agony under this desecration of her maiden self. In rapture, I continued toying with her virgin globes, all the while gloating on Alice's image in the mirror, twisting and contorting in the most lasciviously ravishing way under her varying emotions!

At last I tore my hands away from Alice's breasts. I slipped my left arm 'round her waist, drew her tightly against me, then while I held her stomach and slowly approached her cunt, Alice instantly guessed my intention! She threw her weight on one leg, then quickly placed the other across her groin to foil my attack, crying, "No, no, Jack! Not there . . . not there!" and at the same time endeavoring frantically to turn herself away from my hand. But the close grip of my left arm defeated her, and disregarding her cries, my hand crept on and on till it reached her hairs! These I gently pulled, twining them 'round my fingers as I reveled in their curling silkiness. Then amorously I began to feel and press her gloriously swelling Mount of Venus, a finger on each side of its slit! Alice now simply shrieked in her shame and distress, jerking herself convulsively backwards and twisting herself frenziedly! As she was forced to stand on both legs in order to maintain her balance, her cunt was absolutely defenseless, and my eager fingers roved all over it, touching, pressing, tickling, pulling her hairs at their sweet will. Then I began to attack her virgin orifice and tickle her slit, passing my forefinger lightly up and down it, all the time watching her intently in the mirror! Alice quivered violently, and her head fell backwards in her agony as she shrieked: "Jack don't! Oh . . . for God's sake, don't! Stop! Stop!" But I could feel her cunt opening under my lascivious titillation, and so could she! Her distress became almost uncontrollable. "Oh, my God!" she screamed in her desperation as my finger found its way to her clitoris and lovingly titillated it, she spasmodically squeezing her thighs together in her vain attempts to defend herself. Unheeding her agonized pleading, I continued to tickle her clitoris for a few delicious moments, then I gently passed my finger along her cunt and between its now half-opened lips till I arrived at her maiden orifice, up which it tenderly forced its way, burying itself in Alice's cunt till it could penetrate no further into her! Alice's agitation now became uncontrollable; she struggled so violently that I could hardly hold her still, especially when she felt the interior of her cunt invaded and my finger investigate the mysteries of its virgin recesses!

Oh! My voluptuous sensations at that moment! Alice's naked quivering body clutched tightly against mine! My finger, half-buried in her maiden cunt, enveloped in her soft, warm, throbbing flesh and gently exploring its luscious interior!! In my excitement I must have pushed my inquisitiveness too far, for Alice suddenly screamed, "Oh! Oh! You're hurting me! Stop! Stop!" her head falling forward on her bosom as she did so! Delighted at this unexpected proof of her virginity and fearful of exciting her sexual passions beyond her powers of control, I gently withdrew my finger and soothed her by passing it lovingly and caressingly over her cunt; then releasing her from my encircling arm, I left her to recover herself. But, though visibly relieved at being at last left alone, Alice trembled so violently that I hastily pushed her favorite armchair (the treacherous one) behind her, hastily released the pulley-ropes and let her drop into the chair to rest and recover herself, for I knew that her distress was only temporary and would soon pass away and leave her in a fit condition to be again fastened and subjected to some other torture, for so it undoubtedly was to her.

5.

On this occasion, I did not set free the catch, which permitted the arms of the chair to imprison the occupant. Alice was so upset by her experiences that I felt sure she would not give me any trouble worth mentioning when it became time for her torturing to recommence, provided, of course, that I did not allow her too long a respite, and this, from my own point of view, I did not propose to do, as I was wildly longing to play again with her naked charms!

I therefore let her coil herself up in the chair with her face buried in her hands, and greedily gloated over the voluptuous curves of the haunches and bottom she was unconsciously exhibiting, the while trying to make up my mind as to what I should next do to her. This I soon decided. My hands were itching to again handle her virgin flesh, and so I determined to tie Alice upright to one of the pillars and, while comfortably seated close in front of her, to amuse myself by playing with her breasts and cunt again!

She was now lying quietly and breathing normally and regularly, the trembling and quivering that had been running intermittently through her having by now ceased. I did not feel quite sure she had recovered herself yet, but as I watched her, I noticed an attempt on her part to try and slip her wrists out of the silken nooses that attached the ropes to them. This settled the point, and, before she could free her hands, I set the ropes working, remarking as I did so: "Well, Alice, shall we resume?"

She glanced at me fearfully, then averted her eyes as she exclaimed hurriedly: "Oh, no, Jack! Not again, not again!" and shuddered at the recollection of her recent ordeal!

"Yes, my dear!" I replied, "the same thing, though not quite in the same way; you'll be more comfy this time! Now, Alice, come along, stand up again!"

"No!" she cried, fighting vainly the now fast-tightening ropes that were inexorably raising her to her feet! "Oh, Jack! No! No!!" she pitifully pleaded, while opposing the upward pull with all her might, but to no avail! I simply smiled cruelly at her as I picked up a leather strap and awaited the favorable moment to force her against the nearest pillar. Presently she was dragged off the chair, and now was my time. I pounced on her and rushed her backwards to the pillar, quickly slipping the strap 'round it and her waist and buckling it, and thus securing her. Then I loosened the pulleys and, lowering her arms, I forced them behind her and 'round the pillar, till I got her wrists together and made them fast to a ring set in the pillar. Alice was now helpless: The whole of the front of her person was at my disposal. She was securely fastened, but, with a refinement of cruelty, I lashed her ankles together and bound them to the pillar! Then I unbuckled the strap 'round her waist and threw it away, it being no longer needed; placed the armchair in front of her; and sitting down in it, I drew it so close to her that she stood between my parted legs and within easy touch, just as she did when she was being indecently assaulted before she was undressed, only then we both were fully clothed, while now we both were stark naked! She could not throw her head back because of the pillar, and if she let it droop, as she naturally wanted to do, the first thing that her innocent eyes would rest upon would be my excited prick in glorious erection, its blushing head pointing directly towards her cunt as if striving to make the acquaintance of its destined bride!

Confused, shamefaced, and in horrible dread, Alice stood trembling in front of me, her eyes tightly closed as if to avoid the sight of my naked self, her bosom agitatedly palpitating till her breasts seemed almost to be dancing! I leant back in my chair luxuriously as I gloated over the voluptuously charming spectacle, allowing her a little time in which to recover herself somewhat, before I set to work to feel her again!

Before long, the agitations of her bosom died away; Alice's breathing became quieter. She was evidently now ready for another turn, and I did not keep her waiting, but gently placed my hands on her breasts.

"No, Jack, don't!" she pleaded piteously, moving herself uneasily. My only response was to stroke lovingly her delicious twin globes. As her shoulders were of necessity drawn well back by the pull of her arms her bust was thrown well forward, thus causing her breasts to stand out saucily and provokingly; and I took the fullest advantage of this. Her flesh was delicious to the touch, so smooth and soft and warm, so springy and elastic! My fingers simply reveled in their contact with her skin! Taking her tempting bubbies between my fingers and thumbs, I amorously pressed and squeezed them, pulled them this way and that way, rubbed them against each other, finally taking each delicate nipple in turn in my mouth and sucking it while my hands made as if they were trying to milk her! Alice all the while involuntarily shifted herself nervously as if endeavoring to escape from my audaciously inquisitive fingers, her face scarlet with shame.

·After a delicious five minutes of lascivious toying with her maiden breasts, I reluctantly quitted them, first imprinting on each of her little nipples a passionate kiss, which seemed to send a thrill through her. As I sank back into my chair she took a long breath of relief, at which I smiled, for I had only deserted her breasts for her cunt!

Alice's legs were a trifle short, and her cunt therefore lay a little too low for effective attack from me in a sitting position. I therefore pushed the chair back and knelt in front of her. My intentions were now too obviously plain to her and she shrieked in her dismay, squirming deliciously!

For some little time, I did not touch her, but indulged in a good look, at close quarters, at the sweet citadel of her chastity!

My readers will remember that immediately after I had stripped Alice naked, I had closely inspected her cunt from a similar point of view. But then it was unsullied, untouched; now it had experienced the adoring touch of a male finger, and her sensitive body was still all aquiver from the lustful handling her dainty breasts had just endured! Did her cunt share in the sexual excitement that my fingers had undoubtedly aroused in her?

It seemed to me that it did! The hair seemed to stand out as if ruffled, the Mount of Venus certainly looked fuller, while the coral lips of the cunt itself were distinctly more apart! I could not see her clitoris, but I concluded that it participated in the undoubted excitement that was prevailing in this sweet portion of Alice's body, and of which she evidently was painfully aware, to judge by her shrinking, quivering movements!

I soon settled the point by gently placing my right forefinger on her slit and lovingly stroking it! An electric shock seemed to send a thrill through Alice, her limbs contracted, her head fell forward as she screamed: "Don't, Jack! Oh, my God! How can you treat me so!!" while she struggled frantically to break the ropes that lashed her legs to the pillar to which she was fastened!

"Don't you like it, dear?" I asked softly with a cruel smile, as I continued to gently play with her cunt!

"No, no," she shrieked. "Oh, stop! I can't stand it!" And she squirmed horribly! The crack of her cunt now began to open visibly!

I slipped my finger in between the parted lips: Another despairing shriek from Alice, whose face now was scarlet! Again I found my progress barred by the membrane that proved her virgin condition! Reveling in the warm moistness of her throbbing flesh, I slowly agitated my finger in its delicious envelope, as if frigging her: "Jack! Don't!" Alice yelled, now mad with distress and shame, but I could not for the life of me stop, and with my left forefinger, I gently attacked her virgin clitoris!

Alice went off into a paroxysm of hysterical shrieks, straining at her fastenings, squirming, wriggling, writhing like one possessed. She was a lovely sight in herself and the knowledge that the struggling, shrieking girl I was torturing was Alice herself and none but Alice added zest to my occupation!

Disregarding her cries, I went on slowly frigging her, but carefully refrained from carrying her sexual excitement to the spending point, till I had pushed her powers of self-control to their utmost. I did not want her to spend yet, this crowning humiliation I intended to effect with my tongue. Presently, what I wished was to make Alice endure the most outrageously indecent indignities I could inflict on her virgin person, to play on her sexual sensitiveness, to provoke her nearly into spending, and then deny her the blessed relief. So, exercising every care, and utilizing to the utmost the peculiarly subtle power of touch I possessed, I continued to play with her cunt using both my hands, till I drove her nearly frantic with the sexual cravings and excitement I was provoking!

Just then I noticed certain spasmodic contortions of her hips and buttocks, certain involuntary thrusting out of her belly, as if begging for more close contact with my busy fingers; I knew this meant that her control over her sexual organs was giving out and that she would be driven into spending if I did not take care. Then, most reluctantly, I stopped torturing her for the moment, and, leaning back in my chair, I gloatingly watched Alice as little by little she regained her composure, my eyes dwelling delightedly on her trembling and quivering naked body so gloriously displayed!

She breathed a long sigh of heartfelt relief as she presently saw me rise and leave her. She did not, however, know that my object in doing so was to prepare for another, and perhaps more terrible, ordeal for her virgin cunt!

From a drawer, I took out a long glove box, then returned and resumed my seat in front of her with the box in my hand. She watched me with painful intensity, her feminine intuition telling her that something horrible was in store for her, and she was not wrong!

Holding the box in such a way that she could see the contents, I opened it. Inside was about a dozen long and finely pointed feathers. Alice at once guessed her fate—that her cunt was to be tickled. Her head fell back in her terror as she shrieked: "Oh, my God! Not that, Jack! . . . not that! . . . you'll kill me! I can't stand it!" I laughed cruelly at her and proceeded to pick out a feather, whereupon she frantically tugged at her fastenings, screaming frenziedly for mercy!

"Steady, dear, steady now, Alice!" I said soothingly, as if addressing a restive mare, then touched her palpitating breasts with the feather's point.

"Jack, don't!" she yelled, pressing herself wildly back against the pillar in an impotent effort to escape the torture caused by the maddeningly gentle titillation, her face crimson. For response, I proceeded to pass the tip of the feather along the lower portion of her glorious bubbies, touching the skin ever so lightly here and there, then tickling her maiden nipples! With redoubled cries, Alice began to squirm convulsively as much as her fastenings would permit, while the effect of the fiendishly subtle torture on her became manifest by the sudden stiffening of her breasts, which now began to stand out tense and full! Noting this, I thought it as well to allow her a little respite; so I dropped my hand, but, at the same time, leaned forward till my face touched her breasts, which I then proceeded to kiss lovingly in turn, finally sucking them amorously till they again became soft and yielding. I then made as if I would repeat the torture, but after a touch or two (which produced piteous cries and contortions) I pretended to be moved by her distress, and again dropping my hand leaned back in the chair till she became less agitated!

But as soon as the regular rise and fall of her lovely bosom indicated the regaining of her composure, I proceeded to try the ardently longed for experiment: The effect of a feather ap-

plied to a girl's cunt! And no one could have desired a lovelier
subject on which to test this much-debated question than was
being offered by the naked helpless girl now standing terrified
between my legs!

Pushing my chair back as much as was desirable, I leant
forward, then slowly extended my right arm in the direction of
Alice's cunt. A great cry of despair broke from her as she noted
the movement, and she flattened her bottom against the pillar
in a vain attempt to draw herself back out of reach. But the
only effect of her desperate movement was to force forward her
Mount of Venus, and thereby render her cunt more open to
the attack of the feather than it previously was!

Carefully regulating my motions, I gently brought the tip of
the feather against the lowest point of Alice's cunt hole, then
very softly and gently began to play up and down, on and
between its delicate coral lips! Alice's head had dropped onto
her breast, the better, I fancy, to watch my movements; but as
soon as the feather touched her cunt, she threw her head backwards, as if in agony, shrieking at the top of her voice, her
whole body twisting and contorting wildly. Not heeding her
agonized appeals, I proceeded to work along her slit towards
her clitoris, putting into play the most subtle titillation I was
capable of, sometimes passing the feather all along the slit from
one end to the other, sometimes tickling the orifice itself, not
only outside but inside, then ascending towards her clitoris, I
would pass the tip of the feather all 'round it, irritating it without so much as touching it. The effect of my manipulation soon
became evident. First the lips of Alice's cunt began to pout,
then to gape a little, then a little more as if inviting the feather
to pass into it—which it did! Then Alice's clitoris commenced
to assert itself and to become stiff and turgid, throbbing excitedly; then her whole cunt seemed as if possessed by an irresistible flood of sexual lust and almost to demand mutely the

immediate satisfaction of its cravings! Meanwhile Alice, firmly attached to the pillar, went into a paroxysm of contortions and convulsions, wriggling, squirming, writhing, tugging frantically at her fastenings, shrieking, praying, utterly incoherent exclamations and ejaculations, her eyes starting out of her head, her quivering lips, her heaving bosom with its wildly palpitating breasts all revealing the agony of body and mind that she was enduring! Fascinated by the spectacle, I continued to torture her by tickling her cunt more and more scientifically and cruelly, noting carefully the spots at which the tickling seemed most felt and returning to those ultra-sensitive parts of her cunt avoiding only her clitoris—as I felt sure that, were this touched, Alice would spend—till her strength became exhausted under the double strain! With a strangled shriek Alice collapsed just as I had forced the feather up her cunt and was beginning to tickle the sensitive interior! Her head fell forward on her bosom, her figure lost its self-supporting rigidity, she hung flaccidly, prevented from falling only by her wrists being shackled together 'round the pillar! There was nothing to be gained by prolonging the torture, so quickly I unfastened her, loosed her wrists and ankles from their shackles, and carried her to the large divan-couch, where I gently laid her, knowing that she would soon recover herself and guessing that she now would not need to be kept tied and that she had realized the futility of resistance.

6.

The couch on which I had placed Alice was one of the cunning pieces of furniture that I had designed for that use, should I succeed in capturing her. It was unusually long, nearly eight feet, and more than three feet wide, upholstered in dark green satin and stuffed in such a way as to be delightfully soft and springy and yet not to allow one's body to sink into it. In appearance it resembled a divan, but in stern reality it was a rack, for at each end, there was concealed a mechanism that worked stout leather straps, its object being to extend Alice flat at full length either on her back or her front (as I might wish) and to maintain her fixed thus, while I amused myself with her or worked my cruel will on her! From about halfway down the sides, there issued a pair of supplementary straps also worked by a mechanism, by which means Alice's legs could be pulled widely apart and held so, should I want to devote myself to her cunt or to, dare I actually say it, fuck her against her will!

I did not wish to fatigue her with another useless struggle, so before she recovered the use of her faculties, I attached the corner straps to her wrists and ankles, leaving them quite loose and slack, so that she could move herself freely. Hardly had I effected this when Alice began to come to herself; immediately I quitted her and went to a part of the room where my back would be turned to her, but from which I could nevertheless watch her by means of a mirror.

I saw her take a deep breath, then slowly open her eyes and look about her as if puzzled. Then, almost mechanically, one of her hands stole to her breasts and the other to her cunt, and she gently soothed these tortured parts by stroking them softly, as if to relieve them of the terrible tickling to which they had been subjected! Presently she rose to a sitting position, then tried to free herself from the straps on her wrists and ankles.

I now considered that she must have fully recovered, so I returned to her and without a word I touched the spring that set the mechanism working noiselessly. Immediately the straps began to tighten. As soon as she observed this, Alice started up in a fright, at once detecting that she would be spread-eagled on her back if she did not break loose! "No, no, no!" she cried, terrified at the prospect; then she desperately endeavored to slip out of her fastenings, but the straps were tightening quickly and in the struggle she lost her balance and fell backwards on the couch, and before she could recover herself, she was drawn into a position in which resistance was impossible! With cruel satisfaction, I watched her, disregarding her frenzied appeals for mercy! Inch by inch, she was pulled flatter and flatter, till she rested on her back, then, inch by inch, her dainty legs were drawn asunder, till her heels rested on the edges of the couch! Then I stopped the machinery. Alice was now utterly helpless! In speechless delight, I stood gazing at her lovely body as she lay on her back, panting after her exertions, her bosom heaving and fluttering with her emotions, her face rosy red with shame, her lovely breasts and virgin cunt conspicuously exposed, stark naked, a living Maltese Cross!

When I had sufficiently gratified my sense of sight and she had become a little calmer, I quietly seated myself by her waist, facing her feet, then, bending over her, I began delightedly to inspect the delicious abode of Alice's maidenhead, her virgin cunt, now so fully exhibited! With sparkling eyes, I noted her full, fleshy Mount of Venus, the delicately tinted coral lips quivering under sensations hitherto a stranger to them, the wealth of close-clustering curly hair; with intense delight, I saw that, for a girl of her height and build, Alice had a large cunt, and that her clitoris was well-developed and prominent, that the lips were full and her slit easy to open! Intently I scanned its every feature, the sweet junction of her belly and thighs, her smooth plump thighs themselves, the lines of her groin, while Alice lay trembling in an agony of shame and fright, horribly conscious of the close investigation her cunt was undergoing and in terrible dread of the sequel!

Shakespeare sings (in *Venus and Adonis*):

> *Who sees his true love in her naked bed,*
> *Teaching the sheets a whiter hue than white;*

But when his glutton eye full gorged hath fed,
His other agents aim at like delight!

So it was with me! My hands were tingling to explore the mysteries of Alice's cunt, to wander unchecked over her luscious belly and thighs. My prick was in a horrible state of erection! I could hardly restrain myself from falling on her and ravishing her, as she lay there so temptingly helpless! But with a strong effort, I did suppress my rioting lustful desires and tore myself away from Alice's secret charms for a brief spell!

I turned 'round so as to face her, still seated by her waist, and placed my hands on her lovely breasts. As I lovingly squeezed them I lowered my face till I almost touched hers, then whispered, "You delicious beauty, kiss me!" at the same time placing my lips on hers. Alice flushed hotly, but did not comply! I had never yet either kissed her or received a kiss from her and was mad for one!

"Alice, kiss me!" I repeated somewhat sternly, looking threateningly at her and replacing my lips on her mouth. Reluctantly she complied, I felt her lips open as she softly kissed me! It was delicious! "Give me another!" I demanded, putting my right cheek in position to receive it. She complied. "Yet another!" I commanded, tendering my left cheek. Again she complied. "Now give me two more, nice ones, mouth to mouth!" Again came the sweet salute, so maddeningly exciting that, hastily quitting her breasts, I threw my arms 'round her neck, drew her face to mine, then showered burning kisses on her mouth, eyes, and cheeks till she gasped for breath, blushing rosy red! Reluctantly I let her go; then to her dismay, I again turned 'round and bent over her cunt, and after a long look at it, expressive of the deepest admiration, I gently placed my hands on her belly and after softly stroking it, began to follow the converging lines of her groin. Alice shrieked in sudden alarm!

"No, no—Oh! My God, no, no . . . don't touch me there! Oh! No! Not there!" and struggled desperately to break loose. But I disregarded her cries and continued my invasion; soon my itching fingers reached the forest of hairs that covered her mons veneris, she squirming deliciously, then rested on her cunt itself. An agonized shriek of "Oh! . . . Oh!!" from Alice, as she writhed helplessly with quivering hips, proclaimed my victory and her shame!

Shall I ever forget the sensations of that moment! At last, after all that longing and waiting, Alice's cunt was finally at my mercy, I not only had it in the fullest possible view, but also was actually touching it! My fingers, ranged on each side of the delicate pinky slit, were busy amorously pressing and feeling it, now playing with its silky curly hairs and gently pulling them, now tenderly stroking its sweet lips, now gently opening them so as to expose its coral orifice and its throbbingly agitated clitoris! Resting as I was on Alice's belly, I could feel every quiver and tremor as it passed through her, every involuntary contortion induced by the play of my fingers on this most delicate and susceptible part of her anatomy, the fluttering of her palpitating and heaving bosom! I could hear the involuntary ejaculations, the "ohs" and the "ahs!" that broke from her in her shame and mental anguish at thus having to endure such handling and fingering of her maiden cunt and the strange half-terrifying sensations thereby provoked.

Half-mad with delight, I continued to toy sweetly with Alice's cunt, till sudden unmistakable wriggles of her bottom and hips and her incoherent exclamations warned me that I was trying her too much, if not goading her into spending, and as I had determined that Alice's first sacrifice to Venus should be induced by the action of my tongue on her cunt, I reluctantly desisted from my delightful occupation, to her intense relief!

Turning 'round, I again clasped her in my arms, rained hot kisses on her unresisting lips and cheeks, murmuring brokenly: "Oh, Alice! Oh, Alice!" Then pressing my cheek against hers, I rested with her clasped in my arms, her breasts quivering against my chest, till we both grew calmer and her trembling ceased.

For about five minutes there was dead silence, broken only by Alice's agitated breathing. Soon this ceased, and she seemed to have recovered command of herself again. Then softly I whispered to her: "Will you not surrender yourself to me now, Alice dear! Surely it is plain to you that you cannot help yourself?"

She drew her face away from me, and murmured: "No, no, I can't, I can't . . . let you . . . have me! Oh, let me go! Let me go!!!"

"No," I replied sternly, releasing my clasp of her and resuming my sitting position by her waist, "No, my dear, you shan't go till you've been well-punished and well-fucked! But as I said before, I think you will change your mind presently!"

She looked questioningly at me, fear in her eyes. I rose. Her eyes followed me, and when she saw me select another fine-pointed feather and turn back to her, she instantly divined my intentions and frantically endeavored to break the ropes that kept her thighs apart shrieking: "Oh no, no, my God, no, I can't stand it! You'll kill me!"

"Oh, no, I won't!" I replied quietly, seating myself by her knees, so as to command both her cunt and a view of her struggles, which I knew would prove most excitingly delicious! Then without another word, I gently directed the point of the feather against the lowest part of her cunt's virgin orifice, and commenced to tickle her!

7.

A fearful scream broke from Alice, a violent quivering spasm shook her from head to foot! Her muscles contracted, as she vainly strove to break free! Arching her back she endeavored to turn herself first on one side and then on the other, tugging frantically at the straps, anything as long as she could dodge the feather! But she could do nothing! The more she shrieked and wriggled, the greater was the pleasure she was affording me; so, deaf to her cries and incoherent pleadings, I continued to tickle her cunt, sometimes up and down the slit, sometimes just inside, noting with cruel delight how its lips began to gape open under the sexual excitement now being aroused and how her throbbing clitoris began to erect itself!

Alice presented a most voluptuous spectacle; clenched hands, half-closed eyes, heaving breasts, palpitating bosom, plunging hips, tossing bottom, jerking thighs—wriggling and squirming frantically, uttering broken and incoherent ejaculations, shrieking, praying.

I thought it wise to give her a pause for rest and partial recovery, and withdrew the feather from between the lips of her cunt, then gently stroked them caressingly. "Ah! . . . Ah!" she murmured half-unconsciously, closing her eyes. I let her lie still, but watched her closely.

Presently her eyes opened half-dreamily, and she heaved a deep breath. I made as if to resume the tickling. "No, no," she murmured faintly, "it's no use! I can't stand it! Don't tickle me any more!"

"Well, will you yield yourself to me?" I asked.

Alice lay silent for a moment, then with an evident effort said, "Yes!"

Letting the feather fall between her parted legs, I leaned forward and took her in my arms: "There must not be any mistake,

Alice," I said softly, "are you willing to let me do to you anything and everything that I may wish?"

Half-opening her eyes, she nodded her head in assent.

"And do you promise to do everything and anything that I may wish you to do?"

She hesitated. "What will you want me to do?" she murmured.

"I don't know," I replied, "but whatever it may be, you must do it. Do you promise?"

"Yes," she murmured, reluctantly.

"Then kiss me, kiss me properly in token of peace!" I whispered in her ear, placing my lips on hers; and deliciously she kissed me, receiving at the same time my ardent reciprocations. Then I unclasped her and began to play with her breasts.

"May I get up now?" she murmured, moving herself uneasily as she felt her breasts being squeezed.

"Not just yet, dear," I replied. "I've excited you so terribly that it is only fair to you that I should give you relief, and as I know that in spite of your promise you will not behave as you should do, simply from inexperience, I will keep you as you are, till I have solaced you!"

"Oh, what are you going to do to me?" she asked in alarm, in evident fear that she was about to be violated!

"Restore you to ease, dear, by kissing you all over; now lie still and you will enjoy the greatest pleasure a girl can taste and yet remain virgin!"

With heightened color she resigned herself to her fate. I took her again in my arms, and sweetly kissed her on her eyes, her cheeks, her hair! Then releasing her, I applied my lips to her delicious breasts, and showered burning kisses all over them, reveling in their sweet softness and their exquisite elasticity. Taking each breast in turn, I held it between finger and thumb, then enveloping the dainty little nipple between my lips, I al-

ternately played on it with my tongue and sucked it, all the
while squeezing and toying with the breast, causing Alice to
experience the most lascivious sensation she had yet known,
except perhaps when her cunt was being felt.

"Stop! Oh, for God's sake, stop!" she ejaculated in her confusion and half-fright as to what might happen, "For heaven's
sake, stop!" she screamed as I abandoned one breast only to
attack the other. But the game was too delightful: To feel her
glorious throbbing ripe bubbies in my mouth and quivering
under my tongue, while Alice squirmed in her distress, was a
treat for a god; so disregarding her impassioned pleadings, I
continued to suck and tongue-tickle them till their sudden stiffening warned me that Alice's sexual instincts were being roused
and the result might be a premature explosion when she felt
the grand assault on her cunt.

So I desisted reluctantly. Again I encircled her neck with my
arms, kissed her pleading mouth and imploring eyes as she lay
helpless; and then with my tongue, I touched her navel. She
cried "No, no, oh! Don't," struggling desperately to get free, for
it began to dawn on her innocent mind what her real torture
was to be.

I did not keep her in suspense. Thrusting my hands under
her and gripping the cheeks of her bottom so as to steady her
plunging, I ran my tongue down lightly over the lines of her
abdomen, then began to tenderly kiss her cunt. She shrieked
in her terror as she felt my lips on her cunt, and with frantic
wriggling endeavored to escape my pursuing mouth. At this
critical moment, I lightly ran my tongue along Alice's slit. The
effect was astounding! For a moment she seemed to swoon
under the subtle titillation, but on my tongue again caressing
her cunt, only this time darting deeper between its lips, she
went off into a paroxysm of shrieks and cries, wriggling and
squirming in a most wonderful way, considering how strongly

I had fastened her down; her eyes seemed to start out of her head under the awful tickling that she was experiencing; she plunged so frantically that although I was tightly gripping her buttocks, she almost dislodged my mouth, the rigid muscles of her lovely thighs testifying to the desperate effort she was making to get loose. But the subtle titillation had aroused her sexual desires, without her recognizing the fact in her distress. Her cunt began to open of its own accord, soon the clitoris was revealed turgid and stiff, quivering in sexual excitement, then her orifice began to yawn and show the way to paradise; deeper and deeper plunged my tongue into its satiny recess, Alice mechanically and unconsciously thrusting herself upwards as if to meet my tongue's downward darting and strokes. Her head rolled from side to side, as, with half-closed eyes, she struggled with a fast-increasing feeling that she must surrender herself to the imperious call of her sexual nature, yet endeavoring desperately not to do so, hampered by long-established notions of chastity. Her breath came in snatches, her breasts heaved and panted, half-broken ejaculations escaped from her quivering lips. The time had arrived for the sacrifice and the victim was ready. Thrusting my tongue as deeply into her cunt as I could force it, I gave her one final and supreme tickling, then taking her clitoris between my lips, I sucked hard on it, all the while tickling it with my tongue.

It was too much for Alice. "Stop . . . stop . . . it's coming! . . . it's coming!" she gasped. An irresistible wave of lust swept away the last barriers of chastity, and, with a despairing wail of, "Oh . . . Oh! I can't help . . . it! Oh . . . Oh . . . Oh!!!" she spent frantically!

Feeling her go, I sprang to my feet to watch Alice as she spent. It was a wonderful sight! There she lay on her back, completely naked, forced to expose her most secret charm, utterly absorbed in the sensations of the moment, her body pulsating and thrilling with each sexual spasm, her closed eyes, half-open lips, and stiff breasts indicating the intensity of the emotions that possessed her. And so she remained for a minute or two, as if in a semi-swoon.

Presently I noticed a relaxing of her muscles; then she drew a long breath and dreamily opened her eyes. For a moment she seemed dazed and almost puzzled about where she was: then her eyes fell on me, and in a flash she remembered everything. A wave of color surged furiously over her face and bosom at the thought that I had witnessed her unconscious transports and raptures as she yielded herself to her sexual passions in spite of herself. Stirring uneasily, she averted her eyes, flushing hotly again. I stooped down and kissed her passionately; then, without a word, I unfastened her, raised her from the settee and supported her to the large armchair, where she promptly curled herself up, burying her blushing face in her hands.

I thought it wisest to leave her undisturbed for a brief space, so I busied myself quietly in pouring out two glasses of wine, and knowing what severe calls were going to be made on Alice's reproductive powers, I took the opportunity to fortify these by dropping into her glass the least possible dose of cantharides.

8.

My readers will naturally wonder what my condition of mind and body was after both had been subjected to such intense inflammation as was inevitable from my close association with Alice dressed and Alice naked.

Naturally I had been in a state of considerable erotic excitation from the moment that Alice's naked charms were revealed, especially when my hands were playing with her breasts and toying with her cunt. But I had managed to control myself. The events recorded in the last chapter however proved too much for me. The contact of my lips and tongue with Alice's maiden lips, breasts, and cunt and the sight of her as she spent were more than I could stand, and I was nearly mad with lust and an overpowering desire that she should somehow satisfy for the time this lust after her.

But how could it be arranged? I wanted to keep her virgin as long as I possibly could, for I had not nearly completed my carefully prepared program of fondling and quasi-tortures that gain double spice and salaciousness when perpetrated on a virgin. To fuck her therefore was out of the question. Of course there was her mouth, and my blood boiled at the idea of being sucked by Alice; but it was patent that she was too innocent and inexperienced to give me this pleasure. There were her breasts: One could have a delicious time no doubt by using them to form a tunnel and to work my prick between them, but this was a game better played later on. There were her hands, and sweetly could Alice frig me, if she devoted one dainty hand to my prick, while the other played with my testicles, but nothing would be easier than for her to score off me heavily, by giving the latter an innocent wrench that would throw me out of action entirely. The only possible remaining method was her bottom, and while I was feverishly debating its advisability, an innocent movement of hers and the consequent change of attitude suddenly displayed the superb curves and general lusciousness of her posteriors. In spite of my impatience, I involuntarily paused to admire their glorious opulence! Yes, I would bottom-fuck Alice: I would deprive her of one of her maidenheads.

But would she let me do so? True, she had just sworn to submit herself to my caprices whatever they might be, but such a caprice no doubt never entered into her innocent mind, and unless she did submit herself quietly, I might be baffled and in the excitement of the struggle and the contact with her warm naked flesh, I might spend, "waste my sweetness on the desert air!" Suddenly a cruelly brilliant idea struck me, and at once I proceeded to act on it.

She was still lying curled up in the armchair. I touched her on the shoulder; she looked up hurriedly.

"I think you have rested long enough, Alice," I said, "now get up, I want you to put me right!" And I pointed to my prick now in a state of terrible erection! "See!" I continued, "you must do something to put it out of its torment, just as I have already so sweetly allayed your lustful cravings!" She flushed painfully! "You can do it either with your mouth or by means of your bottom. Now say quick—for I am just bursting with lust for you!"

She hid her face in her hands! "No, no," she ejaculated. "No. Oh, no! I couldn't, really I couldn't!"

"You must!" I replied somewhat sternly, for I was getting mad with unsatisfied lust. "Remember the promises you have just made! Come now, no nonsense! Say which you'll do!"

She threw herself at my feet: "No, no," she cried. "I can't!"

Bending over her, I gripped her shoulders: "You have just sworn that you would let me do to you anything I pleased, and that you would do anything I might tell you to do, in other words, that you would both actively and passively minister to my pleasures. I have given you your choice! If you prefer to be active, I will lie on my back and you can suck and excite me into spending: If you would rather be passive, you can lie on your face and I will bottom-fuck you! Now which shall it be?"

"No, no, no!" she moaned in her distress. "I can't do either. Really, I can't!"

Exasperated by her noncompliance, I determined to get by force what I wanted, and before she could guess my intentions, I had gripped her firmly 'round her body, then half-carried and half-dragged her to the piano duet-stool, which also contained a hidden mechanism. I forced her onto it, face downwards, and in spite of her resistance, I soon fixed the straps to her wrists and ankles; then I set the mechanism working, sitting on her in order to keep her in the proper position, as she desperately fought to get loose. Cleverly managing the straps, I soon forced Alice into the desired position, flat on her face and astride the stool, her wrists and ankles being secured to the longitudinal wooden bars that maintained the rigidity of the couch.

Alice was now fixed in such a way that she could not raise her shoulders or bosom, but by straightening her legs, she could heave her bottom upwards a little. Her position was perfect for my purpose, and lustfully I gloated over the spectacle of her magnificent buttocks, her widely parted thighs affording me a view of both of her virgin orifices—both now at my disposal!

I passed my hands amorously over the glorious backside now at my mercy, pinching, patting, caressing, and stroking the glorious flesh; my hands wandered along her plump thighs, reveling in their smoothness and softness, Alice squirming and wriggling deliciously! Needless to say her cunt was not neglected, my fingers tenderly and lovingly playing with it and causing her the most exquisitely irritating titillation.

After enjoying myself in this way for a few minutes and having thoroughly felt her bottom, I left her to herself for a moment while I went to a cupboard, Alice watching my movements intently. After rummaging about, I found what I sought, a riding whip of some curious soft substance, very springy and elastic, calculated to sting but not to mark the flesh. I was getting tired of having to use force on Alice to get what I wanted and considered it would be useful policy to make her learn the result of not fulfilling her promises. There is no better way to bring a girl to her senses than by whipping her soundly, naked if possible! And here was Alice, naked, and fixed in the best possible position for a whipping!

As I turned towards her, whip in hand, she instantly guessed her fate and shrieked for mercy, struggling frantically to get loose. Deaf to her pitiful pleading, I placed myself in position to command her backside, raised the whip, and gave her a cut right across the fleshiest part!

A fearful shriek broke from her! Without losing time, I administered another, and another, and another, Alice simply now yelling with the pain, and wriggling in a marvelous way, considering how tightly she was tied down. I had never before whipped a girl, although I had often read and been told of the delights of the operation to the operator, but the reality far surpassed my most vivid expectations! And the naked girl I was whipping was *Alice*, the object of my lust, the girl who had jilted me, the girl I was about to ravish! Mad with exultation, I disregarded her agonized shrieks and cries. With cruel deliberation, I selected the tenderest parts of her bottom for my cuts, aiming sometimes at one luscious cheek, then the other, then across both, visiting the tender inside of her widely parted thighs! Her cries were music to my ears in my lustful frenzy, while her wiggles and squirms and the agitated plunging of her hips and buttocks enthralled my eyes. But soon, too soon, her strength began to fail her, her shrieks degenerated into inarticulate ejaculations! There was now little pleasure in continuing her punishment, so, most reluctantly, I ceased!

Soothingly I passed my right hand over Alice's quivering bottom and stroked it caressingly, alleviating, in a wonderfully short time, the pain. In spite of the severity of the whipping she had received, she was not marked at all! Her flesh was like that of a baby, slightly pinker perhaps, but clean and fresh. As I tenderly restored her to ease, her trembling died away, her breath began to come more freely and normally, and soon she was herself again.

"Has the nonsense been whipped out of you, Alice?" I asked mockingly. She quivered, but did not answer.

"What, not yet?" I exclaimed, pretending to misunderstand her. "Must I give you another turn?" and I raised the whip as if to commence again.

"No, no!" she cried in genuine terror. "I'll be good!"

"Then lie still and behave yourself," I replied, throwing the whip away into a corner of the room.

From a drawer I took a pot of cold cream. Alice, who was fearsomely watching every movement of mine, cried in alarm: "Jack, what are you going to do to me? Oh, tell me!" My only response was to commence lubricating her arse-hole, during which operation she squirmed delightfully, then placing myself full in her sight, I set to work anointing my rampant prick. "Guess, dear!" I said.

She guessed accurately! For a moment she was struck absolutely dumb with horror, then struggling desperately to get free, she cried, "Oh! My God . . . no, Jack . . . no! You'll kill me!"

"Don't be alarmed," I said quietly, as I caressed her quivering buttocks. "Think a moment: Larger things have come out than what is going in! Lie still, Alice, or I shall have to whip you!" Then placing myself in position behind her, I leant forward till the head of my prick rested against her arse-hole.

"My God! No, no!" she shrieked, frantically wriggling her buttocks in an attempt to thwart me. But the contact of my prick with Alice's flesh maddened me; thrusting fiercely forward, I, with very little difficulty, shoved my prick halfway up Alice's bottom with apparently little or no pain to her; then falling on her, I clasped her in my arms and rammed myself well into her, till I felt my balls against her and the cheeks of her bottom against my stomach!

My God! It was like heaven to me! Alice's naked quivering body was closely pressed to mine! My prick was buried to its hairs in her bottom, reveling in the warmth of her interior! I shall never forget it! Prolonging my rapturous ecstasy, I rested motionless on her, my hands gripping and squeezing her palpitating breasts so conveniently placed for their delectation, my cheek against her averted face, listening to the inarticulate murmurs wrung unconsciously from her by the violence of her emotions and the unaccountably strange pleasure she was experiencing, and which she confessed to by meeting my suppressed shoves with spasmodic upward heavings of her bottom—oh! It was paradise!

Inspired by a sudden thought, I slipped my right hand down to Alice's cunt and gently tickled it with my forefinger, but without penetrating. The effect was marvelous! Alice plunged wildly under me with tumultuous quivering, her bosom palpitating and fluttering: "Ah! . . . Ah!" she ejaculated, evidently falling prey to uncontrollable sexual cravings! Provoked beyond endurance, I let myself go! For a few moments there was a perfect cyclone of frenzied upheavings from her, mixed with fierce down-thrustings from me, then blissful ecstasy, as I spent madly into Alice, flooding her interior with my boiling tribute! "Ah! . . . Ah! . . ." she gasped, as she felt herself inundated by my hot discharge! Her cunt distractedly sought my finger, a violent spasm shook her, and, with a scarcely articulate cry but indicative of the intense rapture, Alice spent on my finger with quivering vibrations, her head falling forward as she half-swooned in her ecstasy! She had lost the maidenhood of her bottom!!!

For some seconds we both lay silent and motionless save for an occasional tremor; I utterly absorbed in the indescribable pleasure of spending into Alice as she lay tightly clasped in my arms! She was the first to stir (possibly incommoded by my weight), gently turning her face towards me, coloring furiously as our eyes met! I pressed my cheek against hers; she did not flinch but seemed to respond. Tenderly I kissed her; she turned her face fully towards me and of her own accord she returned my kiss! Was it that I had tamed her? Or had she secretly tasted certain pleasure during the violation of her bottom? Clasping her closely to me I whispered: "You have been a good girl this time, Alice, very good!!" She softly rubbed her cheek against mine! "Did I hurt you?" I asked.

She whispered back: "Very little at first, but not afterwards!"

"Did you like it?" I inquired maliciously. For answer she hid her face in the settee, blushing hotly! But I could feel a small thrill run through her!

After a moment's silence, she raised her head again, moved uneasily, then murmured: "Oh! Let me get up now!"

"Very well," I replied, and unclasping my arms from 'round her, I slowly drew my prick out of her bottom, untied her—then taking her into one of the alcoves I showed her a bidet all ready for her use and left her. Passing into the other, I performed the needful ablutions to myself, then radiant with my victory and with having relieved my overcharged desires, I awaited Alice's reappearance.

9.

Presently Alice emerged from her screen, looking much freshened up by her ablutions. She had taken the opportunity to put her hair in order, it having become considerably disarranged and rumpled from her recent struggling.

Her face had lost the woebegone look, and there was a certain air of almost satisfaction about her that I could not understand, for she smiled as our eyes met, at the same time faintly coloring and concealing her cunt with her left hand as she approached me.

I offered her a glass of wine, which she drank, then I passed my left arm 'round her waist and drew her to the armchair, into which I placed myself, making her seat herself on my thighs and pass her right arm 'round my neck. Then, drawing her closely to me, I proceeded to kiss her ripe lips. She made no resistance; nor did she respond.

We sat in silence for a minute or two, I gently stroking her luscious breasts while unsuccessfully trying to read in her eyes what was her present frame of mind. Undoubtedly, during the ravishment of her bottom, she had tasted some pleasure sufficiently delicious to make her condone for its sake her "*violation à la derrière*" and practically to pardon her violator! What could it be?

I thought I would try a long shot, so presently I whispered in her ear, "Wouldn't you like that last all over again?"

I felt her quiver. She was silent for a moment, then asked softly, "Do you mean as a further punishment?" steadily keeping her eyes averted from me and flushing slightly.

"Oh! No," I replied, "it was so very evident that it was not 'punishment' to you" and I tried to catch her eyes as I pressed her amorously to me! "I meant as a little *entr'acte*."

Alice blushed furiously! I felt her arm 'round my neck tighten its embrace, and she nestled herself closer to me! "Not all!" she murmured gently.

"How much then? Or which part?" I whispered again.

"Oh! How can I possibly tell you!" she whispered back, dropping her face onto my shoulder and snuggling up to me, then throwing her left arm also 'round me, thereby uncovering her cunt!

I took the hint! "May I guess?" I whispered.

Without waiting for a reply, I slipped my right hand down from her breast and over her rounded belly, then began gently to toy with her hairs and caress her slit! Alice instantly kissed me twice passionately! She was evidently hot with lust, inflamed possibly by the dose of cantharides she had unknowingly swallowed!

"Then let me arrange you properly," I said. "Come we'll sit in front of the mirror and look at ourselves!" Alice blushed, not quite approving of the idea, but willing to please me!

So I moved the armchair in front of the mirror and seated myself in it. I then made Alice place herself on my thighs, her bottom being right over my prick, which promptly began to return to life, raising its drooping head until it rested against her posterior. Passing my left arm around her waist, I held her firmly to me. Then I made her part her legs, placing her left leg between mine while her right leg rested against the arm of the chair, my right thigh, in fact, separating her thighs.

Alice was now reflected in the mirror in three-quarter profile, but her parted legs allowed the whole of her cunt, with its glorious wealth of hair, to be fully seen! Her arms hung idly at her sides—I had made her promise not to use them!

We gazed at our reflection for a moment, our eyes meeting in the glass! Alice looked just lovely in her nakedness!

"Are you ready?" I asked, with a significant smile! Alice wriggled a little as if to settle herself down more comfortably, then turning her face (now all aflame and rosy red) to me she shamefacedly nodded, then kissed me!

"Keep your cheek against mine, and watch yourself in the glass, Alice," I whispered, then I gently placed my right hand on her sweet belly and slowly approached her cunt!

A thrill, evidently of pleasure, quivered through her as she felt my fingers pass through her hairs and settle on her cunt! "Ah!" she murmured, moving deliciously over my prick as I commenced to tenderly frig her, now fingering her slit, now penetrating her still-virgin orifice, now tickling her clitoris—causing her all the time the most deliciously lascivious transports, to which she surrendered herself by licentiously oscillating and jogging herself backwards and forwards as if to meet and stimulate my finger!

Presently Alice became still more excited; her breasts stiffened, her nostrils dilated! Noting this, I accelerated the movements of my finger, at the same time clasping her more firmly to me, my eyes riveted on her image in the glass and gloating over the spectacle she presented in her voluptuous raptures! Suddenly she caught her breath! Quickly I tickled her on her clitoris! "Oh! . . . Oh! . . . Oh! . . . Oh!" she ejaculated—then spent in ecstasy, maddening me by the quivering of her warm buttocks, between which my now rampant prick raged, held down!

I did not remove my finger from Alice's cunt, but kept it in her while she spent, slightly agitating it from time to time, to accentuate her ecstasy. But, as soon as I considered her sexual orgasm had exhausted itself, I began again to frig her. Then an idea flashed through my brain: Why should I not share her raptures? Carefully I watched for an opportunity! Soon I worked her again into an awful state of desire, panting with unsatisfied lust and furiously excited, obviously the result of the cantharides! Alice jerked herself about madly and spasmodically on my thighs! Presently an unusually violent movement of hers released my prick from its sweet confinement under her bottom; promptly it sprang up stark and stiff!

Quick as thought, I gripped Alice tightly and rammed myself fiercely into her bottom!!

"No! No! No!" she cried and strove to rise and so dislodge me, but I pressed her firmly down on my thighs and compelled her to remain impaled on my prick, creating a diversion by frigging her harder than ever!!

"Kiss me," I gasped, frantic with lust under my sensations in Alice's bottom and the sight of her naked self in the glass, quivering, palpitating, wriggling!! Quickly Alice pressed her lips on mine, our breaths mingled, our tongues met, my left hand caught hold of one of her breasts and squeezed it as her eyes closed. An electric shock ran through her! Then Alice spent frantically, plentifully bedewing my finger with her virgin distillation—at the same moment receiving inside her my boiling essence, as I shot it madly into her, my prick throbbing convulsively under the contractions of her rear sphincter muscles agitated and actuated by her ecstatic transports!!

Oh! The sensations of the moment! How Alice spent! How I discharged into her!!

It must have been a full minute before either of us moved, save for the involuntary tremors, which, from time to time, ran through us as our sexual excitement died away! Alice, now limp and nerveless, but still impaled on my prick, reposed on me, my finger dwelt motionless in her cunt, luxuriating in its envelope of warm, throbbing flesh! And so we rested, exhausted after our lascivious orgy, both half-conscious!

I was the first to come to myself, and as I caught sight of our reflection in the mirror, the licentious tableau we presented sent an involuntary quiver through me that my prick communicated to Alice, thus rousing her! As she dreamily opened her eyes, her glance also fell on the mirror! She started, became suddenly wide-awake, flushed rosy red, then hid her face in her hands, murmuring brokenly: "Oh! . . . How horrible! . . . How horrible! . . . What . . . have you . . . made me do?" half-sobbing in her shame; now that her sexual delirium had subsided and horribly conscious that my prick was still lodged in her bottom and impaling her! Foreseeing her action, I brought my right arm to the assistance of my left and held her forcibly down and so prevented her from rising and slipping off me! "What's the matter, Alice?" I asked soothingly, as she struggled to rid herself of my prick!

"Oh, let me go! Let me go!" she begged still with her face in her hands, in such evident distress that I deemed it best to comply and let her hurry off to her bidet, as she clearly desired.

So I released Alice; she slowly drew her bottom off my prick and rushed behind her screen. Following her example, I repaired to my corner and, after the necessary ablutions, I awaited Alice's return.

10.

Pending Alice's reappearance, I asked myself the important question: "What next should I do to her?" There was no doubt that I had succeeded in taming her, that I had now only to state my wishes and she would comply with them! But this very knowledge seemed to destroy the pleasure I had anticipated in having her in such utter subjection, the spice of the proceedings up to now undoubtedly lay in my forcing her to endure my salacious and licentious caprices, in spite of the most determined and desperate resistance she could make! Now that she had become a dull passive representative of the proud and voluptuous girl I had wanted, I should practically be flogging a dead horse were I to continue my program!

But there was one experience which on no account was to be omitted, forming as it did the culmination of my revenge as well as of my lust, one indignity which she could not and would not passively submit to, one crowning triumph over her which she could never question or deny—and this was . . . her violation! The ravishing of her maidenhead!!

Alice was now fully educated to appreciate the significance

of every detail of the process of transforming a girl into a woman; my fingers and lips had thoroughly taught her maiden cunt its duty, while my prick, when lodged in the throbbing recesses of her bottom, had acquainted her with the phenomenon of the masculine discharge at the crisis of pleasure, of the feminine ecstasy in receiving it, while her transports in my arms, although somewhat restricted by the circumstances, had revealed to her the exquisitely blissful sensations mutually communicated by such close clinging contact of male and female flesh! Yes! I would now devote the rest of the afternoon to fucking her.

Hardly had I arrived at this momentous decision when Alice came out of her alcove after an unusually prolonged absence. She had evidently thoroughly refreshed and freshened herself, and she looked simply fetching as she halted hesitatingly on pressing through the curtains, shielding her breasts with one hand and her cunt with the other, in charming shamefaced confusion. Obedient to my gesture, she came timidly towards me; she allowed me to pass my arm 'round her waist and kiss her, and then to lead her to the table where I made her drink a small tumbler of champagne that I had previously poured out for her, and for which she seemed most grateful. Then I gently whispered to her that we should lie down together on the couch for a little rest, and soon we were closely lying at our ease, she pressed and held amorously against me by my encircling arms.

For a minute or two we rested in silence, then the close conjunction of our naked bodies began to have the inevitable result on me—and I think also on her! Clasping her closely against me, I murmured: "Now, Alice, darling, I think the time has come for you to surrender to me your maidenhead . . . for you to be my bride!" And I kissed her passionately.

She quivered, moved herself uneasily as if trying to slip out of my encircling arms, trembling exceedingly, but remained silent.

I made as if to place her on her back, whispering: "Open your legs, dear!"

"No! No! Jack," Alice ejaculated, struggling to defend herself, and successfully resisting my attempt to roll her over onto her back. "Let me go, dear Jack! Surely you have revenged yourself on me sufficiently!" And she endeavored to rise.

I held her down firmly, and, in spite of her determined resistance, I got Alice on her back and myself on top of her. But she kept her legs so obstinately closed, and, in that position, I could not get mine between them! I began to get angry! Gripping her to me till her breasts flattened themselves against my chest, I raised my head and looked her sternly in the eyes.

"Now, Alice, no more nonsense," I said brusquely. "I'm going to fuck you! Yield yourself at once to me and do as I tell you— or I shall tie you down on this couch and violate you by force in a way you won't like! Now, once and for all, are you going to submit or are you not?"

She closed her eyes in an agony of distress!

"Jack! . . . Jack!" she murmured brokenly, then stopped as if unable to speak because of her overwhelming emotion!

"I can only take it that you prefer to be ravished by force rather than to be treated as a bride! Very well!" I rejoined. And I slipped off her as if to rise and tie her down. But she caught my hand; looked at me so pleadingly and with so piteous an expression in her lovely eyes that I sat down by her side on the couch.

"Upon my word I don't understand you, Alice!" I said, not unkindly. "You have known all along that you were to lose your maidenhead, and you have solemnly promised to yield it to me and to conform to all my desires, whatever they might be. Now, when the time has arrived for you to be fucked, you seem to forget all your promises!"

"But . . . but . . ." she stammered, "I didn't know . . . then! I thought . . . there was only one way! So . . . I promised! But you . . . have . . . had me . . . twice . . . another way! Oh! Let me off! Do let me off! I can't submit! Truly I can't . . . have me again . . . the . . . other way . . . if . . . you must! But not . . . this way! Oh . . . not this way!!!"

With my right hand I stroked her cunt gently, noting how she flinched when it was touched! "I want *this* virginity Alice! This virginity of your cunt! Your real maidenhead! And you must let me have it! Now am I to whip you again into submission? Don't be foolish! You can guess how this whip will hurt when properly applied, as it will be. You know you'll then have to give in! Why not do so at once, and spare yourself the pain and indignity of a severe whipping?"

Alice moaned pitifully: "Oh, my God!" There was silence for a few seconds, her face working painfully in her distress! Then she turned to me: "I must give in!" she murmured brokenly, "I couldn't endure . . . to be whipped . . . naked as I am . . . so take me . . . and do what you desire! Only treat me as kindly as you can! Now . . . I don't know why I ask it . . . but . . . kiss me . . . let me think I'm your wife . . . and on my wedding night!" She stopped, struggling with her emotions, then bravely put up her mouth with a pitiful smile to be kissed!

Promptly I took her lovely naked form lovingly in my arms, and pressing her to me till her breasts flattened against me, I passionately kissed her trembling lips again and again, until she gasped for breath. Then stooping, I repeated the caress on each breast and then on her quivering cunt, kissing the latter over and over again and interspersing my kisses with delicate lingual caresses! Then I succeeded in soothing her natural agitation at thus reaching the critical point of her maiden existence.

11.

Thus, at last, Alice and I found ourselves together naked on the Couch of Love! She, ill at ease and downcast at having to thus yield up her virginity and dreading horribly the process of being initiated by me into the mysteries of sexual love, and I, overjoyed at the prospect of ravishing Alice and conquering her maidenhead! Side by side on our backs, we lay in silence, my left hand clasping her right till she had regained her composure a little.

As soon as I saw she had become calmer, I slipped my arms 'round her, and, turning on my side towards her, I drew her tenderly to me, but still keeping her flat on her back; then I kissed her lips again and again ardently, murmuring lovingly between my kisses, "My little wife . . . my wee wife!" I noted delightedly how her downcast face brightened at my adoption of her fantasy, and felt her respond almost fondly to my kisses.

"May I learn something about my wife?" I whispered as I placed my right hand on Alice's maiden breasts and began feeling them as if she were, indeed, my bride! Alice smiling tenderly, yielding herself to my caprice, and quivering anew under the voluptuous sensations communicated to her by my inquisitive fingers! "Oh! What little beauties! Oh! What darling bubbies!" I murmured amidst fresh kisses. Alice was now beginning to look quite pleased at my using her own pet name for her treasures: She joined almost heartily into my game. I continued to fondle and squeeze her luscious breasts for a little longer, then carried my hand lower down, but suddenly arrested it, whispering: "May I?"

At this absurd travesty of a bridegroom's chivalrous respect to his bride, Alice fairly laughed (poor girl, her first laugh in that room all day!) then gaily nodded, putting up her lips for more kisses! Overjoyed to see her thus forgetting her woes, I pressed my lips on hers and kept them there, punctuating the kisses with feignedly timid advance of my hand over her belly, till it invaded the precincts of her cunt! "Oh! My darling! Oh! My sweetheart, oh, my wife!" I murmured passionately as my fingers roved wantonly all over Alice's virgin cunt, playing with her hairs, feeling and pressing its fleshiness insidiously, and toying with her slit—but not yet penetrating it! Alice all the while abandoned herself freely to the lascivious sensations induced by my fingerings, jogging her buttocks upwards and waggling her hips, ejaculating, "Ah!" and "Oh!" in spite of my lips being glued to hers, nearly suffocating her with kisses!

After a few minutes of this delicious exploitation of the most private part of Alice's body, I stopped my finger on her virgin orifice! "Pardon me, sweet," I whispered; then gently inserted it into Alice's cunt as far as I could, as if to assure myself as to her virgin condition, all the time smothering her with kisses. Keenly appreciating the humor of the proceedings, in spite of the serious lover-like air I was assuming, Alice laughed out heartily, unconsciously heaving herself up so as to meet my finger and slightly opening her thighs to allow it freer access to her cunt. My tongue took advantage of her laughter to dart through her parted lips in search of her tongue, which she then sweetly resigned to my ardent homage! "Oh! Wife . . . my wife! My sweet wife, my virgin wife!" I murmured, as if enchanted to find her a maiden! "Oh, what a delicious cunny you have— so fat! so soft, so juicy!—my wife, oh, wife," I breathed passionately into her ear, as I agitated my finger inside her cunt half frigging her and stopping her protests with my kisses, till I saw how I was exciting her! "Little wife," I whispered with a grin I could not for the life of me control. "Little wife, shall I make you come?"

In spite of her almost uncontrollable and self-absorbing sexual irritation, Alice laughed out, then nodded, closing her eyes as if in anticipation of her now-fast-approaching ecstasy! A little more subtle titillation and Alice spent blissfully on my finger, jerking about lasciviously and evidently experiencing the most voluptuous raptures and transports.

I waited till her sexual spasm had ceased. "Wife," I whispered, rousing her with my kisses. "Little wife! Oh, you naughty girl. How you seemed to enjoy it. Tell me, wife, was it then so good?"

As she opened her eyes, Alice met mine brimming with merriment: she blushed, then clasped me in her soft arms and kissed me passionately, murmuring: "Darling, oh, darling!" Then she burst out laughing at our ridiculousness! And so we lay for a few delicious moments, clasped in each other's arms.

Presently I murmured: "Now, wife, you'll like to learn something about me, eh?"

Alice laughed merrily at the quaint conceit, then colored furiously as she remembered that it would mean the introduction of her virgin hands to my virile organs. "Sit up, wife, dear, and give me your pretty hands," I said.

Alice, now glowing red with suppressed excitement and lust, quickly raised herself to a sitting position at my side. I took her dainty hands, which she yielded rather coyly into mine, turned on my back, opened my legs, and then guided her right hand onto my prick and her left to my testicles, then left her to indulge and satisfy in any manner she saw fit her senses of sight and touch, wondering whether it would occur to her that the fires she was about to excite in me would have to be extinguished in her virgin self when she was being ravished, as before long she would be!

For certainly half a minute, Alice intently inspected my organs of generation, leaning over me and supporting herself by placing her right hand on my stomach and her left on my thigh. I wondered what thoughts passed through her mind as she gazed curiously on what very soon would be the instruments of her violation and the conquerors of her virginity! But she made no sign.

Presently she steadied herself on her left hand, then timidly, with her right hand, she took hold of my prick gently, glancing curiously at me as if to note the effect of the touch of her soft hand on so excitable a part of my person, then smiling wickedly and almost triumphantly as she saw me quiver with pleasure. Oh! The exquisite sensations that accompanied her touch! Growing bolder, she held my prick erect and gently touched my balls with her slender forefinger, as if to test their substance, then took them in her hand, watching me eagerly out of the corners of her eyes to note the effect on me! I was simply thrilling with the pleasure. For a few minutes she lovingly played with my organs, generally devoting a hand to each, but sometimes she would hold my prick between one finger and thumb, while with her other hand, she would amuse herself by working the loose folds of skin off and on the knob! At another time, she would place my prick between her soft warm palms and pretend to roll it. Another time she seized a testicle in each hand, oh, so sweetly and gently, and caressed them. Had I not taken the edge off my sexual ardor by the two spendings in Alice's bottom, I would surely have discharged under the tenderly provocative ministration of her fingers. As it was, I had to exercise every ounce of my self-control to prevent an outbreak.

Presently I said quietly but significantly: "Little wife, may I tell you that between husband and wife, kissing is not only sanctioned but is considered even laudable!"

Alice laughed nervously, glanced quickly at me, then with heightening color, looked intently at my prick, which she happened at that moment to be grasping tightly in her right hand, its head protruding above her thumb and fingers, while with her left forefinger she was delicately stroking and tickling my balls! After a moment's hesitation, she bent down and squeezed my prick tightly (as if to prevent anything from issuing out of it) then softly kissed its head! Oh, my delicious sensations as her lips touched my prick! Emboldened by the success of her experiment, Alice set to work to kiss my balls sweetly, then passed her lips over the whole of my organ, showering kisses on them, but favoring especially my balls, which had for her a wonderful attraction, burying her lips in my scrotum, and (I really believe) tonguing them! Such attentions could only end in one way. Inflamed almost beyond endurance by the play of her sweetly irritating lips, my prick became so stiff and stark that Alice, in alarm, thought she had better cease her ministrations, and with blushing cheeks and a certain amount of trepidation, she lay herself down alongside of me.

By this time I was so mad with lust that I could hardly control myself, and as soon as Alice lay down I seized her by the arms, drew her to me, showered kisses on her lips, then with an abrupt movement, I rolled her over onto her back, slipping on top of her. In an effort to counteract my attack she separated her legs the better to push me back! Quick as thought, I forced myself between them!

> Now I was in the very lists of Love,
> Her champion, mounted for the hot encounter!

(Shakespeare, in *Venus and Adonis*.)

Alice was at my mercy! I could not have her at better advantage. She struggled desperately to dislodge me, but to no avail.

Gripping her tightly, I got my stiff and excited prick against the lips of her cunt, then pushing steadily, I drove it into Alice, burying its head in her! Despite her fearful struggles and rapid movements of her buttocks and hips, I made another thrust, entering still further into her cunt, then felt myself blocked! Alice screamed agonizingly, "Oh . . . oh, stop, you're hurting me!" throwing herself wildly about in her pain and despair, for she recognized that she was being violated. Knowing that it was her maiden membrane that was stopping my advance into her, and that this now was the last defense of her virginity, I rammed into her vigorously! Suddenly I felt something give way inside her. Finally my prick glided well up her cunt and it did not require the despairing shriek that came from Alice to tell me that I had broken through the last barriers and had conquered her virginity!

Oh, my exultation! At last I had ravished Alice. I had captured her maidenhead and was now actually fucking her in spite of herself! She, poor girl, lay beneath me tightly clasped in my arms, a prey to the keenest shame, deprived of her maidenhead, transfixed with my prick, her cunt suffering martyrdom from its sudden distension and smarting with the pain of her violation! Pitying her, I lay still for some seconds so as to allow the interior of her cunt to stretch a bit, but I was too wrought up and mad with lust to long remain inactive in such surroundings.

With a final thrust, I sent my prick well home, Alice's hair and mine interweaving. She shrieked again! Then agitating myself gently on her, I began to fuck her, first with steady strokes of my buttocks, then with more rapid and uneven strokes and thrusts, she quivering under me, overwhelmed by her emotions at thus finding her pure body compelled to become the recipient of my lust and by the strangely delicious pleasures that the movements of my prick inside her cunt were arousing within her. Alice no longer struggled, but lay passive in my arms, unconsciously accommodating herself to my movements, and involuntarily working her hips and bottom, instinctively yielding to the prompting of her now fast-increasing sexual cravings by jogging herself up as if to meet my downward thrusts!

Shall I ever forget my sensations at that moment? Alice, the long-desired Alice, the girl of all girls, the unconscious object of all my desires—Alice lay beneath me, tightly clasped in my arms, naked, quivering, her warm flesh throbbing against mine, my prick lodged in her cunt, her tearful face in full sight, her breasts palpitating and her bosom heaving in her agitation!—gasping, panting in the most acute shame and distress at being violated, yet unconsciously longing to have her sexual desires satisfied while dreading the consummation of her deflowering! I could no longer control myself! Clasping her yielding figure still more closely against me, I let myself go! Thrusting, ramming, shoving and agitating my prick spasmodically in her, I frenziedly set to work to fuck her! A storm of rapid tumultuous jogs, a half-strangled, "Oh—oh! Oh!!" from Alice as I spent deliriously into her with my hot discharge, at the same moment feeling the head of my prick christened by the warm gush that burst from Alice as she also frantically spent, punctuating the pulsations of her discharge by voluptuous upheavings of her wildly agitated bottom.

I remained master of myself, notwithstanding my ecstatic delirium, but Alice fainted under the violence of the sexual eruption for the first time legitimately induced within her! My warm kisses on her upturned face, however, soon revived her. When she came to and found herself still lying naked in my arms and harboring my prick in the freshly opened asylum of her cunt, she begged me to set her free! But she had not yet extinguished the flames of lust and desire her provocative personality and appetizing nakedness had kindled and which she had stimulated to white heat by the tender manipulations and kisses she had bestowed on my testicles and prick! The latter still remained rampant and stiff and burned to riot again within the deliciously warm and moist recesses of Alice's cunt, while I longed to make her expire again in the sweet agonies of satisfied sexual desire and to witness and share her involuntary transports and wondrous ecstasies as she passed from sexual spasm while being sweetly fucked!

So I whispered amidst my kisses: "Not yet, Alice! Not yet! Once more, Alice! You'll enjoy it this time." I then began gently to fuck her again.

"No, no," she cried, plunging wildly beneath me in her vain endeavors to dislodge me. "Not again, oh, not again. Let me go! Stop! Oh, please, do stop," she implored, almost in tears, and in terrible distress at the horrible prospect of being ravished a second time.

I only shook my head and endeavored to stifle her cries with my kisses! Seeing that I was determined to enjoy her again, Alice, now in tears, ceased her pleading and resigned herself to her fate!

In order to more easily control her struggles, I had thrown my arms over hers, thus pinioning them. Seeing now that she did not intend to resist me, except perhaps passionately, I relaxed my embrace, set her arms free, passed mine 'round her body, then whispered: "Hug me tightly, you'll be more comfy, Alice!" She did so. "That's much better, isn't it?" I murmured. She tearfully smiled, then nodded affirmatively, putting up her lips to be kissed.

"Now just lie quietly and enjoy yourself," I whispered, then began to fuck her with slow and steady piston-like thrusts of my prick up and down her cunt! At once Alice's bosom and breasts began to flutter deliciously against my chest. Exercising the fullest control I possibly could bring to bear on my seminal reserves, so that Alice should have every opportunity of indulging and satisfying her sexual appetites and cravings and of fully tasting the delights of copulation, I continued to fuck her steadily, watching her blushing upturned face and learning from her telltale eyes how she was getting on. Presently she began to agitate her hips and jog herself upwards, then her breath came and went quickly, her eyes turned upwards and half-closed, a spasm convulsed her. She spent! I stopped for a moment. After a few seconds, Alice opened her eyes, blushing rosy red as she met mine. I kissed her lips tenderly, whispering: "Good?" She nodded and smiled. I resumed. Soon she was again quivering and wriggling under me as a fresh wave of lust seized her; again her eyes closed, and again Alice spent blissfully! I saw that I had now thoroughly roused her sexual desires and that she had surrendered herself to their domination and that they were imperiously demanding satisfaction!

I clasped her closely to me and whispered quickly: "Now, Alice, let yourself go!" I set to work in real earnest, thrusting rapidly and ramming myself well into her! Alice simply abandoned herself to her sensations of the moment! Hugging me to her, she agitated herself wildly under me, plunging madly, heaving herself furiously upwards, tossing her head from side to side. She seemed as if overcome and carried away by a torrent of lust and madly endeavoring to satisfy it! I could hardly hold her still. How many times she spent I do not know, but her eyes were constantly half-closing and opening again as spasm after spasm convulsed her! Suddenly she ejaculated frenziedly: "Now! Now, let me have it! Oh, God! Let me have it all!" Immediately I responded—a few furious shoves, and I poured my boiling essence into Alice, spending frantically in blissful ecstasy. "Ah! Ah!" she cried, quivering in rapturous transports as she felt herself inundated by my warm discharge! Then a paroxysm swept through her, her head fell back, her eyes closed, her lips opened as she spent convulsively in her turn!

She fainted right away; it had been too much for her! I tried to bring her to by kisses and endearments, but did not succeed.

So I drew my prick cautiously out of Alice's cunt, all blood-stained, stanched with a handkerchief the blood—unimpeachable evidence of the rape that had been committed on her virginity. When she soon came to, I assisted her to rise, and as she seemed half-dazed, supported her as she tottered to her alcove, where she half-fell into a low chair. I brought her a glass of wine, which she drank gratefully, and which greatly revived her. Then I saw that she had everything she could want: water, soap, syringe, and towels. She asked me to leave her, adding she was now all right. Before doing so, I stooped down to receive the first kiss she would give as a woman, having had her last as a girl. Alice threw her arms 'round my neck, drew my face to hers, then kissed me passionately over and over again, quite unable to speak because of her emotion! I returned her kisses with interest, wondering whether she wished to pardon me for violating her!

Presently Alice whispered: "May I dress now?"

I had intended to fuck her again, but I saw how overwrought she was; besides that, the afternoon was late and there was just comfortable time left for her to catch her first train home. So I replied: "Yes, dear, if you like. Shall I bring your clothes here?" She nodded gratefully. I carefully collected her garments and took them to her, then left her to herself to dress. Pouring out a bumper of champagne, I celebrated silently but exultingly the successful completion of my vengeance and my victory over Alice's virginity, then retired to my alcove and donned my own garments.

In about a quarter of an hour Alice appeared, fully-dressed, hatted, and gloved. I threw open the doors and she passed without a word but cast a long glance 'round the room in which she had passed so memorable an afternoon. I called a hansom, placed her in it, and took her to her station in comfortable time for her train. She was very silent during the drive, but made no opposition when I took her hand in mine and stroked it gently. As the train started, I raised my hat with the customary salute, to which she responded in quite her usual pleasant way. No one who witnessed our parting would have dreamt that the pretty ladylike girl had just been forcibly ravished by the quiet gentlemanly man, after having first been stripped naked and subjected to shocking indignities! And as I drove home, I wondered what the outcome of the afternoon's work would be.

"Frank" and I

by Anonymous

This delightful novel of hidden sexuality and erotic escapades was first published in England in 1902 in an edition of 350 copies. The narrator, a wealthy young man, meets a youth— the "Frank" of the title—and, taken by his beauty and good manners, invites him home. When his young charge disobeys him, he commences to flog him. One can imagine his surprise when the young man, confounded in dishabille, turns out to be a young woman of surpassing charms. Given the period, the following excerpt is interesting because the female partner is the initiator, and because oral pleasure is her preferred means of seduction. Under the circumstances, it is no surprise that she is a domestic servant, and not a "woman of quality."

As I had as much poking as I ever wanted with Frances, I entirely neglected my buxom housemaid, Lucy, whom I had formerly poked pretty regularly, and who was, I think, fond of me. She could not understand why I had suddenly given her up, so she used frequently to come to my room on some pretense or other, when she knew I was there. On those occasions, I always had a talk with her, and sometimes gave her a kiss, but nothing else; so, when she saw that I was not going to "have" her, she would go away, looking very disappointed. However, she was a persevering woman, and one day, she regularly forced me to satisfy her desire.

I had gone up to my room shortly after breakfast to change

my coat and, having done so, I sat down in an easy chair to read a letter I had received that morning from Maud. She wrote telling me that she was going to be married in a month's time; and she asked me to come and see her as soon as possible, so that we might settle our little affairs. I was not surprised at the news, for she had before hinted that she was thinking of leaving me.

I had just finished reading the letter when Lucy came into the room; she was looking, as usual, very nice in her neat print frock, white apron, and cap with long streamers. She went through the form of arranging the things on the dressing-table; then coming to where I was sitting, she looked at me wistfully with her big hazel eyes, and said: "You never give me a proper kiss now. Have I offended you?"

"No, Lucy, you have not," said I, stroking her plump cheek, but not kissing her, as I did not feel the least inclined to make love of any sort at that moment, owing to my having poked Frances several times during the night and morning.

"Why, you haven't even kissed me!" she said, pouting her full red lips and holding up her face invitingly. I smiled, but did not touch her.

"Well, I'll kiss you, till you give me a proper kiss." So saying, she dropped on her knees in front of me and to my astonishment—for she had never done such a thing to me before—she unbuttoned my trousers, took out my tool, and began manipulating it with a skillful touch, saying with a laugh, as she noticed its very limp condition: "Oh! How miserable and flabby it looks; but I'll soon make it stiff." Then, bending down her head, she took into her mouth my drooping prick, and began tickling the tip of it with her hot tongue and drawing the foreskin backwards and forwards over the nut with her lips; soon causing the member to spring up in full erection and giving me an intense sensation of lascivious pleasure: so much so, that I felt the premonitory symptoms of the discharge. I exclaimed hurriedly: "Stop! Stop, Lucy! Or you will make me go off in your mouth. Put it in the right place. Quick!" She let it go, and jumped up, with flushed cheeks and sparkling eyes, laughing gaily; and at once pulled all her clothes up above her waist; and as she was wearing no drawers, I had a full view, for a moment, of her massive thighs, her big legs, and the forest of curly brown hair that hid her cunt. Then she turned round and, striding over me backwards as I sat in the chair, she put her hand between her legs, and taking hold of my prick, guided it into its proper place. Then she gradually lowered herself down till every inch of the stiff column of flesh was buried in her cunt and her naked bottom rested on my thighs. I then unfastened the whole front of her dress; and as she had no stays on, her luxuriant bubbies were only covered by her chemise, which I soon pushed down out of the way; then holding one of her big titties in each hand, I said: "Now Lucy, you must do all the work."

"All right," she replied, giggling. Then she began moving herself up and down on the points of her toes; at one moment raising her bottom till only the nut of my tool was left between the lips of her cunt, then at the next moment letting herself down with a flop on my thighs; each time driving the weapon up to the hilt in the sheath; while I sat still, enjoying the exquisite sensation and playing with her large red nipples. Up and down went her bottom, her movements gradually became more rapid, and when she felt the "moment" was at hand, she worked with increasing vigor, her titties undulating like the waves of the sea. In another instant, I spent, and the spasm seized her: I could feel a thrill pass over her body; her nipples seemed to stiffen in my fingers; her thighs gripped mine tightly; and she wriggled on the dart that was impaling her, till all was over. Then she leant back against my breast, the pressure of her thighs relaxed, my limp prick dropped out of its place, and the thick, white stuff trickled out of the orifice, down between the cheeks of her bottom as she sat straddled on my lap. She burst out laughing, and said: "I thought I could make you do it to me!" I also laughed, remarking: "I did not do it to you. You did it to me, you naughty young woman. In fact you have committed an indecent assault upon me, and I am going to give you a good spanking for your misconduct." Then I placed her in position to receive the punishment.

"Spank away. I like having my bottom warmed," she said, pulling her chemise and petticoats well up out of the way, and settling herself down across my knees . . .

SADOPAIDEIA

by Anonymous

Edwardian in tone and Rabelaisian in content, this under-
ground English classic, first published in 1907, relates the
bawdy adventures of a young gentleman, Cecil Prendergast.
While a student at Oxford, Prendergast succumbs to the erotic
charms of the domineering Mrs. Harcourt. Under her careful
tutelage, he learns both the art of submission and the joys of
sadism in dalliances with Muriel, Juliette, Gladys, and other
adventurous young women Mrs. Harcourt sends his way. In
this excerpt, our hero experiences mutual oral pleasure for
the first time.

I first met Mrs. Harcourt at my College Ball, my last term at
Oxford. She had come up for "Commem" to chaperone the
cousin of one of my chums. Only the blessed ceremony of
marriage gave her this right, for she was still well under thirty.
I learnt from Harry that she was a widow, having married an
elderly and somewhat used-up brewer who most considerately
died quite soon after marriage, having, I have every reason to
believe, decidedly shortened his life by vain, though praise-
worthy, attempts to satisfy his wife's insatiable appetite.

She was a little woman, beautifully made, with magnificent
red-brown hair, the fairest possible skin, a bust that was abundant without being aggressively large, a neat waist with splendidly curved hips, and in a ball dress—discreetly yet alluringly
cut—she fired my passion at once.

Harry was very *épris* with his cousin and so was only too glad for me to take Mrs. Harcourt off his hands. We danced one or two dances together. She had the most delightful trick in the boston of getting her left leg in between mine now and then. At first I thought it was an accident, but it happened so repeatedly that I began to suspect, and my old man began to suggest, that more might be intended. At last I felt what seemed a deliberate pressure of her thigh against my left trouser. John Thomas responded at once, and I, looking down at my partner, caught her eye. There was no mistaking the expression. She gave a little self-conscious laugh and suggested that we should sit out the rest of the dance.

Now I had helped to superintend the sitting-out arrangement and knew where the coziest nooks were to be found. After one or two unsuccessful attempts, when we were driven back by varying coughs or the sight of couples already installed (in one case, a glimpse of white drawers showed that one couple had come to quite a good understanding), I succeeded in finding an unoccupied Chesterfield in a very quiet corner of the Cloisters. Here we ensconced ourselves, and without further delay I slipped my arm round my partner's back, along the top of the couch, and, bending down, kissed the bare white shoulder.

"You silly boy," she murmured.

"Why silly?" said I, putting my other arm round her in front so that my hand rested on her left breast.

She turned towards me to answer, but before she could speak my lips met hers in a long kiss.

"That's why," she said, with a smile, when I drew back. "Kisses were meant for lips; it's silly to waste them on shoulders."

I needed no further invitation. I pressed her close in my arms and, finding her lips slightly parted, ventured to explore them just a little with my tongue. To my great joy and delight, her tongue met mine. My hand naturally was not idle. I stroked and squeezed her breast, outside her frock first, and then tried to slip it inside, but she would not allow that. "You'll tumble me too much," she murmured as she gently pushed it away. "I can't have my frock rumpled; people would notice. Take that naughty hand away."

As I didn't obey, she took it herself and placed it with a dainty little pat on my own leg above the knee. "There it can't do any harm," she added with an adorable smile. She was going to take her own hand away, but I held it tight. I drew her still closer to me and kissed her again and again, my tongue this time boldly caressing her own. She gave a little sigh and let herself sink quite freely into my arms. By this time the old proverb that "a standing prick has no conscience" proved its truth. My right hand released hers, and I took her in my arms, my right arm this time encircling her below the waist, with the hand clasping the left cheek of her bottom. Modern dresses do not allow of much underclothing, and I could distinctly feel the edge of her drawers through the soft silk of her frock. "Oh, you darling," I murmured as I kissed her. By my taking her close to me, she naturally had to move the hand that had gently held mine. It slid up my leg and at last met John Thomas, for whom my thin evening-dress trousers proved an altogether inadequate disguise. She gave a little gasp, and then her fingers convulsively encircled him and she squeezed him fondly.

That was enough for me. My hand slid down her frock and up again, but this time inside. It found a beautifully molded leg sheathed in silk, dainty lace, the smooth skin of her thigh, and at last soft curls and the most delightfully pouting lips possible to imagine. My mouth remained glued to hers, her hand grasped my eager weapon, and I was just about to slip down between her knees and consummate my delight when the lips that I was fondling pouted and contracted, and I felt my hand and fingers soaked with her love, and I realized that her imagination had proved too much for her, and that while I was still unsatisfied, she had reached at least a certain height of bliss.

She pulled herself together at once, and just as I was unbuttoning my trousers she stopped me. "No, not here," she said. "It's too dangerous, and besides, it would be much too hurried and uncomfortable. Come and see me in town, there's a darling boy. Now we must go back and dance. This naughty fellow," she added, playfully patting my trousers, "must wait." She then got up, arranged her dress, and, giving me a lovely kiss with her tongue, led the way back to the ballroom. I followed, but do the best I might, John Thomas took his revenge on me by weeping with disappointment, which made me extremely sticky and uncomfortable, and but for Mrs. Harcourt's invitation to see her in town, my evening would have been spoilt.

I "went down" the next day, and on arrival in town lost no time in calling on Mrs. Harcourt at her little house on South Molton Street. When I rang at her door, it was opened by a very neat though not particularly pretty maid, as I thought. She had, however, quite an alluring little figure and a perky naughtiness in her face that is perhaps more fascinating even than mere beauty.

"Is Mrs. Harcourt at home?"

"I will see, sir. Will you come this way? What name shall I say?" She showed me into a delightful little morning room, very tastefully furnished, and disappeared. She did not keep me waiting long, but returned and said:

"Will you come this way, sir? Madame is in her boudoir. Shall I take your hat and stick?"

She took them from me and turned to hang the hat on the stand. The pegs were rather high, and in reaching up she showed the delightful line of her breast and hips and just a glimpse of a white petticoat underneath the skirt.

"Is it too high for you? Let me help," I said.

"Thank you, sir," she said, smiling up at me.

I took her hat over her shoulder and hung it up. She was between me and the hat-stand and could not move until I did. I lowered my arm and drew her towards me. She looked up at me with a provoking smile. I bent down and kissed her lips, while my hand fondled the delightfully plump breast.

"You mustn't," she murmured. "What would mistress say, if she knew?"

"But she won't know," I answered as my hand went further down to her bottom, which her tight skirt made very apparent.

"She will if I tell her," she smiled, "you naughty boy." She playfully patted my trouser leg as she passed me.

"Which, of course, you won't," I said lightly, as I followed her. She laughed rather maliciously, I thought, though I didn't pay much attention to it at the time. I had reason later, though, to remember it.

We went upstairs, and I was shown into a lovely room where a log fire was burning, although it was no colder than most June days in this country. There was a splendid deep low couch, or rather divan, for it had no back, facing the fire, covered with cushions, which took my eye at once, and I mentally promised myself what should happen on it. My expectations fell far short of the reality, as will be seen.

Mrs. Harcourt was sitting on a low chair near the couch. She was in a delightfully fitting teagown, cut fairly low at the neck, with very loose sleeves. It clung to her figure as she rose to greet me, and being made of chiffon with a foundation of pink silk, it gave one the idea at first that she was practically naked.

"Bring up tea, please, Juliette," she said to the maid, who disappeared.

"So you have found your way here," she said, coming to-wards me with outstretched hand.

The room was heavily scented with perfume, which I learnt came from burning pastilles, and she herself always used a mix-ture of sandalwood and ottar of roses. As she approached me, her perfume intoxicated me, and without saying a word I clasped her in my arms and pressed long hot kisses on her lips. To my intense delight, I found she had no corset on, and her supple body bent close to mine, so that I could feel every line of it. My hands slipped down and grasped the cheeks of her bottom as I pressed her stomach against my trousers.

"You rough impetuous bear," she smiled at me. "Wait till the tea comes up." And she disengaged herself from me, playfully slapping as she did so, John Thomas, who was naturally quite ready by this time for anything. "Oh, already," she said as she felt his condition. "I told this naughty fellow at Oxford that he would have to be patient, and he must learn to obey."

Tea appeared most daintily served, and on the tray I noticed a delicate Bohemian-glass liqueur carafe and two liqueur glasses.

"Do you know *crème de cacao*?" asked Mrs. Harcourt. "It's rather nice."

She poured out tea and then filled each liqueur glass half-full of the dark liqueur and poured cream on top.

"*Á votre santé*," she said, touching my glass with hers. Our fingers met and a thrill ran right through me. I drank the li-queur off at a gulp and leant towards her.

"You greedy thing," she laughed. "That's not the way to drink it. No, no, wait till we've had tea."

As I tried to get her in my arms, she said, "Naughty boys must not be impatient," then slapped John Thomas again and somewhat harder this time.

I sat back on the couch and drank my tea rather gloomily,

Mrs. Harcourt watching me teasingly. At last she put her cup down and, reaching for her cigarette box, took one herself and offered me one, then leant back in her chair and looked at me with a smile.

"It's a shame to tantalize him so, isn't it?" she said at last.

I did not answer, but jumped up and threw my arms round her, kneeling in front of her, and covered her face and neck with kisses. She tossed her cigarette into the grate and undid the silk tie of her gown. It fell back and showed that all she had on was a dainty chemise of the finest lawn and a petticoat. My right hand immediately sought her left breast and, pulling it out, I kissed and sucked the dainty nipple, which responded at once to my caress, stiffening most delightfully. My left hand then reached down to the hem of her petticoat and began to raise it.

I felt her right arm round my waist and her left hand began to unbutton my fly from the top. Before she had time to undo the last button, John Thomas leapt forth ready and eager, but she slapped it and pushed it in again and undid the last button and fumbled for my balls and gently drew them out. I drew back a little from her and lifted her petticoat right up, disclosing the daintiest of black silk openwork stockings with pale green satin garters, and above them filmy lawn drawers with beautiful lace and insertion, through which the fair satin skin of her thighs gleamed most provokingly. At the top there appeared just between the opening of the drawers the most fascinating brown curls imaginable.

I feasted my eyes on this lovely sight, undoing my braces and slipping my trousers down. Her hand immediately left my balls and began to fondle my bottom, stroking and pinching the cheeks while she murmured, "You darling boy, oh, what a lovely bottom."

I was eager to be in her, but the brown curls fascinated me

so much that I could not resist the temptation to stoop down and kiss them. I was rather shy of doing this, as I had never done it before, and though I knew it was unusual with tarts, I was not sure if it would be welcome here. Judge of my surprise, then, when I felt Mrs. Harcourt's hand on my head gently pressing it down and heard her saying, "How did you guess I wanted that?"

She opened her legs wider, disclosing the most adorable pussy, with pouting lips just slightly opening and showing the bright coral inner lips, which seemed to ask for my kisses. I buried my tongue in the soft curls, and with eager tongue explored every part of her mossy grot. She squirmed and wriggled with pleasure, opening her legs quite wide and twisting them round me. I followed all her movements, backing away on my knees as she slipped off the chair, until at last, when she drenched my lips with love, she slipped on the hearthrug. Then, as I could scarcely reach her with my tongue in that position, and didn't wish to lose a drop of the maddening juice, I disengaged my legs from hers and knelt down to one side so that my head could dive right between her legs. This naturally presented my naked bottom and thighs to her gaze.

"You rude naughty boy," she said, smacking me gently, "to show me this bare bottom. I'm shocked at you."

Her hands again fondled my balls and bottom, and I had all I could do to prevent John Thomas from showing conclusively what he had in store for her.

I had no intention of wasting good material, however, and was just about to change my position so that I could arrive at the desired summit of joy when I felt her trying to pull my right leg towards her. I let myself go and she eventually succeeded in lifting it right over, and we were in the position I knew quite well from photographs, known as sixty-nine.

My heart beat high. Was it possible I was to experience this supreme pleasure of which I had heard so much? I buried my head between her thighs, my tongue redoubled its efforts, searching out every corner and nook it could find, and just as it was rewarded by another flow of warm life, I felt round my own weapon, not the fondling of her hand, but something softer, more clinging, and then unmistakably the tip of a velvet tongue from the top right down to the balls and back again, and then I felt the lips close round it and the gentle nip of teeth. This was too much. John Thomas could restrain himself no longer, and as I seized her bottom with both hands and sucked the whole of her pussy into my mouth, he spurted forth with convulsive jerks his hidden treasure. When the spasm was over, I collapsed limply on her, my lips still straining her life.

VOLUPTUOUS CONFESSIONS

By Anonymous

From The Boudoir

*The Boudoir was a nineteenth-century underground peri-
odical that featured erotic art and literature. The following is
the complete text of a serialized novella in three parts that
chronicles a young woman's initiation into sexual pleasure,
first as a voyeur of her aunt's adulterous affair, then as the
wife of a husband of mediocre talents (and proportions), and
then with Stefan, her dream lover.*

PART I

The chateau of my grandfather was situated outside the city
in a delightful country setting. The grounds, shaded by
scattered trees, mostly splendid oaks, or chestnuts, were of
great extent and enclosed by walls. The grounds immediately
around the house itself were laid out in splendid patterns of
the finest flowers, and watered by a little river, which became
lost in the country by capacious meanderings.

My old grandmother, mostly confined to the house, never
went much further than the beautiful nearby lake fed by the
river. As for me, my greatest happiness was to wander alone in
the most uncultivated parts of the property, and indulge in the
reveries of my eighteenth year. These reveries, I ought to confess, were always of the same nature. A strange feeling invaded

112

my soul, my young imagination reveled in unknown regions and presented before my eyes images of tenderness and devotion in which a young man was always the hero. Although profoundly ignorant as to the differences between the sexes, my already awakened feelings moved the whole of my body and spirit. A secret fire circulated in my veins; often dimness came over my eyes, my limbs trembled, and I was obliged to sit down, a prey to a weakness that combined both pleasure and pain.

It was the month of June and the weather was magnificent. My walks were mostly in the morning when I was sure to be alone.

We received a letter from Madame Terlot, my aunt, who, replying to my grandmother's invitation, announced her imminent arrival.

Madame Terlot was about twenty-six or twenty-seven, and had been married at the age of twenty to an old man who had left her a widow two years since, the mistress of a great fortune, and without children. She was a delightful person. She had hair black as ebony, contrasted with the whiteness of her complexion, which was lighted up by her beautiful deep blue eyes. Her mouth, small and pleasing, was set off by adorable teeth, as white as the purest ivory. She had a fine figure, perfectly formed and graceful, with medium-sized breasts and shapely hips. She dressed with taste and elegance.

I loved her very much. Her lively and playful disposition had long captivated me. Accustomed to living with my grandmother, whose age prevented her from affording me any amusement, deprived of companions, I was very happy at the arrival of a youthful relation who would be a friend to me.

A marriage arrangement had been spoken of between my aunt and Monsieur Bonbier, which my grandmother immediately approved. Aunt Bertha wrote at once to him, with an invitation to pass some time at the chateau, and in consequence he arrived a few days after her.

What I am going to relate now is very delicate and difficult. I have hesitated a long time! But the chances are nobody will read it; these lines are for my own perusal, after all. The pictures that I am going to draw are very lively, but they will be true. What lovers—real lovers—in each other's arms have not experienced the same? I will add that, even though now I am past kissing, I feel a veritable pleasure in recalling the soft enjoyment.

One morning very early, according to my custom, I had gone a long way in the park and sat down at the foot of a tree plunged in my usual reveries.

I saw my aunt, whom I thought in bed, some distance off, evidently coming to the little eminence where I was. She was dressed in a fresh peignoir of white and blue. Monsieur Bonbier was with her, dressed in a suit and a straw hat. They seemed to be having a lively conversation.

I do not know what secret instinct impelled me to avoid their presence. I hid behind a big tree that completely shielded me from their sight.

They soon arrived at the spot I had just vacated, and stopping for a moment, Monsieur Bonbier looked all around, and convinced that at this hour no one could see them, threw his arms around my aunt. He drew her to him and pressed her to his breast, their lips so joined that I heard a long kiss, which struck to the bottom of my heart.

"My dear Bertha; my angel; my sweet darling! I love you. I adore you. What a frightful time I have passed without you; but soon it will be over! Stop, that I may embrace you again! Give me your beautiful eyes, your lovely teeth, your divine neck! How I could eat them!" he exclaimed.

My aunt, far from resisting, gave herself up to him, returned kiss for kiss, caress for caress. Her color heightened; her eyes sparkled.

"My Alfred," said she, "I love only you. I am all yours."

One may judge the effect such caresses had upon me. I felt as though I had been struck by an electric spark. I seemed unable to move, and almost lost the use of my senses. I recovered myself promptly, however, and continued to be all eyes and ears. Alfred wanted something, which I did not understand, and seemed to insist on it.

"No, no, my love," replied Bertha. "No! Not here, I beg you. My God, I would never dare! If anyone should surprise us, I should die!"

"My dear, who can see us at this hour?"

"I don't know, but I'm afraid! I couldn't. I would have no pleasure. We will find a way of doing it; have patience."

"How can you speak of patience in the state I am in! Give me your hand; feel it yourself!"

He then took the hand of my aunt and placed it in such a curious place that it was impossible for me to understand the reason. But it was worse when I saw this hand disappear in a certain slit in his trousers, which she had presently unbuttoned, and seized an object I could not see.

"Ahh," said she, "I see very well how much you want me. How beautiful it is, and I like it so big and hard. If we had only some privacy, I would soon put you to the proof."

And her hand moved softly up and down, to the apparent pleasure of Monsieur Bonbier, who stood immovably erect, his leg a little open.

"Ah!" suddenly exclaimed my aunt. "What an idea! Come, Alfred, I recollect there is near here a small pavilion, you know. It is a curious place for our love, but no one will see us, and I can be all yours. Come on."

I must explain that the pavilion of which my aunt spoke was

simply a poor gazebo constructed like a thatched cottage.

Protected by some big brambles, I could approach them without fear of being seen. This I did with infinite precautions, and got to the back of the pavilion at the moment when Bertha had already entered and Monsieur Bonbier, after looking all around, also came in. I sought out a convenient hole and soon found one, as the planks and beams were badly joined, sufficiently large to enable me to see everything. I applied my eye and held my breath, and was witness to what I am going to relate.

Bertha, hanging on the neck of her lover, devoured him with kisses.

"My darling, I was very unhappy to refuse you, but I was afraid. Here, at least, I am assured. This beautiful rod, what pleasure I am going to give him. I come already in thinking of it! But how shall we place ourselves?"

"It is all right," he said. "Let me see again your mossy valley. It is such a long time I have wanted it."

You may guess what my thoughts were at this moment. But what were they going to do? I was not left long in suspense.

Monsieur Bonbier, going down on one knee, raised Bertha's skirts. What charms he exposed! Under that fine cambric chemise were legs worthy of Venus, encased in silk stockings, secured above the knee by garters the color of fire. Above that were two creamy thighs, round and firm, surmounted by a fleece of black and lustrous curls. The abundance and length of them were a great surprise to me, compared to the light chestnut moss that covered my own mount.

"How I love it," said Alfred. "How beautiful and fresh your pussy is! Open yourself a little, my angel, that I may kiss those adorable lips!"

Bertha did as he demanded. Her thighs, in opening, made me see a rosy slit, upon which her lover glued his lips. Bertha seemed in ecstasy! Shutting her eyes, and speaking broken words, she seemed transported by this curious caress. I could see Alfred's tongue moving over her flesh, licking and darting like that of a snake.

"Ah, you kill me . . . go on! I . . . I . . . I'm coming! Ah, ah!"

What was she doing? Good God! I had never supposed that any pleasure pertained to that part. Yet, at that moment I began to feel myself in the same spot some particular titillations, which made me almost understand it.

Alfred got up, supporting Bertha, who appeared to have lost all strength. She soon recovered herself and embraced him with passion.

"Come, let me put it in," she said. "But how are we going to do it?"

"Turn yourself, my dear, and incline against this unworthy wall."

Then, to my great surprise, Bertha, by rapid and excited movements, undid the trousers of Alfred. Lifting his shirt above his navel, she exposed to my view such an extraordinary object that I was almost surprised into a scream. What could be this unknown thing, the head of which was so rosy and exalted, its length and thickness threatening to make me dizzy?

Bertha evidently did not share my fears, for she took this frightful instrument in her hand, caressed it a moment, and said, "Let us begin." She pulled Alfred to her by this organ. "Come into your little companion, and be sure not to go away too soon."

She lifted up her clothes behind and exposed to the light of day two bottom globes of dazzling whiteness, separated by a crack of which I could only see a slight trace. She then inclined herself, and placing her hands against the wall, presented her adorable bottom to her lover.

Alfred, just behind her, took his enormous pole in hand, and wetting it with a little saliva commenced to introduce it between the two rosy lips that I had perceived. Bertha did not flinch, and opened as much as possible the part that she presented. It almost seemed to open itself, and at length absorbed this long and thick piston, which appeared monstrous to me. It penetrated so well, however, that it disappeared entirely, and the belly of its happy possessor came to be glued to the buttocks of my aunt.

There was then a conjunction of combined movements— Alfred pushing against her, Bertha falling back on him—followed by broken words: "Ah! . . . I feel it . . . it is getting into me," said Bertha. "Push it all well into me . . . softly . . . let me come first. Ah! . . . I feel it . . . I'm coming! Quicker! I come . . . stop . . . there you are! I die . . . I . . . I . . . Ah!"

As to Alfred, his eyes half-closed, his hands holding the hips of my aunt, he seemed inexpressibly happy.

"Oh," he said, "my angel, my all, ah! How fine it is! Push well! Do you feel my prick in you? Yes! Yes! Do come! There! You're coming, aren't you? Go on . . . go on . . . I feel you're coming . . . push well, my darling!"

Both stopped a moment. My aunt appeared exhausted, but did not change her position. At length she lightly turned her head to give her lover a kiss, saying, "Now, both together! Let me know when you're ready."

The scene recommenced. After several minutes during which Alfred virtually slammed his belly against Bertha's bottom, he in turn, cried out, "Ah, I feel it coming. Are you ready, my love? Yes, yes, there I am . . . push . . . again . . . go on . . . I'm coming, I'm yours. I . . . I . . . Ah! What pleasure! I . . . I'm coming!"

A long silence followed. Alfred seemed to have lost his strength, and practically fell over Bertha, who was obliged to put her arms straight to bear him. Alfred recovered himself, and I again saw the marvelous instrument coming out of Bertha's slit, where it had been so well-treated. But how changed it was—its size diminished to half, it was red and damp, and I saw something like a white and viscous liquid come from it and drop to the floor.

Alfred began to put his clothes in order, during which my aunt, who had straightened up, put her arms around his neck and covered him with kisses.

What had I been doing during this time? My imagination, excited to the highest degree, made me repeat one part of the pleasures that transported the actors.

At the critical moment I lifted petticoat and chemise, and my inexperienced hand contented itself by exploring my tender slit. I thus assured myself that I was made the same as Bertha, but I knew not yet what use or consolation that hand could give. This very morning was to enlighten me.

After plenty of kissing, Bertha said to Monsieur Bonbier, "Listen, my dear, I have been thinking. You know that my apartment is quite isolated. Since my chambermaid sleeps in the anteroom, no one would know if we rendezvous, and we could pass some adorable nights together.

"Under a pretext of wanting something for my toilette, I will send Julie to Paris tomorrow afternoon, and after dinner we can join each other. Be on the lookout; you can give me a sign during the day of the hour when you can slip away to me. I beg you to take the most minute precautions."

It was then decided that Monsieur Bonbier should go first. He was to take a walk out of the park, and during that time my aunt would regain her room by the private staircase. Alfred went out, and I remained hidden in my brambles until he was sufficiently far off not to have any fear of being perceived by him. Observing that my aunt had not yet come out, I stopped and looked again. I saw Bertha stoop right in front of me, so nothing could escape my view. As she did this her slit opened;

it seemed to me a much more lively hue than before. The interior and the edges, even up to the fleecy mound that surrounded it, seemed inundated with the same liquor that I had seen come from Monsieur Bonbier's rod.

I was going to leave my place as softly as possible when I was drawn back by what I now saw. The hand of my aunt refreshed with care all the parts that had been so well worked. All at once I saw her stop, then a finger fixed upon a little eminence which showed itself prominently. This finger rubbed lightly at first, then with a kind of fury, sometimes slipping into the same slit that had been occupied by Alfred's pole. At length Bertha gave the same symptoms of pleasure that I had seen before.

I had seen enough of it! I understood it all! I retired and made haste to take a long path that brought me back to the chateau. My head was on fire, my bosom palpitated, and my steps tottered, but I was determined at once to play myself the last act I had seen, and which required no partner.

I arrived in my room in a state of near madness, threw my hat on the floor, shut and locked the door, and put myself on the bed. I turned up my clothes to the waist, and recollecting to the minutest details what Bertha had done with her hand, I placed mine between my legs. My efforts were at first fruitless, but I found at length the point I searched for. The rest was easy; I had too well observed to deceive myself. I moved my fingers back and forth over the nub of flesh. By varying the speed with which I manipulated it I could alter the intensity of the feelings that began deep in my belly. A delicious sensation seized me; I continued with fury and soon fell into such an ecstasy that I lost consciousness.

When I came to myself I was in the same position, my hand all moistened by an unknown dew.

I sat up quite confused, and it was a long time before I entirely came to myself. It was nearly time for lunch, so I made haste to dress and went down.

My aunt was already in the salon with my grandmother. I looked at her on entering; she was beautiful and fresh, her color in repose, her eyes brilliant, so that one would have sworn she had just risen from an excellent morning's sleep. Her dress, in exquisite and simple taste, set off her charming figure. As for me, I cast down my eyes and felt myself blush.

My grandmother noticed my agitation and told me so. I replied that I had overslept, and contrary to habit had not taken my morning walk.

My aunt embraced me, and as she talked of one thing and another I recovered myself completely.

Monsieur Bonbier arrived soon, telling us of an excursion to a neighboring village, and we sat down to table.

I took care, without being seen, to notice everything that passed between Alfred and my aunt. I must acknowledge I was disappointed and greatly surprised. Not a look showed there was anything whatever between them.

About the middle of the repast my aunt carelessly remarked to my grandmother, "Mother, I was so forgetful on leaving Paris that I am missing several necessaries. Have I your permission to send my chambermaid tomorrow to fetch them? I can attend to myself, and it will only be a short absence."

The day passed quietly. Monsieur Bonbier took a long ride on horseback. Bertha and I sat by the water, amusing ourselves by needlework. Some neighbors came to visit my grandmother, and she invited them to dinner.

In the evening we had music, and I sang a duet with my aunt. Although already a good musician, and having a fine voice, I was not equal to my aunt, who gave me some excellent lessons in taste and feeling.

Monsieur Bonbier played whist with my grandmother, and was completely reserved.

I retired at about eleven o'clock. I was impatient to be alone with my thoughts, so I went to bed quickly and dismissed my maid. I had no doubt that the next evening would be the time for a serious meeting between Monsieur Bonbier and my aunt. I burned to assist at the delicious scenes that would be enacted. I contemplated how to be there.

Knowing all the ways of the house, I thought over the plan of Auntie's apartment. It was situated on the second floor, the same as mine, but at the opposite extremity. A corridor gave communication to all the rooms on this floor. Monsieur Bonbier was also lodged on the same flight, in a turning off the principal corridor.

My aunt had at her disposition a little room in which a bed was made up for her chambermaid, a beautiful bedroom and a dressing room. I recollected that this dressing cabinet, which occupied about one-third of the side of the room, used to be contiguous to an alcove, now closed by a strong partition. I also remembered a small hole in the upper part of the alcove, only stopped up by a small and very indifferent oil painting of a pastoral scene. A door in an unoccupied room gave access to this dark closet.

It was on these recollections that I arranged my plan, then went to sleep, full of resolution and hope for the following day.

Julie, the servant, started for Paris, as had been arranged. Alfred and my aunt were more reserved than ever. However, I found out what I wanted to know as the day wore on.

After dinner Monsieur Bonbier leaned negligently on the mantelpiece, pretending to admire the pendulum of a superb ormolu clock. He placed his finger for a moment on the figure XI, then on the figure VI; it was easy to understand that he intended to say half-past eleven. My aunt responded by a slight movement of her eyes. I knew then all I wanted; it only remained to make my preparations.

When we were seated in the garden Alfred offered to read to us, which was accepted.

I soon slipped away under some pretext, and sure of being unobserved on the second floor, went to the little door of the dark closet.

Everything was in the same state as I have described, but a ladder was necessary, and I knew that there was one to be found in a passage near a linen cupboard. The wooden steps were very heavy, but the burning fire of curiosity that animated my movements doubled my strength. I dragged them into the alcove, found the hole and the canvas that was stretched in front of it, and with a pair of scissors I cut a small piece out of the picture. To my satisfaction, I found I could thus have a good view of the entire room, and above all—of the bed. I came downstairs quickly, shut the door, took the key, and returned to the garden. Everything had been executed so quickly that no one had noticed the strange fact of my absence. The whole of the day and the evening seemed to me to be mortally long.

At last, about half-past ten, my grandmother retired to rest, and we all followed suit. Alfred off to his room; my aunt remained with me for an instant and saw me safely into my bedchamber. I kissed her and said "good evening."

I undressed without delay and dismissed the maid. Then I drew on my stockings again, put on a pair of velvet slippers and a nightgown of a dark color, and waited.

At about a quarter after eleven, I slid like a shadow into the corridor, reached the little door without interruption, opened it, and locked myself in, noiselessly and without difficulty. Then I mounted the ladder, settled myself down as comfortably as possible, and looked through my peephole.

My success was complete; I could see distinctly. The clean

white bed seemed like an altar decked out for a sacrifice. A lamp placed on the night table inundated the brilliant linen with an intense flood of light. Bertha was in the adjoining room, where I heard her performing her ablutions.

She came back into the room at last, with nothing on but her nightgown. Going to the bed, she turned it down, arranged the pillows, and placed the lamp so as to throw a still greater light upon it. Then she took a delicate cambric chemise, trimmed with lace, and advanced towards the full-length mirror of the wardrobe. She looked in the glass for a minute or two, and by a graceful movement of her shoulders let slip the chemise she had on, which was arrested in its downward course for a second by the swelling of her hips, though it soon fell twisted at her feet. She had already put off her gown and now appeared completely naked before my startled eyes.

No one could dream of anything finer! Her breasts, firm and high, stuck out boldly, and were surmounted by two strawberry nipples of a bright rose-pink; the fall of her back and her backside were both admirable.

At the bottom of her white and polished belly, her luxurious ebony fleece, the thickness of which constituted a true rarity, could be plainly seen. The contrast of this enormous black spot upon a body so white gave to Bertha a peculiar appearance of strange voluptuousness.

She drew her lace shift over her head, put on her nightie again, and then walked into her parlor, holding the door ajar. A moment afterwards I heard cautious footsteps. The door was shut and double-locked, and Bertha and Alfred appeared in the bedroom. He had slippers on his feet and was dressed in a summer smoking jacket, under which was only his shirt. Bertha made him sit upon a sofa and she took her place on his left knee. Their mouths met in a lingering kiss.

"My dear angel," said he, "how I thank you for having had

sufficient confidence in me so as not to have made me languish and wait for your precious favors! You lavish them on your true spouse, who will reward you by his everlasting love."

As he spoke he opened the top of Bertha's dressing gown and alternately kissed the two firm globes, while my aunt, reclining backwards, shuddered beneath the caresses that seemingly caused her to shiver voluptuously in every vein. He moved to her nipples, licking, biting. Then, taking advantage of Bertha's position, he once more opened the gown, but this time at the bottom. Lifting up her chemise he toyed a moment with the lovely black hairs, of which he appeared dotingly fond. Then I noticed his finger slip upwards a little and renew the playful friction that I had seen my aunt practice herself, and the imitation of which had procured for me such great enjoyment.

As for Bertha, she had seized upon and displayed the splendid pole. I could not take my eyes off it. It appeared to me to be longer and bigger than the first time I had seen it. It was fully eight or nine inches long, and as big around as my wrist.

My aunt opened her thighs, and therefore stretched her slit, which did not appear longer than my little finger. How is it possible, I said to myself, that an instrument of that size can penetrate entirely into such a little place? I concluded that my aunt, by the position she was in the first time, had doubtless received that great rod not in her body, but between her thighs, and that it must have been its rubbing against her that had rendered her so happy. My error was soon rectified, as during my reflections the two lovers had continued their sweet dance in silence with Alfred's mouth still teasing the spot between her legs.

"Ah," said Bertha, "my husband . . . my darling . . . go on . . . I am so happy! How lovely your cock is! Oh, how I shall come! I'm coming already! Do it a little longer! Ah! I die!"

There was a long and silent pause while Bertha seemed quite overcome, her body arched back, her head hidden on her sweetheart's shoulder, her glorious thighs still wide apart. Monsieur Bonbier gazed at her intently, ravished at the sight.

"Come, now, come!" cried Bertha, rising. "Come and put it into me. I must have it all. I want it all! Come, I'm on fire. I'm burning up! Flood me with your bounteous liquor."

Bertha threw off her dressing gown and stretched herself upon the bed. Alfred did the same, but before putting himself near Bertha, he lifted his shirt and rolled it under his armpits. How beautiful he was, built like Hercules and Apollo; his proud pole stood up stiffly growing out of a thick bush that showed it off splendidly.

Bertha was lying on her back, her legs parted and lifted a little. Alfred got between, on his knees, and lifted his darling's chemise right up to her neck, again exposing her naked form to my gaze. I expected to see her get up and turn her backside to her lover as before, as I thought that was the only way it could be done, but to my great astonishment I found it was not so. Alfred stretched himself upon her; Bertha lifted her legs and crossed them on his back in such a manner that nothing escaped me. I could distinctly see Bertha's hand capture the pole and direct its head to the center of the little slit that opened to receive it. Alfred gave a vigorous stroke of the loins, to which Bertha answered, and at least half of the rod penetrated into the little hole, which dilated and began to engulf it. A few more moments completed the insertion, and I saw their two growths of hair mingle together. At last I knew all about it.

Now there was nothing but movements, sighs, inarticulate words, and maddening shivers. I could see that he was pushing what Bertha had called his "cock" into and out of her grasping slit. When the shaft emerged it was shiny with her juices.

"Let me have it all . . . Ah! How fine it is . . . go gently . . . let us come slowly . . . hold me tight."

"My sweet darling! Lift up your thighs so that it can get right in. There! Do you feel it? Ah! how delightful!"

"It's wonderful! Are you ready? My Alfred, I'm going to come. I—I—make haste!"

"I'm ready. It's coming. There, it comes. Come now. I'm coming! I'm coming!"

Both remained quiet for a moment, then Alfred rose and I saw the dear sausage as before, coming out little, red, and dropping a tear.

Bertha remained a little longer without giving signs of life, but she got up at last, and after smothering Alfred with kisses went for an instant into her dressing room.

I thought it was all over and began to arrange my retreat, but a secret presentiment made me stop.

Bertha went to bed again, embraced by her lover in her arms, and they engaged in sweet conversation.

"I have been so happy, dear! It is so much better when we are quite at our ease, and you do it so well."

"My darling, there is not a more perfect woman than you in the whole world! I want to eat you up bodily!"

Once more pushing up Bertha's chemise, Alfred covered with kisses the whole of the beautiful body that trembled beneath his caresses. When he arrived at the center of bliss, he opened it, bit it gently, and kissed it passionately.

"Stop, dear," said Bertha. "Stop! You will fatigue yourself. Rest, rest!"

"No, darling, look! See? My prick once more asks permission to go into its little companion. You won't refuse me?"

"Let me see. So you've come back to your splendid state? Yes, indeed. Well, well, I'll allow you in once more. There, place yourself like that, and don't move!"

"What are you going to do?"

"You know, dear, how I like a change. Remain on your back and I'll do it to you!"

So saying, my aunt straddled Alfred's hips, and taking his rod in her hand, plunged it into her up to the hilt. Then gently moving she pushed on, stopping a little, and remained thus spitted by the enormous spindle. She teased Alfred, blew him kisses and showed him her adorable titties, smiling and pouting to him all the time.

"I have *you* now," she said. "You are my little wife. See how well I do it!" She bobbed up and down on his pole, raising herself so that the swollen head almost was withdrawn, then impaling herself fully once again. She thrust and ground her hips while sitting against his belly, rotating his staff within her while he lay her helpless prisoner.

After a few minutes of this dalliance, it was easy to see that the supreme moment was reached. She fell upon her lover, who received her in his arms and pressed her to him, as he took hold of the white cheeks of her bottom one in each hand. Pleasure seized them together in great spasms; then Bertha left his embrace and again lazily stretched her at her lover's side.

It was late. I was crushed with fatigue, emotion, and the cramped position I occupied, yet I would not go before I knew if the amorous couple meant to arrange another appointment. I had the satisfaction to hear them fix a rendezvous for the next evening at the same hour.

I regained my room and went to bed tired out, but I slept soundly. I woke at about seven o'clock perfectly refreshed. I ruminated over all I had seen and heard the day before; my imagination became inflamed, my bosom panted, an active fire coursed through my veins. Mechanically, I took up a position on my back, as I had seen my aunt do, then I drew up my chemise, as Alfred had done to her. I alternatively touched each breast, and thrilled as the nipples swelled up. Feeling my body I reached the delicate spot, and rummaged there with great curiosity. It seemed to me that a slight change had taken place. The lips of the little nook were plumper; I sought the place that in my aunt's case had greedily swallowed up the monstrous sausage, but I only found a little hole that my finger could not penetrate without pain. I pushed up my finger a little and shuddered when an indescribable sensation invaded my entire being. I rubbed softly first, then quicker, afterward slower, and again with more activity as I repeated my aunt's words: "I'm coming! I'm coming . . . ah!"

At length a nervous spasm overtook me. I felt transported with immense pleasure that I could fully appreciate, as I did not faint this time. When I had gathered my scattered senses, I drew away my wet hand. I rose and dressed myself and went downstairs, fresh and happy at having enjoyed such a sweet morning's diversion.

I shall not speak of the events of the day, which was an uninteresting one, as I am in haste to come to the scene of the evening. I took the same precautions, and had safely reached my observatory when Bertha and her lover met once more.

The preliminaries were much the same, but instead of going to bed afterwards, Bertha said, "I have a whim, dear. Let us do it like the other morning in the closet. We are more comfortable here and it will be nicer still!"

With these words she divested herself of her gown and pulled up her shift behind. She placed a big cushion in front of the mirror of the wardrobe and knelt upon it, her head and arms much lower than her buttocks, which, thrown out and accentuated by this ravishing position, presented the path of pleasure well in view and largely open.

Alfred, far from idle, had made his preparation. He had taken off his jacket and placed the lamp on the floor, so as to light

up perfectly the delicious picture that the mirror reflected in
every detail. Then he placed himself behind her, and began to
get into her with the pole that bobbed forth from his belly.

"Oh, you can see too much of me!" said my aunt.

"How can I see too much of such beauty? Look in the glass!"
He began to thrust into her with even strokes.

"No, it's too bad! Ah! It's going into me! Stop a little. What
a fine fellow you are!"

"My adored one, how lovely you are! What admirable hips.
What an adorable—ass!"

"Oh! Alfred! What is that naughty word?"

"Don't be frightened, darling; lovers can say anything. Those
words, out of place in calmer moments, add fresh relish to the
sweet mystery of love. You will soon say them too, and understand their charm."

While he spoke he continued his movements. Bertha, in silent enjoyment, said nothing, but devoured with eager eyes the
scene in the mirror. I was stupefied to hear her say to him a
minute later, "Do you love it so very much?"

"What?"

"Why . . . my . . ."

"Your what?"

"Well . . . my . . . ass!"

"Ah, Bertha, how sweet you are to me. Oh, yes, I love it. Your
beautiful ass—I adore it!"

"Feel it then. It's yours—yours alone. My ass—ass—ass."

As she concluded her broken utterances, she let herself go
until she reached complete enjoyment. Alfred, who was rapidly
arriving at the height of sovereign pleasure, reached the desired
goal with her and fell upon her completely overcome.

They went no further than that delicious encounter; they
could not fix a fresh meeting as they feared the return of the
maid. Instead they arranged certain signals, and, if the worst

should come to the worst, they made up their minds to fall back upon the pavilion in the park. I went to my room. Julie returned the next day, so that the nocturnal assignations came to an end, but I sought to discover the signs that were to have been exchanged between the lovers. Much to my disappointment I discovered nothing.

Four days went by in like manner. I was vexed and had once again renewed my morning walks, directing my steps always to the gazebo in the grounds.

During the afternoon of the fourth day, I had gone there and I was surprised to find a garden chair that had evidently been brought from the house. I concluded therefore, and rightly too, that something would take place the next day, and I was at my post long before the arrival of the actors in the drama of love.

They approached with caution, one after the other, and shut themselves in. Bertha sat upon the chair, saying, "You did well to think of this piece of furniture; my position of the other day was somewhat uncomfortable. But what are you doing on your knees?"

"You know I must greet your lovely cleft, my dear."

"Very well then, give him a kiss quickly and let us do it. It is late. You shall sit on the chair, and I'll ride upon you!"

Alfred undid his trousers after planting a lingering kiss on Bertha's muff, then sat upon the chair. Bertha pulled up all her petticoats and got on top of her lover. She then seized his vigorous pole and commenced the introduction by pushing down her bottom as it slowly entered. The chair was so placed that I could enjoy the sight from behind, and consequently could not miss the slightest detail. The enormous tool soon disappeared completely. Bertha lifted up her legs, placed her heels on the bars of the chair, and began to rise and fall in turn.

The accustomed sighs and words rose to their lips; their souls melted in mutual enjoyment. I had intended, this time, not to

rest content with the part of simple spectator. I had made ar-
rangements in advance and chose the most comfortable position under the circumstances.

I began to do it to myself at the precise moment that Bertha
introduced the cock into her slit, and then, regulating my
movements with theirs, operating slowly or quickly, I came at
the same moment as they did, and my sighs of pleasure mingled
with those of the happy couple.

When all was over, Bertha left the lap of her lover, and during
her movement I saw Alfred's cock drop out of its retreat. A
large quantity of the milky liquid, the cause of which I as yet
ignored, trickled along her thighs and fell to the ground. The
lovers readjusted their dress.

Monsieur Bonbier communicated to Bertha that in three
days' time he would make the official demand for her hand,
and should then leave to make all requisite preparation. They
further arranged to meet at the pavilion for the last time two
days later, in the morning. I went away, sadly, to the house. I
was to fall back once more into the dead calm of my life, but
still the hope of being soon married and tasting in my turn the
divine pleasures I had witnessed sustained my spirits.

On the third day I was in my hiding place; Alfred came first,
and Bertha a minute later. There seemed a slight cloud on her
beautiful countenance, yet she threw herself into her lover's
arms, and he, after a few caresses, tried to put his hand up her
clothes. This time she prevented him.

"No, dear. Today is impossible! I am sorry, I assure you, but
there are womanly obstacles in the way. We must put it off till
you return."

"How unlucky for me."

"And how about me?"

"Take hold of it. Look how it throbs for your touch!"

Alfred drew his splendid instrument out of his trousers. Bertha fondled it, saying, "No, no, not without me!"

"But I beg you."

"You insist? Well, I suppose I must not be selfish. But I assure you that I am grieved to see such good cock wasted. And you must not get into the habit of doing it without your companion."

With these words, Bertha had turned up the sleeve of her dressing gown. Alfred had dropped his trousers and lifted the tail of his shirt as he stood up.

"No!" said Bertha. "Take your trousers right off. Since I am to have nothing, I will at least enjoy a good view."

Alfred did as she desired and gave himself up to her. She placed herself a little behind him, put her left arm around her lover's waist, and with the right began a soft movement of the wrist that seemed to procure extraordinary pleasure to Monsieur Bonbier. She pumped up and down, uncovering and covering by turn the head of Alfred's tool.

"Ah! How finely you do it!" said he. "Gently, my angel. Uncover it well. Now, quicker . . . stop . . . go on again! Ah! I feel it coming! Quicker . . . I . . . I . . . I'm going to come!"

He gave two or three strokes of the loins, and Bertha, who had carefully followed his instructions, pressed the instrument higher in her hand. Suddenly, to my great stupefaction, I saw a jet of white liquid spring out in jets and fall full three paces off, the emission seeming to drive Alfred mad with joy.

After a few moments Bertha wiped the rod herself with her embroidered handkerchief. Then she thrust the diminishing organ away, saying, "You are a naughty boy to have spent without me. You owe me one for this, and you shall pay for it at the first opportunity."

I let them both depart, and when they were far off I entered the pavilion and closely examined the fresh traces of the ejaculation I had witnessed. The sight inflamed my imagination. I pulled up my clothes and got astride the chair, placing my hand on the seat, my middle finger upraised. I pressed myself down upon it, found the little orifice, and imitating Bertha's movements stretched myself as widely apart as possible. Working my bottom up and down, I imagined I was taking in the coveted instrument.

A lively sense of pain did not stop me; I redoubled my efforts and got in nearly half of my finger.

Then I repeated Bertha's words: "I'm coming . . . I come . . . my ass!" until suddenly the spasm seized me and I twisted my body about in an agony of pleasure.

My hand and the chair bore the marks of my enjoyment. I hastily wiped them away and returned to the house.

In the course of the day, Alfred had an interview with my grandmother and formally asked for my aunt's hand. All was arranged, and he left for Paris to press on with the preliminaries. It was decided that Bertha should remain with us for a few days. I was to assist at her marriage as bridesmaid, so she took me away with her.

The ceremony was celebrated with pomp, and, for the first time in my life, I attended a grand ball, where I may say without vanity that I attracted a pleasing degree of attention. I should have liked to have been present when the bride and bridegroom were put to bed, but my observatory was far away and I had to put up with solitary pleasures.

Three days afterwards Monsieur Bonbier took me back to my grandmother's, and went off to Italy with his wife.

PART II

I was returned once more to the monotony and dullness of my early life, only with my senses now quickened and the knowledge that my temperament required perhaps much more than many women. I dreamed of nothing but marriage, and Monsieur Bonbier remained my ideal of a husband.

I often made visits to the pavilion in the park and became engulfed in the recollections that hovered thickly there. I had left there the chair used by Bertha and Alfred, which often became my throne of solitary pleasure.

This means of relief was not only necessary, but I may say indispensable, as raging fits of love would sometimes come over me. My eyes would grow dim, there would be a ringing in my ears, my legs would totter beneath me, and simply by pressing my thighs together I would feel that charming part that makes women get wet and palpitating.

In those moments no resistance was possible; I was obliged to give way! My finger was my master; when I came fully once, I experienced a wholesome calm, and a delicious languor overwhelmed me. I am convinced that without this practice I would have fallen dangerously ill, though I did not do it too often.

Thus I attained my twentieth year. I was truly beautiful, and I will here trace my portrait. It shall be an exact resemblance, without false shame or ridiculous self-praise. My stature was a little above medium height; my hair was abundant and of a fine, dark-chestnut color. My eyes, with long lashes, were hazel, brilliant, and swimming with voluptuous moisture. My mouth, rather large and very sensual, was furnished with fine teeth; a black mole, on the right side of my upper lip, gave piquancy to my physiognomy. I had an admirable bust, the breasts apart, firm and well-placed; my figure was neat and supple with shapely buttocks that were perfectly handsome; and my mount of Venus, very much pronounced, protected a nook that it appears was a rare and pure pattern, both in form and exceptional voluptuous quality. While not possessing the rare bush of my aunt, I was well provided in that way with a pretty pelt of silky fur.

How often, dear Stefan, you have placed me so as to enjoy
the view of that mossy growth! What caresses! What kisses! But
let me not get ahead of myself.

My grandmother felt her end approaching, and fearing for
my future tried to get me a husband without letting me know.
An old friend of hers made her a proposition one day that
seemed to suit her hopes and my dearest wishes.

Monsieur de Cocteau was introduced to us. He was twenty-
eight years old, of medium stature, very genteel in manner, with
a graceful bearing and regular features. His family was a good
one, and his fortune satisfactory. He did not present such a
manly appearance as Monsieur Bonbier, but as he was he
pleased me and I secretly gave him my heart from the first
moment.

As for his heart, he was dazzled by my beauty, and his mind
was made up as soon as he saw me, so that we were all agreed.
The marriage being decided, we were to be united two months
afterwards. We resolved to pass a short time with my grandmother, and then depart for Nice, where my husband was employed.

Bertha came to assist at my wedding with her husband. She
was as pretty as ever, and quite as happy. I told her my little
secrets, and how I felt inclined to love my husband with all my
heart and soul. A single thing vexed me, however, and that was
that I found him rather cold and reserved, although always
affectionate and gallant. Bertha burst out laughing and assured
me that all would soon change.

The important day arrived; she acted as my mother and
dressed me herself. I felt the day get shorter and shorter with
unspeakable desire and fear. The act that I was about to accomplish, although well-known to me in theory, filled me with
terrible apprehension.

The ceremony proceeded without mishap, and when the evening came to an end at last, Bertha led me to the nuptial chamber. It was her room, and on the bed where I had seen her so bountifully treated I was to be made a woman.

Bertha put me to bed and sat by my side to instruct me with what in her idea I was profoundly ignorant of. She went through her lesson with tact, but left nothing unexplained, kissed me, recommended obedience, and went away.

A minute afterwards my new husband came in, clothed only in a dressing gown. He drew near to me, kissed me heartily, said some very affectionate things, took off his garment, and got into bed. I barely had a glimpse of his manhood, so quickly did he jump beneath the covers.

Charles, for that was his name, pressed me in his arms; the contact of his naked flesh against mine made me jump! He kissed me softly, telling me to fear not, and drew still closer. I trembled all over, I didn't dare speak, and yet I desired to. He whispered: "Would you like to have a little baby?" and at the same time his right knee insinuated itself between my thighs, so as to separate them. I resisted at first, then little by little I gave way. Soon Charles was on top of me, and I felt the head of the much-coveted object.

This first contact acted upon me like a spark upon gunpowder. All the warmth of my being was concentrated in the besieged nook—I almost came! Charles was awkward, either too high or too low. I couldn't move; I couldn't help him! I was panting and on fire! At last I felt him in the right place. He pushed on vigorously; I felt a sharp pain, started violently and drew back, on the point of shrieking.

Charles, bewildered, asked my pardon, supplicated me to have a little courage, and took up his post once more. I remained still and was artful enough to creep into a better position. He pushed again and the pain came back. I resisted it, and shoved my body up to meet the blows, so as to finish

quicker. It seemed to me that Charles did not act very vigorously, and that there was a great difference in size between the
instrument that perforated me and that of Monsieur Bonbier.
Moreover, Charles did not speak, he did not utter one of the
words I had heard, which I believed were part and parcel of
the operation.

Charles, at last, seemed to gather a little strength. He gave a
solid stroke of the loins and I did the same, stiffening my body.
The pain was so great that I cried out, but I had the satisfaction
to feel myself penetrated, for the whole instrument—thin as it
was—was sheathed within me! My husband continued his
backward and forward movement a moment, then shivered,
sighed several times, and stopped short. I felt a hot liquid in-
undate me and diminish the smarting to a slight degree.

Charles got off and lay down by my side, visibly fatigued.

In spite of my desires and my imagination, I had felt no
pleasure. That did not astonish me, as I had been taught so by
Bertha. Charles kissed me, and wishing me good night turned
his back and fell asleep.

I was very much surprised and quite embarrassed. I fully
expected we should begin again, and in spite of the pain was
quite ready to do so. At last I resigned myself to the inevitable,
and slumbered too.

I awoke the next morning very late—I was alone. On hearing
the sudden movement I made in sitting up, Charles came out
of the neighboring room and approached me. He was completely dressed already, and he kissed me on the forehead, uttered a few kind words, and asked me if I had slept well. But
all this was cold and distant. My heart, ready to spring towards
him, stopped in its flight. It seemed to me that he should have
waited until I awoke to take me in his arms and speak of love
and happiness, and then recommence the caresses of the night.
A doubt for my future flashed across me; this was not what I

had dreamed! Charles went out, saying that he left me to dress, but I had no thought of doing so. I busied myself in sad thoughts. The next moment, a well-known voice called me, and Bertha ran to embrace me.

I put my arms around her neck, held her tightly, and began to cry.

"Gracious me! What is the matter, dear child?" she said.

I didn't know how to answer her, as I had no complaint to make. I only felt that I was not loved as I had hoped to be and that my ardent furnace would never be able to burn freely.

Bertha thought that I was simply hysterical and calmed me by gentle joking.

My natural gaiety soon got the upper hand; I rose and took a bath that my maid had already prepared.

The day passed slowly. Everybody was happy around me; my husband seemed enchanted, acting as tender and gallant as his nature would permit. I was pleased with him and timidly responded to his distant caresses. Night came; he led me away at an early hour and we went to bed. Less timid than the night before, he took me in his arms, said that he loved me, and kissed me tenderly. I was bold enough to tell him that I also loved him, and gave him a kiss that electrified him. Already I felt on my naked thigh something hard that promised much.

As on the preceding evening he placed his lips to my ear and said, "Shall we do like last night?"

I could not answer, but I also could not help opening my thighs and lifting my nightgown in secret. He got over me and I held him fast in my embrace, waiting and impatiently desiring the supreme moment.

I soon felt the head of his cock. A shivering fit seized me, during which I took care to introduce it as far in as possible. I still felt a tolerably severe pain, but that did not stop me; the happy fire that circulated through my veins made me support all. Already I felt the advance symptoms of enjoyment. I tried all I could not to speak; I wanted to cry out and tell all I felt. I now perfectly understood my aunt's words, but the silence of Charles, who seemed wrapped up in himself, prevented me from giving vent to my feelings.

He continued his movements and kissed me, but he did not seem overwhelmed with passion, as I would have wished. I could not resist the impulse to push up my bottom and cry out! Then I remained perfectly still. I was coming, so intensely that I almost lost my senses.

Charles stopped for a second and seemed astonished at my response. I curbed myself, and he resumed his pleasures.

He was a long while performing his sweet duty, though machine-like, and I poured out the sweet dew four times! At last I felt him shudder and sigh, and a fiery, flaming jet inundated my entrails.

We both remained quiet. I was exalted, in a fever, but ready to begin again; he was broken down and only required rest. So we fell asleep.

The next morning, on awakening, I found myself once more alone. I was not sorry, and my brain replayed the scene of the night, till I felt a curiosity that impelled me to examine my body. I sat up on the pillows, my legs well apart, and with my hands opened the lips of my crack. I found a great change— the interior was much more rosy, the opening was wider, and my entire finger easily plunged within it. This examination amused me, and would have produced certain consequences, but a discreet rap at my door made me cover myself up hastily and take a natural position in bed.

It was Bertha, who found me fresh and gay, and when I smiled she kissed me. We gossiped like sisters as I dressed. I was a real woman now, and my pretty aunt treated me as one. She drew certain secrets from me that seemed to interest her gently. I told her what took place. She seemed much surprised when I said that I had felt great pleasure four times, while Charles had only done it to me once. Evidently the slight amount of my husband's virile strength, compared to the vigor of hers, surprised her greatly.

The day passed away, and, as my husband was a great sportsman, he went out shooting. I took a walk with Bertha. We all met at dinner and passed the evening with a little music.

Night arrived, but how different from the two preceding ones. Charles popped an ugly silk handkerchief on his head, chatted about our early departure, about our new house, and so on, but never mentioned a word about love. He simply embraced me coldly and slept.

I awoke on the morrow before he did, and a terrible longing seized me to look at the instrument that I had only felt twice, and which did not much resemble Monsieur Bonbier's in size or strength. I was favored by circumstances. It was warm, and Charles had thrown off the sheet, that only just hid the particular part. Luckily, his shirt had been pulled up; I had only to draw down the sheet a little, with infinite prudence, before I caught sight of the sad tool that was to be my only consolation.

What a difference, indeed, to that of Alfred! Small, wrinkled, and in a shriveled skin, one could hardly guess at the presence of its limp head. Henceforward, I believe, my destiny was fixed.

Charles stirred. I made haste to turn around and pretended to sleep, and he left the bed first, as was his habit.

The limit fixed for our sojourn at my granny's house drew near. I was far from being unhappy, as my husband was good to me and loved me as heartily as his cold nature allowed him. He was proud of my beauty and refused me nothing, but all this did not suffice. It was not what I had so much desired— namely, a voluptuous, lascivious, ardent love, for which I would have sacrificed everything, for which I was capable of real devotion! I could see laid out before me a monotonous life, probably without the birth of a child, but too difficult to support for a temperament like mine.

Charles did it to me once or twice a week, and always in the same despairingly reserved style. He only kissed my cheeks or my forehead—my firm young breasts received no caresses. His hand seemed to flee those charming places that would have so gladly welcomed its touch. In turn I felt that I dared not try to feel him, as instinctively I knew he would have repulsed me.

After two years of marriage my temperament was in full blast and had increased in passion, instead of growing calmer! My husband did it less and less, and as I feared I had no child. A baby would have changed my one fixed idea.

My grandmother had been dead a year. We had a lovely home in Nice, where Charles occupied an exalted position that obliged him to be frequently absent. These little journeys suited his taste for hunting and shooting. Therefore I was often alone, and in spite of music, which I continued to love and successfully cultivate, my brain was always at work picturing scenes of delirious love. What fearful nights I used to pass alone, writhing between the sheets in lascivious positions that I instinctively invented!

My finger was powerless to satisfy me now. I would take my pillow, and embrace it with twisted legs and twining arms, as if it could realize my desires. I would rub against it and reach a degree of comparative enjoyment that drove me still madder. I would change my position and get astride it, rubbing myself, till the sluices of pleasure, swollen to the utmost by this stimulant, burst open and procured me some relief.

These nervous fits brought on hallucinations that manifested themselves by an inconceivable state of hysteria. My calm and gay temper became unequal and capricious. I resisted as well as I could, but at last I avowed myself vanquished. Was I very, very guilty?

I was very friendly with Madame Dumond, wife of the principal magistrate, a slight blonde who may have been pretty once, but who was already beginning to fade. I thought that she must have had many intrigues when young.

One day, when visiting her, she informed me that Monsieur Fanon had come to take command of the garrison. He was a young officer who had been much talked about. He had fought with rare courage on the battlefield, and had rapidly earned the rank of lieutenant colonel. He was about thirty-six and unmarried.

Madame Dumond told me that she had invited him to dinner and that my husband and I were to meet him. Was it a presentiment? I knew not, but I returned home quite pensive and slightly jealous of Madame Dumond.

I must confess, I prepared what I thought was a most ravishing dress, and three days afterwards the dinner came off. When we entered the drawing room, Monsieur Fanon was already there. In a moment, I had examined him. He was tall, vigorous, and well-built, his countenance frank and open, and his manner well-bred. He was introduced and his sweet persuasive voice charmed me. My heart grew cold, and then all the blood in my veins rushed to my face. Oh! I was a captive caught in the toils at last, and I did not even seek to combat the influence that invaded my soul.

The dinner was served and it turned out a very gay affair. Monsieur Fanon was able to show his brilliant and cultivated wit. He sat at Madame Dumond's right hand. I could have killed her!

After dinner, he approached me, asking if he might be allowed to pay me a visit, and talked to my husband, whom he pleased vastly. Madame Dumond sat down at the piano and played a lively waltz; Monsieur Dumond said that I was a good partner and asked me to take a turn with him, but he was old and soon fatigued, so Monsieur Fanon offered to take his place.

As I felt his arm encircle my waist I was taken with a nervous tremor that evidently did not escape him.

I gave myself up to the charm of the hour. Monsieur Fanon boldly profited by the embrace in which he held me, in spite of the spectators. As he turned a corner of the drawing room, he was able to press me so tightly to him that I felt for a second against my belly a certain object so hard and stiff that I nearly fainted.

That waltz was the signal of my defeat!

The happy evening was too soon over. Once more at home I undressed quickly, and pretending fatigue said good night to my husband and jumped into bed, not to sleep, but to dream.

I was placed on my left side, my bottom turned to Charles. A caprice seized him; I felt him softly lift my linen, and then pressing against me, he tried to get into me from behind. I was vexed at first, but, my temperament overpowering me, I gave way to his designs. Unfortunately, he could not manage it, and he did not get in.

I lost all patience and rapidly threw off the sheet by a sudden movement. I passed my hand behind me, seized the tool, which was useless without a guide, and stuffed it into my slit to the last inch. I was thinking of Monsieur Fanon the whole time. I imagined that he was behind me, and that he was doing it to me. Under my breath I addressed to him all that I was burning to say at such a moment. I pushed back against Charles, pretending it was another belly that slapped my buttocks. I rolled my hips passionately, imagining it was a different pole stretching my crack.

Three times the dew of love gushed out for him, for him alone! My husband, profiting unwittingly by the result of my thoughts, did his duty a little better than usual, and refreshed me with a copious ejaculation.

When he had finished, I feared that, with his habitual ridiculous reserve, he was going to make a fuss about the spontaneous movement that made me seize and imprison his cock myself. But he seemed, on the contrary, grateful to me. I made a note thereof for the future.

The next day, Monsieur Fanon came to pay us a visit, but we were out and I was really grieved when I found his card. He returned on the third day, and his persistence pleased me greatly. My husband was at home; we received him as cordially as possible and pressed him to come often.

I fancied that he treated me with particular warmth of feeling, and I was happy at the thought!

A gentle intimacy quickly sprang up between us, my love grew greater each day, and I already saw that my adored Stefan reciprocated the feeling. Although he had said nothing as yet, I was sure of it—what woman ever makes such a mistake?

We had, as yet, never been alone together. I ardently desired and yet feared that moment. I did not wish to abandon myself entirely at the first opportunity, though I felt that it would be impossible for me to resist one single instance! I resolved to know more of him, to try him . . . but all my strength of will melted away as soon as I saw him. In such a state of mind, how could I resist his attack?

That was quickly proved! One day, he came at three o'clock. My husband was away, but I had a visitor—a wearisome female who had no idea of getting up and going. I could see my dear Stefan waiting and suffering, but at least, not being decently able to remain any longer, he took his leave, giving me a supplicating look that I was powerless to resist.

I said to him, "Has not my husband promised you a certain book?"

"Yes, madam, and I had hoped to be able to take it with me today."

"I will give it you. Pardon me, madam," I said to my eternal bore, "and permit me to leave you for an instant."

We were in a small reception room that served as my boudoir. Stefan, who understood me, went out and waited for me in the big drawing room, where I rejoined him with an odd volume in my hand.

In an instant he declared his passion. What he said, what I answered, I do not know. I remember nothing.

I led him towards the hall for fear we should be overheard. There was a double door between the drawing room and a little vestibule, where I would be able to hear an approaching servant. As we reached there, Monsieur Fanon, beside himself, seized me in his arms. A lingering kiss, a kiss of fire, a kiss that penetrated to my soul, arrested a shriek that I would not have been able to stifle.

At the same time, his prompt hand had lifted my petticoats and was caressing my burning slit, that quick as lightning poured out upon his fingers palpable traces of the love potion that filled it to overflowing.

"Begone . . . begone . . . away," I said, with stifled breath. "Go . . . tomorrow . . . three o'clock." Then I fled in a state I cannot describe.

Happily, the lady who was waiting was not very clever and did not notice my disordered state.

I shall not undertake to narrate my feelings till the next day. All that I can remember is that I firmly resolved to satisfy my erotic longings.

My husband intended to absent himself for two or three days on business matters, and I arranged so as to send my servants on different errands. I dressed myself carefully and waited.

My dear Stefan arrived. I opened the door to him myself and led him to my boudoir.

We sat down, much embarrassed. He was very respectful and asked my pardon for what he had done the day before, saying that he was unable to master the delirious rage that had seized him, and that his love for me was such that he would die if he was unable to enjoy me.

I knew not how to answer. Both our hearts were too full. He took my hand and kissed it. Shuddering, I rose. Our mouths met. I confess I made no more attempts at resistance. I had not the strength to do so.

I fully enjoyed this intense happiness. I felt that he was carrying me along—but to where? What were we to do? In my boudoir there were only a very narrow low sofa, some armchairs, and ordinary seats without arms.

Stefan, still holding me in his arms, sat on a chair, so that I found myself in front of him, leaning over his head and face. I felt one of his arms at my waist; soon my clothes were all up in front and Stefan tried to pass his knees between my legs.

"Oh, no," I said, between two sobs. "No, please, have pity. I am a married woman."

Stefan made efforts to pull me down so as to straddle across him; but on instinctive feeling, although I longed for it, I still resisted, and stiffened myself against him. We soon became exhausted. At last, having dropped my eyes a little, I saw something that put an end to the struggle.

He had taken out his prick for the fray. Its ruby, haughty head stood up proudly. In length and thickness it was truly uncommon; it vied even with that of Monsieur Bonbier. I had no strength to resist such a sight; my thighs opened by themselves. I slid down, hiding my face on my lover's shoulder, and I gave myself up to him, opening myself as much as possible, desiring, and yet fearing, the entrance of such an imposing guest.

I soon felt the head between the lips of my grotto, which the thin tool of my husband had not accustomed to such a bountiful measure. I made a movement to help him, and had hardly introduced the head when I felt myself flooded by a flaming jet of loving liquor that covered my thighs and belly.

The prolonged wait, and his own passion, had made the precious dew pump up too quickly, and I had not been able to enjoy it as I should.

I could not help showing a little disappointment, but my lover, covering me with kisses, told me that I need wait but a brief period of repose, and that I should soon be more satisfied with him.

We sat on the sofa, entwined in each other's arms, telling one another of our love and happiness. We had fallen in love at first sight, and both had given way to irresistible passion.

In a few moments I saw that my lover was ready to begin again, and I asked myself how we were going to do it. I did not wish to try again that posture that had turned out so badly for me, and I could see Stefan also looking about him.

An idea struck me. I rose, smiling, teasing him. When he rose too, I retreated, and he eagerly pursued me, till at last I went and leaned with nonchalance upon the mantelpiece, presenting my bottom, that I wriggled like a cat, and at the same time turning my head and throwing him a provocative glance.

Ah, how he understood me. Stefan rushed upon me and kissed me, saying, "Thank you."

Then he got behind me and threw my petticoats over my back. When he saw the beautiful shape of my bottom, he gave a loud cry of admiration. I expected as much, but did not dream of the homage he paid to it.

He threw himself onto his knees, and after having covered

my backside with kisses he drew the globes apart, just at the top of the thighs, and I could feel his lips, even his tongue. I shrieked and was overcome.

Stefan rose up and began to put it in. His enormous instrument could not easily penetrate, in spite of our mutual efforts, so he drew it out, put a little saliva on the head and shaft, and soon stabbed me to the very vitals. I was filled and plugged up, and in a state of unspeakable ecstasy.

My lover, leaning over me, glued his lips to mine, which I offered to him by turning my head; his tongue dallied with mine. I was beside myself. I felt myself going mad. He plunged his tool into me again and again, drawing it out nearly to the tip before driving it in to the balls. I felt those twin plums slap my buttocks with each stroke and so great became my excitement that I reached down and began to massage the throbbing nub of my clit. I could feel my juices running down my thighs as that great prick continued to ravage me. The supreme moment arrived. I writhed about, uttering inarticulate sounds.

Stefan, who was reserving himself, was delighted at my joy; he let me calm down, and then I felt his sweet movement again.

Ah, how he knew to distill pleasure, and double it by a thousand delicate, subtle shades. That first lesson: I can feel it, as I write, between my thighs.

"Dear angel," he said, "tell me what you feel. It's so nice to enjoy each other's soft confidence when we form but one body, as at this moment."

Oh, how his speech made me happy. I, who had always wished to hear and say those words that had almost driven me wild when my aunt was at work! I did not hesitate an instant longer.

"I must do it again," I said, "It's coming—push in—again—right in—finish me—ah! I'm coming!"

"My adored one, I'm coming too—it's bubbling up—Oh! Oh! I'm going to explode!"

Stefan gave a final push and fell against me. I felt his ejaculation, and nearly fainted under the force of the jet.

How was it that I did not die during that embrace? Nothing that I had imagined at the sight of my aunt's sweet struggles could approach this reality! I remained overwhelmed, my head in my arms, my bosom heaving, incapable of movement.

Stefan drew out. I still spent. I kept on spending. I stood as I was, without sense of shame, naked below the waist, trembling, mechanically continuing the movement of my bottom, and causing the overflow of liquid to fall to the ground.

Stefan took pity on me. After rapidly adjusting himself, he pulled down my petticoats, and taking me in his arms sat by my side on the sofa. I was delirious for a second. He calmed me; his sweet voice was a song. I begged him to leave me to myself, and he went away.

I at last regained full consciousness, though my heart still pounded and threatened to burst I was in an extraordinary state of disorder and was obliged to change my linen. My chemise and stockings were not only stained by loving liquid, but by numerous spots of blood. My womanhood could not accept such a full-sized cock with impunity.

When I had set in order my toilette and my ideas, I went to bed and slept soundly, my husband not intending to return till late in the evening. I awoke at about seven: happy, fresh as a lark, and stronger than I had felt for many a day.

I will not restate all the thoughts that crowded in upon my brain, as I have already said that I had been drawn on by my irresistible feelings, and above all by a natural absolute craving for the sexual act. It was as necessary for my life as simple food.

Yet I was far from depraved! I loved my husband as a sure friend, as the companion of my existence, and if he had possessed the manly vigor that was necessary for me, or if even he had known how to answer my clever caresses, I should never have dreamt of being unfaithful to him! I resolved to spare him all sorrow, and I have fully succeeded, as he has never had the least suspicion!

This torrid affair demanded much care, trouble, and discretion. The community was much inclined to scandal, and it was very difficult for me to hide my connection, so I had to take endless precautions.

I warned my lover, who, wishing above all to save my reputation, promised to do all in his power not to excite suspicion. I knew I could rely on his honor.

A few days went by without our meeting; I suffered greatly, and he as much as I! A sign, a look during our walks was our only consolation for eight long days!

At last, Stefan could bear it no longer and came to pay us a visit. We chatted in an ordinary way. A business associate arrived and Stefan decided to leave; my husband showed him out and returned to the room. I don't know what instinct warned me that Stefan had not left the house! I got up with some excuse that seemed all the more reasonable as the visitor was keeping up a technical conversation with my husband, and went into the vestibule. I was not mistaken. Stefan, seeing no servants about, was waiting by the side door.

As soon as he saw me, he threw himself upon me, clasped me in his arms and with violent passion exclaimed, "Darling angel, how I suffer!"

"No less than I."

We were once again between the double doors. Before I knew where I was, our mouths were glued together, my petticoats were up to my navel, and his finger pushed itself into my burning slit, which opened beneath its pressure. My hand had seized the darling object between his thighs.

What more can I say? In a second or two—after a few movements of our hands took place—I nearly swooned with joy. I drew away my own hand, bathed now with an abundance of Stefan's warm liquid.

Yet a few more days went by without our being able to meet, till at last a happy moment of liberty was granted to us. A whole hour was ours.

Ah, how we profited by it! My lover came into my boudoir. I rushed to receive him, and I devoured him with caresses.

"Let us do it quickly," we both exclaimed together. "Let us enjoy to the utmost our secret happiness."

I tore myself from him, removed my clothes, and getting onto the sofa on my knees, presented my bottom.

He put his throbbing cock in at once. There was little in the way of reservation or prolongation. We had been apart so long our passion would permit no delay. Stefan simply rammed his wonderful cock into me and pistoned it in and out until I thought it must emerge from my belly. His balls slapped my bottom, and his hands reached around to crush my trembling breasts as he continued his shattering strokes. I very soon swooned beneath his copious discharge. We then sat down, but my lover was not satisfied. Despite my fears I could not refuse. He went on his knees between my legs, then he made me stretch wide apart. I took his vigorous firebrand in my hand; it was already as hard as ever. I stroked it a second, then pushed it gradually into my slit, while I savored slowly the delightful pleasure.

When the arrow had completely disappeared in its quiver, Stefan leaned over me, and lifting my two legs over his arms, threw me backwards. He went to work so lustily, ramming and pumping, that soon a second ejaculation became added to the first, with which I seemed to be already filled.

I do not intend to retrace day by day all our delicious meetings. I will limit myself to a description of the most striking facts of the adorable liaison that I wished would last out my life! My lover knew how to vary our pleasures without ever reaching satiety, he felt a singular pleasure in teaching the art of enjoyment, and he found in me a most docile and willing pupil.

He taught me the names of everything, sometimes making me say them, but only in the whirl of passion; he used them himself in supreme moments of bliss, proclaiming that such spice should never be too overused, or it would lose its flavor!

What cunning caresses! What lascivious postures he taught me! What whims, infantile play, and even prolonging on both sides! What refinements of pleasure we realized as soon as we'd thought of them! I made such progress, under such a good master, that often I surpassed him.

I used to vastly like to change the way of doing it. For instance, sometimes when plugged from behind, one of my favorite positions, I would unhorse my rider, turn around quickly, give a kiss to my still-erect conqueror, wet with my passion cream, and escape to the other end of the room. I would place myself in an easy chair, my legs upraised and my pussy quite open, while I gave it a provoking twitching movement. My lover would be hardly in me again, when by a fresh whim I would draw it out, make him sit on a chair, get on his knees, my back turned towards him, and taking his tool, plunge it in my body to the very hilt.

His cock, the splendid instrument of my joy, became my passion, the object of real worship. I never tired of admiring its thickness, its stiffness, and its length, all equally marvelous. I would dandle it, suck it, pump it, caress it in a thousand different ways, and rub it between my titties, holding it there by pressing them with both my hands. Often when captive in this voluptuous passage it would throw out its thick offering of sperm.

My lover returned all my caresses with interest. My pussy was his goddess, his idol. He assured me that no woman had ever possessed a more perfect one. He would open it and frig it in every conceivable way. His greatest delight was to apply his lips thereto, and extract, so to speak, the quintessence of voluptuousness by titillations of his tongue. It almost drove me mad.

I got so fond of this delicious method of procuring orgasm that hardly one of our meetings took place without Stefan making me enjoy it.

I had adopted for this joy a favorite position. I would recline in a large easy chair that I had purposely placed in my boudoir. I would sit on it with my thighs open and thrown over the arms of the piece of furniture; my lover, on his knees before me, would lick and suck and tease my pleasure bud with his teeth. When I wriggled and twisted in the paroxysm of pleasure, pressing his head to my belly, gently pulling his hair and ears, and slapping his cheeks, he would drag himself from my grasp, plunge his cock into my cunny, and enlaced together as one, we would come till we almost lost our reason.

Other times, I would kneel on the sofa and receive his tongue from behind, my lover clamping his face between the cheeks of my bottom and finding the delicate spot that received him with joy.

One day, after a rather long separation, my dear Stefan was able to find me alone. Alas! my monthly obstacle rendered our usual pleasure impossible. I could see he was suffering and looking at my hand in a supplicating way. I was quite disposed to accord him this means of relief when a mad idea crossed my brain! I remembered the last scene between my aunt and Monsieur Bonbier in the pavilion in the park. The situation was identical. I wished to reproduce it in every detail and easily induced Stefan to humor me. I made him get up, placed him in the same position as Alfred had been, and proceeded to do exactly the same as Bertha. I fisted him tightly, drawing the skin of his tool up and down and running my palm over the engorged head. With my other hand I dandled his balls, which hung pendulous and full. I jerked him faster and faster until I could see the color rise in his chest and face. He spurted out his dew afar, and I gathered the last few pearls in my hand-kerchief.

When he had done, I could not help laughing.

He asked me the cause of my merriment.

"Nothing," I answered thoughtlessly. "It reminded me of something."

I saw his face change, and quickly guessed the mistake I had just made and what suspicions were gathering in the mind of my lover. Not wishing to cause him the least shade of vexation, I made him sit close to me, and sure of his discretion, I told him all that had happened to me before marriage. The story amused him greatly; he made me enter into the most minute details. When I told him how I was led on to procure sweet pleasure for myself, he exclaimed, "Ah, darling! What I would have given to see you frig your delicious little cunt!"

He asked me more questions about my solitary habits, and I went so far as to tell him that on the day of our meeting at Madame Dumond's, I was so full of thought of him that I had done it that very evening.

"Why," he answered, "this is truly curious! Confidence in return for confidence, dear angel. Know that the same night and probably at the same hour, we were exchanging our souls in mutual spending!"

"What do you mean?"

"Listen. I went home, madly in love with you. I wanted you

as soon as I had seen you. I could not yet believe that I would be lucky enough to posses you, but all my efforts tended to that desired end. I went to bed and thought only of you! I was in a fearful state. I put out my light and conjuring up your image, covered your face with imaginary kisses. Then I did what you were doing, and the pleasure was so great that I am sure we came at one and the same time."

"What? Can men frig themselves as we do?"

"Certainly. Why should this natural means of relief be denied to them? What your pretty hand has just done for me, my ugly paw provides for my solitary gratification."

"Really? Well, I should like to see that!"

"Nonsense! You don't want me to . . ."

"Yes. You must show me how you do it!"

"But you know very well how. I do it like you . . ."

"Oh, please! Grant me this little pleasure!"

So saying, I gathered up his meatpole, which, excited by our conversation, had once more shot up to its most splendid proportions. I took his hand and placed it upon it.

"No, really, this is rank folly!"

"No, sir!"

"But I would sooner have your fingers, or your beautiful tits, if you will only use them instead."

"Give me no buts! I command you to make haste and do it to the very end, or I will no longer love you."

My dear lover could refuse me nothing, and after a little more hesitation he said, "I consent, but on condition that you in your turn shall give me as soon as feasible a representation of your own pleasures."

"To that I consent, but do what I want at once!"

He began, and leaning over him, I followed his convulsive shaking with a singular feeling of pleasurable curiosity. I was fascinated by the way he manipulated his own tool. He used his thumb and three fingers on the shaft, rather than his entire fist. He moved the skin up and down slowly, maintaining a steady rhythm. His breathing was increasing in tempo as his pole twitched in his gentle grip. It hardened still more and was now enormous. I soon took pity on him, however, and unlacing my stays I knelt down before him and made him finish between my breasts.

Shortly after this caprice of mine, my dear Stefan had his revenge upon me. He reminded me of the promise I had made, and despite a certain amount of shame, I stretched myself on the sofa and prepared to satisfy him.

"No, not like that," he said. "You placed me as you liked; let me do the same."

"What do you mean?"

"You shall soon see. Get astride of that chair!"

I obeyed.

"Yes, that will do nicely. Now show me your little cunt, and frig yourself with your left hand."

Again I obeyed, wondering greatly.

During this exercise Stefan unhooked my dress and stripped me to the waist. I now wanted to spend fearfully. My lascivious instincts began to blaze. The operation that I had begun jokingly to perform, only to please him, had become serious in the extreme. Suddenly I felt that Stefan was behind me, with his trousers down, and pressing the upper part of my nude body to him. He had insinuated his organ under my right arm. The originality of this fantastical idea inflamed my imagination more than ever. I bent my head and avidly contemplated the beautiful tool, the head of which appeared and disappeared at each stroke of my dear lover, who kept his eyes fixed on my left hand that was massaging my dripping cunt.

Soon we warned each other that the end was near and our double discharge took place simultaneously!

A few delicious months went by in like manner!

Our love increased daily, instead of becoming feeble or worn out by the frequency, the subtlety and the complete liberty of our connection! The precautions we so carefully took assured us perfect secrecy, and once only were we almost caught in the act.

We thought that we were certain not to be interrupted, as my husband was away from home and all the servants out.

That time, after a chat and a few caresses, I had, by a well-known sign, made my lover aware of what I wanted. He placed me as he desired, my body reclining in the large chair, my legs stretched asunder, and he had begun his adorable, lecherous licking.

I was about to come in his mouth! My eyes were closed and I was wrapped up in my enjoyment, tasting every one of the thousand delicious sensations that his tongue conjured up, when suddenly we heard footsteps and voices in the adjoining room. Quick as lightning, we were on our feet, our clothes arranged, and seated at proper distance.

My maid, who had returned without my knowledge, opened the door and announced the visit of a lady of our town.

I felt terribly giddy, but the cool presence of my lover, who knew the lady, gave me time to collect my scattered senses.

We were saved!

PART III

It was summer. It had been planned that I would vacation at a seaside village a little distant from my residence. I was not looking forward to it, for it would momentarily separate me from Stefan.

My lover was in despair, but this journey was arranged, and Charles wished me to go. He could not accompany me, as business kept him at Nice, but he was to visit me frequently and came to me as soon as possible. It would have been too imprudent to receive Stefan when alone there.

I went off very downcast and passed the first moments at my new dwelling in absolute privacy.

My husband came to see me at the end of a week, and told me that he would bring with him next time Stefan and two other friends, to spend a day. That hope sustained me; I awaited the blessed moment with feverish anxiety.

At last, ten days later, I received a letter announcing that the journey was arranged.

The gentlemen arrived at four o'clock in the morning, and my husband came at once and got into bed with me.

I soon saw that absence had awakened a rare longing in Charles, and although I expected to be bountifully feasted by my adored Stefan, I must here confess that I willingly lent myself to these desires.

I clasped Charles to my arms, slipped my hand under his nightshirt, and taking hold of his member gently pumped it for a few minutes. When I had encouraged it into a most glorious state of erection, I popped it into my slit.

Charles did it better than usual, fucking me with unusual energy, and confessed that the caresses of my hand had afforded him the most vivacious sensations of pleasure. I have often used the manual exercise with him since and whenever he asked me.

We slept till eight o'clock.

We breakfasted at a restaurant in the town with the gentlemen; the meal was good and we were all very happy, my dear Stefan brimming over with wit and good spirits. Our eyes only spoke, but how we understood their language! His seemed to say, "When can we meet?"

My husband, involuntarily, fixed our assignation.

He proposed a picnic in the woods when the heat of the day

should abate, and said that after having seen me home he would go to sleep and so work off the fatigue of the preceding night's journey.

Stefan said that during that time he would make a few visits to some old friends, and the other gentlemen went off to bathe in the sea.

A glance at my lover and all was understood.

At one o'clock in the afternoon my husband was snoring downstairs and Stefan had slipped into my room. Knowing his taste, my hair was carefully arranged; I had put on pink silk stockings and high-heeled shoes. I only had a slight dressing gown thrown over my shoulders, and I awaited his coming with delirious impatience. As soon as he appeared I hung myself around his neck and kissed and bit him. "At last, I've got you, my angel, my love! How I wanted you! Let me devour you!" I said, as I locked the door and drew him towards me. "Come to my arms! Fifteen days without you. I shall die, I'm sure. How I've suffered!"

"And I've been just as badly off, darling. We have but little time to spare, so let us make the most of it. Suppose we are interrupted?"

"He will sleep for hours. I am yours. Do with me as you will."

As I finished speaking, my gown was already on the ground. My lover, undressed, sat me on the edge of the bed and put two pillows behind me. He uncovered my titties, felt and sucked them for some time, then pulled up my chemise. He went on his knees and applied his burning lips to the fiery nook that welcomed the caress with a spasm of happiness.

"Ah, darling," I said. "Ah . . . I'm coming already . . . I'm coming . . . again . . . Oh, what delight . . . enough . . . you'll kill me . . . give me your beautiful cock now! I want to feel your prick inside me. Come into my cunt. Come and fuck me!"

Stefan then rose, lifting my legs over his arms, and brought the head of his cock to my slit. Softly, reposing, I looked down at the sweet introduction with languishing eyes. He pushed his enormous tool in and began shuttling in and out, varying the motion by rotating his hips and alternating short strokes with long ones.

"Do it slowly," I said. "Make it last. Ah, it is so nice! I can feel it penetrating me. It fills me . . . Ah . . . ah . . . I'm dying . . . stop a little . . . ah . . . I'm coming . . . I'm coming!"

"And so do I! Ah! I can't keep up . . . any longer . . . my darling . . . my fucktress . . . I . . . I spend . . . take it all . . . take all my sperm!"

I almost fainted as he shot off into my cavern, but I was not yet satisfied. My love had sunk down upon me. I encircled his head with my arms and glued my mouth to his.

"Ah," said I, in a whisper, "you spent too quickly."

"I could not help it; but don't move now!"

"What are you going to do?"

"You see, I'm still inside."

"But I'm all wet!"

"No matter, I mean to fuck you again without withdrawing."

"That isn't possible!"

"You'll see. What adorable tits you've got, darling. Give me your tongue. That's right. Move your dear ass up and down gently. I'm waking up again. Do you feel it?"

"Yes. It's getting stiff again. Ah! I can't bear it; I just have to come again. Push on once more. Quicker. Ah. I'm going mad. I'm so giddy. I'm coming again. I'm fucking. I'm still spending. Are you ready?"

"Yes. It's coming . . . there! Oh, God!"

A second discharge mingled itself with the first flood. For some time we both remained helpless, and at last Stefan, dropping his hold of my legs, drew out. A veritable deluge of the extract of love came pattering down on the floor.

I rose and took my lover to my heart.

"My adored one," I said, "what a splendid fuck! How happy you make me! I've never come so much in my life! I was coming all the time without a second of interruption."

We were obliged to remove all trace of our prodigious struggles. My thighs and belly were literally covered with gobs of sperm. I had no dressing room, but dared not remain in such a state. I got my wash basin, and making Stefan turn his back, began my ablutions.

My love, far from obeying, did not miss a movement. He took hold of me, with my petticoats still pulled up, and kissed and me as he said, "I must fuck you again."

"Oh, no, please. You'll be ill!"

"But see, it's up again."

The sight completed my madness. I fell on my knees, seized the beautiful head between my lips, engulfed it in my mouth and sucked it with raging delirium. I took it down my throat, pulling and attempting to draw the juice from it. I licked around the head and down the shaft, even taking his balls one at a time into my mouth.

Suddenly, I heard a noise in the passage. I rose with a bound, rushed to the door, and looked through the keyhole. If it was my husband, we were lost. Happily, I was mistaken. It was just the house cat.

I sighed to Stefan that there was nothing to fear. In this position, with my eye fixed to the door lock, my buttocks were exposed, and my shift was all tucked up. In a twinkling, my lover was behind me, and before I had time to collect myself I was penetrated again, filled up by that adorable instrument that seemed to know no rest. Ah! How I helped him by opening and shutting the cheeks of my backside! I writhed, twisted, and swooned with joy.

Our time had passed quickly. In haste, I sent Stefan away,

made the bed afresh, and arranged a neat toilette for the promenade. I was scarcely ready when the carriage drove up and Charles came to fetch me. He found me flushed and lively. I told him that, overcome by the heat, I had fallen asleep.

We went downstairs and I was joyfully saluted by the gentlemen, who complimented me on the good taste of my dress. On the sly, I looked at Stefan, but nothing betrayed that anything extraordinary had taken place. We started off.

The forest we were exploring was deliciously cool and picturesque. We went to the lodge of a gamekeeper where a rustic repast had been prepared. Our picnic was merrily enjoyed; I was forced to drink several glasses of champagne, although I did not require that to stimulate me.

After the meal we set out walking again, my husband gossiping with Stefan. I was with them. The two other guests had strolled onto another path when we arrived at a wild spot, studded with rocks and shaded with large trees.

At this moment one of the gentlemen, who were now far off, called out to my husband, "Come, quick, come and see!"

Charles waved his acknowledgement and left us. No sooner had he disappeared from view than Stefan glued his mouth to mine.

"Angel," he said, "let us profit by this moment!"

"You are mad!"

"No, I love you! Let me do as I will."

"My God, we shall be discovered! I am lost!"

"Not if you hurry. Stoop!"

I did so immediately, lifting my skirts.

"Are you in?"

"Here I am. It's going in!"

"Ah! Make haste."

He thrust furiously, driving his rock in and out so fast that little pleasure could truly be gained in this fashion.

"There, darling . . . spend . . . spend again!"

"Ah! I've come! There! Now go away."

Only just in time. My petticoats, all up behind, were barely readjusted when I heard the rest of the party returning.

I went to meet them, and we found they had fetched us to see a swarm of bees at the top of a tree.

We got into our carriages and returned to the town. We danced the night away and then said farewell to the gentlemen, who went away early the next morning.

It is easy to guess my thoughts when at home once more, as I began to undress for the night. I was brushing my hair in front of my mirror when Charles, delighted with the day's outing, came up behind me.

I was in my shift, which clung tightly to my figure and showed the seductive shape of my backside. I could see in the glass that Charles was looking at it, and that his eyes sparkled.

Aha! I thought. Can it be possible that for once he will be able to do it to me twice in the same day?

I wanted him to fuck me, and coquettishly struck an attitude that threw out into still greater relief what I knew was one of my greatest beauties. Then, negligently putting one foot on a chair, I took care that my chemise would be more raised than was absolutely necessary. I undid my garter.

This ruse succeeded. Charles, also in his shirt, got up, and coming near me kissed me on the neck, then put his hand between the cheeks of my bottom.

"Oh! Oh!" I said, turning round and returning his kiss. "Whatever ails you tonight?"

"My dear wife, I find that you are extremely beautiful!"

"Am I not the same every day?"

"Oh, yes, but this evening still more so!"

"Well, what are you driving at? Come on!"

So saying, I put my hand on his cock. It stood a little, although it was far from being in a proper state of erection.

"You see that you can't do anything!"

"Yes, I can! Caress it a little bit!"

"What makes you excited?"

"Why . . ."

"Well now—what?"

"Your beautiful bottom!"

"Indeed, sir. Well, you shan't see any more of it unless you respond quickly!"

As supple as a kitten, I trussed up my linen with one hand, so that my buttocks were naked, while my front parts were reflected in the mirror. At the same time my other hand had not loosened its grasp, and cleverly excited what it held. I soon had the satisfaction of feeling it get hard. Wishing to profit by his momentary desire, I made Charles sit and got over him, but I soon found that such a position stretched me too much and, widening my slit, was quite unsuited for his thin tool.

I got up and had to begin all over again. I was too excited to be daunted now, and once more started the caress of my agile hand. I resolved to do my best, and he helped, so that soon I was pleased to see it once more in its most splendid state! Then I drew a chair to the glass, placed one foot upon it and the other on the ground, and put his prick in from behind.

Charles, led on by me till he was almost beside himself, did it in such a manner that I spent three times. He thrust up into me feverishly, poking and stroking, using the entire length of this thin rod. He was a long while in coming, but nevertheless finished by discharging, thanks to the clever movements of my buttocks and the talent I had acquired in pressing and pinching his wretched little tool.

Both very much fatigued, we retired to rest. Thus, in this memorable day, I had been fucked six times! I do not exaggerate in saying that I had come more than twenty times!

But such was the force of my temperament and my aptitude for amorous encounters that I rose the next day from my couch as fresh and as well as if nothing had occurred.

I went back to Nice, and Stefan and I relapsed into our sweet habits once more, which, though frequently interrupted, grew more ardent after each successive deprivation.

My husband now rarely went away for more than one day at a time, so that our pleasures only lasted during the short instants snatched during an occasional afternoon. Nevertheless, a few exciting encounters took place, and we profited by them.

One evening, happy in a few hours of security, we determined to completely enjoy our happiness. My love proposed that we should undress and get on my bed. I accepted with avidity. He was soon stripped and laid on his back while I unlaced my stays. I joined him clad in nothing save that with which I had been born. He seized me in his arms and we were clasped together in an instant!

He contemplated my nakedness with ecstasy, then covered my entire body with burning kisses, without omitting one single spot!

I was mad, delirious! In turn I wished to reproduce for him the pleasure I had felt. I kissed with ardor every part of that body, so manly and so handsome. When I arrived between his legs and found that darling jewel that proudly, stiffly stood, I stopped and kissed it, I sucked it, I would have liked to have eaten it!

In this position my buttocks were turned towards my lover's face. I could feel that he had seized my left thigh and was trying to pass it over him.

"What do you want?" I said, turning my head a little.

"Put your legs over me."

"But how? Why?"

"I'll soon tell you. There, that will do!"

I found myself astride his breast, my head still in the same place!

"Now," he said, "bend down, push out your lovely ass . . . there . . . now place your cunt on my mouth."

"Here I am!"

"Good. Now let us both use our tongues. Tell me in time, and we'll come together!"

Although rather puzzled at this new method, I gracefully gave way to him, and soon I felt his clever and delicate tongue travel over my cleft. I went off into a mad rage. I once more took hold of his instrument, that I had let go for a moment, got the entire head into my mouth, and pumped at it with frenzy! An electric current seemed to envelop my entire frame. Each stroke of Stefan's tongue was answered by my mouth!

What delirious joy! I had already spent thrice, and when feeling that the fourth time was near, and that my lover, shuddering and palpitating, was also nearing the supreme moment, I exclaimed, "I'm ready! Come, darling, come in my mouth!"

What happened then? I don't know! I lost consciousness as Stefan's flood of passion exploded down my throat.

My lover's adorable lessons had rendered me very knowledgeable, and I thought I had no more to learn. I was mistaken; there was one supreme lesson left for me to learn.

I have often repeated that my buttocks, or rather my ass, were of rare beauty. The furrow that divided the oval had already received thousands and thousands of my lover's kisses, whose greatest delight was to place me so as to enjoy this spectacle thoroughly. He would then open the lips of the gap of love, caress it, kiss it, and worship it in every manner. Sometimes his finger would wander higher up, and I could feel a strange titillation at the opening of the dark orifice above! Sometimes, even when plugged up to the roots by his magnificent tool, fainting beneath the divine dew that was spouted into me, I felt the finger penetrate far up the narrow path!

That singular caress caused me quite a peculiar erotic joy that I had not sought to analyze.

On one of the rare evenings when we were able to get between the sheets, after having felt each other all over for some time, my lover took off my chemise and looked lovingly at my nakedness.

Knowing his passionate love for my ass, I presented it to him, stretching myself as wide open as I could. Stefan got up behind me, but instead of getting into my cunt as usual, he contented himself with rubbing the head of his prick against my bottom.

"Put it in!" I cried. "You are teasing me dreadfully!"

"Wait a bit!"

"What are you doing? You hurt me. Not there!"

And indeed, I felt the head trying to penetrate the singular aperture I have just mentioned.

"Let me do as I please, my adored one! I entreat you. A delicious woman is cunt all over; no single part of her beautiful body must remain virgin."

"But it's impossible! It can never go in!"

"I can get it entirely in if you will let me."

"But you'll kill me. I'll suffer. I'll scream. I won't come at all."

"Yes you will, and afterwards you'll say how nice it was. I'll wager that you will often ask me to do it."

"No, it's impossible. Come, darling, put it in lower down, it's just as nice for you!"

"But I supplicate you to let me do it. It's the greatest proof of love that a woman can give. I demand that proof."

"Oh, heaven! I can't refuse you. Go along then and do it. How funny all the same." Of course I didn't know what to expect.

I said no more, and remained passive, presenting as well as

I could what was required of me. My lover went to the toilet-table and lubricated his tool with a stick of cosmetic, then, taking up his position again, he once more knocked at the narrow gate. His first attempts did not succeed; I suffered hor-ribly and felt no pleasure at all. Still I loved him so much that I would have suffered greater agonies. And, besides, my curi-osity and a desire for the unknown sustained me. My lover ceased his efforts for an instant, and, passing his hand between my thighs, began to massage my cunt. Symptoms of pleasure now arose, and I myself begged for a second trial, but my lover's leaning posture was too uncomfortable. He took my hand and placed it where his had stroked me. I understood him, and rubbed away myself. Again I felt the terrible point, though the pleasure in front helped to neutralize the agony that my poor bottom still felt.

At last, I felt as if an enormous ring was dilated within me, and suddenly the monstrous cylinder slipped in entirely. I quickened the movement of my hand. An immense . . . twofold . . . sharp . . . extraordinary spasm overpowered me. I almost fainted and fell forward in an indescribable fit.

My lover, luckily, had not been unseated. He followed my movement and laid his full length upon me. He gave a few more strokes in the snug passage and filled his strange shelter with a hot ejaculation that he spurted forth with many groans and sighs.

We remained some time in this position without speaking. I felt a certain shame that I could not explain, and was almost vexed at having spent so well by the ravishing of that unusual nook. On the other hand, I could not prevent myself being delighted by the opening of this new source of pleasure.

Stefan kissed me and whispered, "Well, what do you think of it?"

"I hardly know."

"Did you come?"

"Well, yes!"

"Are you vexed at having submitted to my whim?"

"No."

"Will you ever ask me to do it again?"

"I think I shall, but not often. It is too exciting, too awfully good, and too painful!"

During our chat, the position remained unchanged; my lover's peg was still planted in my tiny hole. I felt it diminishing as he tried to withdraw. I pinched in my buttocks so that I kept him trapped at his post.

"You wanted to get in," I said, "and there you shall stay!"

I relied on his well-tried strength, and while I waited for it to return to its former state I teased him, using all the words he had taught me.

"What do you call this style of fucking?" I asked. "You haven't touched the poor little cunt that has had nothing this time."

"It's called . . . well . . . butt-fucking."

"Well, darling, butt-fuck me again, I begin to like it. Ah! I can feel your nice prick reviving. Treat kindly this ass you love so much. Don't go away yet, I beg of you. I want your sperm once more."

As I rattled out all these little bawdy words, which I knew electrified my lover, I loosened the tightness of my buttocks gradually, so as to leave him full liberty of action.

I began to feel again the advance symptoms of that double pleasure I had just felt. Stefan was not yet quite ready. In fact, I seemed to feel him get weak, so I told him not to leave me as we rose again with infinite care to our first posture.

"Now, my darling," I said, "don't move. I'll do it all myself!"

I began to wriggle my rump carefully backwards and forwards. My lover, on his knees, as still as a statue, was passionately contemplating this libidinous sight. He could see, as he told me afterwards, his cock, held as though in a vice, appear almost entirely, and then be completely lost to view in its narrow sheath.

After a few minutes of this delicious fun, my lover had recovered his pristine vigor. I could tell that by the growing thickness and stiffness of the member that bound our bodies together. I soon felt him shiver; broken utterances issued from his lips. I let him know that I was ready, and a fresh jet of passion potion caused us both to swoon away with joy.

My well-beloved Stefan was right. I grew to like it indeed! How many times since has he not said with his soft voice, as he leans over me, "Where will you have it?"

And how often I have pointed to my bottom, with my finger, and answered, *"There!"*

Suburban Souls

by Anonymous

Suburban Souls is a novel of sex and jealousy, as obsessive in its way as the self-consuming passion of the narrator for Albertine in A Remembrance of Things Past. *A decade before the publication of the first volume of Proust's great novel,* Suburban Souls *explores the true nature of erotic jealousy. Narrated in the first person, it depicts the erotic passion of Jacky S., a middle-aged stockbroker and freelance book editor who becomes obsessed with the coy but highly provocative Lilian.*

I went and found my charmer in a new flaming dress made entirely of vivid red cloth. She had white kid gloves, with a nice hat, and looked very well, being very red in the face too. She had with her the lesbian Lolotte, the ex-mistress and ex-betrothed of her brother Raoul. They were both very jolly. I had never seen Lolotte before, but she knew me by name from Lily. I chaff them about their sexless kisses when alone together, and want to know who is the man of the two. It is the stereotyped stuff that is always poured out to a tribadic couple. Lolotte is a pretty, plump blonde. She was very free and charming; about Lily's age, twenty-two or thereabouts. We are soon very comfortable together in the back saloon of the bar, where, it seems to me, Lily is well-known. It was near the Café de la Guerre, and she went there with her brother on Shrove Tuesday. Directly I saw Lilian, I exclaimed: "Hullo, all up for our luncheon tomorrow!"

"How do you mean?"

"Why, you fetching me out in Paris tonight proves it is all off."

"But that would not prevent us lunching tomorrow, although I can't come for the following reasons. How strange you should have guessed it! I had to take some hats to a customer in Paris on Monday, so I profited by that to get to you. This morning comes a postcard, which Mother sees, to say that the lady prefers to come down to the country. So I can't get out to Paris. My excuse is destroyed. If it had been a letter, I could have suppressed it, and seen the lady today, so as to stop her coming down. Thus our lunch is knocked on the head!"

"Lies!" I thought, but I said nothing. I should have liked to have seen that postcard.

"I have finished Cesarée," said Lily. "It is beautiful. You have marked it well, and scored the best bits, but you are all wrong in one instance."

"About the bedrooms at the Swiss hotel, I suppose?"

"Yes. You know you are quite mistaken in your ideas about me!" She said this slowly and dreamily, not looking straight at me.

"I am absolutely convinced of the truth of my conjectures and stick to every word I have ever said or written on the subject!" I say this firmly, loudly, and impressively.

Charlotte was listening to the conversation, and Lily spoke quite openly, showing that her fair friend knew the secrets of Sonis. I told her that Lily was a liar, and had an awful temper. She knew it, and replied that all women were liars, out of necessity.

Lily's friend talked about London and declared that she would like to go there during the season. I offered, jokingly, to take her. She replied with emphasis, that it would be very nice, and people would take her for a daughter traveling with her

Papa! And she looked fixedly and archly at me. I had enough presence of mind to pay no apparent heed to her bold words, but I felt I had scored again. She knew.

I said I was impotent. Lily cried out: "No, he isn't!"

Lolotte said she was sentimental, and Lily was not.

Nevertheless, the blonde confessed that she liked something stiff and rather long. I could see by the way she spoke that Lily was now like herself; a common, ordinary, middle-class, half-and-half kind of whore, always on the look-out for a man with money, and had I told her the story of her friend's virginity, she would have been quite surprised. It was a great pity that I knew Lily's stepfather-lover and all his connections and history so well. Under ordinary circumstances, they would never have thought of hatching these intricate and silly plots against me.

I spoke of Raoul, but both the girls begged me never to tell him of the meeting of the two beauties in Paris at night.

Lily told us the story of her day: "I got up at nine, had a bath, lunched; then went on my bicycle, came home, dressed again; came to Paris, fetched Charlotte, and we both went to Narkola's to dine. We had lots of nice things: bisque soup and fine wine."

"In a *cabinet particulier*, both alone together?"

"Oh, no, in the public room!"

All lies, but I say nothing.

"How dry you must both be now!"

They roar with laughter, and whisper together, and giggle; and again our conversation about the sexes becomes lewd and stupid. They have two American drinks each. I have a soda and Scotch whisky. Lily amuses herself dropping her saliva in my half-emptied glass, making me drink her spittle mixed with my beverage. She tells me that Gaston taught her that clean manner of showing affection. Lolotte gets on well with me and wants me to take her to London more than ever.

To lull Lily into security, I thank her for having sent for me, and she alludes to how I said she sickened me when she sent me a sudden summons by wire last September. She also spoke of my birthday and remembered the date well. I merely quote these two facts to show that her brain was clear on technical points, and although she was artful enough to give no sign, all I had ever written to her, all I had ever said, had always gone right home to the mark, and remained in her memory. No doubt she read my letters over and over again. Poor, miserable Lily!

The girls kiss and say good night. We put Charlotte in a cab, and off she goes to her home, somewhere beyond the Bastille. Lily has a little jealous scene about my freedom with her friend, as Lolotte had taken off her glove and held my hand and tickled it. We go for a ride to the Eastern station, to catch the 10:30 to Sonis. I am not to get out of the cab at the station, so as not to be seen by the neighbors who might be taking this train, or anybody, or somebody.

"When shall we meet again?" I ask.

"I don't know. You are aware how difficult it is for me to get to Paris."

"It used to be difficult. It ought not to be difficult now."

No answer.

I tell her I shall masturbate her in the cab. We get in. We exchange hot and luscious kisses, as we have been doing all the evening, more or less. After a lot of resistance, with cries of, "People will see us! Oh! They are looking, etc.," I get my hand up her clothes. I pull down the blinds. She pulls them up. At last I overcome her feigned resistance and begin to excite her with my finger.

She has on her best drawers, and to my surprise, her cleft, generally smelling strong of the wonderful odor peculiar to the sex, is quite inodorous. It has evidently been freshly washed after dinner. My fingers afterwards were entirely without any feminine perfume. I knew also that a virgin's vulva is always more fragrant than that of a woman used to coition. I remembered that when her people were at Nice at January, she had a dinner at Narkola's with Madame Rosenblatt and her male relations, who had purposely sent a false telegram to her Granny. Of course that was a cock-and-bull story. Here is Narkola's again! Had I chosen, I could have gone there the next day and inquired about an imaginary earring dropped by the young lady in the red dress, but I really was now quite indifferent and would not have walked twenty yards to find out anything about her. I had spied upon her in Brussels—that was enough.

Suddenly, while gently caressing her clitoris, I turned half round, so as to get almost facing her, and placing my right forearm under her chin, on her throat, I drove her backwards into her corner of the cab, and while she was thus pressed there, unable to move, I thrust the middle finger of my left hand as far up her vagina as I can, until it was stopped by the knuckles.

I measured my finger the next day, finding two and one half inches, and my hand is small. The two and one half inches of medius went up easily. I moved my finger about inside, with a slight corkscrew motion. Within all was soft and damp, but not wet from randiness, only from the drink.

She has not left me to void her urine since 9:00 P.M. She shrieks loudly and says: "You hurt me! You hurt me!"

She struggles, but I have her tightly jammed in the corner.

I find that her grotto is strangely altered. The outer lips were always very fleshy, but inside all was small, and the skin tightly drawn together, as on a thin hand. Now it is very fat, mellow, and as I said, not wet, as she was not feeling "naughty." My finger went in as if in butter, and she has now evidently what I should call a large, fat gap, which has been properly stroked, doubtless by big, manly tools. But then, having been used that evening, it might be a little puffed up, as women's parts are after connection.

I cried out: "You are no longer a virgin! No longer a maid! Now I shall be able to have complete intercourse with you!"

I took my finger out and released her. She made a wry face, as she put down her clothes, saying: "Oh, you did hurt me! But I'm still a virgin. Your finger went in because it was not in the right place. You were between the two!"

Possibly meaning just under the clitoris and above the hymen. I need not stop to point out the absurdity of this anatomical statement.

"You are a virgin? Bosh!"

"I swear I am! On my mother's life, I swear I am still intact!"

I was so delighted at having attained my object that I did not realize the contemptible horror of the situation. It was only afterwards, when I was alone, that I gauged the depths of Lilian's baseness. At the moment, curiously enough, I thought of how I should describe the scene in my book. I saw it all in print, and it seemed comic and unreal, as if it were happening to someone else, and I was but the spectator of my own disgusted self. But there was a glorious warmth of triumph thrilling through my veins. I felt like a detective who after many months has run his man down and at last got the handcuffs on a criminal. I do believe that if I had found she really was a virgin, I should have been disappointed to find a maidenhead. It would have seemed like a monstrosity. Never did a surgeon operating on some special case of hidden cancer feel more awful, intense joy than I did at that critical juncture.

"Come," said I, laughing, "and I'll finish you gently."

She was now quiet and subdued, and expected likely enough a storm of reproaches. She kissed me and let me put my hand up her clothes without any show of revolt. I began again to manipulate her rosebud, but naturally enough she had no enjoyment. Then I got very stiff, but not too much, as I had been indulging that afternoon, and I got it out and put her hand on it.

She caressed and agitated it a little. Seeing we were getting near the station and having a sudden desire for her hot mouth, which I knew would make me ejaculate in a jiffy, better than her awkward pulling at me with her gloved hand, I said: "Give me your mouth, Lily!"

She shook her head, and kept on with the movements of her fingers. I take her hand away and say: "I must have your lips and tongue, Lily!"

She sulks and turns her back to me, looking out of the window.

"Well, I'll masturbate myself!"

"Oh no, don't do that!"

"I will! I'll spend alone! And you can go to the man with no fingernails!"

At this rude remark, which called up the vision of the hands of her mother's lover, to my astonishment she turns round and kisses me. She was so pleased to find I showed jealousy of the wrong person. She was waiting for a scene about the people she had dined with. Out comes her hand again. I push it away and rub my member a little, like a schoolboy. She turns her head away again and to give her a chance, I say: "I suppose your stays prevent you stooping down?"

She, the fool, cannot take my handsome hint, but has turned her back once more entirely towards me and did not answer.

So I, in despair, cover myself up and buttoned my pants. At this moment, we are just nearing the station.

Seeing this, she was evidently delighted that all is over for the evening, and turning, draws me towards her, gently patting my cheek with her hand, her arm resting on my shoulder, as I had often seen her with her Papa. At this Judas-like caress, I confess that I felt myself boiling over with rage. She has disdainfully refused me her lips, without a word of excuse, although I have not spent with her since the first of March, and have not had her mouth since the first of October. If she had said, "I am tired. How can I suck you in my tight stays, new dress, jacket, and hat?" I would willingly have excused her, especially as I was not very lustful just then. But she had not even taken off a glove. Her stroke on my cheek meant: "Now that it is too late to suck him, I'll make it up with the idiot."

My blood boiled at this thought, and I repulsed her, pushing her from me by the shoulder. She was on my right hand. I felt like a brute and behaved like one. I dashed out my right arm and caught her a fearful backhander on the lower part of the left cheek and jaw.

She gasped for breath, and said slowly and quietly in a low tone: "How brutal!"

"I am mad," I replied. "Go and spend when you get home."

This was foolish, as she had freely emitted in Paris, and was not ready for me after her dinner, frolic, and two American champagne mixtures. She had had her enjoyment, and was not yet whore enough to play the proper part with another man at two hours' interval. Besides, her temper would not allow her to do so.

She was on the proper side to leave the cab, as it was now stopped, so she stepped out without a word, and I saw her go slowly and shakily along the station frontage, not boldly entering the first door in front of her, as she ought to have done, but sneaking along slowly, evidently thinking I was going to come after her, or perhaps tipsy, or crying, or mad with rage at being outwitted. Or going to the ladies' W. C. at the end of the building.

I slowly paid the cabman, watching her all the while. I dared not follow her, for I knew that if I did—God help me!—I should have struck her again. So I turned away and walked home. How I got along and what streets I took, I do not know. I am surprised I was not run over. I found myself in front of my door, that is all I can say. It was about 11:30 or 11:45. I got into bed and smoked until 2:00 A.M. I could not settle to read. I could only smoke and stare at nothing. I was very much upset, although I had known the truth all along by intuition.

Then I found that the knuckles of the second and third fingers of my right hand were torn and bleeding. I did not think I could have burst the skin with the force of the blow on her face. I do not suppose I hurt her much, as I had no room to swing my arm in the cab, and she did not put her hand up to her face after the blow. I hoped that I had torn my knuckles on her brooch, or neckpins, or earrings, or garters, or something of the same kind, while struggling with her, and these slight abrasions were only coincidences.

Strange to say, but it is the truth: I had no regret for having struck her and feel none now. When I wrote her that insulting letter about the Belgian trip, and sent the analysis of her own letters, I felt strangely delighted, and was surprised when she was silly enough to answer.

It was the first time in my life that I had ever lifted my hand to a woman in anger.

LILIAN TO JACKY.

Tuesday, January 31, 1899.

Can you come tomorrow night by the nine o'clock train? I shall expect you and do my very best to secure an hour's tête-à-tête in the nasty little dining room you know.

Is Lord Fontarcy still in Paris?

My parents will be back Saturday.

Kisses and love,
LILIAN.

As I went to keep the above alluring appointment, I reflected on the mind and character of my charmer, and the result was far from being complimentary to her. I was surprised to find that she had answered a letter in which I had the sinister audacity to say that I did not wish to return to my vomit! I was opening my eyes at last, and I did not care if she were to be offended with me or not. Still I could not have very deep love for a woman to write to her as I had just done.

Where she made her great mistake, as a trifler with men, and I beg my lady readers to make a note of this, was in not knowing her customers. She used the same bait for all her fish. It was easier for her, but such proceedings savor of narrow-mindedness. A woman is clever who alters her tactics with every lover. A true huntsman uses a different cartridge for each variety of game. Had I desired the complete favors of this hysterical, selfish creature, I should have had to pay a fearful price. And, in return for all my sacrifices, I must have suffered in the terrible bondage that would have held me—a sensitive man—tightly tied, by the links of my own lusts, to this fearful example of a wickedly neurotic female, without reason, without shame, without the slightest particle of self-respect. I was vile enough, in all conscience, and I have little right to judge her, but I had no wish to torture her; I wanted a little love, if it suited her to love me, and that was all. She could do whatever she liked, and enjoy a crowd of miscellaneous lovers, as long as she behaved honestly to me, and when she had enough of me, she was to say so, and I would walk out of her life without a murmur. But this was too simple and sincere for her. There was no money in this, nor any hold on a man. I was not jealous, I had never asked for her virginity. How could such a man be "worked"? It will also be noticed that I asked her in my letter to think of all that might please her in her house. I meant that she was to try and make her Papa like me exceedingly, so as to invite me often, and she accepted all my sly innuendoes on this subject as a matter of course. I wondered, too, why she called her dining room "nasty"? I had never said so, but it must have been because Papa had possessed her in that room, in the evening after dinner, when Mamma had gone up to bed. I also thought, as I sat in the train, that the principal reason for her kind invitation was because I was bringing a little silver purse.

She was waiting for me with her dogs as I came out of the station, and greeted me kindly, affectionately, and with much rapid gossip, so as to prevent me recurring to the harsh part of my letter. I was quite satisfied to have produced my slight effect; I knew—alas!—that all my remonstrances would be soon forgotten.

After a short walk, she told me to keep a sharp eye on the dining-room window, which faced the road. When I saw the light go out, it would mean that she had gone upstairs with her lamp to Granny and would see that all was quiet for the night. I was to go for a little stroll, and when I saw the light reappear, come softly into the house, as that would mean she was back in the dining-room again, waiting for me, and supposed to be writing letters. Everything was arranged as she told me, and twenty minutes later, I was in her arms. She had nothing on but a dove-colored dressing gown of some soft material over her chemise, petticoat, and drawers.

After a passionate bout of kissing, she sat on my knee and chatted gaily, and I frankly confess that I forgot all her wretched shilly-shallying in the joy of holding her loved form clasped in my arms.

Why she had been ill in bed was this: she had suffered agonies through toothache and after trying all the domestic remedies of her grandmother, and obtaining no relief, had fled to

Paris alone, and rushed to a dental institute. There, a young dentist told her she had a very bad abscess of the gums and declared it must be operated at once. On her affirming that she feared suffering, he offered to administer some gas and produce insensibility. To this she had consented.

"Were you not frightened? He might have taken liberties with you and perhaps violated you? Had you no fear, as you say you were all alone with him?"

I watched her narrowly as I said this. She answered me coolly that she had no fear on that head, and I felt more certain than ever that I was right in thinking that her maidenhead had disappeared in October or November.

Duly put to sleep, she remembered nothing more, until she found herself half-undressed and quite dazed, with several windows open, and a crowd of people round her. It appears that the young doctor had administered an overdose, and as an older man who was now in the room told her, her life had been in danger. She had been accompanied to the railway station and was now, although out of bed, still under the care of a doctor.

I told her that she ought to have telegraphed for me, but I did not say how I felt inclined to disbelieve her entirely. Her troubles, to my thinking, might be connected with her womb, and I was afraid that the visit to a dentist meant some uterine exploration. There may have been an abscess as well, and I felt a movement of horror, as I thought of a contaminating contact. It is only just to say that these disgusting thoughts came into my mind later. Everything seemed to conspire against Lilian, and drive me slowly from her: her own conduct and the dread secrets of her prostituted frame.

The operation had taken place during the past week, and Charlotte had spent Sunday with her, sleeping at Sonis, before the return of Lilian's parents. While Lilian talked to me, I had my hand on her naked thighs, and toyed with the luxuriant growth of hair on her mount.

"Charlotte did like that to me the other night as I was falling off to sleep—just the same as you are doing to me now."

"Did you spend with her finger?"

"Certainly not," answered Lily, indignantly. "I turned over, pushed her hand away, and went to sleep."

I have often noticed that if a woman is allowed to talk without being contradicted, she will tell a series of half-truths, relating to what occupies her mind at the time, and an attentive listener is thus often put on the track of secrets he would not otherwise be able to get at. Many men also possess this same grave defect, and lack the retentive power that should prevent them making the slightest allusion to anything they may wish to hide. So I gathered that Charlotte and Lilian had plenty of tribadic fun together.

Still I kept my own counsel, and by laughing and joking, contrived to produce upon her the impression I wanted; that I was a love-sick loon, desiring her madly, full of strange sensual longings, and ready to believe anything she might tell me.

I now began to get rather lecherous and excited, having her half-naked body on my knee, and I made her stand up, while my hands wandered all over her lithe frame. She still kept up a slight show of resistance and I felt greatly irritated and lewd, as I knew that my angel was merely shamming, being by this time expert at every caress. But I played my part, and enjoyed the idea of passing for a fool, especially as I knew that all my sayings and doings would be reported to Papa and Mama on their return. I opened her *peignoir* and was astonished to find that she had grown much fatter in every way and I told her what I thought. She agreed with me, but did not seem to suspect that I noticed she was now a woman. All her girlishness was gone.

As she stood in front of me, I took off her petticoat, and she, in obedience to my wishes, at once dropped her drawers and was naked, with the exception of her loose robe, chemise, shoes, and stockings. I will not weary my reader with an account of my ecstatic caresses, lickings, and feeling of that serpentine body I loved so well, and which I had not seen naked for four months, but I must describe how I fulfilled a strange longing I had felt for some time past.

I had in my pocket the leather belt of which I have already spoken, and she graciously permitted me to clasp it round her naked waist.

I drew it in as far as it would go, and unluckily found I had forgotten my penknife, or I would have made some fresh holes, to tighten it still more, as my idea was to hurt her a little. It excited my passion to a great extent to imagine that a woman could endure a little suffering for my sake. The circumference of her naked waist was about twenty inches, and I could have easily have gained a couple more had I persevered. She complained in a sweet way that she was not at her ease, and that she did not look pretty, as her little belly jutted out in front by the pressure of the girdle. Paying no heed to her peevish complaints, I drew another strap from my pocket, and fastened her legs securely together just above the knee.

Then I forced a passage through her legs from the front, and thoroughly enjoyed the sensation of roughly pushing my hand between her smooth thighs thus drawn together. She seemed to enjoy the fun, especially as I did not forget to caress her clitoris, ever moist, on the way. Now I altered my tactics, and keeping my right hand forced against her slit, my left tried to effect a passage through the strapped thighs from behind.

Directly I began to push my hand under her bottom, she

gradually let herself fall to the ground, and with many a contortion, managed to dislodge my fingers. She swore I tickled
her to such an extent that she could not bear it. I desisted,
having long since made up my mind that I would allow myself
to be made a fool of, until I should tire of the role of victim,
and so I released her legs, but left the belt still round her waist.
I then asked her what I should do to her, and she asked me to
provoke her orgasm with my tongue and quickly installed herself upon the little sofa for that purpose. I was in a good humor
and smiled to myself, as I thought what splendid control I had
over my passions. Here was a woman who swore continually
that she adored me, exercising all her cunning to keep up the
pretense of her virginity, and trying all she could do to present
only a front view of her secret charms. She willingly stood up
naked before me, but when I approached her from behind,
when my fingers could have so easily slipped into an excited
vagina, she artfully wriggled away. I ought perhaps to have
spoken, but I was curious to see what she meant, and where
she was going. Did she know, poor fool that she was?

She reclined upon the couch, and I was soon on my knees,
my tongue sucking and licking all her body, from her breasts
to her knees.

I was very excited, albeit I never lost my presence of mind
with her, and I told her I loved to lick her all over and I felt
certain that at some time or another I had kissed every part of
her body, except her feet.

"Oh! You kissed and licked my feet, too, once!" she exclaimed.

"Did I? When was that, darling?" I knew perfectly well that
I had never done so to her.

"In August, when you slept all night with me."

What strange illusions, and what a quantity of lovers she
must have had to so mix up their caresses! I grunted an answer

that might have meant anything, as my mouth and tongue were busy at work upon her lively clitoris; and I found, being perfectly cool and collected, that her private parts were quite different beneath my lips, being fatter and more open, and my tongue seemed to slip more easily within and penetrate further. I now began to caress her with my hands, while I continued sucking her in the most artistic and elaborate way I could, and I tried to get hold of her two hairy lips and, under pretence of caressing her, force a finger within. But she was too artful for me and, taking my hands in hers, drew them away. She seemed to enjoy my efforts to please her, and kept me between her legs so hard at work that I lost all desire and got quite tired. I remember now how I thought of Charlotte, and guessed she had pumped my Lilian dry on Sunday, and Monday morning too, and I grasped the difficulty of my task with Lilian, having to fight against Papa, Lolotte, and her other lovers.

And so I sucked and sucked, my penis rising and falling, according as my thoughts led me, but Lilian hid with closed eyes, enjoying the sensation caused by my industrious tongue.

Now and then, she would murmur, "Enough! Enough!" and then, of course, I went on more ardently than ever. But the best of everything must come to an end, and she at last pushed me away. I must have been at least an hour between her thighs, which I consider a record time for such a young woman.

She lay panting; breathing heavily, her eyes half-closed, her legs outstretched; all in voluptuous disorder, her shift rucked up to her navel and wide open in front, showing the ruby nipples on her baby breasts.

"Now I am going to see if you are still a virgin, as you agreed to let me do."

"All right," she said, dreamily, raising herself a little, "How will you do it?"

"With my finger," and I went to work and just placed my

index at the entrance of her grotto. She started and drew herself up, out of my reach.

"Oh, it is so tender and sensitive so soon after spending!"

Here was yet another proof of the wrecked virginity, but I took not the slightest notice. I found this useless fencing very curious, but I wanted to ejaculate also and therefore resolved not to quarrel. I drew near to her head as she reclined lazily on the couch, and I rubbed my weapon and my testicles all over her face for a few minutes, reveling in the fascinating contact.

"I shall spend on your face, dear."

"Oh, don't do that!" she cried out in alarm.

"Well then, take me in your mouth."

"I can't, I am still sore about the gums."

She was so indolent, tired, and worn, that I could see she was quite out of sorts, and would have thought it fine fun to let me depart as I had come. But I induced her royal highness to take it in her hand, and she gripped it tightly and manipulated it cleverly enough as I stood by the side of the sofa, my breeches down, while she still lay in the same position.

"Let me see it," she said, turning her face towards its scarlet head.

I was getting near the crisis now, under the influence of her soft hand, and I held her head up and said to her: "Look at it! Keep your eyes on it!"

She fixed her gaze upon it for a second, and then turned her eyes away and released her hold. A tired expression came over her face; she had spent her fill and wished me to finish quickly, or not at all. How selfish she was! How she loved me!

"How shall I spend?"

"With my hand! Make haste!" And she accelerated her masturbating movements.

"Let me spend on you!" I exclaimed, panting with suppressed desire.

She laughed, but opened her *peignoir* and pulled up her chemise, exposing herself completely, as she guessed my wish. She gripped my bursting rod fast, and, shaking it violently to and fro, I felt the most torturing pleasure as the floodgates opened, and the seed flew in the air, to my great delight and relief. She held the red knob well over her belly, but her grasp was so convulsive that the liquor escaped with difficulty and in tiny spurts and clots. As she felt the hot drops fall rapidly, one by one, on her hairy mount and stomach, she uttered a little cry of surprise and dismay at the fall of each one: "Oh! Oh! Oh! What a lot! Will you never be done?"

At last the shower ceased, and she let go my dart. As I recovered my self-possession, I could not help smiling as I noticed that her black bush was covered with little spots of spending, as if snow had fallen. There was some, too, on her smooth belly, and the edges of her dressing gown were also soiled. It is astonishing how the seminal spurt goes far, and lands in all sorts of holes and corners, when allowed to escape in the open.

She arose with a sigh of relief and asked if she might take off her belt. I released her and gloated over the red marks its pressure had left upon her skin.

And now we sat down and talked awhile, as she lazily turned over the pages of *Justine,* and explained to me what awful pleasure that infamous book had given her. She loved the disgusting pictures, too, with which this terrible work is adorned. One character amused her greatly. She spoke quite seriously about it and I could see that this was a deep impression. I allude to Dorothée, or Madame d'Estreval, who appears in the third volume, possessing a clitoris three inches long. It was this malformation that had greatly excited the libertine imagination of my sphinx-like mistress.

Having spent, she once more began to worry about me and

show signs of jealousy, which increased as I told her that I was obliged to go to London shortly for a few days on a matter of business. Indeed, it was a wild-goose chase after some money that was owed me, and which I saw a chance of getting if I went myself. At this tale, her temper increased, and I pulled out my little parcel containing the silver purse, which she was artful enough not to have alluded to as yet, although she was no doubt waiting for it.

"Here it is," I said, "and I had a good mind to throw it in your face and say 'goodbye' forever, if you had not sent me that nice letter."

"It is a very pretty purse," she said dreamily, evading a direct reply.

"What a bad temper you are always in, directly you have spent!" I replied.

"And before, as well!"

"Yes, my darling, you are always out of sorts. You have got a devil's temper, you little whore!"

This was the first time I had ever dared to use such a word to her, or indeed to any woman. To my great surprise, she did not mind. I think she rather liked it; I was coming down to her level, she thought.

"If I am a whore, pray, sir, what are you?"

"A *maquereau!* Your Papa-*maquereau!*"

She started and looked at me strangely, as I had never spoken to her like this before, and I wondered at my own boldness. . . .

Miss High Heels

by Anonymous

Dennis Evelyn Beryl, a young English aristocrat, is trans-
formed, under the supervision of his stepsister, Helen, into a
beautiful young woman. Dressed in the finest silks and satins,
and shod in diamond-buckled satin slippers, our hero(ine) is
initiated into the pleasures of canes, riding whips, and birch
rods. Perhaps the best-known Edwardian cross-dressing novel,
Miss High Heels *delightfully captures Beryl's ambivalent re-*
sistance at the same time as it resorts to science to explain
him (Dennis is born with "milk vessels") and French to cata-
logue his sexual preference.

This story is a reminiscence, a fond recollection of my colorful days as a youth. I can safely say (with the clarity of
hindsight) that my youth was extraordinary. My upbringing
was unlike that of any other young man knew at the time, and
to this day, many years later, I have yet to meet a soul whose
story can compare with mine in its bizarre nature.

My erotic rearing gave me a great sense of alienation, yet also
a feeling of being absolutely rare and precious. Of course, later
in life I learned that I was not alone in my exclusive sexual
proclivities; proclivities that flourished and were fostered from
the time I was very young on through my early adulthood. I
have since had the pleasure of finding others who share the
same delicious tastes that I have enjoyed. I was cared for by my
strange and beautiful stepsister Helen with the delicate atten-

191

tions that one gives a fragile, unique flower. It was my lovely stepsister who helped me to find the "true" self that was hiding inside my male skin.

Ever since I could remember, I had a great fondness for the excesses of women's clothing, of women's finery, and of their ways. It was Helen who really prodded me to discover my true nature and created an environment in which I relished the world of women. Thus, the following words are the tale of what I shall call my "becoming." This is the tale of how I meta-morphosed from Dennis Evelyn Beryl to the lovely Denise Beryl.

The story begins shortly after I had arrived at the manor, having just finished my two years at school. My time at the school is a fraction of this unusual story, spicy morsels that I will elab-orate upon later in luscious detail.

Helen had hired a French maid named Phoebe as my per-sonal servant. A *maid* for a young master of the house, you ask. Yes. Granted, it was a rather strange arrangement for a young gentleman to have a maidservant in his employ, and at his bath and toilet, but as you may have gathered, I was no ordinary young gentleman.

Phoebe, the maid, had the deft, neat hands of a French woman. I watched her, mesmerized, as she threaded pink satin ribbon amongst the shining curls of my coiffure and buttoned the last button of my very long glacé kid evening gloves. She dusted a powder puff lightly over my white bosom and shoul-ders. Then Phoebe tucked a tiny lace handkerchief into my corsage and said, "There, now you are ready, Miss Denise. Stand up!"

"Miss" Denise indeed! And "Stand up!" The insolence of her! I remained seated.

"Ah!" said Phoebe with a malicious smile. "You don't like

being ordered about by poor servants, do you? You are the young master of Beaumanoir, the wealthy aristocrat, the great landlord, *Dennis* Evelyn Beryl," uttering my name with amused contempt.

"Bah! I do not trouble my head about your position. You are in your own house, it is true. It is also true you are under the control of your beautiful stepsister who stripped you of your foolish trousers two years ago to punish you for your impertinence. For two years you have been mincing about in petticoats in a girls' school. A young gentleman, are you? Nobody would believe it. Your hair reaches down below your waist. You have the figure, the face, the soft limbs, the hands and feet *and* the breasts of a girl."

I was dreadfully ashamed at Phoebe's outburst. I could not deny a word of it.

"You are a very important person, I suppose," she went on jeering at me, "with a great career in Parliament! Heavens, how you used to plague my ears with your boastfulness! It may all be true. What I am concerned with is that you should be beautifully dressed as a young lady for the dinner party that your stepsister Miss Deverel is giving. Stand up at once, or I will lace you into a corset one inch tighter than the one you are wearing now."

"Oh, Phoebe," I cried, "I can hardly breathe in this one."

I was alarmed. Her tone was so menacing. She was much stronger than I was. She could carry out her threat if she chose. I stood up. I had a special reason for being obedient tonight.

"That's better, Miss Denise," Phoebe said.

I was dressed in an exquisite décolleté frock of white transparent chiffon glittering with silver embroideries over an underdress of soft white satin. The corsage was cut very low, the sleeves being merely shoulder straps of flashing silver bugles, and my tight, unwrinkled white kid gloves reached up to my shoulders. A sash of white satin encircled my slim waist and was tied in an enormous bow looped through a huge diamond buckle on my left hip, whence the broad streamers fringed with silver floated down to my feet. A bunch of pink roses was pinned on the right of my corsage at the waist. The sheath skirt molded my hips in its gleaming satin and chiffon.

The girlish curves of my figure were caught tightly in at the ankles by a scarf of tulle that passed through a big sparkling diamond buckle in front of the dress and tied in a great bow behind. My legs were quite bound by these dainty fetters of satin and tulle. The skirt was hemmed with tulle and was bordered with a festoon of tiny pink cloth roses, and on the left side a row of flat diamond buttons sparkled up to the knee. The skirt had a long train of white satin, lined with pleats of tulle that rustled deliciously at each movement. Phoebe arranged the train in a gleaming swirl about my feet, and stood up.

Now dear reader, you may be wondering what kind of young gentleman I was, allowing a servant to speak to me thus, mocking and jeering my predicament. Not only that, but what kind of wealthy aristocrat would allow a maid to dress him so fantastically?

I have to admit that I was in a strange state of shock, having just arrived at Beaumanoir that afternoon. It was Helen's birthday, and she was throwing an elegant little party that night to celebrate. I had been away for two long years, and before my absence, I had made a strange arrangement with Helen. I had behaved rather terribly at my first boarding school, and so, rather than attract scandal about our names because of my misconduct, I was sent to a girls' school in the country. I was sent there as a punishment, and worse still, I was to be treated as a young lady.

I had thought at the time that Helen believed that she had

sentenced me to a hellish fate. Not so—I was deliriously happy. Oh, of course I protested and wept and begged, claiming the mere idea was repugnant to me. But deep within my breast, my heart pounded with the anxiety of a secret pleasure. I pleaded with Helen because it began to please me to beg and crawl in her presence, and in turn, I could see that Helen was enjoying her dominion over me. At last I was sent away to bear the delectable torments that awaited me at the school for young ladies.

Two years had passed, and I had returned to my home to claim my birthright. I was eighteen and of age to become master of Beaumanoir. One would assume that this occasion would merit much anticipatory joy on my part. I was to be released from these exquisite bonds of femininity forever.

But I was not happy. I had savored every moment that I was dressed as a lady. I had enjoyed all the privileges that a lovely young girl enjoys, and I was not exactly ready or willing to give that up.

Helen had demanded that I make one more appearance as a young woman, after which I would be released as her charge. I had agreed, and there I stood in the dressing room with Phoebe the maid, my white skin trembling and enervated by the cool luscious silk that rubbed against my body. Knowing that I was wearing the delicate batiste lingerie of a young woman, that I was deliciously confined by the lovely laces and whalebone of the corset for the last time, was a terrible thought. I was nearly aroused by the soft, sweet smell of the lavender powder that Phoebe had lightly dusted my breasts with. I remember that my pleasurable sensations were marked by a bittersweet feeling that all this would end, and I would be forced, by society and circumstance, to return to the world of men; a world I had come to admire from the perspective of a woman.

Phoebe's voice suddenly ruptured these sad thoughts.

"Now Miss Denise, put those smartly gloved hands behind your back!" shouted Phoebe.

"Behind my back! Like a child!"

"Don't argue. Behind your back with them at once, palm to palm, the fingers pointing down."

I obeyed. How humiliating it was!

"Now lift up this pretty face."

She took my chin and tilted back my head.

"I must say, Miss Denise, your governesses have done wonders for you at your school. You always looked like a pretty girl of course, but you are quite lovely now."

I blushed! Was it all from shame, or was there not some thrill of pleasure and of girlish vanity in my reddening cheeks? Oh, my two years at a girls' school had left their indelible influence upon my disposition.

"Now put the high heels of your satin slippers together under your frock."

She looked down to the billowy satin and tulle of my skirt.

"Have you done it? Are the toes daintily turned out?"

"Yes, Phoebe."

"I'll make sure."

She stooped and, thrusting her hand under my dress, felt my feet. The blush deepened on my face, and a soft wave of voluptuous delight swept over me, inflaming my body and exciting my passions. I am to write the truth here. The thought that here, I was dressed with all the dainty luxury of a very fashionable girl, standing obediently with my hands behind me at the bidding of a maid, while she adjusted my satin-slippered feet, troubled my passions. There was something sensuously bizarre in the contrast that fascinated me. Besides, apart from the queer mental impression produced in me, the actual touch of Phoebe's hands on my body, particularly on my insteps and ankles, gave me a delicious physical sensation. I noticed Phoebe was wearing long, white kid gloves. I asked her why, and she glanced at me shrewdly. "Miss Priscilla's orders," she answered. "No one is to touch you, or dress you without long glacé kid gloves on their hands. But why do you ask, Miss Denise?"

I was confused.

"Did the feel of the gloves on your silk stockings please you? Answer at once."

"Yes, Phoebe," I replied shyly.

Phoebe nodded her head with a lewd, knowing smile.

I was tortured by the possibility that she would not touch my ankle again. I feared that she would not stroke the delicate arch of my instep with her soft-gloved fingers. I assumed that she would stop caressing my foot when she realized that she was affording me erotic pleasure. I could tell that she liked the position of dominating me. I could tell it pleased her to see me tortured and willing to be subject to her torments and whims. In fact, I believe Helen hired her because she was capable of severe disciplinarian actions.

As she stroked my ankle, I arched my back ever so slightly, so that the buds of my nipples would rub against the cool white satin of my slip. The sensation made me move involuntarily.

"Miss Denise! If you don't stand still, I am going to be forced to punish you. Not only that, but I must finish my work. Miss Helen will be calling for you soon. Now stand without moving until she comes to inspect you."

Helen had foreseen that the touch of the kid gloves would make its sensuous appeal to me. She had deliberately intended that it should. Why? My old fear returned to me—a fear that she and Miss Priscilla, her aunt, were in a plot together to nullify me, to make me unimportant. Perhaps they had devised some enervating system to reduce me to perpetual subjection. If so, I had reason to shiver. They were so clever. Those two women had shown such insight into my character and failings.

On the other hand, there was the promise that Helen Deverel had given to me in the most emphatic way two years ago. She had promised that the day after I returned from the girls' school I should be allowed to resume the dress of my sex, if the head schoolmistress sent me home with a good report. Well, I had returned this afternoon with an excellent report. Tonight I was to be Miss Denise Beryl, a cousin of Dennis's. But tomorrow I was to resume my liberty. I was to become once more the master of Beaumanoir.

I was turning over these doubts in my mind when Phoebe interrupted my reflections.

"You have moved your feet, Miss Denise," she said sternly. "In that tight, pretty satin frock, every tremor of your limbs is visible."

"I wasn't thinking, Phoebe," I said humbly. "I am sorry."

Phoebe was appeased by the humility of my voice.

"I will forgive you this once," she said. "There's no doubt, Miss Denise, that you ought to be kept in girls' clothes all your life."

"All my life!" I exclaimed.

"You are *so* much easier to manage," she replied. What a selfish argument! All she thought of was her comfort, not one consideration did she give to me, my position, the career that awaited me. No! As a male youth, I should give *her* orders. Under discipline and dressed as a girl, *I* received them from her. That was all she cared about.

I was careful not to move again, and Phoebe busied herself putting away the schoolgirl's dress, the one that I had laid aside so I could appear as a grown-up young lady in a décolleté gown with a long train.

I should briefly explain what had led me to these . . . *unusual* circumstances.

My father, who was probably the wealthiest commoner in

England, had inherited the great estate of Beaumanoir in Hamp-
shire, a house in Park Lane, and a large fortune, which by
skillful business he had greatly increased. He married late in
life and I, his only child, was born when he was fifty-two. I was
baptized Dennis Evelyn, and the second name, which is given
to girls as well as to boys, I always resented. I resented it all the
more, because in complexion, features, limbs, and figure I was,
alas, as the taunts of my school friends assured me, more like
a girl than a boy. My father lost his wife when I was twelve and
a year later married a second time—whence came all my troubles. He married a middle-aged widow, Mrs. Deverel, who had
a daughter, Helen, a girl just four years older than I. She was
a sinister girl with dark hair, a pale lovely face, and a slim figure.
She had the most winning manners and at once set herself to
charming everybody. She succeeded with everybody—except
me. I recognized her game immediately.

I resented my father's marriage and the intrusion of these
new people into the house. I would not call the new Mrs. Beryl,
"Mother," nor Helen, "Sister." Mrs. Beryl was considerate and
Helen set about trying to please me, but I distrusted them both.
I always had a fear that they meant to take my place in my
father's affections and oust me from my inheritance.

I remember particularly one day when I was home for the
holidays. I was thirteen at the time, Helen seventeen; she
stopped me as I was leaving the drawing room and as she was
coming in. Laying her little hand upon my arm, she said with
her eyebrows arched, "Evelyn, can't we be good friends? I am
so *unhappy* that you dislike me."

The name Evelyn irritated me. I looked at her ironically and
I replied, "I suppose that you really want to marry me, to get
hold of my fortune, don't you?"

She laughed coldly, and pinched my arm hard. "How wrong
you are!" If I had not spoken so rashly, I might not be standing

now in the fashionable ball dress of a wealthy young lady, waiting for the moment when I should take my place at Helen's
birthday dinner party. I had become a living tribute to her
domination, from the Louis Quinze heels of my smart satin
slippers to the pink ribbon in my curls, for to that foolish answer, I attribute the beginnings of her hatred and resentment.
She turned away from me that day, and never made advances
to me again.

That same year, in the autumn, my stepmother died, and the
shock of her death prostrated my father, who was then sixty-
five. He had a great affection for Helen and a great faith in her
capacity; at her suggestion, Miss Priscilla Deverel, an aunt of
hers, was introduced into the household to act as companion
to Helen and to assist her in the management of the house.

Miss Priscilla was a remarkable woman, a fully qualified doctor with a great medical reputation. Although she gave up her
practice to join us, to me at this time she seemed merely a
harmless, slightly ridiculous old maid. She was forty-seven or
so when she came to Beaumanoir, a wrinkled, thin, ungainly
woman, who dressed very badly. She was very patient and submissive, and I treated her with the utmost disregard. I did not
resent her presence in the house as I did Helen's. I looked upon
her as of no importance whatever.

The first time I had any doubt about her was a year later
when I was ill with a cold, and Helen brought her to my bedroom. At first I would not allow her to examine my chest, but
Helen threatened to tell my father of my refusal and to send
for a doctor from London. That, for a special reason, I dreaded.
I let Miss Priscilla open my nightgown and I saw at once a flash
of wonder cross her face. I flushed scarlet. I had a secret that I
had always tried to conceal. My bosom was much too developed for a boy's and continuing to develop as I grew. I had not

merely the nipples of a boy, but the white globes of a girl's breasts were threatening to become prominent.

Miss Priscilla examined them carefully. Then she turned to Helen and exchanged with her a significant look. When she looked again at me, a slow smile of triumph was spreading over her face. It seemed to say, "I have got you," and when she went out of the room I remembered with some discomfort the impertinences that I had showered upon her in the past. However, I soon took courage. She could do me no harm, I thought. What a fool I was!

The next term at school, an episode occurred of which it is difficult for me to write. But I must refer to it because it affected my future tremendously. I was, as I have confessed, girlish to look at, although I took my part in the games of the school, and my appearance brought upon me a great deal of chaff and ridicule. It also brought upon me the attentions of the bigger boys in the Sixth Form, especially from Guy Repton, a youth of nineteen, who kept pestering me.

The episode that I am about to relate is a description of my sexual awakening, and the pivotal event that shaped the rest of my life.

As you can imagine, I had been wallowing in a state of some confusion as to the nature of my sexual orientation since the onset of my adolescence. I had been reluctant to leave my home, which had been veritably dominated by women since my father was a widower. Not only was my experience oriented toward the feminine world, but I was slowly developing a pair of budding breasts!

When I was sent away to school, I took great pains to hide my body from the other young chaps, but this did not mean that I didn't take the opportunity to steal long glances at my schoolmates. I quickly noted that I was not growing hair upon my body as some of my companions were, and that my muscles were not turning hard, but quite the opposite. I was becoming softer and more round with every passing month. This gave me a terribly ambivalent feeling, for deep within my heart, I could not help but admire the fantastic changes that were happening to my body. On the other hand, I was ashamed and stood up to much ridicule during my time at boarding school.

My interests were limited when it came to the discussions that most of the other boys delighted in. In fact, even though I had grown to mistrust Helen and Miss Priscilla, I severely missed their gentle company. I found their conversations so much more reassuring and civilized than those of my new companions. I was miserable and terribly out of place. I found that my one solace was daydreaming, and I took to staring out of my window, and the windows of the classrooms, remembering the womanly luxuries that I had once been surrounded with at Beaumanoir.

Many was the night that I lay alone in my bed, creating images of delight, picture-fancies of the lovely gowns that Helen wore and all the accoutrements of her station and sex. I would worry, on such sleepless nights, about my future when I was to take over as master of the household. I felt that I should look forward to that day with much hunger, but in truth, I was not anticipating the day with gladness. In fact, I knew deep within my soul that I had no taste for the powers of my impending manhood, but I did not know how to escape my destiny. If I had only known at that time that my fate was already decided, I would have worried considerably fewer hours away.

But those hours during which I lay awake were not without their pleasurable moments. It was during the secret quiet of the night that I began to discover the pleasures my own body had to offer. Because I was not obliged to share a room with anyone else, I could spend hours lightly stroking my body and bringing myself to pleasure over and over as I massaged my cock and my extra-sensitive breasts. During these wonderful moments, I would always imagine myself to be dressed in the finest of women's clothing. I fantasized that my hands ran over my body encased in kid gloves, and that my breasts were softly caressed by the fine lingerie or the harsh lacing of a corset. These thoughts aroused my fancy almost more than the actual touch of my hand did. The potency that these fineries held for me is impossible to describe in detail. I can safely say that the deep hours of the night were among the only happy ones that I spent at that boarding school.

I devised elaborate passion plays in which Miss Priscilla dominated me, while Helen enjoyed toying with my breasts, or even better still, I liked to imagine Helen's lovely full lips wrapped around my cock while Miss Priscilla lightly abused my nipples with her fingers or her mouth. Of course, during these imaginary scenes, the two women would be dressed in the most exquisite of gowns, while I too was dressed in the dainty underclothes of a young lady. Oh! The hours of pleasure I afforded myself thinking these wickedly delicious thoughts.

I had yet to see a woman naked, so it was hard for me to imagine. But there was an instance that I liked to draw upon during my hours of fantasizing. One time, a few years previous to being sent to school, Helen and I were sent to the shore. I will never forget the moment when Helen bent over and gingerly removed her shoes and then her stockings, revealing the most beautiful pair of feet that I had ever seen. I watched with jealous hunger as she ran to and from the sneaking tide. Oh, how I wished that I were the sea, that it was I caressing her perfect white feet with my tongue, with my hands and fingers.

But I digress! I was to relate the story of the fateful evening in which a turn of events happened that shaped the entire course of my life.

It was a night like any other previous to it. I lay alone in my bed, lightly stroking my cock with one hand, my lovely little breasts with the other. I was recalling an elegant evening dress of satin and tulle that Helen had worn at a spring party the season before. I was enjoying my solitary pleasure so greatly that I never heard the door of my bedroom creak open. As I was quietly moaning into my pillow, I felt a pair of cool hands stroke the soft flesh of my buttocks. I sat up instantly, quietly yelping in surprise when I was met Guy Repton's hungry eyes. Guy Repton! Here was the boy who had taken such pleasure in tormenting me, and now he had caught me in nightly pleasures.

"Guy! What are you . . . ?"

"Shh!" he hissed, and covered my mouth with one hand, while the other began roving around my body freely.

I began to struggle, and he pushed me roughly against the pillows. My heart raced, half in fear and half in a new lust aroused.

"Guy, what do you think you're doing?" I whispered desperately as I thrashed weakly under his body, which was pinning me to the bed.

"I know what you've been doing in here, you nasty little thing," he said. He reached between my legs, and grasped my cock in his strong hand. "I came to join in your fun."

I felt my face flush painfully, especially because my erection showed no sign of quieting. Not only that, but I was painfully aware of my breasts and tried to cover them with my arms.

"Oh, Dennis, don't cover those lovely things. I came to see them too!" Guy laughed, pulling my arm away from my chest with his free hand. "I want to put my lips on your girlish titties, Dennis. Let me suck your titties!"

Without waiting for an answer from me, Guy plunged his

head down upon my chest and hungrily began to suckle at my soft pink nipple.

Oh, if I could describe to you the exquisite joy and heated pleasure that I felt course through every inch of my flesh! No one's hands but my own had ever stroked or paid lusty attentions to my secret boobies. And now, in a moment's time, Guy Repton had fallen upon me, and with his lips he kissed and bit and sucked my tit. With his hand, he reached between my soft thighs and took my cock in his hand and began to stroke and fondle the shaft of my pulsing member. I could feel his strong rod bulging against my thigh and the weight and force of his body and mine; the way he was dominating me was exhilarating. I arched my back involuntarily to meet the kisses that he continued to lavish upon one nipple and then the other.

"Oh! Oh! Guy!" I moaned, my pleasure very nearly exploding.

Just as I was about to shoot my seed into Guy's fist, the door of my dormitory room burst open. There in the frame of the door, his face lit underneath from a kerosene lamp, was the dormitory master.

I shrieked and recoiled from the light that the headmaster brought in with him, while Guy shouted and tumbled off of me and the bed. He tried to madly scramble underneath the bed, but of course it was a futile attempt at escape. I was horrified and utterly shattered that I did not get to finish my passions. And I knew, as did Guy, that we would both be expelled for our "disgraceful" behavior.

The events that immediately followed at the school were dreary, and I was very glad to get away from the dreadful place as soon as I had been booted. Had I known that the episode was the greatest thing that could have happened to me at the time, I would not have been so ashamed. As it was, I feared Helen's wrath, and thought about it the whole ride home. Well, almost all of the ride . . . if the truth be told, I did offer a moment here or there to the delicious memory of Guy Repton's hand on my cock and his pretty mouth clamped upon my nipple.

Accordingly I returned home, and nobody knew what to do with me. I could not go to another school. I was too young for the university. I stayed at home for six months. My father was already sickening with his last illness. There was no one to control me; and no doubt I bullied the servants, was tyrannical and threatening to the tenants, rude to Helen, and contemptuous of Miss Priscilla. Miss Priscilla had precise old-maidish neatnesses that it was a pleasure to me to offend. I would stamp about the drawing room in noisy muddy boots and fling myself on delicately upholstered sofas in dirty football clothes. These things I delighted to do because I saw how much they shocked her and offended Helen. Finally Helen made a suggestion to my father that I should be sent around the world with a tutor for a year. My father was delighted with the idea. He was very ambitious for me. He was unwilling to face the disturbing realities of my unusual feminine persona.

"There is no reason, my boy, why you should make money. I have done that. You must make a famous name. Marry and begin a great family which shall be associated the history of the country."

Oh, how well I remember him saying that! Helen and Miss Priscilla were both at his bedside at the time, and both were looking at me with enigmatic smiles, which, of course, I now understand.

"You must go into Parliament, become a cabinet minister, perhaps Prime Minister. Therefore, go round the world, Dennis, and improve your mind."

I went, grateful to Helen, but after I had started, I began to wonder whether Helen had not some ulterior purpose, whether she had not removed me from my father's neighborhood in order to oust me by slander from his affections and rob me of my inheritance. I wrote to him, warning him against Helen and Miss Priscilla.

"They are, both of them, designing women, I am sure. They wish to intrigue me out of my proper position as your son."

It was an unfortunate letter, for it ultimately came into Helen's hands. But at the same time it had its influence on my father. A couple of months later, I received a telegram announcing my father's death and that he had bequeathed the whole of his immense fortune to me, with a request that I should make Helen such an allowance as I thought sufficient for her and Miss Priscilla. There was, however, a thorn in that, as in every rose. I was not to come into my inheritance until I was twenty-five, and until that time Helen was appointed my guardian. I resented the idea of being subject to Helen, who certainly hated me. At this time she was only twenty years old herself. However I reflected that I had the upper hand. She would be absolutely dependent upon me and my money for her meals.

I returned to London, where I found a letter from Helen asking me to go and see Mr. Willowes, the solicitor. Mr. Willowes was a friend of Helen's, and she had removed the entire affairs of the family from our old solicitor, who had looked after them for twenty years, and put them into this new man's hands. I went to see him in a haughty mood of displeasure.

"I don't approve of the change," I said foolishly, "and I shall restore the business into the hands of our old solicitor when I come of age."

Mr. Willowes, a young sardonic-looking man, twirled his moustache with an ironic smile.

"It is very kind of you to give me warning. Meanwhile here is your first-class railway ticket to Beaumanoir. I have paid off your tutor. Miss Deverel expects you this afternoon and if you will take a word of advice, young gentleman, you will change your tone with her. She has complete control of you for the next several years and I rather think that she has had quite *enough* of your ill manners and bad behavior. Good morning."

Wild with rage, I was shown out of the office. I had hardly any money. I had to go down to Beaumanoir. Immediately upon my arrival Helen threw off her mask. I arrived late, and noticed that all the footmen and menservants had been dismissed. There were only women in the house, plus new women-servants. All of the new maids were big and handsome and strong. I have to admit that deep within my bosom, I felt a renewed vitality being back at Beaumanoir.

"You have just time to dress for dinner," said Phoebe, "if you will hurry."

"I shall be late," I replied. "How is it that there are no valets?"

"You must ask Miss Helen."

I had my bath, and coming back into my bedroom, I found Phoebe still there.

"What are you doing here? You can go," I said and I saw to my confusion that she was holding up a dainty corset of white satin.

"I must lace you into this first, Master Evelyn," she said impudently.

"How dare you? What impertinence!" I began to leave the room and I saw her move to the bell. "What are you going to do?" I cried.

"Ring the bell for some of the other servants if you are going to be silly. I have definite orders from Miss Helen to lace you into a corset and smarten you up."

I remembered with a sinking heart Mr. Willowes' advice. I couldn't have a struggle with a lot of women-servants. It was a question I must settle privately with Helen. A minute's conver-

sation would settle the matter and put a stop to the repetition
of any such nonsense. And so I allowed Phoebe to lace me up
in a woman's corset. What a strange, luxurious feeling it was!
It was an enervating, captivating sensation against which I felt
the strong need to struggle. I had a sense now of truly being in
a woman's power. The delicate corset, all lace and satin outside,
but relentless as steel in its whalebone grip, seemed to me the
epitome of womanhood. I loved the feeling!

I had carelessly allowed my hair to grow long. Phoebe insisted on curling it. I noticed that the dress trousers that had
been laid out had a line of little effeminate black satin buttons
running for a few inches from the hem upward on the outside
of each leg. They were short and exposed my delicate ankles,
which were clad in very fine black silk stockings. My stockings
were attached to my corset instead of ordinary socks and my
shoes were patent leather girls' pumps with neat flat bows and
straight American heels, which were higher, of course, than
those that men normally wear. I was mysteriously excited by
this strange costume. Helen was already at the table when I
went down, seated with five or six of her friends. Mr. and Mrs.
Rivers and old General Carstairs, a regular degenerate, were
there among other guests. I blushed, suddenly ashamed in my
costume.

"Ah, here's the androgyne!" Helen cried as I entered the
room. "Come and sit down! How do you like your corset and
your bright little shoes?"

The company tried not to laugh. I was so confused that I
wished the floor would open and swallow me up. I ate my
dinner not knowing where to look.

"We have just been discussing your future, Evelyn dear," said
Helen.

"I prefer not to discuss my future with *acquaintances*," I replied haughtily, looking at the guests.

"There's no reason to discuss anything," said Helen, "for we have settled it with a unanimous vote. You are too young still for college. For reasons of which you are *aware*, you cannot be safely sent to a boys' school."

I grew scarlet.

"And you are too overbearing and untidy and impossible to remain in this household with a tutor. There is only one thing left for you, dear, and that's a girls' school."

I started up in a rage, although I can now freely admit that my heart soared.

"This is really too much!" I shouted, attempting some modicum of behavior.

"Come with me," said Helen, with a look on her lovely face that frightened me. She had absolute control of me and my inheritance for eight years. She took me up to my bedroom.

"I am quite serious about this, Evelyn," she said in a gentle voice. "It is the only thing to be done. I don't know whether you are aware that I can, if I think you fit for your position, let you come of age when you are twenty-one. If you behave very obediently as a girl for two years at the girls' school to which I am going to send you, I may perhaps shorten your minority."

It was a strong inducement. Besides, she need not have offered any inducement. I actually *wanted* to go pose as a young lady. I desired no escape.

I was deeply, mysteriously thrilled.

"Of course if I go as a girl to a girls' school for two years, I shall be allowed to dress as a man at the end," I said, in case I appeared freakishly happy.

"If your schoolmistress reports favorably."

Of course I consented. During the next day, I was busy with Helen's dressmakers, Helen's milliner, Helen's bootmakers, Helen's corsetière. In ten days I was fetched by a governess. I went by train in the summer uniform of the school—a pretty pink frock of ninon (ankle length), a big white straw hat, long brown glacé kid gloves, and patent leather button boots with *very* high heels. At the school I had a bedroom to myself. No one was to know that I was not a girl.

I went through the most rigid system imaginable, all designed to make me completely girlish in mind and body. Hair was removed from every part of my body, except my head, by electric needles and depilatories. Every morning and every evening I was massaged for an hour to reduce my waist, develop my bust, and soften my limbs. Exercises with the same objective were carefully supervised. I wore facial masks for my complexion, gloves at night to whiten my hands. My skin was very carefully tended. My hair was treated with lotions so successfully that it grew extraordinarily thick. In two years my hair hung down below my waist in luxurious light curls. Of course I was exceptionally aware of the curves that were forming where before there had been boyish angles. The muscles were all vanishing from my legs and arms, which were already naturally round. My breasts were developing into the pretty white, round, delicately veined apples of a girl.

Now back at home, I was waiting for Miss Priscilla to inspect the result of those two long years. I was in a bedroom that had been altogether refurnished in mauve. Over a thick carpet, a covering of mauve kid leather had been tightly stretched, and it was delicious to feel under my sensitive feet. The room was clearly a girl's bedroom, the dressing table covered with feminine bottles of perfume and lotion, jeweled powder boxes, gold-backed brushes. Why, I asked myself, since I was to be returned to the world of manhood again tomorrow? A beautiful little marble-tiled bathroom led from it on one side, and a dainty boudoir flanked the other. The bed was exquisite in the shape of a swan. It was altogether a lovely suite of rooms—for a girl.

"I shall not sleep here tomorrow," I said sadly to myself. I loved the room. The door opened and Miss Priscilla entered carrying a number of leather jewel cases in her hands.

I had despised Miss Priscilla two years ago. I wondered if my feelings had changed. She had not changed. She was the same neat, precise, thin, elderly spinster with a terrifying air of authority. I had changed, and at her bidding. At an age when even the poorest of boys begin to gain their liberty, I, one of the richest in the country, the head of one of the oldest families in the country, had been calmly stripped of my freedom by this old maid and her niece. They had been able to manipulate me through their insight into my true character.

Miss Priscilla was dressed in a high-necked plain gown of gray silk; she wore the flat square-toed ugly shoes that used to excite my ridicule. The solitary touch of luxury on her body was a long pair of white kid gloves. She looked at me coldly, critically. There was no expression upon her cold face, and so much had my two years at the girls' school changed me that I became strangely curious to know what she thought of my looks. I was a little hurt—yes, let me admit it—a little hurt that she was not betrayed into an expression of admiration.

She opened the leather cases and a rippling fire of jewels at once made the room glorious to my girlish eyes. She advanced to me. They were for me, then! Those glittering streams of diamonds, those lustrous rows of pearls! Oh, I loved jewels! She fixed a high collar of diamonds round my throat with a diamond bow and a tiny diamond tassel dangling from it, just behind the left ear. She passed a double row of magnificent pearls round my shoulders. The strand hung down to my waist. She fixed earrings of big pearls set with diamonds in my ears, which had been pierced. She fixed a diamond star amongst my curls, and a diamond brooch amongst the roses at my waist.

"Give me your hands, Denise," she said, and on my wrists, she fastened lovely bracelets of gold flashing with diamonds and rubies. They were very tight and the sensation of confinement thrilled me. And then she fixed another similar pair above my elbows, smoothing up my long gloves carefully before she clasped them on.

"These bracelets will keep your pretty gloves tidy and smooth," Priscilla said. "Now, join your hands again behind your back." With each movement the soft fire of the flashing stones ran over me like water. Oh, how I wished to see myself in the mirror. There were a couple of big full-length mirrors with three panels each, such as one sees in a dressmaker's atelier. But the panels were closed.

"What is Miss Denise's waist-measure?" Miss Priscilla asked of Phoebe.

"Nineteen inches, Miss," replied Phoebe.

"And the height of her heels?"

"Four inches."

Miss Priscilla nodded her head in approval; she turned to me and said, "Have you your big diamond buckles on your satin slippers?"

"Yes, Miss Priscilla," I replied blushing.

"Lift your skirt and let me see!"

With a shy smile of pleasure—I could not help smiling—I raised the hem of the exquisite satin frock in my delicately gloved fingers. There came into view my slender feet in exquisitely cut, new, glistening, white satin slippers with wonderful arched, narrow Louis Quinze heels. They had pointed toes embroidered with pearls and butterfly bows of dainty white tulle. Mounted on the bows were big blazing diamond buckles. The slim little slippers were posed with the heels together and the toes turned out as Phoebe had arranged them. I pulled the skirt higher, exposing a pair of round arched insteps and small finely molded ankles. My flesh showed prettily pink through tightly strained stockings of white silk with lace insertions. I had never before seen such stockings, never even dreamed of things so beautiful. They were of the finest gossamer, transparent as cobwebs. They were filmy delicious ornaments, rather than coverings, with a soft sheen that was lovely. Such stockings and slippers were fit for some blushing beautiful debutante of high birth and enormous wealth, to make her curtsey in before her Queen. No one else could have afforded them.

Miss Priscilla stooped and held out her hands.

"Give me your pretty foot."

Coquettishly, I hesitated, just like a pretty girl who pretends modesty the better to display what she knows to be her best points.

"Oh, Miss Priscilla," I demurred.

"At once, Denise."

I extended a foot. She took it in her hands, tried the buckle to make certain that it was secure, felt the slipper to see that it was tight enough, and measured the heel.

As she took my foot between her two strong hands, I felt familiar erotic sensations aroused in my body and blood. My heart began to move and I felt the heat rise to my head and to my cock, due to the simultaneous pleasure of being ordered to obey Miss Priscilla and the exquisite sensation I was experiencing as she held my foot, admiring its grace and form. It was almost all I could do not to swoon right there as Miss Priscilla held my foot.

I had felt these same stirrings only under very specific circumstances before. There was that experience with Guy Repton, which was quite an adventure. And while I was at the girls' school there was a girl named Nellie who had a great fascination with my body, and whom under the cover of night, I had allowed into all my secrets. Ah, Nellie's hands! She liked to massage my soft flesh so, and she was fond of tickling my titties. She even loved to play with my cock and balls, and on especially randy nights she would let her fingers roam to the little virgin rosette of my bottom. Oh! Oh! But I shall write more of Nellie on pages to follow.

I return our attentions to the strange and wonderful passions that were being excited in my flesh as Miss Priscilla held my foot firmly in her gloved hands. I felt the blood rushing to my loins, and I sensed that my pink nipples were soon erect because of the excitement I was experiencing. I moaned a little, trying very hard to stifle my pleasure, but Miss Priscilla heard me. She looked at my face sharply. I could see in her eyes a form of pleasure and a special kind of powerful recognition that she was giving me great delight by holding my foot thus.

"They are very pretty," she said with cold content. Then: "Put them together again, Denise. You disobeyed me."

"Miss Priscilla, I only hesitated."

"You were trying your little coquetries on me, Denise," she said with a shrewd smile that brought the blushes to my face. "I punish coquetry. You were indulging your vanity by making play with your dainty slippers, and I punish vanity, Denise. You will go down to dinner and sit through dinner with your pretty mouth gagged."

"A very good thing for Miss Denise," said Phoebe delightedly.

I was startled. More than startled, I was appalled, perhaps a little excited.

"Oh, Miss Priscilla! Am I to sit amongst the guests at a dinner party—in this lovely frock—in *these* satin slippers and stockings—with my mouth gagged!"

"Yes, Denise!"

"Diamond shoe buckles and high heels for my feet and a gag for my mouth. Oh, oh!" I gasped.

Poignant emotions stirred me, troubled me, provoked my

passions. I will tell the whole truth. I was ashamed, but I also anticipated the impending punishment with a strange secret thrill of delight. Ever since I had been a boy, I had been besieged with queer fancies that at first I had ignored. Soon the fancies began to fascinate and frighten me. I recognized that my fantasies of correction might be a danger to my character. My fantasies might be an obstacle to the great career that lay before me.

I had dreamed of an exotic, extravagant world in which ladies would punish me. I imagined myself as a girl in the most exquisite of frocks and high-heeled shoes. I imagined gloves and corsets and them laughing at my pretensions to a career. These dominating women would keep me in bondage and subjection. A toy for their amusement. I had fought against these fancies because I felt them to be unusual, impossible, and bizarre. I had ridiculed them in my own mind as preposterous. Yet now these fantasies seemed part of my nature. They were being translated into fact, and in the process, I was fascinated and obsessed with an erotic force a thousand times stronger than before. It had thrilled me with strange delightful emotions to *imagine* myself dressed in the luxurious gowns of a fashionable girl, undergoing punishments and humiliations and dainty tortures at the hands of a laughing beautiful woman deaf to my prayers. How thrilled and excited was I when my dream became true!

I tried, however, to struggle against the strange, sweet pleasure invading my senses. For I knew that Helen hated me, and she thought I had, by inheriting my father's fortune, robbed her. I was afraid that she and Miss Priscilla were seeking to master me completely, therefore getting it back. I was afraid that Miss Priscilla, with her knowledge of psychopathia, had guessed my secret fancies and by translating them into fact was seeking to reduce me to willing servitude. For now, though, the pleasure mastered the fear. It was the scintillating pleasure of a dream fulfilled that had made me offer so miserable a resistance to my first corset and my banishment to a girls' school.

Miss Priscilla had one more question to ask of me as I stood there before the closed mirror with my ivory ankles gracefully together and the big buckles flashing on my glistening slippers.

"There was a *third* tight white kid glove I arranged for you to wear. Have you it on?" I went scarlet. But if I did not answer I should be punished. I hung my head.

"Yes, Phoebe buttoned it on," I replied in a whisper of confusion. Miss Priscilla was content.

"I must see it!" Miss Priscilla charged.

I blushed more deeply than before as I sighed, "Oh, Miss Priscilla, please!"

"I want no disobedience from you, young lady!" she snapped at me.

Her voice terrified me and thrilled me, as there was a subtle form of threat occurring underneath the calm exterior of her cruel face.

"Phoebe, arrange her skirts so I might see that the *third* glove is buttoned and in its place," Miss Priscilla shrilled with authority.

"Yes, Miss!" Phoebe chirped, happily obliging. She went to work carefully lifting my dress and soft white satin slip so that Miss Priscilla could take a look at the little glove that had been sewn especially for my cock.

Miss Priscilla had ordered a tailor to construct this fascinating little belt, suggesting that the piece be sewn from soft kid leather. The tailor had obliged, and had managed to create a fabulous little sheath that kept my cock and balls in place so that the lovely lines of my dresses would not be marred by the bulge that showed without the third glove. Thus the prettiness of my appearance would not be disrupted by the distraction of my male sex. The leather sheath cupped my member closely, while delicate little straps went round the slender part of my waist and met in a V that went down and between the cleft of my buttocks.

I was glad for the tortuously clever device for two important reasons. Firstly, the tight fit of the glove was pleasingly painful, and I enjoyed the secret restraint that was occurring beneath my skirts. I secretly thought of the leather sheath as a modified chastity belt, if you will. The second reason that I liked my special little belt is linked to the first, in that when I was stimulated or aroused and my sex grew hard, the constraint upon my penis was even more excruciating, therefore more pleasant.

Phoebe greedily stared at the delicate contraption that kept secret my cock and balls. I was absolutely blessed to be given both a healthy set of balls and a lovely set of girlish globes. Who could be luckier than I?

"*Everything* is in place, Miss Priscilla," Phoebe muttered as she continued to stare at my cock.

I trembled a little with excitement as I felt Phoebe's hungry eyes devouring my body.

"Stand still!" Phoebe barked. And then she came forward, and rather impudently put her hands near my thighs. She ran her fingers and the palms of her hand slowly over my soft white flesh, pausing for a long moment on my package of love. Her eyes met mine in a devious smile that suggested quite a lot. She grabbed my cock hard and gave it a healthy squeeze. My breasts heaved involuntarily, and I felt my nipples spring to erection in a state of excitement to match my erect penis. I suddenly feared that Phoebe was going to excite my passions beyond all hope, and I would be forced to carelessly spray my seed all over these lovely clothes.

"Oh! Please," I moaned softly. My plea was in part a begging sound for her to cease and in part a desperate call for her to continue. I wanted her to defile me completely with her strong grip.

"It will teach you to be modest in the presence of women, Denise, and to remember that you are under their authority. You will wear it always."

Priscilla pulled down my skirt and arranged it so that the toes of my slippers and an inch of silk-stockinged instep were exposed. As she finished, Helen entered the room. She looked beautiful in a sweeping décolleté gown of black velvet and shoulder-length white kid gloves.

I could not complain of any want of admiration on her part in any event. A look of wonder and delight shone in her face as she approached me. She uttered a rapturous cry. She ran to me, hugged me, and with passionate kisses, bruised my lips.

"Denise! I am so proud of you."

I hung my head, conscious for a moment of the full extent of my humiliation. I was her victim. And I loved my enslavement. I adored her for exposing my true self. I loved and feared her because she dominated me completely.

"Oh, Denise!" She laid her lovely face against mine. "Your cheek is as soft and fresh as a peach. You *are* a lovely girl."

"I am not a girl," I weakly protested. I was becoming drunk with her attentions.

"Aren't you, darling? You shall decide for yourself."

One of the great mirrors was placed behind me. Oh, how excited I became! At last I was to see what they had made of me. The second was placed in front of me unfolded. I stood in a blaze of light. I stared at myself. I uttered a cry and covered my face with my hands.

"Oh, I am! I am a girl!" I admitted with a cry of pure delight. I hoped, for propriety's sake, that I sounded a little shocked.

I saw a girl's face, of fair complexion, mine but more refined and softened. A wealth of fair glinting hair, done up in the most fashionable style, crowned my face. A broad white forehead and arched eyebrows showed darker than my curls. Big, wistful eyes of dark blue with long dark eyelashes flashed. I saw a delicate nose, soft cheeks in which the color came in excitement. Red lips in a Cupid's bow, the color of pale rose leaves. I was smiling and showing a perfect set of small white teeth, a small rounded chin, little ears—such was Dennis Beryl upon his return from school.

I saw in the mirror a girl sparkling with jewels from her feet to her curls, and dressed for a ball in the London season. Helen was in raptures. She might well be, since this was her doing. I was her creation.

"You have exceeded all my expectations, darling," she said.

With little cries of delight, she ran her gloved hands over me, feeling and caressing my skin until I was scarlet with embarrassed desire.

"Oh, Helen. You mustn't," I protested.

"Nonsense, dear! I am your guardian. Keep still, or else I will whip your girlish bottom."

"Oh, oh!" I sighed as an excruciating sensation made me blush more than ever. "Whip me? In this lovely frock?" I whispered shyly.

"Ah," cried Helen enthusiastically, "you do love your exquisite satin frock, darling, don't you?" It rustled delightfully under her hands. "And the tulle band here with the big sparkling buckle in front and the big bow behind?"

"It ties my ankles delightfully," I stammered as she continued to stroke my body. Oh, was it I who was speaking? "The dress is like a soft caress upon my limbs."

Helen applauded me with a radiant face. She ran her daintily gloved hands down the dress across my behind. She felt through its thin texture, squeezing my legs and calves as she teased me.

"They're charming," she cried. "Your legs are as soft as butter. And you love your stockings too, Denise, don't you, the exquisite stockings I deck you out in?"

The feel of her hands affectionately pinching my calves was intoxicating. Her dainty air of mastery wooed me, lulled me into believing that she actually owned me.

"The stockings are deliciously cool," I said.

"And your white satin slippers with the high heels and the pretty bows and the sparkling buckles, you love them too? Lift up her dress to the knees, Phoebe. Don't you love your little girls' shoes, Denise?"

Phoebe raised my skirt to the knees. The white satin garters with the big bows and buckles and the dainty frills of my batiste pantalets were visible.

"Look in the mirror Denise and tell me *gratefully* that you love them!"

"If I must wear girls' shoes," I replied blushing deeply, "they may as well have high heels and diamond buckles." Something much stronger than myself made me speak. In the midst of her delight, Helen exchanged a quick glance with Miss Priscilla. It was a glance of triumph and it put me on my guard.

Phoebe let my dress fall and Helen took me round the waist. "You are delightful, Denise. You are quite a girl now with that pretty white bosom."

"Yes, Ma'am," said Phoebe, "her breasts have come up wonderfully. I think Miss Denise ought to be very grateful to Miss Priscilla for the trouble she has taken in arranging the proper exercises and massage and medicines."

"Oh, there was no difficulty," said Miss Priscilla. "The moment I discovered that Denise had the milk vessels of a woman, I had no doubt that we could fit him with a pretty pair of girl's white breasts. As perfect as any young lady could wish for."

"The milk vessels," cried Phoebe with a laugh. "Then Miss Denise is a freak?"

"Not at all," said Miss Priscilla calmly. "The men of the primitive tribes used to have the milk vessels. Miss Denise may be a chance return to the primitive type. Or originally it might have been that nature was going to give Evelyn a twin sister, and that their embryos got mixed. That happens not infrequently."

Helen laughed, and stroked my cheek lasciviously. I could tell she had further designs on me. But that was later.

"In any case, Denise has a girl's bosom—for life." She touched them with her gloved fingers, and daintily caressed them, ruthlessly titillating my nipples, sending waves of delicious sensation through my veins. "They are a real punishment, dear, for all the trouble you have given us. You can't get rid of them as you could of your girl's shoes and stockings, if we were to let you. They are a permanent proof to you of the *wisdom* of being a woman and the pleasure of being obedient to women."

"But you are going to let me get rid of my girls' shoes and stockings tomorrow. You promised faithfully, Helen," I said.

Helen held me firmly, caressed me, bruised my lips with burning kisses.

"You don't *want* to get rid of them, Denise. You love them! You love your dainty frocks. You will be so much happier as a girl."

As she pleaded with me, her voice, the perfume of her breath, and the feel of her limbs through my dress tempted me. I felt inclined to let myself go in her arms, to say, "Helen, I belong to you." But I remembered my ambitions.

"No, no, I have your word," I cried. "I must be a man. I am to marry and begin a great family."

The three women burst out laughing, confusing me dreadfully.

Helen cried, "Oh, Denise, I would love to see your wife's face when she first discovers your girl's bosom. No, no my dear, you shall love your pretty frocks, your smart corsets, your long gloves, and your lovely little high-heeled slippers."

"No, no," I insisted obstinately, and Helen with an exclamation of annoyance let me go. She had after all only pretended to be affectionate, though she had very nearly deceived me. Now her face became stern with anger. She looked at me with threatening eyes. "Very well," she said, "but I warn you, Denise, you will come on your knees begging me to put you back into girl's clothes. Now go down to the drawing room, and take care how you walk. Point your toes, arch your feet. Take your fan!"

She gave me a lovely fan of ivory and gold. I had turned from her toward the door when Miss Priscilla called me back.

"You forget that you have to be punished, Denise," she said calmly, and she told Helen of my coquetry and of the punishment she meant to inflict.

Oh, how confused the situation had become! There I stood dressed as elegantly as any young woman of fashion, all the while being taunted, molded by the women I had come to love and fear the most in my life. My ambivalence was not only directed toward Helen; I also felt disoriented about the dilemma that I had found myself in.

How right and accurate Helen had been to exclaim that I loved the corsets and dainty shoes, the silk stockings, and the fabulous evening gowns. She knew me well, and between her mind and Miss Priscilla's, they had knowingly awakened the real me that would not lay dormant again. I knew this deep within my unconscious mind, but I had been so stringently conditioned by my father to strive for a career, to build a family name . . . yet I did not protest as I was bullied by Helen and

Priscilla to endure the wonders of their medicines, the massages, the girls' school. In fact, I lived for the hours when I wasn't with Nellie, during which the strong women masseuses would prod and tickle and slap my flesh, slowly forming my body into the feminine shape that it still has to this day. I adored the hours that I lay stretched on my back as a pair of lovely, strong hands kneaded and prodded my wonderfully sensitive breasts into a more full existence. On lovely, rare occasions, the masseuse would be a saucy woman, who would take pleasure in kissing my pink cock, or even lightly stroking the tight little rosebud orifice of my bottom, while she massaged my legs and bum. I never wanted those voluptuous hours to end.

Nor did I want to desire Helen the way that I did. But I knew—as she drew closer to me, letting the tips of her own perfect breasts nearly kiss the tips of my own—I knew that she desired me, too. But as a woman. She only wanted to be near me, to stroke and kiss and fondle me if I were dressed as a woman. This was a sudden realization for me, and I nearly reeled upon discovering this secret fact. I wanted nothing more than to remain in this passive, lovely costume for the rest of my days. But how could I have conveyed that through my shame? The thought of remaining a girl forever was as confounding as it was exhilarating. I wanted to reach out and pull Helen toward me, but I refrained and stood still.

I hadn't really wanted to protest my "humiliating" situation, but I did because I thought that I was supposed to. I was to be punished for my insolence and my ingratitude.

I realize now that it is very likely that I had secretly wished this punishment upon myself, that I had precipitated Helen's response to my insolent mood. I deeply wished the sensuous torments that she was to heap upon me.

Ah, one can never underestimate the power of the unconscious mind, the secret part of our mind that drives so much of our behavior.

"She must be punished," said Helen, pushing me toward a gilt chair with a white satin seat.

"Lift your skirt carefully, Denise, and kneel on this chair," she said sternly.

A little frightened, I immediately obeyed this humiliating order. Helen dipped a pen in the ink upon the writing table.

"It is the rule in this house, Denise," she said, "that one punishment always involves a second to be inflicted later on; and so that we may not forget it, we make a note of it upon the sole of one of the culprit's smart shoes."

"Oh!" I protested. "I am to be punished *twice* for the same fault."

"That is the rule. It teaches pretty young ladies to be careful to avoid punishment altogether."

She took my instep in her hand and stooped over my feet. My position was, of course, extraordinarily humiliating. But the feel of her gloved hand on my round, warm, silk-stockinged instep and the sight of her in the mirror as she wrote the punishment I was to endure upon the new white sole of my dainty satin slipper sent a voluptuous thrill through my blood.

"Now stay as you are, Denise, until the ink is dry," Helen said, and, laying down the pen, she began to adjust my feet. She took great care, with her usual love of neatness, that my ankles were pressed together and my high heels and pointed toes were exactly level.

Miss Priscilla, meanwhile, squeezed and rolled into a ball a small lace handkerchief that she had been soaking in eau de cologne. She came over to me with the ball in her hand.

"Open your mouth, Denise!"

I obeyed. She thrust the handkerchief into my mouth.

"Close your mouth now, dear!"

The eau de cologne burnt my tongue and the roof of my mouth in the most painful way. Tears filled my eyes.

"Oh, oh!" I cried in a stifled voice, wringing my hands.

Miss Priscilla smiled at my sufferings.

"The eau de cologne will keep your mouth fresh and sweet, darling," she said and she took up a bigger handkerchief of the finest silk and carefully folded it. This she adjusted over my lips and tied the end very tightly at the back of my hair, binding my mouth so that I could not utter a sound.

"Now stand up, Denise!" Miss Priscilla shouted.

I stood up and Miss Priscilla carefully smoothed down my shining skirt. What a bizarre spectacle met my eyes in the mirror! I saw a grown-up girl in an exquisite evening gown of white satin with her mouth gagged. Her white throat and bosom were flashing with jewels, while her white-gloved hands toyed with a pretty fan. The delicate bows and bright buckles of her luxurious little slippers were peeping out from delicious billows of white tulle.

Of course what made the spectacle so piquant and seductive to me was the knowledge that the pretty girl was myself. My hands were quite free. I could have torn the gag from my lips in a second. There were only two ladies to prevent me. But I did not dare. I was undergoing discipline in girls' frocks and pearl-embroidered satin slippers at their hands. I was being punished by them and in my subjection I felt powerful and lovely.

"Now go downstairs into the drawing room, Denise," said Helen. "Our guests will be arriving in a minute.

I was to be seen by her guests in this ignominious condition. The shame of it excited me. I looked piteously at Helen. But there was no sign of relenting in her face. I thought the guests would never recognize me. They would see only Denise, a girl.

They would witness Denise's submission, and then Denise would to disappear forever. I picked up the train of my frock and went sadly out of the room. As I turned to latch the door, I heard Helen ask, "Well, what do you think?"

And Miss Priscilla replied, "In a few weeks he will be the prettiest *fétichiste du pied* in the world." And then they both laughed heartlessly.

I was troubled by their words. What was a *fétichiste du pied?* I had to know. I had an intuition that the phrase was the secret to the riddle, was a clue to the plot those two women had concocted to nullify and ruin me. But I had not time to think about it now. My heels were so high and thin and my skirt so tight that I had to be extremely careful making my way downstairs. There were two maids waiting in the hall to receive the guests, and they both burst out laughing when they saw me. They knew who I was, of course, and my cheeks grew hot with shame. I feared I did not look pretty.

There was no one as yet in the drawing room, but my heart sank at the ordeal in front of me. What if I was not as beautiful as I thought?

I heard a light quick step outside and Doris Hind, Helen's cousin, ran into the room. She wore a smart little short frock of pale pink *mousseline de soie* with black silk stockings encased in patent leather slippers. A bright fire was burning in the grate; I turned to it to hide my gag as long as I could.

"Who are you, you pretty thing?" she asked.

I could not answer.

"What's the matter?" she demanded impatiently.

Finally, she turned me around and saw the gag over my mouth. She stared at me astonished for a moment. Then the truth broke in upon her and she clapped her hands with pleasure.

"You must be Denise. Helen has gagged you. How delicious! You *are* a perfect girl now, Denise."

I blushed to the roots of my hair, and unconsciously I placed one foot upon the fender to warm it, lifting my skirt an inch or two. Doris uttered a rapturous cry.

"What adorable feet! And, oh Denise, what divine little satin slippers. Let me see!" I blushed again, but this time it was with pleasure.

"What lovely buckles and what fairylike bows! And those dear little pearl-embroidered toes! And what jolly high heels. Show me your ankles!"

I raised the skirt higher, and the delicate, cleanly rounded ankle in its shimmering cobweb of silk and lace came into view. Doris went into ecstasy. "I should like to perch you on still higher heels dear, and keep you in a glass case to show to my friends. That's really all that you are fit for now. Walk across the room, you exquisite thing, and let me see how daintily you can do it in your beautiful high-heeled shoes." I was delighted with her admiration, but I shook my head at her request.

At once she stamped her foot. "Quick, or I'll punish you," she cried. "Pick up your train and let me see those buckles flashing on your dainty butterfly bows this instant."

I submitted. I was beginning to learn that one of the inevitable consequences of allowing myself to be dressed as a girl was that everyone who knew the secret treated me as a little child in spite of my long décolleté gown and fine jewels. I walked daintily across the room and back. Doris applauded me, laughing.

"I don't know a girl, Denise, who wouldn't envy your figure and your feet and ankles. Oh, but you must be kept in high-heeled shoes all your life! It would be ridiculous now that Helen has got you so smart and pretty to let you go back into stupid trousers. Being a boy would be so tedious for you now."

At that moment Helen and Miss Priscilla came into the room, and the guests began to arrive. There was Mrs. Dawson, the clergyman's wife; Lady Hartley and her pretty daughter; Mr. and Mrs. Charles Rivers . . . about twenty people arrived, mostly young people and all of them neighbors whom I had known as a boy. I was introduced to them as Denise Beryl, a cousin. Helen explained how I came to be punished with a gag. I had to stand and listen, but my cheeks burned with shame.

"Denise is unfortunately very vain," Helen told her delighted guests. "I had to punish her because she kept showing off her feet in a very unladylike way."

"She is very lucky to have gotten off so easily," said Lady Hartley with severity, looking down at my feet through her glasses. "I should not only have gagged her, I should have taken her pretty slippers away from her altogether." Then, to my amazement and horror, "Mr. Guy Repton" was announced and my old schoolfellow came into the room.

He had been expelled in disgrace because of me. How did Helen come to know him? Her first words explained.

"This is my new steward and agent," she said as she introduced him. I was horrified. He was the new manager of my estates. He had turned out to be a handsome young man of twenty-two with a fair moustache. Helen had given him a fine position and a good income. She must have sought him out on purpose because she believed that I had caused his disgrace. She wished to surround me with my enemies, I felt sure. Guy Repton would be grateful to her and presumably he hated me. Helen did not even pretend to conceal the reason for her choice of him. She darted a triumphant look at me. I felt more and more helpless in her hands.

Guy entered the room and dazzled the ladies instantly. He had become the gallant in the past two years. Needless to add, my own heart fluttered wildly as he entered the room, for I

associated some of my most mysterious feelings with him and
the experience we shared at school. I still had fond feelings for
him, even if he was the cause of my expulsion and disgrace
from the academy. I suddenly felt as though I should thank
him for what had happened, because it seemed as if it were an
example of divine intervention. But I realized that Guy did not
recognize me; mentioning anything concerning our tryst at
school would have ruined my feminine effect.

It seemed as though we had both ended up in the proper
positions, though I could not help but smile ironically as he
bent his dark, curly head to kiss my gloved hand.

"Guy," said Helen slyly, "I would like to present to you my
delightful cousin, Denise. Denise, meet Mr. Repton." She
laughed a little, and the sound was cruel and delicious to my
ears. I blushed.

"She is a most delicate creature," said Guy to Helen, as he
continued to hold my hand in his. He turned and met my gaze.
He stared into my eyes for a prolonged moment.

"Helen, are you certain that I have never made the charming
acquaintance of your cousin before? She looks so familiar to
me," he said in all innocence.

"Oh no, Guy. This is her first visit to Beaumanoir," said Helen, laughing gaily.

"But why the gag? Has Miss Denise misbehaved?" asked Guy,
his eyes taking in my person with uninhibited hunger.

"Miss Denise has been a naughty, naughty girl. Her punishment for her impudence is to endure this party wearing that
gag so that she will learn her proper place in this house."

"Well, I must admit," said Guy, "the gag does become her in
a bizarre fashion. It is as though she were meant for it."

"How right you are," cried Helen with delight.

I was miserable, for I wanted to join in the festive repartee of the evening. I wanted to display my feminine charms for all the guests to delight in.

"Come along, Guy, you will have all evening to admire my guests," Helen said, guiding him to another cluster of party guests.

I was grateful for the superb construction of my little leather sheath hiding beneath all my lacy underthings. Seeing Guy Repton had kindled old feelings deep within my soul. I could tell that he fancied me. I could tell that he admired me dressed as a woman much more than if I were the boy he once knew. This recognition of admiration made the blood rush to my face and to my cock simultaneously, and I was glad that my leather pouch kept my feelings from showing.

We were waiting for dinner to be announced when Lady Hartley, a handsome matron of forty-five, came to me and took me by the arm. She led me into a little drawing room situated off of the big one. She pointed to a sofa.

"Lie down there on your face, young lady," and as I hesitated, she pinched my buttock painfully. "At once," she said.

Reluctantly I stretched myself out on the sofa. Oh, what did she mean to do with me? I felt the familiar stirrings of pleasure that accompanied the demands made upon me by strong women.

"I saw something written on the sole of your slipper as you walked across the room," she said. "A punishment, of course." She felt for my foot under my satin gown. Once she located my foot, she lifted it up and read Helen's note. She looked puzzled. "I wonder what it means," she said. "You may get up."

We went back into the big room where all the guests had assembled. Violet, Doris's elder sister, had just come down, and my heart fluttered erratically. Violet looked quite stunning.

"I am very sorry for being late," Violet faltered breathlessly, with a frightened appeal to Helen. She looked perfectly charming in a blue chiffon gown, which set off her porcelain skin and her fair hair to perfection. Helen looked sternly at her, and made no answer.

Dinner was announced.

"Mr. Repton, will you take in Denise," said Helen. "I do apologize to have to give you so silent a companion, but you did seem so *charmed* by her!"

I sat gagged at the dinner table bright with flowers, amongst those smartly dressed people, unable to eat and unable to talk. I felt terribly humiliated. It was cruel to make me come down to dinner at all. I found it difficult to breathe and it was all I could do not to burst into tears. To make things worse the company began to talk about the "other" me, Dennis Beryl. "It is such a pity that he is coming home tomorrow," said Mrs. Dawson. "It has been so pleasant and peaceful here while he has been at his girls' school." Everyone agreed. It was a revelation to me how thoroughly unpopular I was. I felt completely ashamed of my past behavior.

"I think you will all find him *greatly* changed for the better," said Helen with a smile. "His headmistress's report speaks most highly of his docility and his ladylike ways." How I blushed. Luckily no one knew that *I* was present except Helen.

"I can quite believe it," said Guy Repton with a hateful snicker. "I think that you are all a little unjust to poor Dennis. I don't think that his nature is really bad, but as a boy he was not in his proper position. He must have known that dressed in male clothes he looked silly and ridiculous, and no doubt he felt uncomfortable. It was this discomfort that made him arrogant and intolerable. But dressed and treated as a girl he would no longer have that feeling of discomfort. He would probably be quite charming." I could have boxed Guy Repton's ears for his impertinence. "Very likely you are right," said Lady Hartley, "but then he ought to be kept a girl all his life."

"Oh, yes," cried Mrs. Rivers turning enthusiastically to Helen. I had thrown a stone through the drawing room window of Mrs. Rivers' house, just after she and Charles Rivers had gotten married. She had never forgiven me. Helen shook her head sadly.

"I promised him that he should not have to wear girls' clothes after the two years if he behaved himself." She made a sign to Netta, one of the parlor maids, and Netta took the handkerchief from my mouth and the second one from between my lips. My face was revealed, and Mrs. Rivers cried out enthusiastically, "Oh what a pretty girl!"

I blushed with pleasure, and then the most unfortunate event occurred. I had been sitting with my napkin on my lap, although I had no dinner. I had been consumed with curiosity to know what strange punishment Helen had written down on the sole of my foot. So, while the rest were talking I had slipped off my left shoe. Then dropping my napkin, I had stooped to pick it up and, at the same time, I picked up in it the dainty high-heeled slipper. I held it carefully in my lap and read on the new white sole the words "The glass boxes."

I was wondering what strange punishment "The glass boxes" could be with a thrill of awe. I was under the impression that no one had seen my maneuver when Mrs. Rivers uttered her admiring cry; but Lady Hartley had been watching me and she said at once severely, "Yes, a very pretty girl who has kicked off one of her dainty slippers."

I hung my head in shame.

"Is that true, Denise? Let me see!" said Helen sharply.

"Yes, Helen," I said humbly and lifted up the slipper. Helen called to Netta.

"Take a shoehorn and put on Miss Denise's shoe at once."

Netta turned my chair around, drew the slipper on my foot, and put my back to the table. Then she took the bracelets from my wrists, unbuttoned my gloves there. She slipped my hands out and turned the gloves back.

"Yes, a very pretty girl," said Lady Hartley severely, "but if she were *my* pretty girl, I should tie her gloved hands behind her back and stand her in the corner with her face to the wall with her dainty heels together."

My cheeks grew red with shame. But underneath the shame, I was suddenly conscious of a passionate longing to be punished in a childish and humiliating way in front of these gaily dressed people. I tried to shake the obsession off. It felt dangerous and exciting. The venom was in my veins. I tried to think of my ambitions, my career, but I could only think of the little, new, shining satin slippers that so daintily imprisoned my feet under the table, the fairylike bows, the big blazing buckles, the pointed pearl-embroidered toes. I felt the high Louis Quinze heels sinking deliciously into the thick carpet. Oh, to be made to stand upon them publicly in a corner with my face to the wall with my gloved hands tied behind my back like a naughty child. I rubbed my legs together in a spasm of desire. And then as Netta placed my dinner before me and filled my glass with champagne, Helen cried out with a laugh.

"But, dear Lady Hartley, that is exactly what I shall do with Denise."

The men looked sympathetically toward me, but all the ladies were clearly delighted. As for myself, I had to bend my head over my plate to hide a smile of sheer delight. Mr. Rivers actually pleaded on my behalf. Of course Helen would not hear of it.

"And I think Helen is so right," said Lady Hartley. "I support the punishment of young ladies. People allow them such a ridiculous amount of liberty nowadays. It is quite refreshing to find someone like Helen. It is wise to dress them beautifully and treat them like dainty convicts. That is the only way to keep the silly creatures in good order," she said sternly.

I ate my dinner quickly, while the longing to be punished tingled through my veins. Already I imagined that I could feel Helen's quick little daintily gloved fingers binding my wrists behind me with satin ribbons and adjusting my feet in exquisite finery. As soon as dinner was over, cigarettes and coffee were handed round. I lit a cigarette. It was two years since I had smoked one, and oh, how I enjoyed it now! I leaned back in my chair, a smile of delight upon my face, as I relished the rich tobacco.

There was to be a dance for the people of the village after dinner in the village hall, and we were all to go to it. Helen rose.

"Mr. Repton," she said, "will you kindly take the gentlemen down to the village hall when they are ready There are two motorcars. They can come back for us. We ladies will come in for the fun a little while later. After that you are all welcome to come back here; we will have our own little dance and some supper."

"Certainly, Miss Deverel," said Guy Repton. He cast a fiendishly lascivious glance in my direction.

The other two ladies rose and Helen said to them, "Bring your cigarettes, all of you except Denise. I can't have you standing in the corner, Denise, with a cigarette between your lips."

Blushing, I laid my cigarette in the ashtray and followed the ladies from the room.

As they crossed the hall, I heard Lady Hartley say to Helen, "I thought that I read on the sole of Denise's slipper that you were thinking of a quite different punishment for her."

"Yes," replied Helen, "standing in the corner I look upon as a preliminary. The real punishment will be inflicted later on after supper."

"It sounds like a curious one—'The glass boxes.'"

"I think it is interesting and ingenious. You shall see it. I am quite sure you will approve."

I was curious myself as to what the punishment was going to be—curious and frightened.

We all went into a small parlor. It was a lovely little room decorated in white and gold with a polished parquet floor scattered with thick white rugs of Persian silk. It was brightly illuminated with shaded electric lamps, and a cheerful fire burned upon the hearth. The ladies took their seats in comfortable chairs about the fire with an air of eager expectation. They continued to smoke their cigarettes as Helen placed me in the middle and handed a little silver buttonhook to her young cousin Doris.

"Doris, put Denise's hands back into her gloves and button them carefully," she said.

I gave my hands to Doris, who smoothed the tight white kid gloves over my fingers and fixed the buttons while Helen went over to a bureau. She opened a drawer and came back carrying a mysterious leather case and a number of strong black leather straps with big metal buckles shining upon them. Helen placed the leather case on the mantelshelf and the straps on a chair. Her face was radiant, and her eyes danced with pleasure.

"Now, Denise, we are going to truss you up tightly and prettily," she said with a thrill of sinister delight in her voice. From my arms, she removed the gold bracelets that I had been wearing to keep my gloves stretched tight. Then, on each arm, where the bracelets had been, she buckled a broad, black leather strap very tightly. Neither the metal buckles nor the eyeholes were at the ends of the straps so that after the belt had been fastened, two broad ends hung from each of my arms. Helen tied the ends in a knot and passed them back through the oval buckles. The leather straps were on the outside of my arms, and on the inside of each strap, a little steel ring was stoutly sewn. Helen produced a tiny bar of polished steel with a spring hook at each end of it. She forced the hooks to snap onto the steel rings, pushing my arms together with a strength of which I should never have believed her capable.

"There," she said, "I can now tie your wrists comfortably." She sat down.

"Stand with your back to us, Denise." My elbows almost touched in the small of my back and my shoulders were drawn back most painfully. An extraordinary sense of helplessness, delightful and at the same time alarming, overwhelmed me. Slowly and with hesitation I obeyed my cruel feminine tyrant. I stood in front of her chair with my back toward her, and I offered my daintily gloved wrists for her to bind. There were mirrors set into the wall panels and I could see myself in my glistening white frock, which delightfully reflected the lights, from the buckles and pearls gleaming on my satin slippers to the curls of my exquisitely coiffured head, as I stood in this humiliating position of subjection. Yet how the spectacle aroused my passions! I felt dreadfully excited.

"Keep quite still now, Denise," said Helen, with a laugh. "Have you ever had your hands tied together for bad behavior before?"

"Never, Helen."

"It seems a pity that you should have to have them tied up on an evening when you look so pretty and are so delightfully dressed."

My girlish vanity made me answer with a smile of confusion, "If I have got to have my hands tied behind me I would rather be prettily dressed than not for the ceremony." The ladies laughed and I blushed. Lady Hartley cried out, "That is charming of you, Denise."

I felt Helen's hands on my body and suddenly—was it in a panic, or was it to prolong the delight I felt?—I began to struggle. But my arms were already bound, and the struggle was soon over. In the mirror I saw my hands suddenly interlaced with Helen's. They were fluttering like four doves. Our four hands separated. Helen's hands were holding the ends of a black leather strap, which encircled my wrists. She drew it tighter and tighter.

"Oh, oh, you are hurting me, Helen," I protested.

"You shouldn't make it necessary for me to hurt you, darling," she answered. And then she tied the leather and passed it through the oval steel buckle, as she had done with the other straps.

"That will do," she said, rising briskly. My arms hung down behind me in their delicate long kid gloves, inert, useless. She took me by the elbow.

"Take care how you walk on your high heels now that your hands are tied behind you, Denise. Point your toes and arch your pretty insteps!"

She led me to a corner by the fire and placed me in it with my face to the wall. "Hold your head up darling! That's right! Put your high heels together, and turn out the pointed toes. Let me see!"

She stooped down and picked up the train of my dress. She proceeded to wind it tightly round my legs, binding them in its folds and exposing to view my ankles and feet. She fixed it at my knees with a leather strap.

"Now stand without moving," she ordered, and with the handle of her fan, she gave me a sharp smack on my bare white shoulder.

"Take care! If I see a flutter of the butterfly bows or a flash of the diamond buckles on your daintily slippered feet, I will lock a tight pair of fetters over your gossamer silk stockings, locked round your slender ankles. You will be bound so fast that you won't be able to twitch one of your toes."

"Oh, Helen," I sighed. But it was not a sigh of alarm. It was a sigh of voluptuous, languorous desire.

Strange as it may seem, it was absolutely delicious to be standing daintily in the corner with my arms and hands cruelly bound behind me in my exquisite satin frock. I loved the sensation of the long girls' gloves of supple white kid. I was nothing more than a pretty punished thing of ribbons and pearls. But to have my ankles in their girls' lustrous transparent open-worked white silk stockings fettered tightly together too! The thought of standing in a corner with my delicate feet unable to move in their exquisitely cut high-heeled slippers of white satin and delicate bows was nearly more than I could bear. To see my round pink insteps gleaming daintily through the lace insertions of stockings—stockings that only the richest of heiresses would wear at a ball in the London season! The mere thought of it made me almost swoon with delight. This is what I had dreamed of. I could realize my deepest desires by a single movement. An irresistible impulse to act out was upon me.

"I don't see the use of my wearing beautiful satin slippers with valuable diamond buckles if I have to hide them in a corner," I pretended to grumble.

"Nonsense, Miss Denise," replied Mrs. Dawson. "It is delightful for us to see an elegant young lady with pretty feet smartly shod standing *obediently* in the corner." She evoked a picture of myself in my mind that carried me away. I was nearly delirious with pleasure. I wanted nothing more than to feel the binding powers of those fetters.

"Mayn't I even do this?" I asked impertinently, and I stretched out a foot, pointing the toe. I quickly drew it back again. An exclamation of indignation at my willfulness broke from the group of ladies.

"Lock and chain together those satin-slippered feet at once, Helen!" cried Lady Hartley.

"I will indeed," answered Helen. "Come Violet, Miss Hartley, help me please." With the assistance of the two young ladies she literally carried me from the corner and lifted me onto a chair.

"Support her please," said Helen. I was quite helpless, with my satin train swathed around my legs and my hands and arms tied behind me. Helen opened the leather case and took out a pair of bright fetters of thin polished steel.

"Oh, they are too small," I cried. "They will never go around my ankles."

"Hold your tongue," said Helen and she stooped over my little buckled feet. Oh, wonderful blissful moment! I felt the cold, cruel bands close about my ankles, the lock clasp sounding sharply through the room. It was done now, past recall. I was chained and completely at the mercy of these women. Thrills of voluptuous exquisite delight tingled warmly through my body from my high heels to my curls. I looked down—oh, bizarre and entrancing spectacle! I saw the bright bands of steel glistening on my filmy silk stockings, imprisoning my ankles. I saw my small feet in the gleaming, white satin pearl-embroidered slippers. Oh, what waves of sensuous pleasure swept over me! Helen raised her hands and smoothed down my skirt from the waist to the knees. Her masterful hands, having bound my arms and wrists behind me and fettered my ankles, were now engaged in the feminine work of making my frock sit prettily. The blood rushed into my face.

As Helen ran her hands over the front of my lovely gown, her searching hands rested most languorously upon my crotch. Her fingers tickled and grasped at my cock. For the second time during that evening, I thanked heaven for the leather sheath that Miss Priscilla had forced me to wear. I was also cursing it, however ambivalently, because as Helen teased my cock, the sheath forbade me to experience the true pleasures of an erection. Instead the thing caused me great discomfort, which, of course, was not altogether unpleasing to me, but I wished suddenly to be naked and alone with Helen. I imagined her pretty gloved hands stroking and squeezing my cock. I even went so far as to picture her lovely mouth covering my prick, giving it a goodnight kiss. The exquisite torture that Helen had devised for me was more than I had ever expected in my life. Helen continued to lightly tease my rod beneath the folds of my evening gown, and with every stroke I felt the strain of my secret bondage. As Helen tortured me so voluptuously, our eyes met for a long, tense moment.

"Oh, oh," I murmured. I stood quite still, every nerve tense and alive. It seemed to me that Helen's hands had opened the door to an unimagined paradise. She stared into my rapt eyes shrewdly.

Then in a triumphant whisper, she said, "You *wanted* me to chain your feet, Denise."

Her words brought me to my senses. It was part of her plan, I was sure, to produce in me a craving for these delectable punishments. It was part of her plot to keep me in a permanent state of submission.

"Lift the pretty creature down," said Helen contemptuously. When I was placed standing again on the parquet floor, she added with a slow malicious smile, "I think, Denise darling, that since you are so disobedient, before I put you back into your corner, I had better give your fleshy little ass a sound caning."

"Oh, please no," I cried in terror.

Helen turned to Lady Hartley.

"Don't you think that I am right, Lady Hartley?" she asked.

"Certainly. You will be doing Denise a kindness."

"Doris, will you go and find Phoebe and ask her to bring a strong thick cane for Miss Denise?"

"Oh, please, Helen," I whimpered, "I have never been caned. Oh, I will go on my knees to you."

"You can't, darling," said Helen, "you have your pretty feet chained together. Don't be silly!"

She turned me around and ran her hand lightly over my buttocks.

She began laughing with excitement and pleasure. "I am afraid that even through this fabric the cane will hurt and sting you terribly dear. Your flesh is so deliciously soft."

I wriggled and struggled in vain. Oh, what a fool I had been to let her bind and fetter me! I was helplessly at her mercy now. My heart soared with secret bliss.

Phoebe brought in a long, thick bamboo cane. It was a dreadful weapon. Helen made it whistle through the air. I shrank and trembled.

Helen burst out into a callous laugh at my abject entreaties. The other ladies moved excitedly in their chairs, tapping with their heels on the floor, making their pretty dresses rustle. Clearly, all of them were eager to see me soundly caned in my lovely clothes.

"Come, Denise, don't disgrace the smarter sex by so much cowardice!" said Helen.

She seized me. She thrust her left arms in between my bound arms and my back, and lifted my hands off my back into the air.

"Bend over, dear."

She raised the cane high above her head.

How cruel women can be! Helen herself was flushed with pleasure. She grew more severe with each stroke.

"Seven! Oh, I love to see you crying, Denise!" she said. I writhed and screamed.

"Eight!" she cried triumphantly, and the slashing cane burnt my soft buttocks like a hot wire.

"Keep still, Denise! Don't rub your knees together under your frock in that indecent way. You'll tear the lace frills of your drawers if you do."

"Oh, Helen!" I sobbed. "Let me go."

"Nine! And don't squeeze your satin slippers against one another. You'll ruin the butterfly bows. Ten! You are to dance in them tonight and show them off! Eleven!"

I shivered from head to foot, fearful that I was going to shoot my spunk.

"Now for the last! Twelve!"

The last was a dreadful stroke, and I very nearly reached climax.

"Oh, untie my hands!" I screamed. "Take my dress off! Let me plunge my bum into cold water! Oh, my flesh is on fire!"

Helen laid down the cane.

"Shut up," she said. "Violet, Miss Hartley!"

They lifted me up, carried me writhing in agony into the corner, and placed me once more standing with my face to the wall.

"Your head well up! Turn your shoe buckles out!" Helen barked at me. She looked flushed with the pleasure of having completely dominated me. Her eyes were lustily feverish. She looked beautiful.

"Now cry away, baby, as much as you like, while we go down to the village. Aunt Priscilla will sit here while we are away and see that you don't move," she whispered in my ear. "Think of your perfect humiliation! Think of your perfect submission, and my total dominion over your body and your mind," she whispered caressingly in my ear, tempting me with seductive images.

Soon the ladies put on their cloaks and went away. I was left in the little sitting room, standing in the corner, sobbing bitterly while Miss Priscilla sat at the bureau, where she could watch

every movement that I made. She callously ignored my weeping
and wrote letters.

She had no pity for me in my bondage and misery. She was
perpetually chiding me. One moment it would be, "Don't work
your shoulders in that violent way. Keep them still and if you
must cry, sob silently!"

Later she said, "I see your fingers twitching, Denise. Open
your hands and let them lie quiet against your satin dress." And
then moments later, "Your feet are trembling, Denise. Keep
them still. Your slipper buckles are flashing so that they continually attract my eyes. I shall have to cut them off your shoes."

She came over to the corner with a pair of scissors in her
hand. All my vanity, all my love for my dainty slippers, rose in
alarm.

"Oh, please don't cut the buckles off. Please, Miss Priscilla!"
I begged her.

"Be careful, then," she said and rapped my insteps, exposed
in their open-worked thin silk stockings, with the handle of
her fan. My tears broke out afresh.

At last the pain of my burning flesh began to diminish. I
sniffed rather than sobbed. Finally I said in a humble voice,
"Miss Priscilla?"

"Well, what is it?" she answered sharply.

"My hands are tied. Would you be kind enough to wipe my
nose for me?"

She consented. I was eighteen years old, a youth, and the
owner of this house, a young man of great wealth and position.
And yet there I stood in a corner wearing a girl's evening frock
of white satin, girls' gloves, girls' silk stockings and high-heeled
shoes. Not only that, but girls' tight satin corsets and frilled
batiste drawers were secreted under my dress. My long hair had
been done up beautifully in a girls' coiffure. I was bound with

my hands behind me, and my ankles chained, and I had to have my nose wiped by an old maid whom a year or two ago I despised. With what strange paradoxes and twists of fate does life provide us!

SECRET TALENTS

By Anonymous

*This memoir is a coming-of-age story set in a Viennese board-
ing school, where young ladies learn about the art of love and
its attendant delights. In this episode, our heroine, at this stage
of her life an actress and, like many of her profession during
that period, hardly loathe to spend an hour or two with a
well-heeled admirer, relates an unusual incident.*

Now I shall tell you of that strange experience I had and
let you judge for yourself just what temptations lay in
wait for a girl.

The night I have in mind, I received a basket of flowers.
Strangely enough I hadn't sung that night, so I couldn't account
for its reception. In the basket, and well-hidden, was a letter.
It was addressed to me. There being no longer any doubt as to
whom it was intended, I opened it. It was a request that I have
dinner with the sender . . .

In the letter it said that he (the writer) occupied the number
two box, and to avoid mistakes he was wearing a yellow flower
in his buttonhole. It also instructed me how to join him outside
the theater. I was to enter a certain carriage that I would find
at the exit, and here I would find him waiting, and here he
would explain his wishes.

I had little time in which to make up my mind. The play was
almost over, and whatever I did I had to do quickly.

Going to the little peephole, through which the players were able to see out without being seen, I searched the box in question, and there he sat. Naturally, with the theater in semidarkness, I couldn't see very well, but with what I could make out, he didn't look very dangerous. Then, too, I was to talk with him in his carriage, and if I didn't care for his proposal I wasn't obliged to go with him. Any way I looked at it, it had promise of a thrilling experience. As was the habit with me, I made up my mind quickly.

I would go—just for the novelty of the thing!

Following his instructions to the letter, I left the theater and entered the carriage, which was waiting at the exit. Sure enough, the gentleman was within and waiting for me.

"You are prompt, my dear," were his first words, "and I am grateful to you. You will find me a gentleman, so you need have no fear of me. Rest assured I shall treat you with every consideration."

"I am sure of that," I answered, by way of starting conversation.

Little, however, was said by either of us as the carriage traversed through the city, and it wasn't until we had entered a very beautiful villa that he made any suggestion as to what I might expect. Indeed, we were seated at table and had partaken of the delicious foods and the splendid wine before he enlightened me.

Then, quite nonchalantly I thought, he told me that he cared nothing whatever for women; that is, he cared nothing for them in a sexual sense, and only for those who appealed strongly to him.

I must have appealed strongly to him, for he went into the business at once. Rising from the table, he stepped to a closet and brought out a white dress. With almost the same motion, he produced a purse and laid it beside the dress.

"In the purse there are one thousand marks," he said, "and

they shall be yours if you will but don this dress and do my bidding. You have nothing whatever to fear from me. I admit my request is a strange one, but since I have given my word that nothing will happen to you that might harm you in any possible way, I will be delighted if you will but assist me, doing your simple part that I might enjoy myself in the only way I can. Will you do this?"

Really, I was thrilled. I had become reconciled to being alone with him; I could see nothing in his manners that might lead me to believe him insane and, in truth, I was beginning to get a real thrill out of it already. Besides, I would have something spicy to tell my friends!

"Very well," I answered. "I promise to go through with it, providing I might rest assured that you will not whip or hit me or molest me in any other way."

He nodded in agreement, then said: "You will find your task simple, indeed. You have but to go into this room"—pointing to one—"and remove all your clothing. Then you are to dress in this costume. You will find slippers and stockings to match the dress in the room, and you will don them. But remember, you are to wear nothing but the dress, slippers, and stockings."

Without further ado, I picked up the dress and entered the room in question, he holding open the door for me and closing it after telling me to return as soon as I had changed.

I heard the door click shut behind me. It being too late to back out now, I hurried out of my clothes. Then, before dropping my last garment, I looked all about, but could find nothing amiss.

There was nothing but a beautiful bedroom, a dresser and chairs and wardrobe, which contained many other garments, to say nothing of an endless assortment of slippers and stockings. Slippers and stockings seemed to be a weakness with the old boy, I thought.

Choosing a pair suitable to my feet, I sat down to pull on the stockings and slippers when a strange feeling that I wanted to make water came over me. This I thought was unduly strange for I had just attended to my wants before leaving the theater just a short hour before. But the feeling persisted. Indeed, it grew on me as I sat there thinking about it, and I began seeking something into which I might pee. There was nothing I might use, however, so I slipped on the dress.

I tried to dismiss the thought from my mind. Turning to the door through which I had entered, I was about to turn the knob, when I was again taken with the necessity of wanting to pee, and the need of freeing my bladder was so pronounced I couldn't see how I was ever going to stand it until I could get out of the house.

Thinking to hurry the matter, I opened the door and entered the room where I had left him. As he had suggested, I acted the dutiful wife. My hands were clasped in front of me and my eyes were downcast, and all in all I must have looked very funny.

Wishing to say something, I asked him why he had chosen me as his wife. He explained that only such a girl as I could appeal to him, and that since I was an actress I could carry out the part as he desired it. And while he was telling me this I squirmed and twisted about, so great was my desire to pee.

Finally, when I thought I could no longer stand it, I told him that it would be impossible for me to continue until I had been allowed to visit the privy, and I will never forget his answer to this!

"No!" he said, looking at me, a stern look on his face. "And do not mention it again! When the proper time comes you may attend to your want, but not before!"

To say that I was frightened would be putting it mildly. Then he handed me a bridal veil, telling me to put it on. This done to his satisfaction, he said: "Now answer all my questions, just as though you were my legal wife. Will you do everything such as a dutiful wife should do?"

"Yes, sir," I answered, somewhat cowed now.

"You will obey me in everything?"

"Yes, sir," I answered, sure now he must be a mad man. My bladder was almost bursting and, my knees pinched together for fear of spilling it all over the expensive Persian rug on which I stood, I awaited his next command. I didn't have long to wait, either.

"Come," he said, leading me into another room. Here, in spite of the outside warmth, a great fire burned on the hearth, and before this lay a great bearskin rug. Then without further ado he lay down upon this rug, his head resting on the head of the thing.

Then he commanded me to come and stand close to his head.

"Closer!" he cried. "That is right. You are now in the right position. In the future, you must dispense with drawers; they will be in the way while you are acting the good wife."

I knew then that he was looking under my dress, and if he wasn't getting a good look at everything it was his fault, for I was without drawers: I wore nothing, as I said, except the dress, slippers, and stockings.

Then, when I thought I could no longer stand it and would surely pee then and there, he said: "Now step astride me!"

With an effort I managed to do his bidding. It was an effort because now I felt as though I was about to burst, so filled was my bladder. Hurrying to do his bidding, that I might get it over with, I moved up so I stood astride his chest, my feet at his shoulders.

"Now squat down," he said. He kept me thus for fully a minute; it was the longest minute I had ever been called upon to endure. I began to suffer in still another way; I found my legs were hurting me dreadfully; they seemed filled with cramps, and my knees ached. He must have noted my suffering, for he said: "Do you still feel that you wish to make water?"

Snatching my dress away so I could see his face, I nodded.

"Then," he said, a strange light in his eyes, "since you are my dutiful wife I command you to do it right where you are!"

I could hardly believe my ears! Was I hearing correctly, or had the man gone completely insane?

"Could it be possible," I thought, "that this man wants me to do this dreadful thing on him?" I recalled having read something about a certain Russian count who, before he could bring himself to have a sexual connection with his mistress, insisted upon her pissing on him! Could it be possible that this man wanted me to do the same thing, and that afterward he would ravish me?

The thought sickened me! It wasn't that I dreaded the thought of doing this supposedly dreadful thing on him; it was the fear that gripped me that I might in another minute be ravished by him. But my fears and dread were not to be taken into consideration; I had already stood for more than I could stand, and even as I squatted there over him I so lost control of myself that the floodgate was forced open, allowing a solid stream of amber fluid to gush and spatter over his shirt-front!

Suddenly I felt thrilled at it all! The fact that he seemed to enjoy this most intimate thing to be done upon him so aroused my lascivious mind that I deliberately arched my hips that I might dash the stream deliberately upon his face! Nor was I alone in these thoughts. At the first contact his arms went about my naked hips and he quite lifted me directly over his open mouth! His mouth glued tightly to my cunt, he was drinking my fluid in great gulps—

And at last I had no more to give; my bladder was empty.

If my desire to make water had passed, my desire to be sucked had not. I had been greatly aroused; the dreadful act of sickening me had forced my unusually lascivious nature to the limit! One of my hands went to the back of his neck; his hair and the back of his collar were drenched, but I cared not for that!

My desire was then to go-off; that it might not have fitted into his scheme of things I cared not; I was burning hot! Moving and twisting about, rubbing my cunt all over his clinging mouth, I drew him tighter and tighter, and then I felt the time rising within me!

I went-off! I saw him smile with his eyes (that being the only part of his face I could see, since the rest was buried in the thick curls), and I realized then that he was enjoying it all and that I hadn't carried my play too far. But the double shock had been far too great for me to stand.

Instead of mounting me as I thought he would, and which I was powerless to prevent, he satisfied himself with simply rolling off of me, and there, his face still between my naked thighs, he contented himself simply by kissing my aching gap. And it was at his initiative that the play ceased.

Rising to his feet, he stood looking down at me; then he did a strange thing. Bending down, he drew my skirt down over my legs, thus shutting out the sight of my nudity. "You had best rise and take care of yourself," he said in a low voice. "You are quite wet."

Almost reluctantly I rose to my feet. "I am wet," I answered, raising my single skirt to well above my waist with an utter disregard that I might be inviting him to further liberties.

But my guardian angel must have been spending her entire time watching over me that night, for the gentleman made not the slightest effort toward molesting me, and I re-entered the bedroom quite as intact as I had first left it.

Here I bathed myself and hastily dressed. It had been a rare novelty to me, but I would feel better about it when I was safe back in my own rooms. He was waiting for me when I came out of the bedroom. I thought he appeared somewhat crest-fallen, and I couldn't help but thrill inwardly at the thought of the strange story I would tell my friends.

Gynecocracy

by Viscount Ladywood

When Julian Robinson, later Viscount Ladywood, shows too much spunk as a lad, his parents ship him off to a secret and very select private school to learn discipline. Under the stern tutelage of Mademoiselle de Chambonnard, Master Julian is forced to learn a series of entertaining and exciting lessons from the demanding headmistress, the staff of the establishment, his three beautiful cousins, and a unique assortment of others associated with this remarkable school. Written with insight and wit, Gynecocracy is Viscount Ladywood's masterful and candid diary of his unusual education.

A sort of mesmeric influence seemed to have crept into me from that intensely feminine garment that had been in such close contact with Mademoiselle's own person and then so long over my head and face as I stood disgraced in my corner. It seemed to have sapped my strength and all my powers of resistance, to have undermined my self-respect, to have rendered me contemptible in my own eyes; in short, to have completely emasculated me. I had felt my virility ebbing away during the hours I had stood with the red thing enveloping my shoulders, touching my eyes and nose and mouth, conscious all the while that it was a woman's petticoat which had been worn, and that a thing so essentially feminine had, willy-nilly, been forced upon me. I had gradually, step by step, to give in to the flood of feminine associations, which rushed upon me,

254

and yield by degrees to the power of woman. I was keenly aware that nothing could save me, that all opposition was useless and hopeless, and I was slowly drifting towards the knowledge that I must sooner or later abandon myself absolutely to it. I stood before Mademoiselle cowed and humiliated, not so much at the prospect of the beating as at the sense of my own helplessness in her hands, because she was feminine and could therefore do with me what she liked. Whatever it was, I knew I had no power left to resist, and trembled at the inevitable acknowledgment of this fact to myself. She seemed the embodiment of triumphant womanhood as I was hustled into her presence, shaken and pulled about by another woman, to be whipped by her.

As I stood before Mademoiselle, my hands still tied, my ears red and tingling from Elise's rough usage, panting and out of breath, my back sore from the rude thumps of Elise's knees, my courage gave way and my eyes filled with tears, which the poignant sense of my abasement caused to overflow. I could only hold my head and yield in silent resignation and despair.

Let not the reader, however, imagine that I was subdued at once. No, there was many a reaction: a constant revolt of all my manhood that required many severe lessons to quell and conquer finally. But I must confess that as time went on, my disgust lessened, these revolts were divided by longer intervals, and at last I became a wretched petticoat-slave.

Mademoiselle looked on haughtily. Her form dilated and expanded with the sense, so agreeable to a woman, of power over something male. She looked like a magnificent bird of prey, a regal and feminine eagle about to swoop upon her victim. She stood erect, her head thrown back, consciously displaying her well-developed bust and elegant figure, her air of determination and pretty willfulness much enhancing her charms. There was something arch about her manner as she quizzed me upon my first introduction to a lady's bedroom. She asked me, as she significantly handled a light, long, and elastic birch, how I liked the prospect of my first assignation. She remarked that I had been introduced in all due form by her maid, to whom she proceeded to give a guinea out of my pocket money (which Mademoiselle had charge of) in recognition of her services. Mademoiselle produced a sovereign and a shilling and gave them to Elise before my eyes, to my intense and ill-concealed annoyance, which increased her merriment, and Elise thanked me with mock politeness and gratitude.

Mademoiselle promised me by way of consolation that the maid should be sent out and that consequently I should have the advantage of an entirely private *tête-à-tête* with her, and inquired whether I was not rejoiced at my good fortune? I do not know what it was, but something or other in these words, and what they suggested, quite changed my mood, and I let my eyes rest on her affectionately and admiringly, and said that I indeed appreciated the favor; a remark that brought me a sound slap on the face. Again disconcerted, I determined that nothing should allow me to be made a further fool of, and resolved not to utter another word.

The room was a large one and very handsomely furnished. The extremely pretty bed stood under a heavy silk canopy across the angle of the room farthest from the fireplace, the canopy suspended from the ceiling and the carved oak bedstead standing clear of the walls. There were several quaint cozy-looking chairs about, and bowls of spring flowers. Mademoiselle stood between me and the light, tall and graceful in her severely simple *mousseline de laine* dress, displaying her womanly figure to the fullest advantage. As I contemplated her in my wretched condition, I felt yet more abjectly humiliated. A novel sensation of awkwardness again replaced my habitual self-possession, an inveterate stupidity my ordinary sprightliness and vivacity. There I stood, a great boy, trussed like a fowl, with nothing to conceal my bare legs but a shirt, which did not reach to my knees.

Mademoiselle ordered Elise to place a long carved bench of black oak, about a foot wide, in the middle of the room, and to put upon it a feather bolster which Elise, by means of tapes, tied to the bench. I was then compelled to stand across one end while Elise strapped my ankles close together underneath and then left the room. Mademoiselle went to the door, shut and locked it, and then turned full upon me. I could not but note as I trembled how her whole form glowed with smiling and triumphant satisfaction. She walked deliberately up to me, lifted my skirt up behind, and, to my intense shame, intently contemplated my back for some seconds; then, still holding up this undergarment and standing a little way off, she took up the birch and gave me some stinging lashes with it. I had never felt anything like it before. I had no idea that it would hurt one-tenth as much as it did, and was compelled to cry out.

Mademoiselle then, to my horror, unbuttoned my waistcoat and lifted my shirt with both hands high up in front. I could not move. I was speechless as she stood facing me and examining my most secret possessions over which and along the front of she several times passed her dimpled hand. Then she let the shirt fall, untied my elbows, and taking up a lady's jeweled riding whip, she remarked that I should be flogged naked. I hesitated and fumbled. Looking round, she gave me a touch of the whip on my bare legs. If the birch smarted, that vicious little thing bit like fury. I yelled and clapped my hands to my legs, but only to get them lashed also. She went on until, in desperation, I tore off my jacket and waistcoat.

"Now your shirt! Quick!"

Up went the whip, her eyes sparkling savagely. This time, without an instant's hesitation, and without thinking about it,

I whipped off my shirt more quickly than ever I had done before. And there I was, perfectly naked before her, red and overwhelmed with shame and smarting with pain. She leisurely regarded me, evidently intending not to spare me a single pang. She moved her hand along my back and shoulders, remarking that she thought the whip would mark my skin easily, and, by way of experiment, she gave me several more smart cuts with it on various parts of my body, each stroke causing me intense anguish. I cried out, and implored her to desist; but she merely gloated the more over my torture.

"Now," she at length said, "your bottom must be put in a proper position for me to punish."

"Oh, Mademoiselle, forgive me! Oh, I am sorry for my disobedience and folly! Do forgive me!"

"I never forgive! Lie down on your face!"

I saw there was nothing for it but compliance; so, with a sigh like a gasp of despair, I obeyed her. She placed her hand on the back of my head and pressed it into the bolster. The wide bench separated my thighs, pressing my most sensitive parts cruelly. She fixed a strap round my neck and passed it under the bench, placed another round the seat and my waist, and lastly fastened my hands together underneath the bench. My posture and the soft bolster (which soon became pleasantly warm) gave me a certain voluptuous feeling that was soon, however, to be dispelled by my sufferings.

"Now we shall see whether a girl can properly punish a boy's bottom!" How she dwelt on the shameful word! "Whether a youth is or is not to be subject to feminine discipline and rule and to his governess." And, putting her hand between my legs, she caught hold of what I was ashamed she should know I possessed, and pulled it about until I confessed to myself that I was her slave, body and soul. Then, for the first time, was revealed to me the secret source whence woman's power springs. A keen sense of the difference of sex was communicated to me through her taper fingers. Her skirts caused me an electric shock each time they touched me. The feminine characteristics of her form as she stood over me became indelibly stamped upon my being, and acquired for her and for the rest of her sex an absolute dominion from that moment over me. A look or the rustle of a petticoat is enough for me now. At either, I tremble.

This sway was established and emphasized by the cruel punishment of the most secret portions of my body that I then underwent at her hands.

Regularly and deliberately was the birching, the methodical administration of which I could not interrupt. I protested and swore; but I had to learn how cruelly women can punish—how relentlessly they slake their vengeance—what a lust they have to satisfy, when they have a male at their mercy, to deal unmitigated torture over him, how they exercise that dominion over him which is so real, although often unacknowledged. Men are not subject to these motives and never punish so cruelly as women.

Only once was my torture stayed. Mademoiselle had flogged me from my right side and from my left. My sobs had given place to screams and yells, but Mademoiselle said she should insist on my taking punishment quietly, at which threat I gave a delirious laugh. She calmly opened a drawer, and took out a plum-shaped piece of wood with a leather loop at its thickest end, through which loop she slipped one of her scented handkerchiefs. Then she forced the plug into my mouth, and tied the ends of the handkerchief tightly behind my neck. Perfectly indifferent to my sufferings, she resumed the punishment, merely remarking that I should have ten minutes more of it for making the gagging necessary.

When the ten minutes had expired, there came an interval

when the strokes, which fallen with the even regularity and swing of a pendulum, the swing of which I had ascertained to the fraction of a second, ceased. I hoped it was over. I could not express the hope in words, so I groaned. Mademoiselle had been whipping me across both ways. She now came to the top of the bench at my right, daintily lifted her skirts, and put her right leg across me. Then, almost sitting upon my neck and smothering me with her petticoats, the back of which fell to the floor over my head, she proceeded to flog me lengthwise. She was looking down my back, and I knew that behind me the wardrobe mirror reflected my open thighs. Although the strap had been loosened, I could scarcely move my head; when I tried to do so, however, she pressed me more closely. I can give no idea of what I felt at my novel posture underneath a young woman. She now struck lengthwise, more slowly but more viciously; the strokes cut like hot iron, and as the pliant ends of the birch hit what lay between my thighs, I felt I was being murdered. The anguish was maddening, and if I recollected what she could see by lifting her eyes to the glass, it was with utter recklessness to the exposure.

"There, Master Julian, that's enough for the first time. I think I have whipped you pretty severely. You will not care to set me at defiance again," she complacently remarked, throwing herself into a great saddleback easy chair, apparently somewhat exhausted.

I lay utterly prostrate, powerless to speak even had I not been gagged; all my strength was gone, and I smarted as though I had been scared with red hot wires. Presently she unstrapped and ungagged me. I could scarcely move. I was in a cataleptic or comatose state and only semi-conscious.

She resumed her seat and bade me kneel at her feet. I obeyed mechanically. Had she bade me walk into a fire, I think I should have done so. I was so thoroughly exhausted that my head sank upon her lap and my tears flowed softly, but soon I began to feel better. She then bade me kiss her hands and the remains of the rod, and thank her humbly, but sincerely, for whipping me. Whatever she ordered I at once obeyed, deprived altogether of my own volition. She made me stoop down and kiss her feet and legs; for one delicious moment she held my head in soft imprisonment between her thighs. Beside myself from the effect of the pain, I am astonished still at the recollection of how my feelings towards Mademoiselle then underwent a most unreasonable but complete alteration. I loved her as violently as I had detested her before. I loved her because of her cruelty and became suddenly enthralled by a strong and anxious desire to press and fondle her. I worshipped the very ground on which she walked.

BEATRICE
by Patrick Hendon

After her marriage fails, a young woman returns to the bosom of her family, where, far from the city, she encounters beautiful, gentle lovemaking, even with her own father and her sister, Caroline. Richard Manton has rightly praised this novel for its creation of a "haunting evanescent dream of erotic excitement" and it is true that its eroticism is slow to build, almost muted. As lyrical as a waking dream, Beatrice evokes Edwardian decadence through a series of soft-focus chapters that pass no judgment on the characters' activities.

The sun was warm when I awoke. The curtains had been drawn back, the lamps removed. Evidently I had slept heavily. Jenny roused me, smiling from the doorway where she stood. The gong below sounded for breakfast.

"You are late," she said. She wore a long black skirt, the waist drawn in tight. Her blouse was white, the buttons of pearl. Beneath the silk of her blouse, her breasts loomed perkily. A perking of nipples. They indented the material. Like a child late for school, I was hustled into the bathroom and out again.

"I have no dress to wear," I said. Jenny smacked my hand.

"You are late," she repeated. The smell of sizzling bacon came to us. I was hungry. My mouth watered. The wardrobe doors were opened quickly. A thin wool dress of light brown color, rust color, was handed to me. "Nothing beneath except your stockings," Jenny said. She palmed my bottom and my breasts as I raised my nightdress. The sensation was pleasant. The dress cascaded over my shoulders and was worked tightly down over my curves. It was as if I were naked. I was preferred in boots today, Jenny said—black lace-up ones that came to my knees. The heels were high. I feared to fall down the stairs. I told her.

"Nonsense," Jenny said. "Brush your hair quickly. Show me your teeth. Are they clean now?"

I was taken down. Approaching the dining room, we walked more slowly. My legs felt longer in the boots, the high heels. My aunt and uncle and Caroline were already seated. Silver tureens stood on the massive sideboard. Caroline looked up at me quickly and then attended to her bacon. We ate in silence as if some doom were pending. Neither my aunt nor uncle spoke, even to one another. It was a penance, perhaps. I ate voraciously but delicately. The bloom of health was upon me. The kidneys and mushrooms were delicious. The maids who served me were young and pretty. I liked them. They avoided my eyes. They had learned their learning.

With every movement of Jenny's body, her breasts moved their nipples beneath her blouse. Beneath the tablecloth, my uncle's hand stole onto her thigh. She wore garters that ridged themselves slightly through her skirt. He caressed them. His palm soothed from one leg to the other. Jenny parted her legs beneath her skirt and smiled. I wanted to suck the tip of her tongue.

At a nod from my uncle, we were dismissed. Caroline and I rose together and wandered into the drawing room. We were lost in our foundness. We held hands. Our fingers whispered together. In a moment, from a side entrance, my uncle appeared in the garden. A carriage had arrived, it seemed, but the visitors came not to the front of the house. They skirted the side and appeared where my uncle stood.

The woman he greeted was in her early thirties. I had a

vagueness of seeing her before. Her flowered hat was large, of pale straw with a wide brim. She wore white kid gloves to her elbows. Were they my gloves? I had left mine in the sea at night. The fishes had nibbled at them. She was beautiful, elegant. Her dress was of white and blue, the collar frilled. Pearls glinted around the neck. Beside her came a servant neatly dressed in black with velour lapels on his jacket. He had an air of insolent subservience.

"She is beautiful," I said to Caroline. "Do you know who she is?"

Jenny's voice sounded behind us. "What are you doing?" she asked in a sharp tone. A tone that scratched.

"I was asking," I answered.

Caroline moved. Her palm was moist in mine. "I know her. She is Katherine Hayton—an actress. We have seen her at the Adelphi," she said. Her eyes were saucers as she received Jenny's stare.

"You were not told to hold lunch," Jenny said. She jerked her head at me and said, "Come, Beatrice, come."

Forlorn, I relinquished Caroline's hand. Our own house was yet an ocean away. In the bedrooms, women with bronzed skins and supple hips were lying. They would wear my clothes and steal my jewelry.

Jenny led me down the hall. To my astonishment, we entered the linen room. It smelled of starch and nothing. "You must learn—you must both learn, Beatrice. Do you not know?"

I blinked. I did not know who I was. Father had lied, perhaps. He had not gone to Madras. He was with the women in the rooms. They would be French. Their lips would taste of curry. There would be musk between their thighs. I said yes to Jenny. My voice said yes. My hands were at my sides.

"Kneel before me, Beatrice."

I did. My head was bowed, my hands clasped together. I

prayed for goodness. Edward's mother used to undress with her door half-open. We could see her as we went past. Her bottom was big. I told Edward that she should close the door. He smiled. His eyes were small and neat. Like his *pine* when it was not stiff.

"Kiss my thighs," Jenny said. She raised her skirt, gathering up the folds. I was blind. A milkiness, a perfume. Her drawers were split both back and front. It was the fashion then. Women could attend to their natural functions without removing them. In my mother's early days, women had never worn drawers.

The curls of her slit, her loveslot, honeypot, were framed by the white linen. My palms sought the back of her thighs. Her knees bent slightly. I could feel her smile. My tongue licked out, sweeping around the taut tight tops of her black stockings. Her skin—white like my white. She tasted of musk and perfume and the scents of flowers. My lips splurged against her thighs.

"Ah, you lick! Like a little doggy, you lick," Jenny laughed. After a moment or two, she pushed me away with her knees. "It is too soon," she said. I wanted to cry, but she would not let me. I was brought to my feet even as the door opened and Jenny rearranged her dress. My aunt led Caroline in and frowned a little at Jenny, as I thought. The window of the linen room was set high up at the other end from us. The light was morning soft. Caroline wore, as I did, a woolen dress of fine skein.

"You will see to them, Jenny," my aunt said. From our distance, I heard my uncle and Katherine enter the house. There was a tinkling of glasses, of laughter. The door closed, leaving the three of us alone.

"Remove your dresses," Jenny said. My hands went to the buttons of mine, but Caroline hesitated. Jenny smacked her, and she squealed. "Quickly!" Jenny snapped. We stood naked except for our stockings and boots.

Jenny drew us together, face to face, thighs to thighs. From a drawer, she took cords and bound us tightly together: ankles, thighs, waists. We could not move. Our cheeks pressed close. Placing her hands beneath Caroline's bottom, she urged us slowly into a corner. I stood with my back to the meeting of the walls. Caroline's breath flowed over my breath.

"Your bodies merge well together," Jenny said. "Are your breasts touching fully? Move your breasts. Your nipples must touch."

"Yes," I said, "yes, Jenny." Our nipples were like bell pushes together. Mine grew and tingled. Caroline's grew. Her toes curled over mine.

"Please, don't," Caroline whispered. I knew that she wasn't speaking to me, but in her mind speaking. I moved my lips against her ear. Jenny had gone.

"You like it," I said. I wanted to make her happy. I coaxed her. She had had the cane. Was it nice? "Do you like it?" I asked. I made my voice sound as if we were going on a holiday. If she liked it, we would be happy.

"I don't know," Caroline said. Her voice was smudged. Our bellies were silky together. I could feel her slit: warm, pulsing. It was nice standing still. I moved my mouth very slowly from her ear to her cheek. I felt her quiver. Had she sucked his cock? I would not ask yet. I would ask later. The tip of my tongue traced the fullness of her lower lip, the Cupid curve. Caroline moved her face away. Her cheeks burned. Our nipples were thorns, entangled.

"Do not!" she choked.

"Jenny will come," I said. Caroline moved her mouth back to mine. The bulbous fullness of her breasts against mine excited me. Our mouths were soft in their seeking. I sought her tongue with my tongue. It retreated, curling in its cave curling. Sipping at her lips, I brought it to emerge. The thrill made us quiver. Our nipples moved, implored. My belly pressed in tighter to hers.

The door swung open all of a sudden. It was Jenny. She scolded us and said we had been kissing. Working her hand between us, she felt our lovemouths, secretive between our thighs. They were moist. Her hand retracted. Her fingers sought our bottoms.

"You must practice—you must love one another. Caroline, put your tongue in her mouth."

We swayed. Caroline's tongue was small, urgent, pointed in its flickering. Hidden by our lips, our tongues licked. It was a secret. I wanted.

"Open your mouths—let me see your tongues," Jenny commanded. We obeyed.

"Half an hour," Jenny said. She moved to the door and we were alone again. Birds sprinkled their songs among the leaves outside. I was happy. The richness of our bodies flesh to flesh was sweet. Caroline's eyelashes fluttered and tickled against mine. I could feel her belly rippling.

Our tongues like warm snakes worked together. Our thighs trembled. The ridged tops of our stockings rubbed.

Perhaps the door would remain closed forever.

Our minds whispered together like people in caves.

SHADES OF SINGAPORE
by Angus Balfour

In this unusual and provocative fictional memoir, Sister Sarah Balfour describes her experiences in the pre-war South African court system. Her job and her good fortune lay in examining young women and girls prior to their receiving imposed punishments, which consisted of a caning or strapping while fastened nude to the whipping bench. The following excerpt details the first caning she ever witnessed.

Although the first punishment was sixty-seven years ago, and my experience spanned nearly thirty-seven years, in which I was involved in literally thousands of whippings, there are many, especially the earlier ones, when I was witnessing judicial whippings for the first time, which stand out in my mind. Naturally, amongst these was the very first caning I ever attended.

I seemed to sit in that punishment chamber for an eternity, awaiting the knock upon the door, which would herald the first victim. No interview or examination result had ever caused me such anxiety, as I awaited with butterflies swarming in my stomach. Anyone could have been excused for believing that the policewoman would be coming through that door to give me the thrashing.

At last the knock came, and a very pretty brunette was pushed inside the open door, which was quickly re-closed and then locked by a stern policewoman in her forties. The girl had been crying, with tears still wet upon her face. The police-woman ordered her to strip off all her clothes. The girl began to cry and sniffle again, and the policewoman curtly repeated the order, emphasizing that if the girl didn't comply immediately, assistance would be brought in to prepare her, and extra strokes would be laid upon her bottom for her resistance.

The girl was dressed very primly in a long suit consisting of skirt, bodice, and jacket. She was wearing her hair up, with a large picture hat, obviously to impress the Court. The clothes began to be discarded and neatly laid upon the solitary chair, the one I had been sitting upon. I watched with great anticipation.

In my job, I had already seen many young women, and men, naked, and had performed intimate examinations, but all as a mere clinical exercise. Seeing this, and subsequent attractive young women, stripping against their wills, and then fastening them down for a thorough thrashing, was something else entirely. The buttocks became an exciting spectacle. Their exposure was linked with intimacy. There was something ritualistic and sacrificial about it that has excited human lust for centuries. Later, when I began to actually participate in the infliction of the punishment, the feeling of power was very exhilarating. The satisfaction of administering true justice was carried out with great willingness, enthusiasm, and fervor on my part, as I uncompromisingly thrashed the screaming offender with a deep sense of purpose and determination.

But back to the case at hand.

After her well-laced petticoat had been removed, the girl's underclothes consisted of black stockings, gartered just above the knee; loose drawers tied at the waist and gathered with further ribbon ties at about mid-thigh; and a chemise, also with a ribbon tie about the neck.

When left with these last two garments only, she obviously

didn't know which one to remove first. Both were going to reveal something she didn't want to show. A quick, "I'm waiting," from the policewoman saw the chemise urgently pulled over her head, exposing very full breasts, and a very red flushed face once the chemise had cleared her head. Next the drawers were untied and slowly eased down her thighs. With her back to us, I had a perfect view of her bottom as at last it tantalizingly came into view, and I began to breathe very hard indeed.

She was ordered to turn around and approach the Sister, and timidly came towards me. I gave her a quick examination, eager to get on with her punishment, and told her to lean forward against the chair. I then felt her bottom, and was satisfied it could have taken much more than the measly ten strokes to which she had been sentenced for shoplifting.

The policewoman came over, and pulling the pins from the girl's hair, told her, "We are not whipping a young woman, but are about to flog a naughty girl's bare bottom with the cane. You will certainly be acting the part of the girl very well with your screams, so you should also look the part." The girl's hair fell loose about her shoulders.

Taking an arm each, we marched the naked girl across to the whipping bench. She offered no resistance until we were about to fasten the straps around her wrists. She suddenly made to get up, but obviously thought better of it and meekly allowed us to shackle her. Then, with the belt across her waist, she was ready for her punishment.

I remembered all my newfound young policewomen friends had told me of the joys of seeing a bare bottom performing under a well-deserved punishment. Unbelievably, now here was my own opportunity to witness it.

I took up a position standing directly behind our well-secured young prisoner. This was a vantage point later used by many policewomen when I was the one wielding the cane.

It was a beautiful bottom, lying there utterly defenseless. The twin hillocks ivory white, perfectly bent across the end of the whipping bench to show them at their wondrous best, seemed to invite punishment. I don't think I have ever been as excited in my life as I was when viewing this exquisite intimacy, so smooth and feminine.

The delinquent's bosom was probably no fuller and appealing than some of the bottoms of girls I had seen whilst at boarding school myself. But it was the fact that this was a judicial caning, and the offender's bottom was rendered so helpless to receive it, which caused such feelings of lust. I thrilled to watch the squirming buttocks, and was eager and yearning to see the policewoman apply the cane to them, but at the same time wanted to continue to admire such intimate beauty, unwillingly offered by the now-sorrowful girl.

The punisher began tapping the cane across the cringing girl's buttocks, and the shapely young bottom trembled and twitched to the accompaniment of little gasps and whimpers. The policewoman certainly knew how to get the most out of the situation.

Slowly she raised the cane high above her head. The gasps and whimpers stopped, but the awaiting buttocks quivered all the more violently. Rocking forward onto her toes, the policewoman brought the cane down with full force. There was a fearful rush of air as it slashed its way downward. The sound was much louder than the usual noise of the cane when any of our teachers had been using it upon a naughty girl at school, and this girl was no older than some I had seen being thrashed.

Her trembling bottom shuddered and shook all the more. There was a loud crack as the cane landed on it again. The cane seemed to bounce off the twin jellied mounds of the girl's bottom, which immediately leapt upwards. She let out a loud gasp of anguish.

Again the cane was raised, and the girl began begging and pleading for mercy. I found myself saying under my breath, "You deserve all you are going to get, you little thief." I just wanted to see that bottom thrashed and thrashed. It was the most stimulating sight imaginable.

The welt from the first stroke was slowly reddening and was joined by a second, laid slightly lower across the girl's bottom. This time the girl let out a loud scream, then burst into tears, only to choke and splutter on her supplications.

Taking her time between each stroke, and completely unaffected by the screams, supplications, and tearful sobbing of the punished girl, the policewoman efficiently laid a pattern of welts across the wildly kicking and struggling offender's bottom.

I moved about, admiring the proceedings from various angles. It was the most exciting spectacle I had ever witnessed. The girl pulled and tugged at the restraints around her wrists, but there was no way she could break their hold or hope to slip out of it. Her hips twisted one way and then the other, but she couldn't take her bottom from the path of the relentless cane.

Kicking legs added a new dimension to corporal punishment as far as I was concerned. No girl had ever kicked her legs when under punishment at school. For one thing, although she had much of her weight upon her hands or elbows, she would be standing in a bent and leaning position for her punishment.

The girl's legs kicked more frantically at every stroke, shooting out in all directions. As exciting as it was to see her total abandon, I always looked forward to seeing her legs eventually fall to the floor. It was then that I got my best view of her lovely striped bottom, and I also knew that the next blistering stroke would soon be delivered.

I kept careful count of the strokes being applied to the girl's bottom, and was rather sorry when I got to nine. With only one stroke remaining, this scintillating performance was almost over. I wished it could have gone on for much longer.

The policewoman seemed to hesitate over the last stroke even longer than normal. Obviously she also was of the same opinion that she would have liked the caning to go on. She pursed her lips and let the girl have the last of her strokes. This one brought the shrillest scream of all, and the distressed antics from the fastened girl's body perfectly matched the shriek.

Having concluded the punishment, the policewoman lay her hand on the girl's bottom: "Personally, I think you got off far too lightly, but at least next time you have itchy fingers you might remember this smarting bottom of yours, and your screams, and change your mind about stealing."

The sobbing girl retorted: "I'll never do it, again, Madam. I promise I'll never do it again. Honestly."

The policewoman was conversational though authoritative: "Well, my girl, just as long as you remember what will happen to you if you do." Then she added in a sober tone: "It's a nice hot bottom you've got. Here, Sister, come and feel this. You could just about roast chestnuts on her bottom."

It was now my turn to feel that lovely whipped bottom, and the heat radiating from it. The buttocks squirmed as I put my hand to them. The purple welts now stood up in pencil-thick ridges across her very red bottom. Caressingly, I ran the back of my fingernail along one of the welts. The girl winced, but I wasn't hurting her. I just wanted to test the texture of the tortured skin.

Looking at her punished bottom, and feeling the ridged weals, I knew that the girl would be lying upon her tummy that night. I knew from personal experience that her bottom would be throbbing something awful. I had once received a caning of similar severity from our biology teacher.

I can clearly remember both the girl's face, and the face of the policewoman who had so determinedly thrashed her. I had watched in utter fascination as the screaming girl struggled in her fastenings, whilst the stripes were laid so neatly across her quivering bottom.

Now, as I was examining the whimpering girl after her ordeal, I couldn't feel any sympathy for her: only envy for the policewoman who had had the great pleasure of whipping this attractive girl's bare bottom. I decided there and then that if there were any way possible to administer any of the strokes myself, I would jump at the chance.

THE CAPTIVE

By Anonymous

When a wealthy English rake attempts to make advances to the beautiful twenty-year-old debutante Caroline Martin, she haughtily repels him. As revenge, he pays a white slavery ring to have Caroline abducted and spirited away to the remote Atlas Mountains of Morocco. There the mistress of the ring and her sinister assistant, Jason Vanwell, begin Caroline's education—an education designed to break her will and prepare her for her mentor.

PERSONAL NARRATIVE OF JASON VANWELL

I heard a timid knock at my door, and I bade her enter.

She was still naked, apart from a pair of long black nylon hose and fine black pumps, the only clothes—if one can call them that—which I'd allowed her to put on. Impeccably made up, with her hair neatly combed, as ordered under penalty of sanctions. A little pale, her eyes violet-circled, her nervous hands betraying her anguish. Her lovely naked titties, rising and falling quickly, seemed to offer out their rosy points—involuntarily, needless to say!

I pretended that I hardly noticed her, and made a simple gesture toward the little bench placed near my armchair. With a fearful air, she seated herself, her thighs tightly squeezed together, her arms over her bosom to hide those splendid titties of hers.

I smiled with amusement but said nothing, continuing to smoke by cigarette and read the book I held in my hand. Finally I decided to hurl my thunderbolt, and turning towards her, stared her straight in the eyes, inwardly enchanted to see the fear that leaped into them.

I said, "You're not at a tea party in the vicarage, Caroline. So it's useless for you to sit like that, with your arms crossed in that unaesthetic way, your legs pressed together like a holy virgin. You must learn to sit down in a suitable fashion in my presence. Now stand up! Good . . . now, you're going to sit down, as every slave must do before her master. Now sit down . . . very straight . . . hands crossed behind your neck, arms well spread on each side, so as to stick out those lovely little titties you've no reason to hide. Come now, better than that— stick out your titties! Good . . . now open your legs!"

A shiver that announced imminent tears passed over her pale face, but after a few seconds' hesitation, her knees slightly opened.

"Open them! Spread them better than that," I dryly scolded. "Perhaps you'd prefer to have me take the switch and incite you to livelier obedience?"

Her lips began to tremble, but she widely opened her legs, revealing the secret of her cunt, which I knew she would have longed to hide from the gaze I fixed on it.

"Now that's better," I smilingly declared. "But so it will be perfect, sit on the edge of the bench and push out your darling little cunt!"

She could not suppress another sob, but squirmed forward as I'd ordered, and arched out that adorable little quim of hers.

I felt passion rise in my prick. As I was completely naked under a cashmere robe, I should have every license, when the whim took me, to exhibit my big prick to modest little Caroline. For the time being, I leaned toward her, and I caressed very delicately the fawn-hued moss of her armpits, her titties palpitating to the quickened rhythm of her breathing, her belly, which tensed under my fingers, and then the curly fur of her cunt, whose yawning lips no longer concealed the inside of a lovely hole, bright pink and sweet to fuck!

"You're very lovely and exciting, Caroline," I said, tickling her clitoris, which made her start. I stared at her a moment without a word; then, raising my hand, I slapped her twice, first her right cheek, then the left, wrenching a terrified cry from her.

"No! Master! Master!" she cried shrilly.

"Good! Try to continue to call me thus. Besides, to refresh your memory in case you don't, I've the proper stimulant," I told her, reaching behind me and bringing out a superb martinet with an ebony handle and long green leather thongs. I saw anguish and terror mount in her beautiful tear-filled eyes, and I felt my prick lift heavily in its savoring joy.

"Caroline, we're going to proceed to the first stage of your education as a slave. I'm going to teach you certain words and expressions that will be necessary for you to know, so as to employ them at the opportune time. Perhaps you may even already know some of them, but we'll find out. However, I must warn you once and for all that a slave must not, must never, lie to her master. It is an unpardonable fault that is very severely punished. Now then, consider yourself fairly warned."

I then pointed a finger toward her jutting bosom and asked, "Do you know what one calls those lovely things?"

"I-I—don't know," she stammered, red with confusion.

"They're named titties, or bubbies," I said calmly. "And now, tell me what they're called."

"Ah—er—I—m-my—t-titties—my—b-b-ubbies." Her face was as red as a tomato.

Without hesitation, I lifted my arm and slashed the thongs

of the martinet over those lovely globes, which seemed to dance under the clinging kiss of the thongs, while she fell backwards, shrieking with agony, clutching her bosom. Long livid streaks encircled those darling tittles, ornamenting them magnificently to my taste.

I pointed the martinet at her. "Good. Now, we'll proceed the same way for the other parts of your charming nakedness. The place which the Countess and I have already occupied ourselves a good deal with you is called the ass. But you knew that, didn't you?"

"Yes . . . yes . . . m . . . m . . . master."

"Then say it!"

"It is . . . my . . . my ass . . . m . . . master . . . my . . . a . . . ass," Caroline said, beginning to cry.

"Yes, my beautiful miss, it's your ass, your lovely girlish ass, to which I reserve many a surprise, I promise you. But that isn't all. That lovely ass is composed of two beautiful buttocks, and when one spreads them open, these buttocks, what does one see?"

"I—I d . . . don't know . . ."

With a violent backhand twist of my wrist, I furiously whipped her titties. A frenzied shriek tore from Caroline, who again flung herself, crying and sobbing, on the rug.

"Back in your seat, back, at once!" I cried, slashing the cruel thongs right against her tender satiny belly.

Caroline leaped wildly to her place, uttering strident cries, and painfully resumed her seat, thighs open, hands behind her neck.

I examined her titties, which had begun to redden and swell where the leather thongs had traced dark pink striata. I took her nipples between the thumb and forefinger of each hand and I squeezed them with all my might as I pulled on them at the same time.

Under the torture, Caroline began to totter and, leaving her position, she gripped my wrists to try and release those wounded tidbits, uttering clamorous shrieks.

"Answer me," I roared. "What do they call what's between your buttocks?"

Choking with agony, Caroline uttered unintelligible cries, and finally managed to articulate: "Aaagghh . . . no . . . noooooo . . . ooooggghhh . . . aaaanus . . . m . . . my aaanus!"

"Little bitch," I said, releasing her. "Take the position at once. You see, you knew it, didn't you? I warned you not to lie to me."

"Oooh . . . ooooh," she sobbed, enough to move a stone statue—but not myself, I assure you! "P—pardon . . . pardon . . . m . . . master . . . but don't hurt me so . . . oooh . . . oooohhh . . . my b . . . breasts . . . ohh, my breasts!"

"No pity for you if you lie again," I warned as I took up my martinet. "Repeat it now!"

"M—my anus, master," she groaned, then began to sob hysterically.

"Yes, yes, dear Caroline, it's your anus. Your bunghole . . . your asshole . . . and to that dainty asshole of yours I reserve a special treatment all my own. It's a particularly sensitive spot, quite susceptible to be made use of in training a disobedient girl like you. Do you know what one can do to a woman's anus?"

"Nooo, m . . . master, I—I swear it—"

"I believe you this time, dear Caroline, for these are things which well brought up young ladies like you scarcely have occasion to learn, or at least to discuss. That is why I'm going to teach you, so you may be clarified on what awaits you."

I let this sink in for a moment, then pursued: "First, from the viewpoint of punishment, one can bury various stretching objects in the anus, or whip your bunghole with the aid of a special lash made of rubber, which, I must confess to you, is extremely painful. Or again, in case of refusal to obey, thrust in a cotton tampon soaked in hot eau de cologne, a punishment that causes much suffering."

Caroline stared at me, her mouth gaping with terror, but without taking note of her frightened stupor, I jubilantly continued: "However, before all else, your asshole, lovely slave, is made to be buggered. By that I mean for a man, the master, to bury his full prick into it and take his full joy within its dainty depths!"

At this, Caroline couldn't hold back an exclamation full of horror: "Oooh! No, no!" she protested in a suffocating voice. "Oooooh! Why—why do you tell me such horrible things? N . . . no . . . no, I beg you . . . I beg you, sir!"

"Oh, but yes indeed, lovely miss! One day you will be bottomfucked, yes, buggered, and I warn you that generally it hurts . . . a good deal, especially if the slave is buggered as a punishment." I chuckled as she shrank from me. Then I said, "Think now," and I opened my robe to expose my enormous prong standing up like a mule's cock, "think now, Caroline, what you'll feel when this huge thing buries itself pitilessly in your tight, sensitive asshole. Sincerely, I've almost pity for you, and yet, you must receive it all . . . entirely, up to here . . ." At this, I pointed to my heavy balls.

But this time, it was truly too much for her offended modesty and for her pride as a young lady accustomed to the respect and adulation of her admirers.

"Oh, you ignoble brute! How dare you say such things to a young girl? You're low, a shameless creature—oh, I detest you, I hate you!" She burst into sobs and despairing cries.

To tell the truth, I had expected that, for I had purposely used crude, obscene words to excite her disgust. I sprang up and, gripping her by the hair, dragged her head violently back and, with all my might, I began to lash her titties, belly, thighs, and arms, when these latter tried to protect the vulnerable and most tempting portions of her delectable anatomy.

My room was filled with the clamor of her suffering and terror; and the more she cried out, wept and complained, the more it excited me and the more I whipped her, till her titties jiggled from one side to the other under the terrible lashes of the martinet, which I pitilessly applied against their round jutting curves, thrilling with delicious joy to cause her such agony that, at the same time, struck home at her prudery.

The correction was so severe that suddenly she went limp in my arms, and I saw that she had fainted. For I'd forgotten to give her a fortifying injection which would have prevented her losing consciousness under the mounting threshold of the pain I so joyously bestowed upon her.

My prick was on fire and agonized me, so violently had I been roused to a full hard-on, but I was quite able to restrain myself and occupy myself with my victim as had to be done before taking my pleasure with her. I promised myself that pleasure for later . . . in the afternoon. Till then, I preferred to remain in full erection so I might better train my beautiful pupil, for I was far from having finished with her.

For the moment, I gave her a stimulant to sustain her and avoid a new fainting spell. Then, when trembling with terror and half-choked by her sobs, she had satisfactorily come to, I sermonized her in a cross voice while she timidly moved her trembling hands over her poor reddened and streaked titties, marked by the vigorous lashing I'd inflicted on them.

"Filthy little bitch! Is that the way you profit from my lessons? Ah, you rebuff me! So, you call me filthy and low, I, your trainer! Very well, my charming one, I know what has to be done. This evening, I'll lock you up in the Cage of Silver, and not for an hour, nor for even four or five, but for all night long! That will teach you, I wager!"

Only her despairing plaints answered my pronunciation, which reaction, to be sure, I quite ignored. "And now," I continued, "we shall pursue our lesson, but I seriously recommend that you don't try that little comedy again, or you'll have earned yourself a visit to the Room of Punishments."

I glared at her, smiled to see her shrink back, and then resumed: "For now, it's necessary that you learn the art and manner of exhibiting your charms when your master will order you to do so. You'll begin by kneeling and by presenting me with your lovely naked ass!"

"Ooooh! No—n—nooo—oh pl—please," she begged me, clasping her hands and lifting them toward me as in prayer.

I bent over her and, terribly roused, kissed her lingeringly on the mouth. I felt her stiffen with despair when my tongue slithered between her lips; then she passively submitted to that further exquisite humiliation.

I stood up, moved away from her. "Do you want me to take you right away to the Room of Punishments?" I demanded in a harsh voice.

"Nooo! Oh, noo!" she cried, recoiling with fear.

"Very well, then. So do at once what I told you to do. Kneel, or rather put yourself on all fours, and stick your lovely ass out toward me, so as to offer it humbly!" And, making the martinet whistle in the air above her, I added, "Don't try to push my patience to the end, Caroline!"

With a long groan filled with despair, she finally placed herself on her hands and knees.

"Hoist that lovely backside still more!" I threatened.

"Ooooh, please—ohh n . . . not that, pl—please," she kept supplicating, weeping with all her heart.

I swiftly approached her and applied two terrible strokes

across her naked behind, which tore piercing cries from her.

"I told you to present your ass properly to me. You must obey without reservations! Lift your buttocks still more, and present them the way they should be for my inspection!" I waited a moment, glowering at her, watched her shudderingly obey. "There, that's already much better. Now, beautiful little slave, you're going to put your hands behind you and of your own accord open up your lovely little buttocks so that I may properly examine your little cunt and your asshole!"

She seemed to hesitate for a few instants, then suddenly, taking me by surprise, since I believed her mastered, she flung herself forward with a cry of rage and revolt: "No! No!" she began to shriek furiously. "You've no right to make me do that! Filthy swine, disgusting scoundrel, I won't do it! I won't do it, no, no, no!"

And suddenly she ran toward the door of my room and with all the strength of her revulsion and despair she sought to open it. Needless to say, I'd taken the elementary precaution of locking it by key; and when she discovered there was no possible way out, she slumped against the wooden panel, sobbing and weeping with abysmal despair.

I flung myself on her, crying out in a hoarse, furious voice: "Filthy little slut! Ah, you wanted to escape, did you? So, you don't want to obey? Well, I'll make you pay for that! You've just earned yourself a trip to the Room of Punishments, and I beg you to believe that we shall both have fun there!"

Then she threw herself down on the rug, kicking and screaming, "Help! Oh, God, won't someone help me?"

I plunged one hand into her long silky tresses and, slipping my other hand between her thighs, despite the maddened resistance she tried to oppose, dug three of my fingers into her vagina, and having thus harpooned her, lifted her with a sudden jerk of my loins and bore her shrieking and wiggling toward the dungeon and the Room of Punishments.

Once there, I flung her on her belly over the heavy wooden horse and, easily overpowering her kickings and squirmings, buckled round her ankles the leather cuffs sealed into the back legs of the apparatus; then I immobilized her wrists the same way. Next, I tightly buckled down round her waist the broad leather strap, which pinned her tightly down with her belly flattened against the punishment horse.

"Noooo! Ohhh! Help! Help!" she shrieked, absolutely terrorized now, for she was becoming aware that her rebellion was going to cost her dearly.

"Yes, cry out, cry out as much as you want, beautiful bitch! Here, no one will hear you, except me, and the more you cry out, the more it will rouse my prick! Look at this!" I flung off my robe to show her my huge prick: throbbing, swollen, ready to explode its gismic burden. And, stark naked, my prick bobbing as I walked, I strode around the punishment horse.

Because of its special construction, the horse was higher and wider at the rear part than at the front, the purpose being to upraise and totally distend the bottom cheeks of the victim thereto attached. Hence I had under my eager eyes the most intimate view of Caroline's maiden secrets. In the amber cleft of her behind, the delicious bunghole, a dark pink aureoled with silky blonde hairs; and then, beneath, thickly framed by the rich profusion of silky tufts, her vulva, yawning to expose the humid, bright red interior of the vagina, that exquisite channelway for fucking!

What a delicious, exciting spectacle it was!

"So, little whore," I laughed, "you didn't want to show me your cunt and your asshole, eh? But do you know that at this moment I see them as clearly as a doctor examining you would be able to do? I see them, and you can't prevent me," I went on, while she frantically tightened her muscles, groaning and sobbing, in the feverish hope of contracting her bottomcheeks. But the straddle imposed upon her by the contours of the horse was such that she could do absolutely nothing except remain there, opened, offered, powerless to avert whatever I pleased to do to her.

"I'm going to kiss your ass . . . I'm going to lick your asshole and your pussy, do you hear me, Caroline? You're going to feel my tongue in your vagina, your lovely cunt! You're going to feel it dig into that dainty tidbit of an asshole of yours!" I savoringly pronounced.

"Nooooo! Oooooh! Noooooo!" she gasped in a tone full of horror.

With a mocking laugh, I bent over her bottom, till my face brushed the cheeks of her distended nakedness. I kiss that dainty, crinkly little mouth whose silky hairs tickled my lips most agreeably; then with my hardened, pointed tongue, I forced the tender petals to open, and I buried my tongue a little in the warm little canal of soft, quaking flesh. Her asshole rejected my tongue with a violent nervous spasm.

Without wanting to make an issue over this sign of ill will, this time I posed my mouth right against the orifice of her pussylips, and I delectated a long moment in sucking and licking that soft moist flesh; this time my tongue could plunge its entire length into her vagina, and my lips could take hold of the nodule of her clitoris, which began to harden under that intimate caress.

"You've got a hard-on! You've got a hard-on!" I laughingly told Caroline, who burst into tears of shame and confusion. "Now give me that sweet little bunghole of yours," I ordered and, once again pointing my tongue and tautening it as if it were a veritable prick, I tried again to force it through that narrow little slit of crinkly, rosy flesh, but once again a nervous reflex on her part repulsed my tongue.

At once, my sadistic instincts took over. "Ah, you little whore, you squeeze your ass shut, do you? You don't want to let me train you, eh? Well, we'll see!" I angrily cried. Then, posing the tip of my index finger against her asshole, which glistened with my saliva, I applied a violent thrust forward, and brutally buried my finger, up to the very palm, inside her bunghole!

Caroline uttered a strident cry: "You're hurting meee! Ahhh! You're hurting me!" she shrieked, trying to turn her head towards me.

"So much the better," I laughingly replied. "I want to hurt you . . . a good deal more, you'll see!"

I tore my finger out of her anus, wresting simultaneously a new shriek from the young beauty. But I hadn't finished. This time, I stuck both index and middle finger in that dainty orifice. I saw her asshole grow deformed and distend hugely around my two fingers, which I forcibly probed into her recalcitrant rectum. Then, after twisting them about several times, I savagely pulled them out. Her asshole was already reddened and congested; as for Caroline, she shrieked and sobbed, but then she could do nothing at all to prevent my vicious caress.

Now I stuck index, middle, and ring finger all in line, in a sort of cone, which I tried to bury into that bunghole of hers. Her howls of suffering rose louder and louder as my fingers advanced. Her asshole was formless now, abnormally stretched out as it was then, when, with an accentuation of wrist pressure, I almost managed to penetrate the base of my three fingers.

Caroline uttered pitiful cries; leaning forward a little, I could see her fingers madly clawing the legs of the punishment horse under the crisis of suffering that was lacerating her tender behind.

I wished I could have buggered her right then, dry, to make her suffer and bellow a good deal more; but alas, the time had not yet come for that, and so, regretfully, I slowly removed my fingers from that lovely backside, contracting frenetically in its owner's intolerable agony.

For a few indescribably delicious moments, I contemplated that swollen anus, agitated by nervous flexions; then I went to the wall, from which I unhooked the whalebone switch, before moving in front of the punishment horse to show it to my victim.

Her face bathed in tears, Caroline lifted eyes filled with terror on the instrument she already knew so well, alas, and which I sadistically waved in front of her.

"Well, Caroline, this is the first time your titties and belly are in contact with the horse, but you may be sure it is not the last—far from it, my beauty!" I announced. "And now, I'm going to give you an insight into what is called a real whipping; I'm going to lash you without pity, which will teach you, my dear, to profit from the lessons and the warnings that I give you. You're here to be trained, to be whipped, to be conquered, my beauty, and you can believe that from my experience in such matters you assuredly will be!"

While I thus harangued her, I had seized her hair in my other hand so as to lift her head above the horse, and I amused myself with tapping her cheeks with gentle pats of whalebone. When I let her go, her head fell back on the punishment horse while she redoubled her sobbing pleas for mercy.

Every nerve in my body was vibrating with pleasure. This is what I loved above all else, to have a girl at my mercy and to whip her without pity. I had the erection of a donkey between my legs, in full heat, and my prick was enormous. If I had buggered her at this moment, I should have broken her backside for her! Alas, as I've already explained, the time for that kind of amusement was still on the calendar of the future. So I had to content myself with flogging her.

I took my place before the apparatus and there, my legs planted astride to ensure my balance, my prick throbbingly upangling towards my belly, I raised my arm to ascend the supple whalebone, and with all the force of my wrist, I lowered it across her white bottomcheeks.

Instantly, Caroline raised her head with a violent jerk, and a strident shriek sprang from a throat strangled by the horrible searing torment that had bitten into her behind. A long livid weal encircled the lovely bottomcheeks, shuddering and tremoring in a series of rippling spasms of pain; and when she had at last regained her breath, it was to exhale another shriek of agony, which echoed from wall to wall. I pivoted on myself and with all the strength of my arm dealt her a second stroke of the switch that was far worse than the first.

There was a sudden silence, for the excessive agony had momentarily cut off her breath; then, as suddenly, she burst into deafening clamors. I knew that, wielded in this fashion, the whalebone must hurt abominably, but that only excited me the more; and without pausing, I lashed that lovely behind with all my might.

Methodically, spacing the lashes from ten to fifteen seconds apart, I sent her cut after cut. Caroline shrieked with all the power of her lungs. She resembled a madwoman. Her widely open mouth let saliva drip onto her chin, mingling with the tears that streamed down her cheeks; her neck was stretched so extremely that you could see the tendons stand out against the sweating skin, and her eyes were so enlarged by her suffering that one would have thought them about to pop out of their sockets.

Weal after weal, stripe after stripe . . . my strokes fell regularly . . . five . . . then ten . . . from ten to fifteen . . . from fifteen to twenty. You could hardly believe that a lovely young girl could shriek so loudly! My prick was almost clinging to my belly, so exquisitely was I in rut.

Oh, the joy that shook me at each stroke I inflicted. Oh, the exquisite pleasure to hear and see the thin flexible switch bite into the tender flesh of those satiny bare bottomcheeks of hers! Oh, the delicious sensation of hearing her shriek and imagine how she must be suffering under the cuts I was administering to her!

Lash after lash, stripe after stripe, without pity or compassion. Hadn't I told her that I was going to show her what a real whipping was like, so she'd remember it a long while?

By now, the pale flesh of her bare bottom had virtually disappeared under a network of swollen weals that painted her behind a dark pink. In my flagellatory excitement, I didn't notice at once that between the thirtieth and fortieth lashes my victim had finally lost consciousness, despite the injection I had given to prolong her resistance. I stopped, panting, my forehead dripping with sweat, and I went back to the wall, where I hung up the switch that had had done such yeoman service.

Then, too excited to hold myself back any longer, I bent over the burning backside of my victim, and pressing my huge prick between her scarlet bottomcheeks, I deliciously masturbated. I needed only a few rubbing maneuvers along the amber valley between those soft quivering globes to unleash my spunk, and with cries and groans of ecstasy, I spurted copious jets of thick white sperm over the unconscious Caroline's martyred behind.

At last I straightened, and with my palms I rubbed my viscous white semen over her lovely ass, as if anointing her with a soothing balm. When the two globes were thoroughly impregnated with my sperm, I took a flash of smelling salts and held it under her contracted nostrils; then, when she was nearly restored, I left the Room of Punishments.

I wanted a drink to calm my nerves, as well as to give my

pupil time to recuperate after the terrible shock she had just endured.

About two hours later, I returned to see how she was enduring her captivity, for she had remained bound to the whipping horse.

When I entered the Room of Punishments, there was such a silence that I feared for a moment she might still be unconscious, but I quickly realized, much to my relief, that such was not the case. At the sound of my footsteps, I saw her violently start, and all her lovely naked body began to tremble with terror.

Her face reposed on the black wooden side of the forward section of the horse, and one of her eyes fixed me with the terrified expression a rabbit has when fascinated by a snake. I heard her groan in a stifled voice.

"How's your little ass, Caroline?" I asked, feigning compassion.

She began to weep and turned her face to the other side. At once I dug my fingers into her hair, making her cry out with pain. "You mustn't turn your face away when your master or your trainer speaks to you. That's something you must know once and for all," I dryly reprimanded her.

Stretching out my arm, I drew toward me a little adjustable chain dangling from the ceiling and with a rather wide ring at its free end. I thrust a sheaf of her silky perfumed hair through the ring and knotted it all around; then I hoisted up the chain, which lifted Caroline's head and forced her to remain with her neck painfully stretched and her face erect. The poor darling wept like a child who is crushed by grief, and big tears again began to roll down her pale cheeks.

"I'm going to leave you this way till it is time for your meal. I hope this will be salutary to you and that this afternoon, when we resume our lesson in obedience, you'll be a little more supple and docile, my beautiful little miss! Try to be good, now!"

And I left the room, pursued by her lamentations, but not till I had caressed lingeringly and savoringly the sweet little cunt that she proffered to me so prettily.

After the excellent meal that I forced her to eat (for there was no question of restraining her as to diet; quite the contrary, it was important that she regain her strength), I generously allowed her three hours of rest, then went down to take her out of the room and bring her back to mine, as I had done in the morning.

After having made her resume the initial position with hands crossed on her nape and thighs widely spread, I began the educational session that had been so annoyingly interrupted in the morning.

"We shall see if you know your lesson, Caroline. What are those called?" I calmly asked as I fondled her breasts.

"My . . . my t-titties . . . master."

"Very good. And what do they call the little orifice of your behind?"

"I—m—m y—an . . . anus, m . . . master."

"And besides?"

"My b—bunghole . . . my . . . my . . . ass . . . ass . . . assh— hole," she breathed, blushing and lowering her eyes.

"Good, that's very good. Now, name for me the slit that hides under those lovely curly hairs."

Caroline began to tremble a little and raised supplicating eyes to me: "M—my s—sex . . . my s . . . slit . . . or my v . . . vulva?"

"No, that's not it at all!" I said in a cold tone. "Yet you've heard me tell you enough what the word is! All right, I'm waiting!"

She cast a terrified glance and decided itself: "I—it's my . . . my . . . c . . . cunt . . ."

"Say it better than that, three times!"

"My cunt . . . my cunt . . . my cunt . . ."

Already, to my great pleasure, I saw her lips trembling and her eyes mist. I untied the belt of my robe and drew it completely off my body. Already, my big prick was half-erect, like the neck of a swan.

"And that, do you know its name?"

"It—it—it's your s—sex organ, m . . . master," she stammered, turning her head away.

"Look at it! Look at it right away!" I commanded. "It's called a prick, a cock, a whang . . . all right, now repeat all that!"

Eyes fixed with apprehension and revulsion on my stiffening cock, Caroline Martin had to repeat clearly: "It's your prick, your cock, your whang."

"Repeat again! You must know those lovely words, and you know them well!"

"The   p . . . prick . . . t . . . the   c . . . cock . . . the wh . . . whang . . . t . . . the whang." Saying this, silent tears ran freely down her contorted face.

And so, for half an hour, ignoring her horrified stammerings, I taught her and forced her to repeat a lengthy collection of erotic words and expressions. My pleasure was in seeing this young girl, whose lips till now had been so used to the most intellectual and sophisticated phrases, obliged to explain to me, suffocated with shame and humiliation, the meaning of such words and phrases as "fuck," "bugger," "shit," "frig," "brown," "pull prick out of bung," "spurt," "fuck ass," "French," "blow job," "suck balls," and so on. And Caroline was half-dead with shame when at last I judged the moment ripe to pass to a more complicated occupation.

"In spite of your stilted attitude of a young lady of society,

I'm certain that you already know certain of these words," I laughingly remarked. "Besides, you aren't a virgin, so you must already have got yourself fucked, eh?"

She was speechless and could only weep in her confusion.

"Come on, answer me when I ask you a question—and above all, pay attention not to lie, because you know what it costs you, eh?"

"Y—yes."

"Yes, what?"

"I—I—g . . . got my—myself . . . f . . . fucked." As she stammered this out, she burst into touching little sobs. It was easy to see that such an avowal was not easy for a young lady like Miss Martin to make.

I stared at her for a moment, slowly caressing my cock, as her horror-filled eyes watched my obscene maneuver. "And you love to be fucked, tell me, Caroline; you love to feel a big hard prick dig into your cunt, don't you?"

"Oooooh! Ooooohh!! Ooooohhh!!!" She didn't answer, but went on weeping without restraint.

"Look at my prick!" I ordered. "Look at it, doesn't it make you hot? Wouldn't you love to have a thick long hard prick like that in your nice little cunt? Look at that juicy piece—tell me, does it please you?"

"Oooooh! S . . . Sir . . . please . . . n . . . n . . . ooooh . . . n . . . no!"

"What? It doesn't please you?" I feigned anger.

"Y . . . yes . . . Ohhh! Yes . . . it . . . it's . . . l . . . lovely . . . it's . . . it's . . . lovely," she hurried to tell me, her words interspersed with hot tears and choking little sobs.

"And why does it please you so much, this prick of mine, tell me, lovely little fucker that you are?" I went on, without pity for her modesty.

She knew what she had to say to please me, or the whip

would enter into play; so she forced herself to explain to me in a voice broken with sobs: "It's . . . it's b . . . it . . . it's enormous . . . it . . . it's an en . . . enormous p . . . prick . . . th . . . that's w . . . why I . . . love it," and she burst into heartrending sobs.

"And my balls, do they please you too?" I imperturbably demanded.

"Y . . . y . . . yes . . . y . . . y . . . your . . . b . . . balls . . . a . . . are . . . e . . . enormous also."

"I see," I said with a mocking laugh. "I see you're a vicious little whore. You love big whangs, eh? Well, be satisfied, my beautiful Caroline, you shall have it, you shall have it soon, I promise you, and be up to the balls! You'll have it in your cunt and you'll also have it in your ass! I think your ass is still virgin, isn't it?"

"Ooooohhh . . . m . . . master . . . s . . . sir."

"Well, my little one," I went on, ignoring her horrified expression, "I shall take charge of unmaidening that sweet ass of yours. And when you're received this morsel of mine in your asshole, believe me, Caroline, you'll no longer fear suppositories!" I exclaimed as I frigged my huge cock to let her see what she was going to have to swallow when the time came.

She looked ready to be sick from the horror that swelled in her, but I was far from finishing with her, and so I resumed my little discourse. "I understand very well that you're impatient to be buggered by so handsome a shaft as this, but your little hole must wait and content itself for the moment with my tongue or fingers, for the taking of your asshole virginity, my dove, is to be done before the Countess, who dearly loves to witness such a spectacle."

Hearing these last words, the poor little miss was ready to faint, and she redoubled her despairing groans.

"While waiting, we may occupy ourselves in another way," I said to her as if I did not notice her despair. "Stand up and come kneel before me." As I gave her that command, I sat down on the edge of my bed, my legs widely spread. Caroline came to kneel down before me.

"Come closer," I told her, and she crawled forward a little on her knees, her hands still crossed on her nape.

"Closer still! Between my legs!"

"Pl . . . please . . . n . . . no . . . please," she sniffled, but she nevertheless obeyed. She was now kneeling right between my thighs, petrified before my huge prick as a mouse before a hungry cat. My prick was not more than an inch from her lovely contorted face, and its glistening, taut skin was so swollen that anyone would have thought it was on the point of spurting.

"Although you may already be acquainted with spurting," I explained in a doctrinaire and serious tone, as a schoolteacher might to a most attentive pupil, "you've a catalogue of things to learn. Things that your future master will demand of you for his own pleasure. First of all, you must know that a slave must not content herself just to receive her master's prick, though of course it may be for him one of the major pleasures. There are, for example, many delicious preliminaries, tasty perversions, and it is a slave's duty to know how to bring the master's pleasure to the zenith and spice it with infinite variety. I hope I make myself clearly understood?"

A groaning reply escaped poor Caroline's contracted throat, and I knew she would certainly have given a great deal to be anywhere else in the world at that moment.

"Stop sniveling," I severely exclaimed. "Otherwise, I'll give you something to really cry about!" Then I went on: "I'm going to teach you now one of the perversions of which I've spoken. Nature has endowed you with a lovely pair of titties: soft, supple, and firm all at once, delicious to touch and look at. Notably, they can provide a deliciously soft and satiny sheath for

the master's prick. That is what you're going to do . . . right
away!"

She stared at me as if she did not comprehend a word. Smiling cruelly, I went on: "Approach a little more now, and then
take your titties from underneath so as to lift them a bit. Now
approach them together. Then, you'll lower yourself slightly so
that my prick no longer lodges between them; then press them
tightly together to pinch my prick between them. After that,
you'll make them stir gently, while moving your bosom up and
down, so as to frig my cock with your two lovely titties!"

While I thus instructed her, Caroline's face took on a mask
of horrified revulsion!

"No! Ohh! No . . . no . . . no!"

"Come on now, approach and do what I've just explained,"
I said threateningly.

"Oh, pl . . . please, sir . . . I couldn't . . . I couldn't . . . oh, I
beg of you!" she choked, staring at me in the most appealing
way you can imagine.

"I shall give you exactly ten seconds, Caroline," I replied.

"Oooohhh! No . . . ohh! No . . . I can't . . . no, not that . . .
it's . . . it's frightful!!" she began to cry, and half-rose.

As you may imagine, I was in a state of ferocious excitement,
and so with feverish impatience, I awaited that contact that I
divined would be infinitely soft and caressing: the clenching
pressure of her two beautiful titties against my huge throbbing
cock.

To be sure, I hadn't really counted on an immediate realization of my desire, nor one that would take place at once,
docilely and without discussion. But the very notion that my
chaste, haughty new pupil might perform that erotic perversion
on me without hesitation was so stirring that I absolutely
wanted her to do it to me right away.

However, Caroline didn't seem to be so disposed; half-risen, half-squatting, she stared at me with the frightened eyes of an animal caught in a trap.

My frustration was suddenly too great; I quickly leaned over her and, seizing her by her long hair, I dragged her violently towards me, making her cry out and struggle, while I gloatingly rubbed her face against my huge penis and hairy balls.

Then, as she kept struggling, and even clawed my thighs, rage submerged me and, ferociously tugging her hair back, I cried, my face stuck up against hers, my gaze plunging into her terror-dilated eyes: "Very well, little bitch, you asked for it, you're going to get it!"

"Pity—pity . . ." she began to sob while I forced her to rise. Dragging her up by her hair and forcing her over to a leather armchair, I flung her with her belly over the elbow rest. To be sure, she struggled wildly but quite in vain; and on that lovely naked backside of hers, so deliciously upreared by the posture I forced her to retain as I twisted one of her arms behind her back, I began to apply a hail of dry, crisp smacks, applied with my palm and using all the strength of my arm.

Her buttocks were still severely reddened and swollen by all I had made them endure that morning, soon turning as burning a scarlet hue as hell itself.

Caroline yelled and screeched with all the power of her young lungs, and her long, sensually exciting legs waved wildly in empty space as she tried to kick free, while her bottomglobes bounded under my smacks, sometimes contracting till the shadowy groove leading to her virgin asshole almost disappeared, then yawning to expose that dainty, hairy little hole and the base of the plump slit of her cunt, all in the vain hope of attenuating the suffering that kindled a burning fire throughout that voluptuous backside of hers.

Without letting myself be softened by the plaints and shrieks she endlessly emitted, I continued to give her a spanking of exemplary vigor. "I've already told you that a slave must obey, Caroline," I sermonized as I pitilessly smacked that beautiful ass, which was now as red as a ripe tomato. "And as long as you don't obey me, you shall be severely chastised!"

But soon my hand began to burn and hurt me. As I didn't care for that, I halted the correction, to Caroline's great relief, she believing that I had finished with her. What an error that was on her part!

Leaving her to sob and cry over the arm of the chair, so crushed that she didn't even seek to rise, I strode to my dressing table and seized a hairbrush, an oval brush with a rather long handle. Holding it like a little racket, I returned to my disobedient pupil and, placing a hand at the hollow of her loins to immobilize her, I raised my arm and applied the back of the brush against her crimson buttocks.

It smacked like a pistol shot on that burning skin, and it must have hurt a great deal, for my pupil kicked frenziedly and uttered a piercing shriek. My prick gave a convulsive jerk of pleasure, and I applied a second smack as biting as the first on that swollen bottom.

"Well, Caroline, have you changed your mind? You'll tell me when you'll agree to use your big titties to give me pleasure. But take your time, I'm in no hurry." I applied another smack with the back of the brush, this time right at the base of her behind, near the thighs.

The pain was so scorching that it cut off her breath, but as soon as she had regained it, she resumed wailing out her torment—the torment of her charming behind. I gave her another good smack, right over the lower curves of those fiery red bottomglobes of hers, with all my might. And through the shrieks that filled the room, I gathered that she was trying to tell me something.

I stopped smacking her behind and, recovering my own

quickened, panting breath, I waited for more coherent words. But almost with haste, terrified at the idea of receiving more blows from the hairbrush, Caroline, while continuing to sob heartrendingly, gave involuntary vent to her physical reactions from that thrashing; her scarlet buttocks relaxed their contracting tension, yawning to reveal that dainty pink bunghole aureoled with a fine wreath of hairs.

Decided, there's nothing like the whip or a good spanking to master the most recalcitrant and most modest pupils!

I bent over to take better note of the intimate furrow of this lovely little miss, shaken with tears and sobs, while I slowly rubbed my fiercely swollen cock; then, with a luscious smile, I straightened up over that yawning backside and, this time turning the brush to the side with its long nylon bristles, with a sudden deft turn of my wrist I brought the bristles right down into the girl-slave's asshole!

A veritable bellow of agony rose from the armchair, and under that hideous suffering that seemed to tear her anus to shreds, Caroline lunged out of my grasp and fell onto the rug, gripping her bottom with both hands and crying like one possessed.

I let her appease her torment as best as she could; then, when her cries began to diminish, I ordered her to kneel once more, hands again behind her nape.

Still overwhelmed by what I had made her endure, the young English beauty nevertheless hastened to obey and placed herself in the indicated position.

"If I still obtain only disobedience from you, Caroline," I told her gruffly, "I warn you that I'll take you back to the Room of Punishments and administer a whipping that you'll remember till the end of your life. Is that understood, Caroline?"

"Oh! Y . . . yes . . . s . . . sir . . . y . . . yes . . . I promise you to obey!"

"Very well, my darling, then let's go back to the bed and do what I explained to you. Give me pleasure with your lovely titties!"

A moment later, Caroline found herself kneeling between my naked thighs, trying to keep her face as far as possible from my huge prick, which dangled heavily before her tear-drowned eyes. However, the fear of the whip made her act against her very visible revulsion and the obscene affront to her innate modesty. What an exquisite moment when her two soft warm titties were pressed against my cock, providing a wonderfully satiny sheath for it!

"Very good," I complimented her to encourage her. "Now frig me up and down, keeping your tittles nicely squeezed together. All right, go ahead! Unless, of course, you don't think your bottom has had enough yet?"

Her eyes closed to shut out the sight of my enormous prong, which emerged obscenely between those two white globes, she began, sobbing with powerless shame, to manipulate her breasts gently in a soft friction and to undulate her body from upwards down, rather jerkily at the beginning, then according to a slow rhythmic cadence.

I spread my thighs still more to give her room, and I leaned back on the bed to relish the better these marvelous sensations which, through my throbbing, huge cock, invaded every fiber of my being.

As inexperienced as Caroline's first tittie-manipulation showed itself to be, nonetheless it did not take very long before I felt the infallible ticklings that announced the approach of orgasm.

The soft warmth of her body pressed between my thighs, the fact that I was able to compel her to perform that obscene ritual, augmented and unchained my pleasure, as much as did the fact of hearing her sob with useless revolt and feel her tears moisten my big prickhead—which, by the by, they helped, much as an unguent would, my rubbing along that resilient, soft warm sheath. And my gasps of lustful ecstasy mingled with her groans of shame and horror.

Suddenly, to prevent a much-too-rapid termination of the rut I felt surge along my prick, I pushed her away. I didn't want to go off so quickly, not this first sweet time with haughty Caroline!

"It will be better soon," I told her, my voice hoarse and panting, but of course she didn't answer, for the situation had nothing joyful in it for her. I allowed my erotic emotions to ebb a little; then I gave the young girl the order to resume caressing me with her titties. She showed a rather perceptible hesitation; then again I felt those sweet warm globes voluptuously squeeze against my cock, and then she resumed her undulations, pressing her titties together with both her slim soft hands against the burning stiffness of my massive ramrod.

Her head bent down, she seemed hypnotized by the enormous, glistening cockhead that rhythmically emerged from between her bubbies and whose large gism-slit seemed to split in two, exuding this viscous drops as testimony of the intensity of my rut.

Suddenly, I felt it was mounting inexorably; I abandoned myself and cried out with my orgasmic crescendo. But I suspected that Caroline was not yet sufficiently trained to endure that culminating moment of my pleasure without rebelling. I was certain she could not endure it, in spite of all the threats with which I confronted her.

And so, when I felt my moment was at hand, I suddenly gripped her between my knees and, plunging both hands into her disheveled hair, viciously pressed her against my belly, while I jerked my loins back and forth to bring about the orgasm.

Maddened, Caroline began to cry out and to struggle, but in vain; suddenly braying out in glorious rut, I felt myself spurt my essence.

My spunk spattered forcibly against Caroline's titties and neck and, most of all, full against her face. Almost ill and beside herself with abhorrence, she felt my thick warm splashings moisten her eyes, already wet with tears, besmear her nose, and enter her mouth as she opened it to cry out her horror.

After that sensational discharge, I remained a long moment on the bed, mulling over the intense delight I had known, while at my feet, Caroline, plunged into abysmal shame and disgust, sobbed heartbrokenly, her face glistening with tears, saliva, and gism.

THE PRUSSIAN GIRLS

by P. N. Dedaux

In the first half of the eighteenth century, Friedrich William I, the first Hohenzollern ruler of Brandenburg, had established such rigorous discipline throughout his realm that it became known as "the land of the Corporal's stick." In 1729 this self-styled King of Prussia caught his son making eyes at the daughter of a Potsdam rector and ordered the girl to be "whipped first before the town hall, then before her father's house, then in all corners of the town." P. N. Dedaux, a master of traditional historical erotica, is in his element in this classical exploration of the dominance and submission of a group of Prussian young ladies attending boarding school.

It was a long, high room with pointed windows, barred on the inside, and a vaulted oaken ceiling. Ranged in seemingly endless regularity across this space were a number of desks, at which worked girls of various ages. At the far end, under a large oil lamp, stood a mistress, behind a pulpit desk of impressive proportions. Overhead—or rather, behind it—reigned a colossal clock, and by her side was a bucket, in which steeped long birch rods.

In actual fact, there were no more than some thirty-four pupils under her care tonight, this being the evening preparation period for the junior, or *Vorschule*, class in the school. This term the Schloss Rutenberg had swollen, under parental pressure for admittance, to as many as seventy-one girls, who were divided into three classes—senior, junior, and *Schaum* (or scum), as the new girls in their first year were known. This term there were exactly a dozen *Schaum*; there were fifteen senior girls, and ten prelectors. There were eleven mistresses, excluding the school matron and head, or *Direktrice*. Excluding these two, they were all single, young, active, and vigorous. Fräulein Katte, the evening monitor, or *Mahner*, of junior prep was quite typical of these. Twenty-eight years old, dark and broad-browed, she had been at the college—if such it could be called—some seven years already, having graduated from its ranks. She wore her on-duty uniform of soft black leather becomingly. This was no longer than a three-quarter man's court coat. It fit her closely at the bosom, was drawn in by a wide leather belt from which hung, at one side, a bunch of keys, and at the other a ritualistic black leather switch, and its skirt swung its hem higher than her knees. But the mistresses at Schloss Rutenberg did not suffer from cold. They wore thigh-high boots with steeple heels, so highly polished and tightly laced that they shone like black glass.

The girls seated before her, hunched over their bethumbed books, wore a uniform peculiar to the school. Except for that of the prelectors, it consisted in something similar to a Greek tunic or abbreviated dancing costume. For the junior class (and of course the *Schaum*), this was extremely short, hanging just beneath the bottom, and caught in at the waist by a fairly slender chain. For seniors it was gold in hue, for juniors green, and for the scum it was a positive and symbolic brown. Thus were the Hohenzollern colors incorporated, at any rate.

Schaum wore black stockings, impeccably upheld by biting garters; juniors were permitted a moderately lighter shade, and seniors lighter still. All heels were veritable stilettos. As little was worn under these brief woolen tunics, it might be thought that these children of the aristocracy would get cold. The pages that follow will hopefully testify that they were kept tolerably warm. But let us focus to one bent back in a center row, and one pair of pale blue eyes gazing sightlessly at her beseamed and time-worn text, over which her short fair crop would occasionally stir as she tried in vain to memorize her lines of Caesar for the morrow.

A careful observer, one looking over her shoulder, might have noticed the stain of a tear on that monotonous Latin. For Monika Vorst was going to get a whipping. It was not the first she had had, nor the last, but a saying among the sufferers in this school was that a whipping brought on whipping, and she simply couldn't concentrate on her recitation. It was no good. She only hoped and prayed that she would be called on by the mistress. Her mind kept straying, like her eyes, to the clock. It ticked stentorously.

The time was half past eight, and at nine the duty mistress held her notorious session with those unfortunates who had been put up on the duty list. This was one of the most dreaded moments of the day for all concerned. But the women would have to get Monika's individual report over soon. The girl sighed. She shifted her thighs. Under the tight green knickers, her bottom felt shivery and wobbly, and twice as big as usual. She wondered if it showed, behind. A book dropped and she jumped.

It was the girl in the desk to her right. As the book had fallen open near Monika's feet, she reached to help pick it up. A note was stuffed hurriedly in her hand. Two bright eyes caught hers.

Slowly, under carefully cupped fingers, Monika read the single word scribbled in pencil: "*Glück!*" Good luck. She ventured a quick glance across the aisle and caught her friend Barbara Mack's eyes in a sympathetic squeeze of commiseration. Then she swallowed the morsel of paper, barely moving her gullet as she did so. That had been decent of Barbara. If they'd been caught Fräulein Katte would have given Barbara ten with the birch. At least.

The door swung open and Monika's world crashed about her. For a second she couldn't catch her breath. A tall prelector called Else Gundling stroke in, wearing her uniform of office—in her case, of the same soft black leather as the mistresses', but with the skirt in very short pleats falling over smoky stockings, tautly hauled, and knee-length leather boots. These clicked with precision as she went up to the Monitor's desk in silence, curtseyed, and whispered something. Then she was coming along the aisle to Monika, whose heart began to hammer like a . . . like a . . .

"Duty mistress requires to see you. Follow me."

Sickly closing her Caesar, Monika stood up and, with nobody looking at her but everyone looking at her, followed the prelector out of the room. Once outside, Gundling led off smartly down long stone corridors lit by flares. She marched in martial tread—left, right, left, right—and Monika had to keep step with her, just behind. The girls were not allowed to talk. The shadows fled over the strong broad shoulders of the figure leading her, yes, to hell. Round Gundling's thick neck was the gold chain from which hung a "P," the symbol of her office: not for *Präfekt* but for *Pflicht*, since she was duty prefect for the day. Her shoulders tapered to a surprisingly narrow waist, caught in by a broad leather belt, and beneath that the hips thumped out lustily to either side, making the brief skirt swing, as her heels struck sharply at the flagstones. Monika was feeling sicker and sicker: it was all happening so fast, so irrevocably. She tried to breathe in deeply, half-tripped round a corridor, heard an irritated "Come on!" and was soon aware, at the end of their flickering vision, of the long corridor leading to the west wing and the little area, or parade ground, in front of the duty room. Before she knew it, the prelector had reached this, turned completely round, and stood at attention with her back to wall on one side of the door, all the while staring expressionlessly over Monika's shoulder.

"Hurry up. Knock," she hissed in a whisper.

Monika stepped up, shivering, to that plain door whose vision had filled so many Prussian girls with trepidation. She raised her hand. She had to knock. But her fingers refused to function. She bit her lip. She was going to cry. Perhaps to pee. After all, it had been such a very little fault. Hadn't it? Speaking to a mistress without being spoken to. An accident, as a matter of fact, a slip, but as in the Army every accident at Rutenberg was treated as a crime. How many, then? Talking out of turn was surely only six. It couldn't be more than six, could it? Wedell wouldn't give her more than . . .

"Oh, come on," said a voice, and the prelector beat her knuckles on the door. A low "Herein!" resounded in a woman's tone and Monika constrained her fingers to open the door, enter the room, close the door behind her, march to the center, and curtsey to the two women standing there, one slightly behind the other.

It was a large rectangular place with a wooden floor of ebon black and a general impression, at first always, of being without furniture. Like a gymnasium, or a stripped prison antechamber. An air of stern gloom hung over all.

This was not relieved, for Monika, by the sight of the two mistresses. The one who stood closer to the fireplace was Fräulein Holz, of whom Monika had inadvertently raised a question, without being addressed, or raising her hand first, that morning. Thus she had incurred mandatory chastisement. The woman in front was much more impressive, however, since she was not in the customary uniform. Fräulein Wedell, as duty mistress for the day, did wear the gleaming, creaking thigh-length boots, it was true, but above these what she had on was

no more than a most skimpy tunic of spotless white, a heavy
Tours silk, caught in at the waist by the usual wide belt, but
with the skirt falling, in a slight flare, over the firm slopes of
her hips, from which it depended briefly, in suggestive reign,
on the tops of her brilliant boots. She had on the chain of office
and a golden "P" was embroidered between her breasts. At
thirty-two, Fräulein Wedell was a massive beauty with a rather
flat face, slumberous eyes, and a mane of brown hair held back
in a slide. Under her tense, gourd-like breasts, whose nipples
prodded like thumbs at the stuff enclosing them, she bent a
long and springy cane, yellow, highly polished, and concluding
in a knob, at the grasping end. She looked as if she could cane
extremely hard, which she could, and enjoy doing it, which
she did.

All this had Monika's gaze, fixed straight in front of her like
a soldier's, taken in, as well as—to her right—the outlines of a
leather-padded vaulting horse. These occasional punishments
could be treated in various ways. In this case, they had probably
decided to take her over the horse. But her thoughts were interrupted from further speculation on her fate.

"Monika Vorst?"

"Yes, Fräulein."

"You stand accused of speaking to a mistress without permission. Report of Fräulein Holz. What do you plead?"

"Guilty, if you please, Fräulein."

"Have you anything to say?"

"No."

"Do you wish to appeal?"

"No."

This ritual over, Monika waited with bated breath.

How many?

"You will receive eight strokes with the cane."

Eight!

"Thank you, Miss," she said hastily.

"Strip," came the command. Hurriedly, as if there were suddenly no time, Monika reached under her tunic and slid her green knickers down and off, leaving them neatly folded on the floor. Then she tightened up her stockings and folded her skirt into her chain-belt. After which she stood to attention again.

The duty mistress came forward, and for a few seconds inspected her naked front. Monika had a heavy bulging mound adorned with strong curls that were rather darker than her hair; her vulval lips were pulpy and close-seamed. Evidently satisfied, the mistress went behind.

"Lean forward, hands on your knees."

She palpated and pressed the flesh of the young buttocks carefully for a moment. Monika knew she had marks from a previous beating behind and the good Fräulein was feeling the extent of bruise left, if any, in order to see if she should use the same spot again. For maximum pain within the just limits of allotted discipline was a sine qua non of Schloss Rutenberg, as elsewhere in the kingdom.

"Bend over there." The quiver of willow indicated the horse.

It was a low one and Monika stretched over it in the correct pose: feet astride, her belly on the leather top, which inclined slightly down, her arms in front of her, her hands gripping the wood at the side. She stared ahead at a far wall, on which was a rack of canes in parallel lines. She heard Fräulein Holz come forward, the two exchange some comments, and then heard the duty mistress step well back and to one side. Above all, she heard the sudden thumping pace and that tearing of stretched silk which was the noise the cane made as it whirred through the silent air about her. It was more compelling a sound than any in her memory and, indeed, more frightening than the little dry *thuck* of the cane's impact.

By then it had happened. The limber limb thrashed round

her fatted flesh low down, causing her a blaze of excruciating pain. She gasped and clenched her teeth so as not to cry out.

Seven more.

There was a long pause, for these mistresses were experts in the minutiae of physical chastisement, knowing that the feeling of leisurely endlessness was an essential ingredient, and timing their cuts to succeed at the maximum moment of mounted sensation.

Trhhhrrrlll-wuck!

Two.

Monika said nothing. She was being thrashed now, and she knew it. She was a privileged member of a master race, a race of gods and goddesses, descended from the mists of old, ancestors of glory, and she put her tongue between her teeth, bidding herself bite through it rather than disgrace her body and cry out. All she uttered were stomach-deep grunts: "Huink!"

Three . . . four . . . five . . . you could get to five or six with one of these light canes, but anything more began to be a problem.

"Lower," murmured Fräulein Holz from behind her.

Phrrrwuppp!

Only two more!

It was a good thrashing and, though low, well-spaced, so that the whole of her bottom stung, hard. Wedell always had a lot of weight in her cuts. If only she'd get these last ones over with quickly. Monika knew just what she looked like from behind: a pair of welted buttocks which, try as she might, could not keep from squeezing and squirming and rolling, the slotted oval of her sex shamelessly on display beneath. She jammed her knees into the woodwork and found that her fingers were scratching at the same in front.

"That one made her jump a bit."

There was low laughter.

"Anyone would think she wanted it . . . up her."

"One of our Emperor's *lange Kerle!*"

Ph-ph-phrrrrpp!

Monika lost and found her tongue: "Haiee!"

That had hurt her considerably indeed. Oh god, how that beastly cane could sting! She shot out a leg. Christ! Could she hold it for another? She had to . . . for Brandenburg, for . . . Prussia. She knew the prelector outside would be counting the cuts, which would come to her as thin flicks of air, and she wondered if a finger would be under her skirt working up a hungry tongue of gristle in her slit.

Phhhrrwppp!

Over!

But this was the worst! The pain was at its very worst about thirty seconds afterwards, and lasted so for a full minute; she had to show her control by waiting for *Erlaubnis*, the ritual word of permission to get up, and then she had to keep from rubbing herself afterwards. She tried to freeze herself to the horse, tried to still the seething writhing of her ribbed cheeks in the rear.

"All right," she heard.

She stood up a trifle uneasily, clamping hands to her sides to stop them from wandering, out of control, made weakly for her knickers, which she pulled up, shivering. Having frantically tugged down her skirt, she approached the duty mistress, dropped to one knee, said, "Thank you for punishing my fault, Fräulein," and kissed the top of the cane. To her dry lips it seemed somewhat warm. Then she was blundering out.

The prelector, who was waiting outside, just under the well-known duty list, frankly grinned when she saw Monika's writhen lips and miserably fisted hands at her flanks. Although she was not supposed to speak, she said, "Good caning? I hoped you were going to get ten."

She started striding back. Monika stumbled into step behind, but was now able to grab her beaten buttocks and knead them beneath her tunic. The prelector walked fast, knew (as Monika, mewing, knew) that the pain was still mounting nicely in the pair of whipped cheeks and that self-control on re-entering the classroom was going to provide a salutary task of willpower. It was for that one went to places like Schloss Rutenberg, after all.

"Hey, keep in step," she more than once turned back angrily to declaim.

A good caning? Monika knew it had been. Excellent. Eight sweeping strokes right under her chubbiest parted person, a seething cauldron of purplish weals that made her suddenly pant and stop, squirming, her forehead pressed to the ice-cold wall.

"Please, Gundling. Just a second. Honestly. Wedell cuts so tightly."

"Come on. Or I'll have to report you for dawdling."

The prelector was pulling at her tunic when, from an intersection ahead of them, a mistress appeared. She was young and pretty, with rather mousy hair, and under normal circumstances they would have detected her approach by the jingling of keys at her belt. This mistress as yet wore none. She was new this term; her name was Daunitz, from near Gentin. By chance she had got to know Monika Vorst and came forward, smiling shyly, at the already much-embarrassed girls. Stopping in corridors was a caning offense. In some schools, you had to run in all the passageways.

"Poor Monika. Have you just been caned?"

"Yes, Fräulein," came the answer, after both girls had curtseyed.

"Let me see."

The mistress parted Monika's skirt and panties and in-

spected. The weals were thick and hard and hot. Another caning across them could be agonizing, if well applied. Which, at
Schloss Rutenberg, it invariably was.

"Hurt a lot?"

"Yes. I was j-just . . ."

"Well, you'd better be on your way, hadn't you? I know the
head doesn't approve of dawdling in corridors. Any more than
I do."

She tapped the girl's slabbed butt and watched it joggle out
of sight, round another turn of the corridor, as Monika followed
the martial prefect. As the latter finally opened the schoolroom
door for her charge to enter, she too smiled. The girl was doing
well. It might be interesting to find out one day, one night, if
she . . . and what dormitory was Vorst in?

"Thanks, Gundling."

"Just as well it was that new mistress. Or she'd have had both
our hides."

Red of face and wet of eye, her hands at her side, Monika
went up to the monitor and requested permission to return to
prep. It was granted and, when she resumed her desk, she stood
at it, as was required of any girl who had just suffered correction. In the total silence of the softly ticking room, every aspect
of it proclaimed one thing and one thing only: I have been well-
caned across the naked buttocks and it stung like such sheer
hell that I wish I didn't have any. Eight slow juicy strokes,
driving in just above the sulcus until I wanted to scream and
squirm, but I couldn't, because of my country's honor. At Mag-
deburg, a soldier had just had his ears and nose cut off. Probably been decapitated or shot thereafter, she wasn't sure. What
was a trifle of stripes on the seat in comparison? All the same
the tip did eat in like fury. She could feel it still.

Across the aisle, Barbara Mack saw sidelong the little fatty quivers that shot through that jut of rump. Her eyes were moist and gleaming.

Yes, it was still hurting a very great deal—as each single breast, beating beneath those thin green tunics knew. Monika herself bore no resentment. Such a notion never even got near to her mind. She was happy she had again "come through," without disgrace, and that was simply that. It had been a routine beating and thus another ordeal and challenge to rise to. Like an athletic activity, in many ways. She had broken a rule and reaped the consequences. She admired Wedell for making it so painful, so "tight," and knew she had got everything out of her eight strokes that she could. Once or twice she had been a trifle wild, she had "overhit" perhaps at the end, but by and large it had been a methodical, calculated caning of the type that made you feel corrected through and through. Monika's burning bottom now felt thrice its size, heavy as lead, but she knew corporal punishment achieved its goal. If she made that same mistake again, she'd be more likely to get a dozen. And anyway, the worst of the smart was now subsiding nicely, melding into a pervasive heat, and sense of satisfaction at her center. Relaxed and torpid, she stared at Caesar's rank prosaic prose and knew she would have to borrow Barbara's bone thing from her again tonight.

SPRING FEVERS

by Martin Pix

"Spring Fevers" taps into the common male fantasy of having an entire sorority of attractive co-eds at one's disposal. Though not for the faint of heart, this excerpt uncovers the sadism latent in these fantasies. After all, the co-ed is desirable precisely because she is unattainable, and for the particularly crushing way in which she might let an older suitor know that his attentions are not appreciated. As Thomas Mann demonstrates in Death in Venice, *to lust after a young lover is to confront one's own mortality. In "Spring Fevers," the older suitor exacts his revenge, as the object of his lust is forced to perform a number of unsavory tasks; she is ritually despoiled, inside and out.*

Sigma Epsilon Xi's chapterhouse had its social room drapes discreetly drawn. Decorated paddles from classes back to 1935 hung from the picture molding ringing the cavernous room. Judy Latimer seemed pale and frail in the huge, almost empty expanse. Her tawny, dark, California-blonde hair made her skin seem as colorless as her frost-white racer tank top and full-cut cotton briefs. She wore nothing else.

"I'm going to die, Charlotte, I just know it." She cringed, her bare toes curling into the black and gray Navajo area rug. "That wet T-shirt business felt yucky enough at night. In daylight . . ."

"Hey, you'll pick up points toward the Mardi Gras contest." Charlotte Bosk was the only other inhabitant of a room designed to hold eighty at a stand-up social. "Where's Nora?"

Judy betrayed a swallow of envy as she watched the tall soph-omore stride around in her lingerie.

Charlotte's surfer-girl tanned abundance almost burst from a pale gold camisole sewn with diagonal metal threads in rain-drop patterns. Figured fleurs-de-lis ran along the deep neckline and around the flared hem.

The camisole ended just above her sun-ripened thighs. Gar-ter tabs projected from a hidden belt to sway freely along the creamy muscles. Charlotte wore no hose and the dancing cami hem advertised her absolute lack of panties.

"They're just going to parade us around the yard, I'll bet." Charlotte's shrug set her free pectorals bouncing under the filmy camisole. "Show poise in front of the girls from the other houses."

"Yeah, girls with their guys." Judy wilted. The sophomore could be nonchalant. Charlotte had copped nine of the ten possible points for her soaked, T-shirted boobs, their raised aureoles like Bing cherries under the transparent clinging cot-ton.

Judy had just placed a mediocre five. She'd had all of the embarrassment of flashing her pretties under the see-through wet shirt without grabbing any of the glory.

"Thank God for St. Cloud's anti-rape campaign, Nora!" Char-lotte's paralyzing blue eyes had gone round as saucers. "You'd be steak before starving wolves."

"Yeah, Women Against Rape—Daughters on Guard would love me." The twenty-nine-year-old pledge stepped into the social room from the chapterhouse entry hall. "They told us to wear our classiest underthings, without stockings."

Nora Quincannon's rusty hair had been cropped shorter than last term. It cleanly outlined her freckled Celtic face. Equally sharply, a kelly green, bone-ribbed, open-bosomed bustier defined and presented her fully naked breasts. Translucent flesh showed china-blue veins. The mouthable nipple tips stood eraser-thick. The garment outlined but in no way upthrust the freestanding, freely undulant globes.

"Knockers up, as Rusty Warren used to say." Nora grinned. The bustier ended in a lace trim embroidered with bright emerald shamrocks. Her bikini-scant panties had vermicelli-thin straps that hugged her hips and vanished utterly into her gluteal crevice.

At the briefs' pubic center, a tipsily tilted emerald shamrock capped the kelly satin hiding her mons. A straggling wealth of dark russet hairs poked their untrimmed ends from both sides of the bikini-cut triangle.

"I pity the fellows in the audience with those headlights shining in their eyes." Charlotte pursed her lips in a low whistle.

"I guess Delinda's been at it again." Judy studied the reddish violet mottling on Nora's amply visible buttocks. "After that Ken thing, they should have reassigned you to another guardian angel. Donna's not that hard on me, and I screw up all the time."

"Thanks." Nora patted the freshman's shoulder. "I'll complain to Maxine and Gerry when I need to, okay? But not before. And remember, Ken Gormish victimized us both."

"Yeah, but Delinda's taking it out on you . . ." Charlotte suddenly went silent.

"Looks as if some basic board action repainted your aft, Pledge Quincannon." As if cued, Maxine du Pre arrived with a clipboard in her hands. "Since I know you've been ultra-careful about the Bad Word Ban and scrupulous about your conduct since the denim incident last term, those angry stipples must be a token of sisterly concern."

"Yes, Max—I mean, Madam Pledge Trainer."

"Thanks for sharing with the representatives of the other

Greek houses assembled outside. They need to be reminded how Sigma achieved its rep." The Midwestern girl waved her hand at a platinum-haired, demurely sweatered, and skirted senior following her. "Allow me to introduce our special guest, Miss Cynthia Lynch, president of Delta Gamma—hmmmgh."

The sudden throat clearing sounded spontaneous. Nora tried to keep her face solemn. Sigmas invariably called the fashion-snobbish clone sorority Delta Gamma Huche.

"And may I present Miss Arletta Tomasci of Kappa Iota Sigma." Gerry Vestry strode in beside a fox-faced, Mediterranean-complected girl whose hair swirled in a feathery wave reminiscent of Errata Stigmata from the *Love and Rockets* comic book. "She'll act as judge for that house."

Cynthia Lynch seemed fascinated by Charlotte and Nora's outfits, her eyes devouring them as Maxine resumed speaking. "Just to remind everyone, the three girls adjudicating each event have absolute say in all judgmental matters and rules interpretations."

"I am acting as Sigma Epsilon Xi's representative and have one vote, as does Miss Tomasci as Kappa's delegate. Miss Lynch's role of impartial judge from outside the Tri-Sigma houses carries one and one-half votes."

Gerry Vestry took up the recitation. Sigma Epsilon Xi's Greek letters showed low on the left lens of the glasses perched on her heart-shaped face. "Miss Lynch votes in the case of abstention by either Tri-Sigma Alliance judge, or to break any tie. Clear? Good."

"Competition points will be awarded by averaging the numerical evaluation scores given by all three judges," Maxine explained. She consulted the great pendulum clock tick-tocking grandly against the far wall. "In a few moments you'll proceed outside to this afternoon's contest. Once you finish, three Sigma Alpha Delta pledges will follow you in competition, then a trio of Kappa Iota Sigma aspirants."

"Followed by the next three in our own pledge class." Gerry Vestry's honey-light hair looked rich enough to spread on English muffins. She concluded, "And so on until all nine girls from each Tri-Sigma house have been tested and scored."

"Pledges, at attention!" Maxine ordered crisply in her flat farm-girl voice. "Now, slow-time, march!"

The bare-footed girls traipsed out of the social room and down the hallway toward the back yard at a deliberate pace. Their hips wobbled in steady sways, Nora's spectacularly so.

"Do you think she had that custom made?" Cynthia's whisper to Arletta could be heard the length of the corridor. "Or did she buy it off the race from the pro shop at MacArthur Boulevard, where the Oakland working women hook their 'dates'?"

"I hope that greasy barbecue smoke doesn't collect on my cami," Charlotte murmured to Nora as they waited inside the door to the back porch. "I want to wear it tomorrow on a very special all-night field trip."

Nora's body suddenly felt the man-hunger that had plagued her ever since Scott Madrigal turned out to be Ken Gormish, Delinda's two-timing beau. She recalled the languid evenings she'd spent in bed with him at her apartment in San Francisco, or out at his place in Walnut Creek.

The ache of betrayal had almost subsided enough for her to begin responding to the void he'd left in her life.

"Sigma pledges, outside!" Maxine had mastered the drill sergeant crackle in a command.

The three girls stepped out onto the porch. To the left lay the flagstones of the pledge patio, reserved by tradition for their exclusive use. A frowning pillory stood not more than six feet

from the patio's flat stones. Actives and pledges alike atoned
for sins between its boards at various times.

The Sigma House yard stretched on before the girls, protected from street view by a nine-foot adobe wall topped by
slick red tiles.

Smells of slow-cooking ribs, grilling frankfurters, and sput-
tering lamb-chunk shish kabobs poured over the three pledges.
Voices chattered from the milling sorority and fraternity actives.

"Nooo!" Judy shrieked, hands suddenly at her drawn, horrified cheeks.

"Gerry!" Charlotte gawked in a rare moment of uncool stupefaction.

"Shit on a prick procto!"

"That's two swats next Thursday come the Bad Word Ban
payoff, Pledge Quincannon," Maxine frowned. "That sounds
most unlike you. Have you been consorting with Susie Salton?"

" 'Smatter, girls, don't you remember the fun you had last
term clambering up the greased poles?" Gerry Vestry's silver-
rimmed spectacles caught the sunlight merrily. "It was the social coup of the fall semester."

"Last time we did that in our grungies," Judy's voice accused.
She sounded as if she teetered on the brink of tears. Her face
flamed as the fat boys slowly wheeled around to ogle the
pledges.

"T-shirt and jeans," Charlotte whispered. Her elegant gold-
threaded cami rippled with shudders. Shrill whistles of ribald
appreciation began. Her shoulders automatically straightened,
thrusting out her prize pectorals and lifting the fleur-figured
hem.

Then revulsion wracked her as she stared helplessly at the
three upright posts. Not quite as broad as a telephone pole,
each one reached eight feet above ground level. A plywood

platform shaped like a horned quarter moon had been nailed to each summit.

January had brought a false, warm spring to exacerbate California's drought. The shirtsleeve weather sunshine sparkled on the heavy yellow grease slathered thickly along each post, from the packed dirt it sat in to the arcing platform. A low-lipped crescent serving dish lay on the plywood, as the girls knew from bitter memories of the fall semester pole climb.

"We've arranged for your pledge meal at the top," Maxine declared in her emotionless Midwestern tones. "No more cold oatmeal. We've diced and boiled chitterlings—"

"Pig's guts?"

"Exactly, Pledge Bosk," Gerry Vestry nodded. "Cold as earthworms, but much more nutritious."

"Garnished with braised octopus eyes," Maxine continued impassively, "and served in a delicate sauce of cod liver oil and overaged white vinegar, seasoned with horseradish and a soupcon of Boraxo."

Cynthia Lynch made a startled face and nudged Arletta. She whispered, "We threaten them with live banana slugs at Delta G, but only make them eat dead ones. Just one each."

"Keep lots of sawdust on hand for the queasy tummies, too, I'll bet," Gerry Vestry commented. "Sigma girls know how to face adversity forthrightly. Correct, pledges?"

Three mumblings of assent followed.

"Uh, Madam Pledge Trainer, if we are sick—" Charlotte's beach-bred tan seemed strangely pallid and greenish.

"You'll smell foolish for the rest of the afternoon. As judges, we may subtract points, but that'll be adjudicated on a case-by-case basis, with appropriate voting." Maxine gestured toward a croquet-style rack holding field-issue sorority paddles. Each had been deeply branded with a sigma, an epsilon, and a xi.

"Of course, bowel or bladder incontinence will earn a supplementary reminder."

"Publicly," Gerry Vestry supplied.

"And the three worst times by each house's pledges merit a trip down the paddle line," Maxine stolidly declared. "Bare bottom, of course, and we've invited the fraternity actives present to participate."

"Time's a-wastin', girls." Gerry Vestry's delicate face tried to be stern as she pointed to the waiting posts. "Mount up and chow down. You must stay on the pole until your lunch is entirely consumed."

"That means entirely," Maxine emphasized. "Although we don't expect you to lick the plate."

"Any more than you have to while scarfing up the goodies. What, Pledge Quincannon? Speak up."

"Sorry, Madam Vice-President. I just said that octopuses are thought to be intelligent—the large ones, at least."

"We'll have to check that with Lucretia Sue Meredith, our alumna adviser." Gerry Vestry glanced right and left. "I don't see her. But that should add the spice of potential cannibalism to your meal."

Maxine pursed her lips. "Amy Morgenstern might be able to beg off on religious grounds. I'll ask Reverend Roundsong, since she's our spiritual adviser."

The senior efficiently bustled toward a large woman in corduroy robes cut to a semi-Medieval ecclesiastical pattern. She had a plate of ribs and beans, with bright grease spots and brown sauce flecking her double chin. Braids fringed a motherly face.

"I don't know why St. Cloud lets that flake teach her silly goddess worship." Cynthia tried to pitch her voice beneath any notice save one.

Arletta looked indignant, however. "I thought her Introduction to Religion lectures were the most inspirational things I've heard since Father McElroy gave our parish Lenten talks."

The Kappa Iota Sigma girl pointedly walked several steps away.

Meanwhile, the doomed Sigma House pledges approached the goo-laden uprights.

"Hey, shake your stuff up there, Blondie!"

"Flaunt 'em, honey. You sure got 'em!"

"I know the pair I wanna date! How about it, angel cheeks?"

Judy seemed oblivious to the raucous taunts. She appeared mesmerized by the oozy pole, a virgin faced with the sudden matrimonial demands of a cyclopean lover. With a flutter at her throat, she embraced the over-lubricated girth. Guck instantly seeped through her cotton undies.

She tucked her legs around the smooth trunk and tried to hoist herself aloft. Her neck craned sharply as she tried to keep her face away from the sickly yellow grease. Her shoulders strained away as well and she lost her grip.

Mouth twisting, she hugged the phalliform wood and worked her body like an inchworm. Her cheek and the corner of her lips became instantly slimed. Her hair slid through the goo. Her tummy squeezed against her backbone and her gorge rose.

It would be worse when she got to the top and had to . . . had to . . .

Her struggling body began to slide downward. Limbs churned against gravity and the purulent goop. Like a Victorian bride surmounting her first-night malaise, Judy rose to the occasion inch by hard-won inch.

Maxine du Pre watched Charlotte's laid-back cool peel away in shredded layers as the sophomore struggled up the slimy pole.

The elegant camisole all but dripped grease, the front clinging like a second, soiled skin.

The girl began to drift earthward. The hem rode up, exposing the fleurs-de-lis ornamenting her garter belt. An inch of loose fabric patterned with gold-thread raindrops fluttered above her frantically working bare buttocks.

The spread hindcheeks showed everything to the watching Greeks, without mercy.

"I see asshole!"

"Hey, I'd like to grease that beaver the way that pole's doin' it!"

"You can lick her off afterward!" a Kappa Iota active catcalled, before peeling the pop-top from a Coors can with her teeth.

"Points to the little one on style," Arletta sotto voce'd. "She tackles it and does the job."

"She's ready to barf, too," Cynthia sniffed. "Look at her."

"That's what I mean. She's ready to upchuck and she does what she has to do." The wavy-haired senior watched intently.

Nora felt grateful to whoever'd lavished the grease on her post. It prevented her naked breasts from chafing as she wriggled up the smooth wood. The satin bustier's ribs bit into the under-sides of her bosom and prodded into her soft underarms as she struggled frantically.

She felt an absolute fool for having made such a sexy show of herself. Trust Sigma to take a girl down a peg . . . five pegs. Scott Madrigal (the beastly Ken Gormish) had betrayed her for making herself erotically available. She flaunted herself again and Sigma disciplined her folly, spitting on her flagrant femi-ninity with bilious guck.

Served her right. The only thing more fitting for her was the vomitous banquet awaiting her in the bowl at the top of the post. Silly woman, trying to show the world that Charlotte Bosk wasn't the only train-stopping sensual beauty around here.

Chitlins, here I come, she vowed, as she felt herself slide downward. Angrily she checked the drop and squirreled her body higher, the bustier stays jabbing her as she undulated.

Her eyebrows reached the quarter-moon platform. Luncheon beckoned.

Ugh! They hadn't lied. Bulbous, ink-pupiled dead eyeballs regarded her from a mess of bite-sized hog intestines. She could smell the nauseous sauce above the stink of grease and the gritty barbecue smoke. Cod liver vinaigrette. Boraxo. Horseradish.

Enough for a feast. Her legs clung to the pole. She clutched the platform edge with slippery, sliding fingers. A breath . . . two breaths, and she plunged her mouth into the hideous repast like a dog muzzling slops in an alley.

Charlotte Bosk's sun-browned buttock rounds mashed against the ground as she rested her matted forehead on the greasy pole, ignoring further indignities to her slime-straggled hair. Long furrows in the post's slick coating traced her hard rise and precipitous fall.

Air, she needed cold air . . . her limbs felt hot, her tummy swollen with fire. The front of her destroyed camisole showed that she'd been spectacularly ill. She only inhaled acrid bile when she breathed.

"Hey, honey buns, stop layin' it in the mud. You're losin' the race. Shake your pussy up that big, long stick again." A raw, guffawing voice encouraged her.

Mud? Her naked seat did seem to be planted in something wet.

Her muscles carried the memory—her sudden loss of grip as nausea had convulsed her at the top of the pole. The frantic writhing that barely slowed her slide down the post. The noisy upchucking of that rancid pledge "luncheon" and her breakfast and every scrap she'd eaten for a week.

She pulled herself to her knees and embraced the pole. It no longer looked as slippery as it had been. She carried half its guck on her person, like a greased pig.

She'd seen the film *Dead Birds* in her cultural anthro class. The New Guinea locals had arrow-shot a shoat at their feast and let it gallop around in panic, fountaining its blood for their edification as it died.

Now she knew how the poor thing had felt. She only wished she could definitely, completely die at the end of her degrading display. She doubted that she could be so lucky.

Her lush body moved inch by filthy inch up the smeared post. Her throat already contracted in anticipation of the hog guts and chokingly thick, pungent cod oil, vinegar, and soap. The horseradish almost numbed her sinuses and made the mess tolerable.

"Angel ass is back in the race!"

"Shake it, sister! You've got a chance. That puny one looks ready to puke her guts out."

Charlotte's abdominal muscles locked as she shinnied higher. Poor Judy: that kid would be green. Those octopus eyes! The girls hadn't been kidding! No hardboiled eggs with dye for irises—no peeled figs doctored with egg white—not Sigma; real eyeballs sautéed in olive oil and marinated in stinking swill.

She dragged her fouled body up to the top again. She curled her cold fingers around the plywood platform's edge and faced the mess in the quarter-moon bowl.

The eyeball she'd spat out when she'd started retching lay atop the diced chitterlings. It stared to one side in shame.

She gathered her strength and tried to put her lips around it . . . just like some stud's nuts getting a Saturday Night Special tongue massage . . . she kept her mind blank.

Too big to swallow whole without choking. It half-filled her mouth. She hesitantly bit. Something awful and gelatinous squirted vengefully along her palate. Bile rose to meet it.

Her legs weakened. She hung by her desperate fingers, eyes screwed shut as gastric juices splashed out her nose. Don't let go—don't let go—don't drop!

She sucked air through her mouth around the ruptured lump. Cold tears drizzled from her face onto the bile-stained, snot-clotted chunks of intestine. She swallowed.

Her tummy rumbled, then subsided. Pressing her chill face into the waiting bowl, Charlotte began to eat once again.

"Ten points for Judy, definitely." Arletta rested a plastic plate of mushroom-heavy potato salad and thick shish-kabob chunks on the porch rail. "She looked like death, but overcame it. She didn't barf; she just did the job, much as she hated it. I say ten."

"I agree with what you say." Maxine brushed her foot against the racked sorority paddles. Her fingers toyed with well-ravaged ribs, picked clean of meat and membrane. Some sauce-dark gristle remained at the ends. "I'd still go for nine. Save ten for something extraordinary."

"Four." Cynthia sniffed. Her plastic fork toyed with cole slaw and prodded at a wienie barred with black grill marks. "Well, okay, maybe five. I mean, it did look better than that Charlotte's exhibition, but your girl Nora—"

"Nora's more than ten years older. Judy's just fresh out of school." Maxine shook her head. "I think she did a really strong thing."

"Subtract points because of that tacky outfit she wore?" Cynthia daintily nibbled at the end of her skewered hot dog.

The Sigma Epsilon Xi pledge trainer laughed. "That is her

best lingerie. We'll have to work on her wardrobe once she's initiated, come March."

"That Charlotte could give her lessons, but your Nora—" The Delta president rolled her eyes. "Strictly H-house City."

"Whore is spelled with a 'W,' dear," Arletta observed. "Have we final scores on Judy? I still push for ten."

"Nine."

"Okay, maybe a six—I just can't get behind that outfit being the nicest thing she could come up with." Cynthia tapped at a pocket calculator. "I think that averages out to eight, rounding down. Now, how about that Charlotte?"

"Mediocre climbing," Arletta evaluated. She squinted. "She's just sitting off by the wall, not mingling or anything. Four, with two points off of that for tossing her cookies."

"You're right about the climbing, but I'd call it five, with two points off." Maxine tapped her shoe against the paddle rack. "Three."

Cynthia seemed troubled. "Her clothes, though. I mean, she really messed up something really nice. I'd go for seven, with two down for becoming sick. Five total. Come on guys, she ruined a really great cami without whining."

"Two."

"Three."

"Okay." The Delta pecked at the calculator, visibly irked. "That rounds to three."

"An obvious candidate for the paddle line." Arletta turned to Gerry Vestry, who stood by the doorway with Sarah Bothington. "Who's next?"

Maxine stepped off the porch to announce the final scores.

Nora Quincannon drank some warm cider mulled with cloves and slices of Valencia orange. The sweet, citric nip almost purged that ghastly vinaigrette taste from her mouth. Her cramped, queasy stomach began to sail on an evener keel.

She watched other lingerie-clad girls squirm through the same ritual defilement. Some trouble erupted briefly, foolishly. A Kappa Iota Sigma Dutch-cut blonde with rising panic in her eyes refused to mount the freshly regreased pole. She curled into a ball, clutching her knees and jerking her head in terse, hard shakes.

Her sorority's actives clustered in consultation. One ran to the paddle rack on the porch. It took nine thumping slaps across the satin-pantalooned bottom to bring the pledge to her feet. Another five swinging whacks sent her scrabbling up the yellow-slimed post toward the top.

She slipped back, shinnied up, and slowly reached the platform level. She only stared at the cold, smelly mess in the half-moon bowl and wept, her fingers white talons on the plywood.

Finally the disgusted actives let her slide down to the ground. The two other pledges continued to gobble their bilious luncheons.

Nora suspected the crying girl who shivered on the unfriendly earth at the base of her post would be awarded a flat zero score. So it proved.

"Charlotte Bosk, Mona Forbes, and Francesca uh . . ."

Sigma Epsilon Xi's unlucky candidates stepped forward. Their greasy underpants had been stripped away. Bare bushes and buttocks diverted the multitude as the three sank onto knees and elbows for the classic sorority centipede crawl. Wide spacing allowed other girls to fit between them.

"Leyla Khalid, Sophia Withers, Lena Minski."

Sigma Alpha Delta frosh Khalid's fathomless black almond eyes studied the ground with rue as she took her place on all fours behind Charlotte. Her tawny Fertile Crescent hindcheeks mirrored the bounty of the naked moon that hovers at the nocturnal horizon.

"Samantha and Tabitha Tang, Marianna Trek."

The dainty Samantha crouched in line, her nose to the Arab student's gibbous wealth. Her own panther-sleek androgynous tail rounds twitched ahead of Mona Forbes's face. Fine sable pubic growth never disciplined to the rigors of a bikini cut proliferated between her trim thighs.

The vivid Tang girl-fur presented a near vista for Mona. Her own honey hair had matted badly, and her bruised-mauve irises expanded as she squinted briefly at the lingering afternoon sun.

Those softly submissive rounds so feelingly plastered by cousin Rita's leather and board—plus the beastly length of garden hose—and by Professor Porter's whispering tutorial cane, those hindmost loveglobes once gripped and crammed by her impetuous lover Ron: those fair peach-curved hillocks now dimpled and twinkled in abject fear.

A line of grinning guys, glossy-faced with barbecue fat, breath rich from Coors and Heineken, stood swinging long-bladed Greek paddles. Their legs stretched far, far akimbo in invitation, and they seemed to extend to infinity in daunting succession.

"A stately procession, now, girls," Gerry Vestry instructed firmly. "Any rushing will only earn you a second trip, baby seal bare from chin to toe. Get ready, get set . . ."

Charlotte's fluttery jaw jutted upward, its aim centered between the college boy's arched legs.

"On the count, Go!" Maxine's steady voice set the cadence. "Right knee . . . left knee . . . right knee . . . left knee . . ."

The nine pledges shuffled forward at her command, their enticingly stark haunches swaying.

"Nothin' personal, nookie-tookie." The bright, scalding *Swat!* punctuated a moron's laugh. Charlotte ground her teeth and concentrated on Maxine's impassive tone. The board caught her twice more before her stinging hindquarters swayed through the guy's legs and she approached the next member of the paddle line.

"Right knee . . . left knee . . ."

Pain had all nine pledges in sobbing tears halfway through the paddle line. Nora wondered if poor, distraught Mona had ever had her rumpsteaks grilled quite as thoroughly, even given her ex-roomie Rita's disciplinary pranks.

The drunken frat rats callously walloped the provocative bare bottoms and thighs wiggling between their vaulting legs. The air rang with the solid Splat! Splat! Splat! of heinously applied hardwood.

Nora saw that Samantha Tang's pert Asian buttocks had already gone beet-dark, with bluish streaks. No matter. The paddle-fire crackled as she writhed onward.

Leyla Khalid's desert mare crupper wore the sizzling sheen of a naked houri cast out into the sands to blister for her sins under the penitential sun. Her long black hair dragged along the grass as she kept her face respectfully low. Lucretia Sue had spoken to Sigma House about her own sojourn in a Persian Gulf prison just last summer. Had Miss Khalid known the masculine weight of a camel's whip across her shoulders or rump?

Nora pondered on the differences between the arrogant male East and comfy, American Orinda, California.

"May I get you some more cider? Uh, miss?" A crop-haired jock with a quivering Adam's apple appeared at her elbow. Adoration and uncertainty warred in his face as his eyes took in her bedraggled charms. "Please?"

"Thank you." She tried not to laugh as she melted him with a smile. He couldn't have been much more than ten years younger than she was. She set her hips in a bold slant, aware of her own barely hidden muff and paddle-dappled rear.

He galloped to oblige her.

The line of college boys wielded the boards in a mocking chorus. "You chose this! You chose this!" they chanted.

The crawling pledges wavered a moment, then pressed on as the last girl, the Dutch-cut Kappa Iota, collapsed and groveled in yipping hysterics.

"I've never had the board so bad." Marianna Trek mournfully clutched her plum-blotched hams. Not a shade of color showed in the quivering face under her platinum Dutch-cut locks. "Does Sigma Epsilon Xi treat you like—"

"Yeah." Mona Forbes did a shuffling dance in the upstairs room as she eased her paddled bottom into panties. "Often."

Samantha and Tabitha Tang exchanged tear-dried looks. "I guess Kay-Eye isn't so bad."

"I thought that pole and that dog's vomit luncheon would kill me," Lena Minski declared. She had her grease-filthied lingerie in a shopping bag. She appeared reluctant to don the dress she'd arrived in.

"My mom never used her own sorority board on me that hard," she continued, "and I got it almost weekly, bending over the arm of the couch with my panties down to my knees, all the way through high school—"

"And still get your ass tanned on vacations. Yeah, yeah." Sophia Withers' boy-cut punk hair had been lovingly streaked with ripples of bright fuchsine never found in nature. On closer examination, her inverted cross earrings turned out to be Batman, suspended by his heels, his cape spreading behind his body, his arms and head composed of tiny silver skulls. "Such a production."

Leyla Khalid contributed an exquisite shrug of her tawny nude torso. "In Qu'imram, our women do not have the freedom to wiggle their bare bottoms before mixed gatherings. You should reverence the opportunity. It is unique to your Western lands."

"I'll kiss the ground when I get out to the street." Sophia unrolled the midnight black corduroy jumpsuit she'd arrived in. She didn't bother to peel off the guck-slimed lavender satin corselet. She carefully fit one foot in a leg and started to pull up the outfit.

"Humiliated, poisoned, and paddled to a pulp," Lena encapsulated. "Except for the toxic diet, I could have gone home to my parents' for the holiday weekend. I don't know that this is such a great testament to freedom, Leyla. My tushie feels like I sat in that barbecue fire and packed a load of hot coals with me. I don't need the joys of sweet Greek sisterhood to have that."

"I won't be able to sit a minute during my date tomorrow," Charlotte mourned. She shimmied her sore, bewitchingly burgundied nethercheeks into a white wool skirt and buttoned it snugly at the waist.

"He won't want you sitting anyway." Sophia zipped the corduroy jumpsuit shut over her soiled corselet. She faced the disapproving stares of girls who'd discarded their own slimed underthings. "Hey, I'm going to burn every stitch I have on once I get back to my apartment. I'm going to forget today happened, okay?"

"Sigma House never lets you forget," Mona winced as she tentatively rubbed a swollen gluteal mound.

THE DAYS AT FLORVILLE
by Richard Manton

With many novels to his credit, including the best-selling The Captive *series, Richard Manton is a mainstay of the Blue Moon library.* The Days at Florville *has been a reader favorite since its publication. Let us allow Manton himself to set the scene: "Half an hour before midnight, Lesley is secured face down on a black leather sofa, her bottom bare. It is more than three hours later when the last strokes of the whipping are given. In the manner of a roman nouveau, the whipping is not directly described. The reader sees it through the camera lens, its photographs studied through the eyes of an adolescent boy." The central act of the drama begins with the audiotape accompaniment to the fifth photograph of the sequence, which appears after the first break in the following excerpt.*

As summer turned to autumn, the stars glittered more coldly above the tide-washed sand and the white terrace of the casino. By late afternoon the sun was low in the sky and the wide boulevards of Florville were empty of all movement but the dry scuffling of fallen leaves.

The Villa Rif stood untenanted and desolate in its deep gardens. Those whose voices and passions animated it in summer had gone, some to the winter city and a few to that other house beyond frontiers and a mountain range. The very furniture had been removed from the spacious rooms, leaving only the bare floors and the walls and ceilings from which footsteps rang harshly.

A boy of fourteen, a solitary youth with private dreams and passions, noticed the open and untended gates on a fine autumn afternoon. Unchallenged, he walked along the driveway to the house, the grass and weeds already luxuriant after several weeks of neglect.

The windows of the house were shuttered and its doors still locked. Yet the first of the equinoctial storms had blown down a small tree and broken a catch on one of the window shutters. The boy heard the irregular clatter of the hinged wood, swinging back against the stucco of the wall.

No one would come there again until the winter was past and the early spring brought a time for refurbishing and painting the villa in readiness for the new season. The boy followed the sound and found the open shutter. It could only be secured from the inside. The boy knew that it would be an easy matter to open the window, close the shutter and the catch from within, then let himself out by one of the doors which would lock again by means of its Yale fastening.

As he swung himself through the space of the window and into the first room, the boy paused and gazed at the ghostly grandeur of the bare walls, dimly lit by the light which filtered through the slats of the closed shutters. He walked slowly through the echoing apartments until he came at last to a room that was brightly lit by contrast with the others, for its windows were covered by an iron grille and it needed no shuttering.

The floor of this room was paved in marble and the walls with their white tiles seemed like those of a prison or institution. It was strangely furnished. A hand basin and a toilet pedestal gave it the appearance of a washroom. Yet there was also a padded leather sofa with no back but having a heavy scroll at one end. This was almost the only piece of furniture left in the villa and stood at the center of the paved floor. At intervals on its mahogany frame, restraining straps had been strongly riveted to the wood.

The boy was intrigued by the disorder of this room, as if it had been left forgotten by the occupants of the villa. No attempt to tidy it had been made in the days before their departure.

On the sofa lay a young woman's panties, a brief film of apple-green translucence. The boy's interest quickened as he picked them up. A bamboo cane and an open jar of Vaseline were on the floor beside the divan. As he lifted up these curious items, he noticed that where the restraining straps were low down, beneath the padded scroll, the varnished wood bore sheaves of tiny scratches, as if from the frenzied nails of strapped hands. The wiping rag and a box of tissues lay on the sofa. A pulse of excitement and curiosity beat harder in the boy's throat as he tried to conjecture what had been done to the young woman in this room. On the padded leather sofa lay a soft pliable gag strap, upon which it was just possible to see the impress of her teeth clenched in desperation. A pencil-shaped glass squirt and the liquid soap dispenser from the hand basin had been left on a nearby stool.

Entranced by these objects, the boy examined the brief silk panties eagerly. They were not the knickers of a schoolgirl or a teenage nymph, but belonged, he thought, to a mature young Venus.

The rest of the villa was empty, devoid of furniture or even discarded clothing. It was only as the boy walked through the rooms for a last time that he noticed the white leaves of paper in a grate.

There was no doubt that the bundle had been placed on the fire in order that it should be burnt. Some charring of the paper suggested that a match had been set to it and that it had been left to blaze. Whether it was carelessness in arranging it or some quirk of downdraught in the chimney would never be known.

Yet the boy picked the papers out and found them unharmed. There was also a small package, which when unwrapped contained a recording.

The boy's heart jumped as he saw that most of the papers were full-plate photographic prints, ten inches by twelve. At the top of the pile was a surreptitiously taken picture of a young woman standing in a garden with a child of ten or eleven. The boy looked at her firmly mature young figure, the fair urchin crop, and the regular fair-skinned features. He turned the print over and saw the name "Lesley" penciled on the back.

There was no time to examine the rest in detail. A glance at them proved that most had been taken in the tiled room of the villa at night. They showed Lesley stripped and at the mercy of two sadistic prison guards. Anticipation rather than unease made the boy collect these discarded treasures quickly and make his way from the Villa Rif.

Returning home, he locked the door of his room to guard against parental intrusion, and began to investigate the photographs and the recording . . .

The preliminaries were over, and Lesley was sprawling on her belly over the cushions, still strapped by one ankle. Her face was turned in dismay towards her ravishers, one of whom had now picked up a long slim cane. The light caught a trace of wetness in the rear parting of her thighs and a slight oily smear at the meeting of Lesley's buttocks.

"Take your hands away from your bottom, Lesley," said the voice of the man on the recording. "You won't like the cane across your knuckles."

"Wait," said the second man. "She needs more cushioning under her belly, so that her arse is properly lifted. Lift your hips a little, Lesley! At once! Or must we add a refusal to your punishment?"

There was a sound of the cushions being arranged and the cane being lightly touched across the young wife's buttocks. Then the cane lashed down in a vicious stroke across the bare pale cheeks of Lesley's bottom. There was a split-second's pause of total silence. And then Lesley screamed.

Again the bamboo rang out across the firm pallor of Lesley's bottom-cheeks—and again she screamed at the swelling agony of the impact. Eagerly the boy counted the strokes to himself to see if it would be six—but it was more—or twelve—but that passed, too.

The clock in this photograph showed that it was half an hour after midnight and that a dozen strokes or so of the caning had been given. The bamboo had left deeply colored weals across the firm erotic maturity of Lesley's bare bottom, as well as two marks across the backs of her thighs. Frantic with the burgeoning smart, the young woman had twisted round on her hip and was clinging hard to the arm of her chastiser to prevent him from raising the cane. Under the parted fringe, her blue eyes were imploring him as if her life depended on his answer. Her mouth had the woebegone, downturned shape of a penitent little girl who pleads with her teacher.

The next camera study was made only a few moments later. Yet there was a significant and predictable change in the scene. To avoid such an interruption as had taken place, Lesley's wrists were strapped together to the far end of the sofa frame and the caning had continued. Her fingernails clawed at the polished wood until they broke in the agony of the thrashing. Her hands clenched into fists until the nails drew blood from her palms.

Her head was still turned, her mouth and eyes wide under the fringe of her short-cut fair hair as she screamed for a respite. But the two men replied to the desperate appeals of the promiscuous young wife with smiles that promised a long ordeal. The man with the cane had thrashed the crowns of Lesley's twenty-eight-year-old bottom-cheeks to deep crimson. Now he was measuring the bamboo across the softer, sensitive under-curve of her backside, just above the crease dividing her buttocks and thighs.

On the recording, the boy heard Lesley scream at the first of these savage lashes of the cane. Yet even so he was able to hear how the men had taught her to accept the inevitability of her punishment. Half an hour before, under the first stroke, he had heard the young woman cry out not to be caned. It amused him now to hear Lesley screaming instead only to have her strokes delayed. The boy hoped this would be denied—and it was.

It was almost one o'clock and the boy felt a stiffening excitement in his loins at the knowledge that the two men had made Lesley's punishment last so long. Indeed, it was by no means over, though the scene had once more altered. From the voices on the recording, the boy had heard that Lesley was crossing her legs desperately, jamming one knee into the back of the other to contain the appalling smart of the bamboo. The men had already denied her this relief by strapping her ankles a few inches apart to the sofa frame.

To take the cane upon the flank of her hip was painful enough. Yet the boy had counted at least fifty strokes of the bamboo across Lesley's bottom and knew how frantic she must be to shield it from further punishment. So she had begun to twist on her side, away from the man with the cane. It was the second man who came to his colleague's assistance. Smiling at the folly of Lesley's attempted evasion, he perched on the edge of the sofa, tightened his arm over her waist, and turned her seat back to face the punishment. He remained like this, holding her, so that only Lesley's bottom and legs were visible in the photograph. It was on the recording that the chastiser's voice explained the consequences of her disobedience.

"Your punishment will continue in a moment, Lesley. First of all, you must receive properly the extra stroke that you tried to avoid. Then there will be six extra strokes for your failure to keep still."

The boy listened with his pulse racing to the sounds that followed these words. He heard the extra strokes given with vicious skill. Lesley screamed for her husband, her lovers, her children, as if one or all of them could hear her and would come to her rescue.

It was also in this photograph that Lesley, in her writhing, had thrust her bottom out to its fullest extent and thus offered her most complete rear view. The boy took a magnifying glass and scanned the picture with prurient curiosity. He saw, between the rear of her thighs, the light pubic hair matted by the moisture of sexual excitement. Between her buttocks, the few stray hairs near Lesley's anus were plastered flat on the smooth skin by the sheen of the Vaseline.

At this point, for the prison thrashing was still continuing after one o'clock, the boy could not resist glancing at the piquant contrast offered by Lesley in the days before her enslavement. There was a photograph of her gardening in the black coolie-suit, not long before she had renounced her married life and children. Her present ordeal was all the more exciting for this portrait. The picture showed Lesley standing to face the camera, holding a child with its back to her; the arrogant blue eyes were looking a little away from the lens, and the fair-skinned facial beauty under the parted fringe was marred by her customary sulkiness, seen most clearly in her mouth and chin. How much more the boy preferred to see her contrite and weeping under the bamboo.

From this portrait of an emancipated young woman, the boy turned to a full-plate study of Lesley's face during the present caning. He held the two pictures side by side and saw how the arrogant self-possession had crumbled at the first strokes of the cane. The picture of Lesley's face while she was chastised was one that any true disciplinarian would have hung among the treasures of his collection. Under the long fair-haired fringe, the aloof blue eyes were now wide with pain, the mouth forming a howling oval of torment.

Like the chastiser in the next picture, the boy had to undo the front of his trousers at this point in order to ease the discomfort of his erection.

Lesley's bottom was once again the center of the composition. Now, however, tight strapping round her waist held her down without the need of a man's arm. The hands of the clock showed that the picture had been taken at just before half-past one in the morning.

There was no longer any part of Lesley's behind that was not deeply colored by the cane, except for a strip of whiteness where her buttocks curved in together. The cane was unable to touch her there and, for that reason, a whip was kept in readiness.

The chastiser was now caning her hard and sharply across the earlier weals of the bamboo. Lesley's voice was shrill with panic: "Don't cane me anymore! Not yet! Please! Oh, please!"

"Lie forward properly over the cushions, Lesley," said the man impatiently. "Don't clench your buttocks like that!"

"I'm being tortured!" Her cry made the stone walls ring.

The other men laughed.

"You shall learn the true meaning of that word, Lesley, in the place to which you are being sent."

With astonishment and delight, the boy saw that the caning had still not finished. The supple bamboo rod smacked and lashed across the woven crimson that marked Lesley's buttocks.

For the first time, the boy paused to consider his own reactions as he followed the events of the photographs and the recording. In truth, he had first heard Lesley's cries and out-bursts with a profound shock. By now, however, he was in-trigued enough to consider them more rationally. He noticed, from the intensity of her screams, that the initial impact of the cane across Lesley's bottom seemed to swell for several seconds to an unbearable torment, sharpening her cry to a wild shriek.

It was also evident that her screams were now more abrupt than they had been at first, perhaps from so much crying out and pleading. It could scarcely be that she noticed the pain less. Between the strokes and the screams, Lesley gave vent to a storm of sobbing, rising in shrillness of falling in despair, like the arpeggios of punishment.

The boy wondered if the drama was merely acted for camera and recording. Perhaps it was. Yet he knew by instinct that no actress, of however consummate ability, could mimic such a performance as Lesley's. In the photographs, there was a sense of authenticity that the onlooker saw immediately.

In the present photograph, Lesley's high-crowned head was turned, so that she faced her chastisers in pain and panic.

"You've cut me!" she cried out. "I can feel it!"

The boy looked quickly at the photograph. Where the bam-boo had landed aslant Lesley's right-hand bottom-cheek it had raised a well-marked weal. It was plain to see that several ruby dots had welled up along this line, and that the largest of them was trickling down the lower curve of Lesley's backside to gather in the crease that divided her thigh and her behind. The men dismissed her frantic cry.

"You have much to learn about prison thrashings, Lesley. You are not a little girl being smacked by a teacher. A young married woman of your age and type must expect a prolonged judicial punishment. A well-used bamboo will cut your back-side a number of times before the thrashing is over. Lie forward properly over the cushions. There is much worse to come yet!"

There was much following this which had not been photo-graphed, yet was to be heard in fragments on the recording. At one moment it seemed that Lesley was undergoing a softer or-deal in the hands of the two men, for she sounded like a spanked little girl now pleading affectionately to be loved and forgiven.

Soon after this, she cried out in panic and seemed to wrestle vainly with the men who positioned her. A man's voice said, "Don't be foolish, Lesley. You're here to be punished. We want you strapped bottom-upwards over the sofa-scroll, bending very tightly forward."

It was shortly before two in the morning. Lesley was indeed strapped down and kneeling very tightly forward over the heavy padded scroll at the end of the sofa, her arms strapped at full stretch to the base of its frame. In this posture her firm pale buttocks were pulled hard apart, showing the yellowed-ivory smoothness of Lesley's bottom-crack where the skin curved in towards her anus.

They were punishing the young wife for her promiscuity, using a pony lash with a stout handle and a short tail of braided leather. It was the second man who whipped her now. He cracked the snakeskin lash across the bare pale moons of Les-ley's bottom in a sinuous weal. The whip curved and clung agonizingly to her first seat-cheek, curled down into Lesley's bottom-crack, and then curved up over the further cheek of her behind.

Lesley's high-crowned urchin-crop was turned, and the blue eyes under her parted fringe matched the expressive frenzy of the shriek on the recording. Every muscle in her thighs and hips seemed contracted by the anguish; her knees were jammed urgently together and her toes curled with the sheer intensity of the impact.

Unmoved by this, the man who held the lash took aim across

Lesley's backside, even including the rear of her thighs, and whipped, and whipped, and whipped.

There was a pause in the discipline, allowing Lesley to check her sobs a little. It seemed that the men wished her to understand exactly what was going to happen.

"Now you must undergo the last part of your threshing, Lesley. It will be the hardest for you to bear. The full rigor can only be exercised when you are already supremely sensitive from the previous strokes. Let us have no hypocrisy about punishment. I want to take you far, far beyond the limits of punishment, into a twilight world where nothing exists for you but the anguish of the whip across your bare buttocks. Don't twist your mouth from the cotton wad, Lesley! It is prudent that you should be gagged for this last adventure!"

Even before the first stroke was given, the recording caught the small sounds of Lesley's frenzy. Her shrill pleading and protests were reduced by the gag to an urgent mewing. The sofa springs echoed the strapped writhing of her thighs and hips. He heard the young wife's bare belly slithering vainly on buttoned leather in the sweltering southern night. Unable to contain her panic, there was a short sound of feminine rudeness from Lesley's behind.

Was it all a charade or did it truly happen as the man promised? The boy heard a wild mewing as the smack-cuts of leather across Lesley's bottom made the stones ring. As for the next photograph, it had been taken just after half-past-two.

In this full-plate study, the whipping was over, the last stroke just given. Lesley was unfastened and her gag removed. Indeed, the two men had raised to her feet this urchin-cropped young wife, her firm erotic maturity laid pale and bare. As they assisted her upright, it seemed that Lesley's bottom had patterned the floor with red petals from the final tapestry of the pony lash.

There was one more detail, deeply exciting to the boy as

proof of how far the men had taken her. Lesley's head drooped on the man's shoulder as he held her, her arms limp at either side. The second man stared in wide-eyed admiration and open-mouthed delight. Like a ravished virgin bride, Lesley had swooned in her chastiser's arms!

CHRYSANTHEMUM, ROSE, AND THE SAMURAI

by Akahige Namban

On her way from Britain to a mission in China, Rosamund is swept ashore on the coast of Japan following a shipwreck. Held captive by thugs, the innocent girl is tattooed and sold to a brothel. From there her adventures multiply, as she encounters the full range of seventeenth-century Japanese society, from enlightened Buddhists to roughs and rogues. Unusual in its setting and wealth of historical detail, Chrysanthemum, Rose, and the Samurai is a fast-paced adventure story, the erotic equivalent of Shogun.

The young man clutched at his loose trousers as he watched the old man enter the maid. She lay there, struggling awhile as the thick pale flesh pole entered her. The old man pushed on her inexorably, his massive member disappearing gradually in her dark cleft, barely painted by a brush of black hair. The boy could see the sweat on her brow as finally the hair at the root of the man's cock melded with her own, and she took the full weight of the old sea rover on her slim body. The old man began moving. He drew his prick out so that it showed over her thighs, and then thrust himself home again with a massive grunt. She raised her brown stocky legs over his massive back. He thrust his tongue into her mouth as she began moaning, whether with the weight or with pleasure, the boy could not tell. The old man's rhythm increased, and the girl raised her body to meet his. The rice bales on which she was lying shifted under the pounding pressure. The man slid his hands down her haunches and hid them under her ass. She moaned again and the tempo of the fuck increased. He changed the speed of his thrusts. They became slower but deeper, almost brutal. His belly slapped down onto the girl's, and she cried, "Please, please," asking him to stop or continue, the watcher could not tell. The man raised his head from the girl's and his face became red and apoplectic. "I'm coming, I'm coming," he cried. His loins slammed into the girl's and she raised her head in ecstasy. The man shot off his load and his body jerked with the power of it. The girl drew her fingers hard against the man's shoulders, but made no impression with her short nails on the thick hide, darkened by sun and wind.

The old man lay on the girl as if dead. His thick white-streaked beard tickled her shoulder. At last, impatiently, she twitched her leg. He grunted and rolled off of her. He was a giant of a man, and her figure, a golden brown color, looked like a doll's next to his. He tweaked a dark brown nipple on the almost flat breast, and she stretched voluptuously, then lay her hand on the limp soggy prick beside her. He grinned, said something in a low voice the young watcher could not hear, and stood up. After adjusting his clothing, he walked out of the barn. The girl lay there, her flat-nosed face calm, her eyes almost closed.

The young man stared at the wet dribble on the cracked wooden wall of the barn before him. He shivered, and then his eyes hardened with resolve. Restoring his still hard prick to his trousers, he walked around to the entrance to the barn. He could still see the tall broad figure of his father walking towards the villa they lived in. He marched into the barn to confront the maid. She had dressed by then, wrapping her gown tightly around her, and was now adjusting her sash. She looked at him as if in surprise, and then, noting the look on his face, grinned slyly.

"Well, young master, enjoyed the show?"

The young man tried to swallow, found his throat dry. Faced with the reality, he could barely get a word out of his mouth. His hands leaped forward as if on their own, and he seized the girl's small breasts for an instant, their prominent nipples burning his palms. She slipped aside, slapped his groping hands.

"No, no. Still too small for me. I prefer bigger men." Her hand snaked out and grabbed him by the crotch. Not hard enough to really hurt, the movement was a surprise to the boy, who was still confused both by his lust and his inexperience. She ran to the door.

"When you grow older, young master," she said, flipping her skirts at him, "and bigger!" With a giggle, she was gone. The boy was left alone in the barn with his painful erection.

Okiku was breathing evenly, unlike the man she was riding. Her thighs gripped him unmercifully as her hands traced patterns on the muscled chest. The man beneath her she had met on the road, and liking his looks, she had made advances: breathed harshly and arched her back. He tried to stab her innards with his prick, but she rode so skillfully that he was never able to reach the orgasm he craved. His prick, she noted, did not give her as much pleasure as she had hoped. She rammed herself hard down on him, leaning forward to bring her clit into contact with his erect maleness. That last motion was too much for him. He exploded wildly, wetting her insides with a torrent of juice. With disappointment she felt his prick shrink inside her as soon as he had finished. She ejected his cock with her interior muscles and rose to her feet. He rose after her, fumbling at his loincloth.

"Well, sweetie," he said. "How was it? Good?"

She snorted in derision. "It was probably the worst fuck I've ever had." She turned to get her clothes and brushed the leaves off her knees.

"Oh, yeah?" he said. He had the rough accents of a southerner. "Come here, and I'll show you what's what."

"Oh, go and play with yourself." Okiku was too confident of her abilities to assume the attitude of servility and helplessness expected of women. Angered, he tried to seize her and instead of pulling back, she leaned forward. With her two hands, she grasped his thumb and little finger, and then throwing her weight to one side, she held her elbows and shoulders rigid. There was a snap, and the man screamed in a high-pitched voice. His wrist dangled. Quickly, Okiku snaked a hand into the cloth belt he wore around his middle. While riding him she had felt the wallet there. Before the hurt man could do a thing, she had leapt back, the heavy wallet in her hand. She extracted the three silver pieces it contained and threw it contemptuously back in his face. Grabbing her clothes, walking stick and bundle, she skipped back through the bushes in the direction of the dimly seen village of Miura, tugging her robe around her as she walked. Not satisfied, except financially, by her exercise, she rubbed her mound pensively as she walked, the thrills continuing to race up her spine the closer she slid down the slopes to the village.

Rosamund woke gradually. The pounding she noticed first was that of the surf, roaring in behind her as it had roared when the ship went down. She had thrown off her habit when she tried to swim to shore, and was now naked but for her shift. The warm sand gritted on her fair skin. She picked herself up, spitting out sand grains. She was in a small rounded cove, bounded on either end by piles of gray rock. Before her rose a steep slope covered with bushes and trees. Feathery plumes of some paler green growth she could not identify waved in the wind. She rose completely and took stock of herself. Her crucifix and habit were gone. Besides a thin transparent shift, she had only herself. Full white breasts topped by cherry-like nipples hid a smoothly sloping stomach, which funneled into a generous stretch of hair, a darker version of the gold on her head. Long legs, pale except for their backs, where they were burned from overexposure, completed the ensemble.

She wondered where she was. Her upbringing and subsequent life had been sheltered. She knew little of the world beyond that which she had been taught at the convent. She had been on her way to Cathay to establish a mission to the heathen Chinese when the ship had foundered in the storm. Perhaps she was already in China, or much better, the Philippine Islands, ruled by His Most Catholic Majesty Philip III of Spain. That would be nice, she decided, being rescued by a handsome don, who would take her away from her expected fate as a nun.

Still unsteady, she began walking towards the shade of the trees before her. As she approached, she stepped on a dry branch, which broke under her feet. A human figure popped up suddenly from behind a bush. She gave a short surprised yelp, and then paused to look before fleeing. The young man had a smooth bronze-colored face with almond-shaped eyes and high cheekbones. He wore a blue kerchief folded over his head in a peculiar three-cornered fashion and loose colorful clothes, and carried a short curved sword in his sash. A staff with a gnarled top and a bag of checkered blue cloth lay at his feet.

Goemon, for so he now called himself, watched the apparition before him. She was, he decided, a woman of the Southern Barbarians. But she was dressed, or undressed. He licked his lips slowly. The pale cotton shift barely went to her knees, and being slightly wet, was transparent throughout.

He reached out a hand and said, "Don't be afraid." Mistaking his motion and not understanding his words, Rosamund turned and ran. Goemon, intending to explain, leaped after her. She ran across the sands, her shift flying. He closed in on her easily, but as he closed, he began noticing the details of her body. Her high pale ass swung before him, now hidden, now exposed. Beneath it he could see the tufts of the delicate golden beard she wore between her legs. Her heavy breasts enticed him as they bobbed from side to side. He made a flying leap, and they tumbled together into the sand, he on top. At the feel of her skin, his prick rose and knocked against her exposed belly. Not pausing, he loosened the ties of his trousers, and his magnificent erection swung free. She tried to push him away, and her hand slipped, sliding down to grab his swaying stick unintentionally. They both gasped: he with pleasant anticipation, she with surprise. The prick was almost the thickness of her wrist. She stared at it in dread mixed with anticipation. Having seen the eagerness gleam in his eyes, she knew what lay in store for her. The prick rose, a dark brown column nesting in black hairs. Below it dangled a soft-looking pulsing bag covered with the same dark hairs. The wide dark tip of the prick seemed to stare at her blindly from one eye. She shrieked and let go, but he held her hand fast and brought her soft white palm up and along the length of the shaft. He was grinning. She struggled and squirmed to extricate herself, but his knees forced her legs apart. He wedged himself between her knees as she struggled desperately to escape. He pushed. His prick missed its target and ploughed its sticky way up her pussy. Excited by the roughness of the hairs, he tried again. Her movements while trying to escape excited him. He pinned her to the ground with his body and stuck his fingers into the pink opening of her cunt. Dry and virginal, the cunt twitched in his grasp, and she screamed. He laid his index finger on the nub of her clitoris,

then folded the thick labial lips over his finger with delight.
The little hole moistened lightly. He kept on moving his hand
while pinning her down with his body. Releasing her hands,
which commenced to beat on his shoulders ineffectually, he
pushed her thighs apart. Spread beneath him, thighs wide, the
pink framed with gold lips presented a target that could not be
missed. He slammed his body forward from his position on all
fours. His prick hit the mark. She screamed again, louder this
time, as his lance entered the smooth channels of her body. He
surged upwards and inwards, digging toes into sand as his prick
burrowed into her belly. Their hair meshed and he drove their
pelvic bones together. He rotated his loins in delight as she lay
moaning beneath him.

His prick began the familiar pumping motion, almost too
excited for him to control. He drew it out almost to the tip,
then thrust home once more. Again and again he repeated his
action, as her pained stare began to change into a look of not-
unpleasant surprise. Before she could explore this sensation
further or begin to understand it, he exploded. Clouds of sperm
flew from his prick, inundating her insides, smoothing their
membranes. He bored into her, uncaring, his eyes open and
staring as if in a fit, his hands seizing and crushing her tits until
she cried again in pain.

When it was over, he lay on her belly, idly sucking her nipples. She whimpered and moved slightly beneath him. Oblig-
ingly, he rolled off her and smiled happily. He examined her
bloom-and-come stained thighs, her wet matted hairs, and
smiled with satisfaction and delight. His hand roved over her
full breasts, smacking her fingers aside as she tried to stop him.
He then delved again into her sopping cunt, spreading the
hairs. She tried to move away from his touch. A cuff on the
nearest fat firm breast put an end to that.

"You are interesting-looking," he said, and leaned over to

suck a nipple rising cheekily near his face. "In a while I'll do it again, and this time you will enjoy it."

She answered in a language he did not know. He tried Dutch.

She looked at him in surprise. The nuns who had raised her had spoken High German, and the language he was speaking sounded like a variant of that. After a fashion, his hands still exploring her ripe body, they began to communicate.

"That was terrible, a sin."

"So, you are a kerisitan?"

The question surprised her for a minute, but then she answered: "Yes, a Christian. A Christian nun." Or at least, she thought, a novice. "It is sinful to abuse me as you have done."

He grinned at her. "Here in Nippon, the kerisitan sect is banned. I would not admit to membership in it if I were you. You would be crucified."

She shuddered with fear. The thought of holy martyrdom rose before her eyes for a moment, and was then overcome by the fear of death.

"What is this horrible place where men . . . where men . . ." She couldn't express the word in her limited German, and even in her native tongue, the word would not have come easily to her lips.

He grinned again and patted her belly. "Before you go to the cross, I will make use of you again." She stared in fascinated horror as the glistening length of his prick began to swell again.

He spread her thighs brutally once more, taking in with his eyes the sight of her bleeding and sopping cunt. Then, leaning forward, he lapped at the lips and commenced sucking at the prominently erect clitoris. Her hands groped in the sand, not knowing how to react to the sensation—painful, but overcast with a new emotion she knew somehow was sinful—the lingual massage roused in her. He delighted in his power. Drunk with the smell and taste of her awakening cunt, he fell prostrate by the blow from the piece of driftwood she had found in the sand.

The chase this time was a repetition of the first, but both participants moved slower. His kerchief absorbed the blood from his scalp wound, and the pain from the blow dissolved into the pleasure of pursuit as the white thighs, now speckled with a few drops of blood, fled before him. He caught up with her in the shade of the woods. He threw her on the ground and buried his face in her heaving and sweaty breasts. Her gasps were compounded of pain, fear, and a newfound delight as he bit her nipples and tits, bringing blood. Her nipples sprang erect. She closed her thighs forcefully, but they were dragged apart. He shoved his rampant prick into her torn hole. The burning sensation from the unhealed wound overcame her for a minute, but then the delight of the sharply biting teeth and sucking lips, and above all, the monster serpent in her pussy, drove all thoughts from her head. Her head began twisting from side to side, a twin to her hips that swiveled and tried to swallow more of the meat shoved into her. Unfamiliar waves rose from her cunt to her spine and head. The pleasure became unbearable as he bore into her. She dug her heels into the ground, not to push him off, but to force more of him into her. The pain of the drilling rod did not disappear, but added to her pleasure.

Goemon collapsed on her. He closed his eyes, allowing his prick and come to trickle gradually out of her cunt and down the crack of her ass. The power of his orgasm made his head throb at the wound, and he slid off her perfect white belly, unconscious.

She shook him off and wiped herself the best she could with her shift. Searching the beach, she found his loose coat-like shirt, and after donning it, began climbing the steep slopes, getting away from the events that had overtaken her.

EROS: THE MEANING OF MY LIFE

by Edith Cadivec

The author of this book was a well-known lesbian Viennese schoolteacher who, during the 1920s, was an outspoken advocate of corporal punishment. Her position provided her with a steady supply of female "culprits" to satisfy her psychosexual needs. In 1924, she was arrested and, after a sensational trial, sentenced to six years' imprisonment. Discovered in the original German and published for the first time in English by Blue Moon, Eros: The Meaning of My Life provides an authentic look at female sadomasochistic sexuality during the first quarter of the twentieth century. The following scene, in which a protagonist is moved to erotic fantasy via contact with a "forbidden" book (in this case, by Casanova) and is subsequently exposed to flagellation early in life, is apocryphal, appearing in works by authors as wide-ranging as Austen and Rousseau.

FROM MY CHILDHOOD

I am fully under the sway of your personality as I commit these reminiscences to writing for you. Under the spell of the descriptions of the impressions of your own youth, I am driven by an overwhelming desire to disclose to you the deepest human frailties of my innermost being, free of any false shame. You offer me the happy occasion to bring to mind all the voluptuousness that life has so richly poured over me like a libation—and to sing a hymn of praise to existence.

I could never have done this without you. The scenes of my childhood rise before my mind's eye when I converse with my soul, after being so carried away by the impact of your book. Now I wander hand in hand with you along blessed paths back to my paternal house, which I find again only when I go in quest of it together with you.

Today I am as old as you and no longer speak so disdainfully of childhood as I once did when I wished to be "grown up." When are we really grown up? It is almost fifty years since I was born, but what does that prove? My feelings have remained the same, and I perceive no contradictions between the past and the present.

My father was a top-level civil servant. He was a gentleman of the old school, conservative in character, methodical to the point of pedantry, precise as clockwork, strict with himself and others. He scarcely bothered with us; Mother had been placed in complete charge of our upbringing. We were six sisters, no brothers. Mother shared Father's high sense of duty, and she wore herself out in its service. She raised us very strictly, demanding instant obedience and industriousness, and she was not sparing in the matter of corporal punishment.

I was the third-born child and wholly different from my sisters. I had no idea of how to play with dolls. I was tough and quarrelsome, and was generally avoided as a mischief-maker. I liked best to play with boys, where things were generally more wild, and I got my greatest fun fighting and wrestling with them. The thought of the thrashings that were waiting for me at home threw me into a state of fear and confusion; nevertheless, I would not want to escape them at any price because they did me good.

Out of respect for our parents, we were not permitted to dare oppose their discipline. Father and Mother had grown up in a tradition of exaggerated strictness and authority in the matter of morals and manners, which lives on to this day in solid, old bourgeois families. As long as we were small children, my mother used the disciplinary instrument of her ancestors, the birch rod. But as the child of her age, besides the old-fashioned birch rod, she also used a French whiplash with long wide strips of hide. She always dealt out corporal punishment to her six daughters on their bare buttocks, completely exposed to view.

Since my earliest childhood, the corporal punishments so frequently administered in the family with the birch rod were what made my heart beat faster with excitement and what gave a goal and direction to my sensuality. They deeply affected my innate character traits and awakened my dormant feelings. At first I did not see the things at all, but only imagined them in my fancy. Without any knowledge whatsoever, I surmised what many, indeed all of the things, would be—a kind of foreshadowing. I veiled them in tender and mysterious words and I first had to tear this veil from them in order to find their true secret.

I was left entirely to my own resources in coming to terms with these bewildering thoughts and feelings. Nobody talked about them because everything was in appearance so matter-of-fact and natural. Gradually, however, the many corporal punishments that I witnessed transmitted to me the knowledge and experiences that I was unconsciously searching for. How often I stood on the lookout, trembling from head to foot, in order to see how my siblings, my schoolmates, or other children received the birch rod on their naked bottoms. My sensuality grew apace with the preparations. The strict order by my mother, the tearful pleas of the culprits, the unbuttoning of the bloomers, the sight of the stark-naked bottoms, the swishing sound of the birch rod in action, the shrill shrieks of the children being flogged, and the wild dance of the glowing buttocks all fused into an intoxicating symphony that gave me a thrill I found enigmatic to the extreme, accompanied by the most wonderful sensations . . .

Never was I satiated by these exquisite excitements. Little by little the voluptuary sensations increased in intensity and deliberateness until finally they broke out of me in the most violent, irresistible way. One day, after watching a corporal punishment, I suddenly experienced for the first time the wildest sexual excitement.

From this day on, I grew to full awareness of the enigmatic connection between the flagellations and my voluptuous feelings. In my imagination, I lived over and over again through all the ecstasies of the corporal punishments that I had witnessed and suffered. In a low tone of voice, I recalled to memory the exciting images and sounds of such scenes, and the mental representations of them plunged me into abysses of bliss.

I remember that as a young girl I both feared and craved birchings. Mother, and Father, too, gave me solid spankings on the behind as punishment for being a mischief-maker. On such occasions, I shrieked and kicked wildly about and was inwardly truly shaken, but I deeply loved the convulsions that shook my entire being. I felt eased; they were for me unforgettable sensations. I was simply compelled to think about them, and I spent many sleepless nights recalling all the delights I had felt. Thereupon all my blood rushed to my head and my body was as hot as if in fever.

At times, the mere sight of the birch rod or whiplash that shortly before had been on one of my sisters hypnotized me. My thoughts became uneasy, and a wave of excitement swept over me. I felt a tickling sensation in my sex parts, and all my nerves tingled as a chill voluptuously ran through them.

In order to get on with my description, I shall pass over the events of my childhood and begin to tell the story of my schooldays. As you know, corporal punishment was generally the rule and enjoyed great esteem as a pedagogical discipline at the time when we were very young. Corporal punishment was administered as a matter of course in the schools just as in the homes. I can cite such examples from my own experience and will tell you about them in today's letter.

One day when classes were over, Dora, a friend of mine, came to me and proposed that I follow her to a classroom on the third floor. She acted very mysterious, placing a cautioning finger on her pretty mouth, looking me squarely in the eyes, and whispering in a very confidential tone: "Will you promise to keep a secret?"

"Why?" I asked.

"I will lend you a book, such as you have never read in your life. A book by Casanova! You'll see . . ."

I followed Dora, who led me to the empty cloakroom. She pulled a thick book out of her coat and, after a moment of reflection, said to me very forcefully: "But be careful that your mother doesn't discover anything—or your sisters. Otherwise, I wouldn't even dare to think of the consequences. You must under no circumstances say that I lent it to you. Oh, the pictures in there! You'll see: they're all naked."

I took the book, my blood again rushing to my head and my cheeks blushing a fiery red, and hid it in my knit satchel. I rushed down the stairs and left the school building.

My mother, who had already begun to be impatient over my tardiness, was waiting to the school gate. She had come to take me and two of my sisters for a walk.

"Have you had your fill of silly chatter?" she called out to me from where she was standing when she saw me coming. "Hurry up, let's go!"

A mad fear suddenly choked my throat. I had just noticed that my knit bag clearly showed the outline of the forbidden book! I collected all my wits to contrive a convincing excuse so that I could escape from them and be alone at last to enjoy its contents in complete seclusion and security.

"We were assigned lots of homework, Mama: an essay to write and very difficult problem in arithmetic. May I have your permission to go home right away?" I asked, stuttering with a hypocritical air of innocence and daughterly deference.

"Your diligence positively moves me, child. Go home and prepare your homework. We'll be back in about an hour," answered my mother as she turned into an avenue and disappeared from sight.

The moment I was in my room, I began to leaf through the book, page by page. The adventures of this voluptuary instantly gripped my interest, although I found them obscure and incomprehensible. Some passages, however, enticed my nascent perversity more than others. While reading the book, I panicked at the slightest sound and quickly hid it in a drawer. Despite these interruptions, I managed to read the cavalier's romantic tales to the end. Suddenly, Mother appeared in the room at the very moment that my mind was most deeply engrossed in what I was reading. My father traipsed in behind her, followed by my sisters.

It is impossible for me to describe the deadly fear that seized me at that moment. I literally slumped to the floor in confusion and embarrassment at this surprise intrusion. Wholly immersed in my reading, I had heard neither their footsteps on the stairs nor the creaking of the doors on their hinges; nor had I noticed Mother's sudden, threatening apparition. When I did become aware of her presence, it was already too late.

Mother remained standing in front of me to observe me for a moment. Indignation had darkened her features; I, the little liar, was not doing my homework. Instead, I was reading! Moreover, she recognized at a glance that I was reading a forbidden book. She sprang at me like a tiger and tore the book from my hands. In the first phase of my horror over the sudden attack, I rose, terrified, and in a wild panic over what was now in store for me, I retreated to the farthermost corner of my room.

Mother turned the book around this way and that and examined it from all sides. It did not take her long to grasp the dimensions of the disaster.

"Casanova! Casanova!" she shrieked wrathfully to the rest of the family members present. Her horror before this state of affairs choked her breathing; her pale face had flushed crimson. Finally she regained her self-control and, turning towards me, asked: "What kind of book is that, you depraved child? Where did you find it? Was this the so-called homework that worried you so much? Answer me now!"

So saying, she gingerly took the infamous book between her fingers and held it under my nose. Defiantly, I turned my back on her. The others just stood there as if rooted to the floor, gaping at the scene. If I had been alone with my mother, I would have found impudent excuses and answered her boldly and brazenly. But the shaming reprimand in the presence of my father and my smirking siblings, this public disgrace, totally disarmed me. Tears welled up in my eyes and I remained in my corner, burning with shame and in a state of utter confusion.

"Speak up! Answer me! Where did you find it? I'll give you the birching you deserve in front of everybody here."

The threat of the rod on my naked backside was not the worst threat that loomed before me. Face to face with my mother alone, I had humbly submitted to the most violent of floggings. But now, older, I defended myself against a flogging in the presence of my father and sisters. Mother perceived the reason for my refusal to submit and observed me with an icy

stare. Then her eyes glinted with fury and in a sudden movement, she tore out a handful of pages from the disreputable
book. She turned to my father and declared in a tone of great
resolve, not without a touch of hypocrisy: "This has to stop
once and for all. If you don't take energetic steps now, we'll
have worse trouble later with our little hoydens. And this one
here is more trouble than all the others."

"It's true," my father agreed. "The others don't give you half
the trouble that this devilish Senta does. I believe she deserves
a thorough arse-warming—right here and now. But I shouldn't
be the one to do it."

"Why not? After all, you're her father, aren't you?"

"Indeed, but I can't punish her because I'm not angry enough
with her. You can punish her in my presence; that will shame
her all the more and take some of the arrogance out of her.
Whip her behind to shreds . . ."

The maid appeared on the threshold to announce that dinner
was ready at the very moment my father pronounced the last
word. The whole family left for the dining room on the floor
below; only I remained in my corner, in defiance of them all.
Mother was the last to leave; at the threshold, she turned
around to me once more and, after taking cognizance of my
stupid stubbornness, in a very severe and peremptory tone she
declared: "As punishment you will not eat with us today. You
will remain in your room until I come back. Is that clear? Don't
drive me to extremes or I'll let you have here and now what
you certainly can expect later."

Shame welled up in me. I felt my face glowing like a red-hot
coal. I could only stammer contritely: "Oh, Mother, please forgive me."

She came up to me and tried to bend me under her left arm.
But she quickly realized that my resistance blocked her from
carrying out her obvious intention. When I broke free of her

grip, she released me and slapped me resoundingly several times on both cheeks with all her might, temporarily deafening and blinding me. I reeled back under the blow, half-dazed, sobbing and inwardly seething. My mother took advantage of this moment to leave the room.

Hastily, I hurled myself at the door in an attempt to hold her back, but she was already outside and had locked me in the room, turning the key in the lock twice. Full of anger and shame, my senses in a tumult, I threw myself on the bed. Through my brain raced the wildest thoughts of revenge against Dora. I imagined myself flogging her naked backside to shreds, and this image suffused my whole being with pleasurable sensations.

Little by little, however, a deep depression came over me. I rose from my bed and went out on the balcony, where I sunk into a wicker chair. The fresh air cooled my brain and cheeks. I could hear the loud conversation from the dining room, which lay directly under my room. I leaned over the side of the balcony and saw that the window was open. I heard my mother's voice saying: "It's absolutely impossible to get on peacefully with Senta. Who owns the book? Who lent it to her?"

My father's voice followed hers through the open window. Instead of trying to answer her rhetorical question, he struck a warning note: "You mustn't hesitate for an instant to use the rod unsparingly, and sooner or later the children themselves will be thankful for it. Mere words, tossed out like bubbles in the air, have no effect on them. A good arse-warming helps them remember warnings better than anything else."

This exchange was followed by complete silence. The noon-day stillness was broken only by the clink of the cutlery and the clatter of dishes. My anger reached a pitch of absolute fury. I was hungry, sleepy, and utterly exhausted.

I was suddenly awakened from my drowsiness by the rattle

of the key in the door. Blinking, I recognized my mother's silhouette. She was standing in front of me, holding a long birch rod. The whole family followed behind her like a pack of sensation seekers, my father and my five sisters. Their faces mirrored the singular prurience that I myself felt at the prospect of witnessing a flogging.

My mother came up to me without uttering a word and grabbed me firmly by the wrist. With a jerk, she tore me away from the chair and boldly swung me to the center of the room, whereupon she said in an icy command: "Unbutton your bloomers and lie face down and straight across the bed. Out with your naked bottom. I'll give it the whipping it deserves because of your shameful deed!"

Her wicked words plunged me into an abyss of shame. I also realized that any resistance would be useless, since I deserved the thrashing and therefore had to submit to my mother's commands. Trembling, I stuck my hands under my clothes, fingering them confusedly as I tried to find the buttons of my bloomers. My mother waited in front of me impatiently, the birch rod poised in readiness to strike, accompanying the mute scene with utterances that deepened and intensified my shame.

My hands, hidden under the dress, finally found the buttons of my bloomers. I undid them, and my underclothes rolled down to my ankles. Then I bent over the edge of the bed and lifted my dress high above my arched bottom, exposing it fully to the view of all those present. Mother came to my side, and after raising all encumbering pieces of clothing still higher, she began to swing the rod viciously.

Swish! Huit! Swish! Huit! Huit! soughed the thin birch branches as they landed on my exposed buttocks. Each blow seared my flesh like a hot iron, and the wild sensation of pain first elicited plaintive whimperings from me. Although I squirmed and twisted like a snake and kicked wildly in all directions, I could not ward off this hail of hissing blows as it fell mercilessly on my tender backside. I burst into a terrifying scream and rolled up into a ball in a desperate effort to defend myself.

My father spontaneously rushed to her help; he grabbed me around the waist, and his powerful arms easily bent me into a position that inflected my body in the correct angle. Then, in a state of great excitement, he belabored my already burning buttocks with his strong hand.

Under his crackling blows, I began to scream, to kick about again, and to defend myself with all my might. My screams were so loud that the cook came running upstairs and stuck her head through the chink of the door to find out what the uproar was all about. When she saw that Father was giving me a sound thrashing, she went back to her kitchen pleased with the sight.

I find it very unseemly for a father to inflict corporal punishment on his daughter's naked bottom. A girl can be punished by birching up to the time of her marriage—this I believe is a sound and salutary practice—but always on condition that it is the mother or the governess who administers the beating.

My father released me only after his rage subsided. I slumped to the floor and rolled on the carpet. I rubbed my sore buttocks without thinking of the indecent spectacle I was offering the onlookers in view of my wild despair and confusion. It was the most terrible birching I had ever received. Never in my life had I ever received a similarly sound thrashing, in double portion to boot.

"Get up now and pull on your bloomers, Senta. I hope you will take good note of this," said my mother in a soothing tone of voice. I got up dizzily and felt my backside; it was heavy and swollen, like a red-hot ball. I pulled up my bloomers with a feeble motion and arranged my clothes properly.

Father came up to me, and in a pacifying tone of voice he admonished me emphatically: "This should teach you a lesson, child. You have been very severely punished, but eventually you will see that your parents have acted correctly. And now, try to mend your ways."

Overcome by tender family feelings, I took a few steps toward my mother, threw my arms around her neck, and hid my face in her bosom. I sobbed heartrendingly. She loosened herself from my embrace, kissed me fleetingly on the forehead, and left the room with the others.

Once I was alone, I fell prey to an extraordinary sensual excitement. A tickling stimulus in my private parts threw me into a turmoil. I pulled down my bloomers, threw myself on the bed, lifted my clothes over my head, and spread my legs. I daydreamed wonderfully about Dora's stark-naked bottom being flogged as never before. Fancy conjured up the most voluptuous images of a birching. My fingers unconsciously played with my clitoris, the area around which was moist with sexual excitation for a long time, until my consciousness was buried under an avalanche of voluptuousness.

When I went to school the next day, the teacher made it quite obvious that she was fully and exactly informed about the disagreeable story of the forbidden book. She pointed at Dora and branded her as an evildoer before the whole class. Someone had taken the trouble to hand the book over to the teacher and to disclose the secret to her with all proper discretion. She took the Casanova book from her desk and fastened it up on the wall.

At that time, thrashings were not only administered in families, but also in schools. Dora had not only lent the book to me but had secretly removed it from her father's library. When the teacher called her to account for it, Dora flatly denied it and named as the real culprit another girl who had nothing at all to do with the matter. After reaching the end of her patience, the teacher announced that Dora was to be punished before the whole class.

During this announcement, all eyes in the classroom fell on Dora, whose pretty face reddened with shame. She bowed her head with a saintliness that was hypocritical shame, because I could note that under her lengthy whimpers she was winking over at me and striving mightily to suppress an outburst of mocking laughter. She believed that I had betrayed her. I was in a state of wild excitement and trembled all over with a lustful craving for a look at her naked bottom.

At the close of the lesson, the teacher pulled from her desk a fresh birch rod, obviously prepared in advance, summoned Dora to stand before her, adjusted a chair, and then ordered her to kneel on the seat. In a trice, the poor girl's clothes were flung high above her back, her bloomers were pulled down, and her rotund buttocks revealed to view. Dora remained in this position for several minutes, exposed to the scrutiny of all her classmates. She had a white, well-formed bottom, voluptuous and beautiful in its lines, as I had envisioned in my fantasies. Dora contracted the charming buttocks so close together that the dividing line almost disappeared, and she sobbed bitterly into her handkerchief.

As the teacher's rod swished on the smooth, white rotundities, Dora grew desperate and began to scream so loudly that the nerves of all the onlookers quivered with excitement. Her screams ring in my ears to this very day: "Forgive me . . . Fraulein teacher . . . please forgive me! . . . oooh. . . . ooh . . . ohohoh . . . I won't . . . do it . . . again . . . oooooo . . . forgive me . . . ooooooo."

Her act of contrition, however, had come too late, because the teacher now took no notice of her shrill screams. Unflinchingly, she landed spirited blows on the repentant sinner's scarlet red buttocks. Swish! Swish! Her flogged bottom danced and hopped according to this beat time, now expanding and contracting, now spreading the hams apart, now protruding towards the class and pulling itself in, only to meet again with the pitiless birch.

As if in a frenzy, the teacher counted, loudly and slowly, the blows that she landed on Dora's bottom, so slowly indeed that she always counted two blows for one. She lashed Dora's red-hot and well-covered buttocks pitilessly and vigorously without pause, and her frenzy seemed to know no bounds.

Finally the procedure was over.

The teacher looked as though she was drunk, and she was breathing heavily. Dora rose to her feet with feeble movements, dried her tears, and rushed, unnoticed, out of the room. I, however, had enjoyed this punishment scene.

It had a terrific impact on me and sent me into raptures. Even long afterwards, I fed upon the remembered voluptuousness of the scene. I clearly saw the glowing, welted, dancing, twitching buttocks. I distinctly heard Dora's mad moaning in my ears, and with this vision in mind I sexually excited myself.

At this moment, of course, it is not possible for me to report on each case in which our teacher's birch rod threatened the smooth bottoms of her charges of both sexes, and just as little on the many pretexts which our parents knew to find when it was a question of administering our favorite arse-warmings to us. But the older I grew, the more intensely I felt that I was no longer able to separate my sensual excitements from the corporal punishments administered to stark naked bottoms.

OUR SCENE
by Wilma Kauffen

Our Scene, Wilma Kauffen's finest novel, wittily depicts the erotic fantasies of Jim, who is at his best when spanking an ample pair of female bottoms. That Jim knows his fantasies are clichés is of a piece with the narrative's ironic and amusing tone. In this scene, he indulges in—and then replays—an interlude in which he is a headmaster who must punish a group of very naughty schoolgirls.

It came to me while waiting at a table in the rear of Uncle Ned's for Lucy to find me. Every once in a while a fat black fly flew by, always in the same direction, bumping the kitchen side of the greasy, diamond-shaped window in the swinging door. Since whatever lovers do is mutually pleasurable, then, by symmetry (so goes the Mirror Principle), a lover exists who wants to give what you want to take, and to take what you want to give. The fly waxed fatter each trip, and older, alas.

I looked it up in the sex survey book by Kase and Bonbornikol: thirty-two percent of men and twenty-three percent of women have fantasies like mine, the good doctors report, and twenty percent of men and eleven percent of women enact them with a lover.

In a corner of my mind, variations of the scene play themselves over and over: The Master prepares to punish a pretty young woman for, say, chattering about some idiotic astrology article in a woman's magazine, or for overcooking the pasta, or for . . . no deviations in conduct pleasing to the Master are too slight to let slip by. The penitent turns her sweet face up to me and says, "You're really going to spank me as I deserve, aren't you?" and presents her naked or lightly covered posterior. I swish my belt in the air inches behind her rear cheeks, which quiver in anticipation of the first stroke. Yes, dear, I shall whip you and humiliate you when I have time for the whole scene. Not during working hours, but having lingered over the delicious preparatory stages all day off and on, when I'm alone in the evening, stroking my cock in rhythm with the whipping, and coming furiously as you submit to one or two of my specialties, or to all of them at once.

What makes the scene work for me is the submissive quality in the young penitent. One day I am the headmaster of a girls' boarding school, and she is a senior caught sneaking out of her dorm to meet a local boy after curfew. Her bouncy breasts and pouty lips had made me long for just such an opportunity. Now, she lies across my lap as I fumble irritably in the recesses of my desk drawer (I *do* have to clean out my desk). The baby-faced tart knows from the other girls what to do to appease me, and she is eager to play along to avoid being expelled just before graduation. At last I find my spanking ruler, which has brought tears of repentance to the eyes of many naughty young girls. Disdainfully I lift the bottom hem of her skirt (school uniform gray plaid) to the small of her back, and lightly tap the full double curve of her coarse cotton panties as I lecture her on her waywardness. I draw the waistband of her panties down a few inches. The skin at the top of the cleft is goose-pimply. She is chagrined about lying across my knees with her rear end about to be bared. "You can't see my bare hiney," she exclaims, clutching at my hand. "Nobody sees my bare hiney, not even my boyfriend!" she cries. An unfortunate reference for her to make just now, even if true, which I doubt. I lower the panties past the hollows of her knees. "I guess you can," she murmurs. I can also see a good bit of her quim, although she attempts modesty by pressing her thighs together. I spank her plump "hiney" until it is hot to the touch. Her calves trapped in her panties, she kicks up her heels (in gray school socks) in tandem. I rest my arm, admonish the back of her head on her lewd behavior. She sighs in relief. I find an extra fillip of pleasure in allowing a penitent to believe her spanking is over before it is.

I resume spanking briskly, pointedly indifferent to her sobs. Her buttocks bounce to the lively rhythm. She bawls and parts her thighs, suffering too much fanny pain to care what I see.

I set the ruler down and massage her red rear cheeks. She wiggles and groans. "Anything else I can't do?" I chuckle, tracing inside her crack with my fingernail and lightly circling her pink-brown asshole.

"No," she sobs.

Down to the little cunt lips, kneading them gently between thumb and finger, with special attention to her swollen clit. "That's nice," she says dreamily, parting her thighs further for me. I roll her clit until she clutches my hand hard between her damp thighs and pants like a bitch.

"Your townie boyfriend," I say, "doesn't he do that?" She pants hard. "What does he do? Out with it!"

"He finger-fucks me," she says.

"With your clothes on?" I shriek, thinking I may still get her for lying about him not seeing her fanny.

"He reaches under my skirt," she says. "Okay? Any more questions?"

"Yes, there are," I say. I insert the tip of my finger into her warm moist quim, reliving the pleasures of adolescence.

"Like that," she says, "but all the way in." I give her a few deep swirls and clit-picks, and I feel her coming again. I let her have that and then withdraw the finger. She sits up on my lap.

"Where do you indulge?" I say.

"At the movies and under a blanket at football games and in the town library and sitting on the floor in his room," she says, "when his family thinks we're studying, but I'm up on my haunches and he's behind me with his hand under my skirt the whole time. And his mother and his sister always come in and talk to me and I try to rise off his finger and close my thighs but I can't because he grabs me underneath by my bush. Last time he used the bowling-ball grip."

"Bowling ball?" I ask.

"You know, with his middle finger in my 'gina and his thumb up my ass—is that very bad? He told his family, 'Can't you see we're studying?' But he fingered and goosed me slowly in and out and as soon as they left he gave it to me fast and furious, and I just had to put my face down on my books and take it until I came."

"Where else do you misbehave?" I say.

"The first time, we'd just met in the grocery, he started feeling me up. There wasn't anybody near the dog food corner. I had just unbuttoned my blouse a little for him when I saw the grocer watching us in the mirror."

"So it was you," I say, "one eager slut disgracing the school uniform all over town." I put her across my knees again and give her a dozen stern smacks with the ruler on her naughty rear. She yowls. It's good that my office is separated by several rooms from the rest of the school. The only ones who can hear the meaty smacks of the ruler and the wailing are my secretary, Ms. Bunn, and the "young ladies" in the anteroom whom she directs to remove their sturdy school shoes and not squirm while awaiting their turns. No wonder even the brashest curtsy timidly as they enter my office.

Begin again: Same girl, pouty lips, uniform disheveled, breasts full, bouncy, jiggling slightly low, brought to me by the security guard who caught her going over the Elm Street fence.

"She sticks her purse and her school jacket through the fence," the guard says, "and starts up over it, so I nab her."

"Good thinking, Nabs," I say.

"You should have a look at her without her jacket," Nabs says. The girl shifts from foot to foot.

"I will, Nabs," I say. "Is there anything else?"

"Sir, when she climbs the fence, and I come up underneath her and grab her ankle, I see that she's not properly dressed, if you catch my drift, sir."

"I think I do," I say. "Anything else, Nabs?"

"She offers me a fiver to let her go on her way," Nabs says.

"You're an honorable man, Nabs. Is that all?"

"No, sir. When I don't take the fiver, she says how about this, and makes an obscene face."

"What's an obscene face, Nabs?" I say.

Nabs opened his hippopotamus mouth and waggles his thick tongue. The young tart would look prettier doing that.

"I wasn't actually going to go down on him," she pouts. "It was just a trick."

"You're not helping yourself, young lady," I say.

When I have dismissed the invaluable Nabs, I tell her to remove her blazer. The pleated front of the school blouse, designed to mask the shape of the wearer's breasts, does not hide the lack of support for this young woman's melons. Her nipples poke into the fabric between the pleats.

"Empty your purse on my desk," I say. A pair of coarse schoolgirl panties and a bra are among the booty.

"Unbutton!" I order her. She obeys. Magnificent pair. "Come here!" I say. I flick her longish pink nipples with my index fingers and watch her get turned on. "You are not worthy to wear our school uniform," I say, and place her across my knees.

"You can't see my bare hiney!" she cries.

I lift her skirt, exposing hiney and more.

"I guess you can," she murmurs. She is naked except for the unbuttoned blouse, skirt around her waist, and her socks. When I have spanked her plump cheeks until they are red and painfully tender, I ask her, "What do you do with your boyfriend?"

"We just kiss," she says. Sharp spank.

"Ow!" she cries.

"What else?" I say. "Why are you sneaking into town with your bra and panties in your purse?"

"He tweaks my titties," she says, "and it takes too long to get them back in the cups if someone comes."

"And?" I ask.

"That's all," she says. I spank her again, as hard as I can.

"Ow!"

"And? And?"

"He puts his finger up in me," she says. "He calls it 'finger-fucking.' I hate it when people catch me trying to pull up my panties in a hurry and him just standing around real innocent."

She admits permitting insertions of the boyfriend's tireless finger in his room, at his high school football games, at the movies, in the town library. I paddle her soundly after each tearful admission.

"Where else have you been carrying on?" I ask.

"In the Sacred Heart Church when nobody was there in the afternoon," she confesses.

"I thought so," I say. Reaching between her hot cheeks and underneath her, I roll her clit with a fingertip. She groans and comes.

"And what do you do for your boyfriend in return for all this fingering?" I say, as though I don't know.

She slides off my lap, removes her blouse and skirt, kneels between my legs. I am amused by the way she leers at me through her tears as she expertly unbuttons my trouser buttons and unzips me.

"You actually sucked him off in the church, didn't you?" I say.

"There was nobody there," she says, "except someone playing the organ."

"That must have been the priest who wrote the letter," I say. "He thought the boy was suffering a spiritual crisis, and came down to comfort him, but he didn't notice you until the last moment. When he saw you kneeling the wrong way in the back pew, with your head bobbing in the boy's lap, he fainted dead away."

I reach for my ruler again, but she lunges forward and fastens her pretty mouth on my cock. She has too clever a tongue to waste on a local boy. As her head bobs, I inform her, "You are hence forth restricted"—spurting down her throat! It's marvelous—"to the campus."

When she is done swallowing, she lies naked, except for her gray socks on the rug of her belly, her chin propped up on one hand. She has a thoughtful (or is it merely digestive?) look.

"That really hurt," she offers, gently rubbing a pink buttock. I assure her that it is merely a touch of what she will get when she reports to my office in a few days to be punished for the indiscretion in the church. I resolve to keep her soundly spanked and gulping like a goldfish for the rest of her senior year.

IRONWOOD

by Don Winslow

In Don Winslow's best-known novel, the harsh reality of disinheritance and poverty vanish from the world of our narrator, James, when he discovers that he is in line for a choice position at an exclusive and very strict school for girls. Ironwood becomes for him a fantastic dream world where discipline knows few boundaries, where the silver is always polished and the food and wine and the best quality, and where his role as master allows him free reign over the willing, well-trained beauties in his charge.

I never knew my Uncle Rupert, except by reputation. He was by far the richest member of our family. He was also the black sheep. Mother would never allow his name to be mentioned in the house. Father, should the subject be brought up, would grumble darkly about blackguards. It was all very vague, yet mildly exciting to a young lad growing up in a house full of secrets. And so it was that while growing up his name seemed to punctuate my life at odd intervals.

As I grew older, I became more intrigued by this mysterious figure, particularly when I found that I was increasingly being compared with him. Usually the sentiments expressed were to the effect that if I didn't mend my ways I would end up like my Uncle Rupert. The tone of warning implied that such an ending would be dastardly. I remember distinctly that my father used the analogy on the day he received the letter notifying him that I would not be welcomed back to college for the fall term.

And so it was that I found myself very much on my own. Father had not, as of yet anyway, disinherited me, but I had been reduced to so meager an allowance that I could barely keep body and soul together. The debts mounted up, and things looked bleak indeed. I still had my circle of friends, of course. A man with friends is wealthy in a sort of way, I suppose, but most of them were tapped out. In at least two cases, their situations resembled mine so that, by comparison, my father seemed exceedingly generous.

These thoughts were running through my mind on that cold, drizzly day in London when my uncle's name once again came into my life from afar. More precisely, one might say that it was his ghost that touched my life at that point, changing its course forever.

It was a late afternoon in March. I was returning to my flat and stopped to rifle through the daily post, left just inside the foyer for the perusal of the tenants. Usually I paid it little attention since my correspondence increasingly consisted of more bills, further reminders, and increased threats of legal action.

So it was with some surprise that I noticed a lavender envelope with my name on it, written in a curious, free-flowing feminine hand. The envelope bore a faint scent, reminding me, on that cold, hard day, of the promise of spring.

The letter was from a Mrs. Cora Blasingdale, who introduced herself as a business associate of my late Uncle Rupert. That I did not know of Uncle Rupert's demise is hardly surprising since, in my family's opinion, he had ceased to exist some years ago. She went on to say that my uncle had spoken of me as someone who might have similar business interests and a willingness to help manage the enterprise, once he might retire from an active role in the concern. He specifically said that for one so young I was already acquiring a certain reputation.

Needless to say, I was quite surprised. Though I was sure my uncle knew of my existence, I could not fathom why he should recommend me for anything. Nor could I understand what sort of reputation he had in mind that might qualify me for any position. Nevertheless, Mrs. Blasingdale asked me to call on her at Ironwood, a remote country estate, where we might talk about the possibilities.

I was intrigued by this letter, and as my immediate prospects in the city looked poor, I resolved to proceed and find what fate had to offer at Ironwood.

And so it was that three weeks later I found myself seated across a massive mahogany desk from the mistress of that estate, a stern, rather austere blonde, who coldly appraised me with steely blue eyes.

At the first sight of her, I lost the image conjured up by her correspondence. Cora Blasingdale was not a retiring, dour, old matron. She was perhaps in her forties and well-built, with short, cropped hair; long, strong legs; and trim thighs wrapped in a pair of tight jodhpurs. She wore a high turtleneck sweater, and long polished boots completed the outfit. She was dressed all in black.

Cora was one of those women who carries herself proudly with an imperious air. In her high-heeled boots, she was almost as tall as I was. When we met, she grasped my hand firmly and stared evenly into my eyes. I found her frank appraisal rather unsettling, as she held me captive for several seconds. Then, seeming to like what she saw, she allowed herself a half-smile and said, "I'm glad you could come."

For the next hour and a half we talked. At first she was cautious, asking many questions. Then gradually, she seemed to gain some confidence in me, and her story started to unfold.

Cora and my uncle had been the proprietors of a sort of trade school where young girls were trained for domestic service. Cora was in complete charge of the girls, their training and discipline. Uncle Rupert found gainful employment for the girls once they graduated from Ironwood, and he collected handsome finder's fees from those eager for their services. One of these domestic trainees had met me at the door. A plain girl in a dour gray uniform and white cap, she greeted me properly and politely showed me to the office. I remarked upon that now, interrupting Mrs. Blasingdale's account.

My hostess acknowledged that some of the girls made credible domestics but, she assured me, by far the greater effort went into teaching the "other" girls a very different set of duties.

It soon became clear that at Ironwood a selection procedure was rigidly adhered to. Newcomers were closely examined by Mrs. Blasingdale, and sometimes by Uncle Rupert, when they first arrived. They were judged by their looks, face, figure, deportment, discretion, spirit, and obedience. Those who passed muster were sent to rooms on the two top floors. Those found wanting were banished to the servant's wing to be taught the domestic skills. These were inevitably referred to as the "staff," and though a rigid order prevailed at Ironwood, they too had certain privileges.

Still it was the upstairs girls, the "students," to whose training the most detailed attention was given. Once a girl was designated as a student, she began a course of rigorous training in the art of lovemaking, each phase of which was closely supervised. Finding the proper situations for these premier graduates of Mrs. Blasingdale's school had occupied much of my uncle's time. It often meant traveling to the Orient, Arabia, or India. But this part of the business was very lucrative indeed, and his efforts were well rewarded. In only a few years he became a wealthy man, and he came to know the rich and powerful on five continents. This was the role now being offered to me.

I was fascinated and wished to eagerly accept, for at the age of twenty-five, I was still rather impetuous. Cora, on the other hand, having learned to be more circumspect about life's choices, urged me to think it over carefully. In order to help me make an informed decision, she suggested that I spend some time getting acquainted with Ironwood and its residents. We would begin by meeting some of the girls.

She led me down the halls to the manor's library, a richly appointed room with shelves of leather volumes and folios. I later learned that this room contained a prize collection of erotica, which was used to further the education of her young charges.

As we passed through the doorway, Cora stopped the little serving girl I had met upon my entrance.

"Darla, send the students down," she said.

In a few minutes, a group of lovely young things began to filter into the room. Chattering in small clusters as they approached, they fell silent upon entering and quickly arranged themselves into a line facing us.

There were eight girls present, although Cora informed me that a few others were about on various duties, while one or two were usually excused should the time of month be inconvenient for them.

Each girl was dressed in the school uniform that they wore during the day while they attended their classes. This consisted of a navy blue blazer with a gold embossed crest over the left breast. Beneath she wore a crisp white blouse, partly obscured by a blue and gold striped tie. A matching loose pleated skirt, long white cotton stockings to the knees, and polished black leather shoes completed the ensemble. This was a standard schoolgirl's uniform, like hundreds of others except for one important detail. The skirt had been shortened to an absurd length, barely covering the top third of their trim, nubile thighs in front, and just failing to conceal the bottom of their small, firm, panty-clad cheeks behind. Arrayed before us, the girls waited in perfect silence.

"Master James, these are my girls. To get to know them better, we'll start with a little display." She turned to face her young charges. "Girls, Master James wishes to conduct an inspection. Strip to the waist. Now!"

The last, a ringing command, hung in the silence of the room. The young girls meekly obeyed, their eyes cast down, their movements slow and deliberate. Blazers fell to the floor, blouses were slowly unbuttoned, and skimpy lace brassieres carelessly discarded, to reveal eight pairs of mouthwatering breasts ranging from the small nubs of budding feminine promise to the fuller roundness of rounded summer apples. The girls stood at attention, hands at their sides, awaiting my inspection.

"Straighten up, girls, shoulders back," Cora snapped. There was some shuffling in the line, the effect being to more proudly display the feminine treasures.

Cora continued the little game, beckoning to me to follow her. "As you can see, Master James, we have no secrets here. Come, let me introduce you to them."

We slowly trooped the line, stopping before each girl, who would stand submissively, head bent, eyes to the floor, awaiting our approach.

"Master James, allow me to present, for your pleasure: Jacqueline, Melanie, Danielle, Vanessa, Jeanelle, Sonya, Erika, and Marianne."

As we would draw near, Cora would snap the girl's name. Each would execute a short curtsy, look up to meet my eyes for just a short moment, and resume the pose at attention, her arms at her side, palms facing outward, as if in offering.

In a line, bare shoulders and slim arms just touching one to the next, they made a most pleasing study of the female form.

Each girl was a unique picture of loveliness, each a singular
example of her type of feminine beauty. I longed to touch what
so far only my eyes had feasted on. Cora sensed my desire.

"You may touch them if you like. Go ahead, feel their breasts,
weigh and compare."

As fate would have it, I was standing in front of the third girl
in the line. She had a bell-shaped helmet of soft brown hair,
with girlish bangs in the front, a small heart-shaped face, an
upturned nose, and dark, elfish eyes. A recent arrival, she still
had to learn the control that the discipline of Ironwood would
instill.

I turned to face her directly, and reached out. My fingertips
tentatively touched the side of a firm, high-set breast the size
of a tennis ball. She allowed herself just the trace of a smile. I
played with her breast for a moment, weighing it in my palm,
running my fingers across and under and then down the top
slope, then finally, brushing several times across the darkened
nipple. Now her mouth was slightly open, revealing a row of
small even teeth. I watched her run her tongue over her lips. I
could hear her breathing. Smiling, I continued the massage of
her left breast, resolving to see how long she could maintain
her poise.

Glancing at Cora, who was watching me closely, I began a
more serious manipulation of the captive tit. Placing my hand
completely over her breast, the soft weight in my palm, I
cupped my fingers to cradle it lightly, and began a slow, circular
motion. She responded almost immediately, shifting her weight
from one foot to the other and pushing her left shoulder forward.

Cora saw the little test for what it was. "Stand still, Danielle.
You were not given permission to move. You are not to respond
until permitted to do so."

Her tone was stern and unforgiving. Cora has since told me

of her theory that women can be controlled even to the point of withholding their own climax, until they are released and allowed to experience it. Since that day, I've seen many experiments in self-control at Ironwood, but I saw the degree of control described by Cora only once. In any case, her warning had only a temporary effect on Danielle.

I gradually increased the pressure into a deeper massage. Heat was radiating in my palm, and the sensitive nipple began to stir between my fingers. Her labored breathing grew quicker and louder, and when I looked at her face, she had closed her eyes. Her mouth was tightly compressed, and two small teeth indented her lower lip as she fought to maintain control over her growing desire.

I knew she was close to the breaking point, so I decided to escalate one step further. First, I removed my hand, allowing her a few moments respite, and then, concentrating my attack on the tip of the heaving breast and straining nipple, I lightly raked it with my fingernails. Then I began to flick the now-erect nipple up and down, barely touching it with the pad of my index finger.

Danielle at first responded with a slight sway of her hips. This swaying motion increased, finally turning into a series of involuntary pelvic thrusts, as her body cried out for that which her mind was trying desperately to deny. Then it happened. She could hold out no longer. A moan escaped her lips, then another. She stepped forward, pressing the breast even deeper into my hand, and with her eyes still closed, muttered, "Oh yes, please, please."

"Enough."

The sharp command shattered the pleasure bond between us, allowing the room's reality to flow into our shared space. My hand lingered and dropped. The girl whimpered.

"This is really disgraceful. I am ashamed that Master James

should have to see such a shocking lack of discipline."

I made to protest, to intercede for the girl, but Cora shot me a meaningful glance that said, "Do not interfere in this." I knew that I too, for now at least, was only a pawn in the elaborate game Cora Blasingdale had arranged.

"Master James, I apologize."

She turned to the hapless girl, who had resumed her humble stance, her breathing quieting.

"As for you, young lady, you will present yourself at punishment call. It may be that Master James will want to witness your punishment so he can see how we deal with disobedience here at Ironwood. Go, you are dismissed. All of you."

With that, she clapped her hands twice. Blouses, brassieres, ties, and jackets were scooped up, and the room emptied in the twinkling of an eye. At such times I often had the feeling that I had awoken from a dream, no trace of which remained in the quiet library of this country estate.

"Well, James, what did you think of our little drama? You found me too severe, perhaps, but I can assure you that the strictest discipline is imperative in these girls. Any shred of rebellion must be driven from their minds, as they are bent to a will far more dominant than their own. Only when they are possessed by the other totally can they go beyond childish selfishness and vanity, their only remaining desire to give pleasure to the other. Ultimately, for a woman, that is the truest happiness of all. But come, let us talk further over lunch. This way."

Lunch was served in a long, narrow dining room cluttered with medieval furniture. A large, sturdy trestle dominated the room, but today only two places had been set. As we entered, a pair of serving girls was closing the drapes, leaving the room in dim light. At the far end of the table hung a brighter light, positioned directly over a small platform, and on this small stage I saw a striking blonde girl. She was thin and tall, her willowy body stretched by the manner in which she had been suspended, her wrists tied over her head to a hook hanging from the ceiling. The rope allowed just enough slack so that her toes just touched the carpeted stage. With the exception of the bands around her wrists and a leather gag in her mouth, she was totally naked.

Cora ignored the nude form as she showed me to my seat, asking after my likes in food, and generally engaging in small talk. Finally, I could stand it no longer. I inquired about the nude captive, who was swaying slightly as she became more fatigued in her demanding position.

It seems the girl had been caught stealing food, a minor offense. As a result, she had been restricted to reduced rations of bread and milk for the next three days. In order for her to more fully appreciate her crime, she was required to be in attendance while the others enjoyed their meals.

As I ate, I found it impossible to take my eyes off the swaying figure. I recognized her as the tall blonde, Erika, whom I had seen in the lineup. She had the high cheekbones of a Nordic goddess, with straight hair falling in a sheet around her slim shoulders. Above the narrow strap of the gag, her icy blue eyes stared at some distant vision. Her face suggested that she had resigned herself to her fate.

She ignored our presence in her unabashed nakedness. My eyes traveled further to her proud, upstanding breasts and down the long lines of her narrow hips, across a flattened stomach made almost concave by her restraints, to the small triangle at the base, slightly etched with soft down. Finally, I examined her long dancer's legs, which trembled with the obvious tension in her thighs and calves as she strained to take some of the unbearable weight off her arms. Her punishment lasted for more than an hour as we lingered over our coffee.

That afternoon, Cora took me on a tour of Ironwood. I saw

the classrooms with their old-fashioned wooden desks bolted to the floors. Cora pointed out that they made a secure platform for a girl to bend over should she have to be punished in front of her classmates. Here I met two of Cora's assistants, women of about her own age, who taught classes and gave demonstrations during the day, and were assigned other duties at night.

The third assistant, a certain Baroness Von Stoffen, was supervising the exercise room, which was the next stop on our sojourn. This cavernous space was large enough to hold the equipment for a modern gymnasium, parallel bars, exercise cycles, a trampoline, etc., and still have room left over for playing games. At the far end, the entire wall had been mirrored, like a dance studio, and completing that analogy, a ballet bar had been erected in front of it. Here the girls were taught poise and balance as they learned to adopt several of the classical ballet positions.

Because of the belief at Ironwood that girls must overcome false modesty and not be ashamed of their nakedness, all exercises were conducted in the nude. In this way, the girls learned to accept their nudity as natural, first in front of their classmates and under the stern eye of Fraulein Von Stoffen, who herself preferred a one-piece black body suit over a pair of matching tights.

As it happened, the class was now in session, and I beheld a roomful of supple young bodies bent and contorted in various positions along the bar. Little Jacqueline was there, an intense look on her childish features as she tried to balance herself on one leg, keeping the other outstretched, her heel resting on the top of the bar, and the reflection of her little pubescent pussy winking back at her.

I left Cora chatting with the Baroness and went to venture among the gymnasts. Further beyond, several girls were sprawled about on thick exercise mats. I watched Jeanelle, an athletic-looking lithe brunette of about seventeen who, starting with legs apart and arms high over her head, bent to touch her right hand to her left foot, and straightening up, repeated the procedure on the opposite side. I was fascinated by the way her breasts changed shape as she assumed the pose. Each time she bent, they shifted from small gourds to hanging tit bags, succulent and crying out to be plucked and sucked. I felt an overwhelming urge to lay into this luscious piece, but I found that I too was learning restraint. Instead, I walked behind her, and found myself equally entranced by the rear view she presented to me. She, of course, ignored me. I had come to expect that by now.

Just to her side, a thin, lissome blonde was lying on her back, her tits flattened by the supine position. Elbows on the mat, her hands were supporting her hips. Her legs steepled high in the air, described a scissors, opening and closing as she treated me to a close-up view of her welcoming netherlips.

To my left, one of the older girls rode astride a bucking exercise bike. Clinging to the handlebars, she was alternately being stretched forward and snapped back to the upright position. The rhythmic motion sent her boobs bouncing in a most delightful way, while behind the piston-like churning of her thighs caused her ass to roll from side to side over the narrow wedge of the seat, firmly embedded in her crotch. I noticed that her eyes were closed and that she had a smile on her face.

As I strolled through this garden of delights, I would pause here or there to admire some nubile female form bent back or stretched and straining to hold a classical pose, as muscles trembled in tense legs and thighs.

Finally, I came to the back of the room, where a large exercise mat had been set up. On this two of the girls were engaged in serious combat. Their wrestling had apparently started playfully enough, but an unfair move on someone's part had invited retaliation, and the intensity had escalated, as each sought to subdue her rival. They emitted a series of animal-like grunts as they grappled with one another, seeking a hold that could cause pain and submission. As their struggle became more earnest, their hair became disheveled, and their faces and chests grew bathed with perspiration. The female scent mingled with the stale gym air as they closed yet again. Breasts crushed against breasts, and arms clutched round narrow backs. I was captivated by this display of raw female aggression.

As the contest became more vicious, it drew the attention of the other girls, and a small circle began to form around the mat, the onlookers cheering on the favorite. This, in turn, drew the attention of my hostess and the Baroness, who hurried over to break up the fight.

It took some time to extricate the girls' tangled limbs, but once apart their tempers quickly cooled and they hung their heads sheepishly, avoiding the stare of the headmistress.

Cora lost no time, but turned her back on her errant charges and, with the Baroness beside her, knew full well what was in store. I brought up the rear of this little procession, and from that vantage point was treated to the two rounded behinds shifting in rhythm as they were slowly marched off to meet their fate.

Our destination turned out to be a long wooden trestle, or gym horse, about waist high, which had been padded and covered in leather. Without a word or command, the penitents draped themselves over the horse, clutching a set of iron handgrips that had been mounted midway up on the wooden legs at the opposite side. Behind them, their mistresses had acquired a set of wooden paddles. These resembled those used in table tennis, but they were slightly larger, and their broad flat blades had been covered with a ribbed hard rubber coating so as to ensure a biting sting.

The other girls gathered around to witness the punishment. The two girlish behinds were placed side by side, their hips barely touching. They shifted nervously in anticipation of the spanking that they knew would be administered with considerable verve by their enthusiastic mistresses.

"Ten of the best, then." It was Cora who set the punishment.

As one, the stern disciplinarians raised their weapons, carefully measured the distance to their targets, hauled back and delivered two stinging slaps that echoed in the rafters and caused their victims to bounce up on their toes. The girls let out howls of pain, but they were allowed no respite, as the stinging blows were repeated like twin gun shots from a rapid-fire rifle. The girls howled in chorus, a curious contralto, punctuated by sobs of pain.

As the pace slowed somewhat, I noticed that their cheeks were acquiring a rosy glow of heat. The blows were spaced further apart until they were made to wait a full thirty seconds for the last whack, which was delivered with extra vehemence. Then they were released. Instantly their hands flew to their behinds to rub and soothe the tortured flesh. They would find it uncomfortable to sit for some time, I was sure.

As the crowd began to dissipate, Cora and I took leave of this charming place. We went through the adjoining hall to the large indoor pool under its glass dome, and then through the double patio doors, and into the garden beyond.

"There are many more things I could show you, James, but I expect you've had enough stimulation for one afternoon. In any case, you may want to return to your room to rest or freshen up. I will have some tea sent up to you. Later, perhaps, we can sit together, let's say at four o'clock, in the sitting room. I have arranged a little demonstration for you so that you may see a well-trained girl at her best."

With that I was dismissed. I wandered back through the

house to the bedroom that I had been given at the top of the stairs.

The room was luxurious, with a huge private bathroom attached. Somewhat at loose ends, I kicked off my shoes and lay back on the silk damask bedspread. Folding my arms under my head, I stared at the ceiling. At various times during this extraordinary day, I had been dragged up the peak of sexual excitement, only to be left standing alone. And the toll was beginning to tell. My cock was stiff and screaming for relief. I resolved that I should find it between the heavenly thighs of one of those lovely creatures down the hall before the night was through. I closed my eyes as visions of naked nymphs danced in my head. Once again I saw cute inflamed asses aching to be touched, caressed, and soothed by hand and tongue. Dreamlike, the images cascaded before me as I went over the day's events and made plans for a pleasure-filled future at Ironwood . . .

THE CORRECT SADIST

by Terence Sellers

With the publication of The Correct Sadist, *Terence Sellers established herself as one of the premier voices of sadomasochistic theory and practice of the twentieth century. This work has been praised as "a search for the ultimate freedom from bondage through an examination of its most intricate and manifest intricacies." Ostensibly a description of masochism,* The Correct Sadist *is framed by a brilliant exploration of the sadistic self, as demonstrated by this classic excerpt, from which the book's title is derived.*

I have always considered myself unknown to others. When anyone attempted to pierce my guardian shell, I never doubted they would soon give up under the strain of so futile and unrewarding a project. Yet I did await the day when I could reveal to someone my soul, that would then burst out so brilliantly white it would annihilate us all . . .

All the so-called terrors of solitude console me. The resonant silence of the evening's end, as the stars come into their own, is a pleasure I cannot share with anyone—though some do seem sensitive enough. I often wake alone, with the echo of an uncertain sound from the house below fading in my ears . . . I leap from the bed directly and rush to meet the intruders. Perhaps once a week I have such an adventure. But no one is ever there.

One evening when I was ten, I embraced the form of the full

white moon as my only "husband." I stretched out on my bed under its sickly light and submitted to a weird alertness. The room fell away and I strained towards the open window. The real world was not of blue walls, books in bookcases, not my sister sleeping in the next bed, not school and my lessons done for tomorrow—but something awful and tense; it was a struggle and the presence of death. The climax of this tremulous dislocation was the palpable knowledge that I was not my body, even if I should try to be. I then realized my bed as the wide end of a great wedge whose blade was buried in the center of the earth—and from my spine fell a plumb line to this single point.

At seventeen I lived in the arid red landscape of New Mexico, whose dry hostility suggested the surface of the moon. Returning from some amusement one night, I crossed a brushy plain and realized too late that I had walked directly into a lunar communion, the submission of that charred land to the violent spew of full moonlight. I panicked and walked faster, and had the misfortune to look down at my feet. Between my raised foot and the ground gaped a vast space. My foot drifted down and hit with a sickening vertigo, my leg turned to amoeba and I fell—and in the luxury of that fall, I wished there were no earth to receive me. Yet once safely prone, I clung to a little stubble of brush and suffered that familiar moonwash of illogic, of confusion, of suspension of every pore. Terror ebbed away, and I was not a multitude of beings, and so I was released . . .

Even though I am well-armored against your interest and violations, never do I suffer slightly an influence from without. I absorb you readily; immediately do I become your subject. Yet I never let you see this. I once thought this was symptomatic of my desire to be of a heart sublime and devoted beyond all others, but were I indifferent or obsessed, all contacts were intimate and excruciating. For once you are admitted, in the effort I make to comprehend your alien soul, I revoke my right to solitude and thus am utterly lost to myself.

In the naive enthusiasm of a new companionship (it always holds the promise of an ideal realized!), I would not notice my new vacancy. I felt far from empty, for I was inhabited by them. My chosen one's gestures, grimaces, turns of phrase, and even laugh, soon replaced my own. It took but one disharmony for the inevitable to occur. With a spasm of self-disgust, I knew the dispensability of the chosen one, and so withdrew profoundly, suppressing my real sorrow . . . But I was unknown to them throughout, and the scourge that is my true and better self rallied against what I could now perceive as their parasitism. Ruthlessly did I expel every drop of their influence from my pores, and by this purging believed I destroyed every quality I had possessed in common with their inferior person.

Why did I continue to seek them out, when my virulent idealism doomed the contact?

Like some exotic monster, I rarely emerged from the green darkness of the ocean floor, where my frail phosphorescence led the way. These light and fluent creatures, who fled easily through watery latitudes to surface and air, I envied; I wondered at their careless trust in a foreign light. I surface slowly into their bright and confused stream to find that they care nothing about my icy home below. They know only that to follow me would be their death as slowly the terrible pressure crushed their bodies. Enough that they are well amused by my lurid coloring and profusion of antennae.

As a child I did not consider myself a child. At birthday parties, I wheedled my way into the room where the adults sat drinking, and I danced and amused them and pretended to understand everything they said. No amount of prodding could induce me to return to the noisy games, and if I was taken forcibly into the children's company, with disapproval and scolding as though I were being punished, they in turn would reject me, and make me the butt of their play.

I used to lie to myself concerning my parentage and true home. Lie? No, I had not the faintest doubt that my parents were not my real ones. As an infant, I had been abandoned by the royal pair who had conceived me. It was all because of the war. I recalled the basket I had been found in: of dark golden straw, decorated with green paint, and swathed in a gauzy protective canopy. A bouquet of violets was tucked in at the foot of the snow-white coverlet. I often dwelt upon the names of the gems—diamond, ruby, emerald, sapphire—for these were the playthings of my lost childhood. By some awful fluke, my true parents had never rediscovered me, and so I was doomed to live out the balance of my early years miserably, within the narrow, institutional, gray walls of a one-bedroom apartment. Mansion, canopy, chandelier, balustrade—I recited these words as an immigrant strives to keep his homeland tongue alive. I considered my adoptive parents malicious in their design to keep me from my proper station in life and felt few qualms at being completely disobedient. Crystal, throne, angel, salon: these were the words of my proper language.

Thus did I reluctantly develop within a childhood fraught with hardship and humiliation. Perhaps it was no worse than any childhood, but to a vagrant princess it was a cruel purgatory. My one consolation was school, where I assumed my natural predominance. Insufferably good at my lessons, a toady to my teachers, I was loathed by my classmates. I detested them as a nest of snakes. I made my closest friend in a girl to whom I had to concede first place from time to time. In that way I leached of its odiousness her occasional triumph over me.

I took as a mark of distinction the scornful treatment, jibes, and petty snubs I received as a consequence of my hauteur. If my blue blood was not recognized, the soul of the beholder was in affliction, not I. This belief in my innate aristocracy and imminent assumption into the airy, ineluctable regions of a spiritual royalty was my solitary and inviolable experience of conviction.

The stories of the lives of the saints never failed to seduce me. Morbidly I was attracted to those that recounted the most horrifying physical trials, the sacrificial punishments endured for the glory of God. The life of an ascetic hermit in the desert I envied; it seemed the most perfect of lives. About these hermits I was extremely curious, but upon their destitution and exalted communion with God the nuns would not remark. Instead of revealing to me the reason behind this behavior, they turned my eyes towards the banal saints, who plodded in their gardens and taught little children. I was left to my own devising, and designed to emulate the holy men's sublime excesses. I believed it was within my power to take up such a life, but the nun to whom I revealed this vocation quickly discouraged me. She falsified a schedule of the arduousness of achieving that "position"; insisted that I would have to enter a cloistered convent; that it took years and years learning how to meditate; that the Vatican now disapproved of people "avoiding their duties in the world, and using prayer as an escape."

I considered a hair shirt. I practiced sleeping on the floor; halfway through the night I relented and stole a pillow from the bed. I settled for buckling my belt too tightly and wearing old shoes. Over and over I read the lives of my favorites—St. Theresa in particular—and gratified myself through evoking their trials. Their torments and ecstasies I rapturously envisioned as other adolescents no doubt call up the phantom arms of film stars. I withdrew from the profane world, "mere material existence," but grew frustrated and languid under the influence of my simulations. The pristine impact of a vision was not forthcoming; Theresa transfigured by a spasm was simpler than I.

I cannot now recall the name of the saint who washed the feet of lepers, who as proof of her humility before the most afflicted of God's creatures drank the dirty bath water. The peril of this did not satisfy, no—she would catch in her throat a loosened scab from one of their incurable sores, swallowing it with thanks, as no different from the Eucharistic body of Christ itself. This accomplishment I admired and dwelt upon. I could not comprehend why the Church did not find glory in these acts. Whatever God had responded to these ecstatic submissions had fallen under suspicion.

Gradually the Church, whose rituals I had ardently observed and whose saints I emulated, came to disappoint me. I began to know the back of the nun's hand as my waxing bad faith sloughed off the restraint of fear. Their displeasure made me cynical as I dispiritedly marked in them a strange repressed rage that focused too avidly upon the palest disobedience.

The terms of my exile grew clearer as my enervate, lonely adolescence dragged on. I asked myself with debilitating frequency: How much longer must I remain on the outside, cut off from the state of grace? The power of the confessional was a confidence trick: There was no one to confide in; certain stains would never fade. A more potent exorcist I required to relieve the brand of strangeness that was upon me. Thus was I compelled to embrace my estrangement, and passionately; beneath its cold triumphant form my moral sense ceased to function.

Due no doubt to my increasing humility, my family expelled me from my home as soon as I was of age. A naive and arrogant confidence in the power of my intellectual ability assured me that this was to my taste, for whatever I wanted I could have by merely willing it. I rapidly discovered that the Philistine considered these cerebral virtues just so much decoration. I had no practical resources upon which to draw, and soon I decided to reconcile myself with the strangers who were my family. But such hostility had I provoked in them that it is no exaggeration to say that they wished me dead, or mad. My letters to them were returned, unopened.

The demeaning job I was reduced to taking was not the worst of it, but that the world had only that to offer I took as a personal insult. My assumption into the company of the Elect was still years away, and I sensed this and so conferred upon myself a tragic air. The money I earned paid for the animal's keep: food and shelter, and nothing else.

Under the influence of the meager meals, the cheap clothes I scavenged, the derelict apartment I barricaded myself in, my nerves' strength declined. I became convinced that luxury held in its symbols the spiritual food for which I starved. To recall that the hermit suffered worse privations failed to console me, for my temperament was in truth sensuous, worldly, and proud. Poverty gave the lie to my power and obscured the nobility I was destined for. There were forces abroad bent on my destruction: jealous ones, lusting after my inheritance. They rejoiced to see my demoralization, and against this vast organization of evil, I was a weak and solitary dreamer.

I renewed my convictions; I shut myself away and devoted all my thoughts and acts to regaining contact with the kingdom of the Elect. From my readings in books of magic ritual, in the histories of foundling empires won by blood, in the brainsick songs of Baudelaire, I came to suspect it was incorrect to sit and wait for the crown to descend from the skies. I had to steal it back from those who kept it from me. What right had they? Through my own devising, I would enter the company of the Elect. Under the spell of this moral imperative I foundered, irritated past breathing, frustrated and sickened by my absolute ignorance of method.

It was in this unbalanced and aspiring mental state that I commenced to read a most malignant writer, but one who unflinchingly proclaimed virtuosity in the use of power. An aristocrat by birth, he was not satisfied by the conventional ascendance he held; his temperament prompted him to delve more deeply into the arts of manipulation, the victorious assault. This philosophy sounded a deep and sonorous knell within me; it freed me, and so condemned me to destroy all I had held sacred—without sentimental retractions. Nor did this resonance fade over several months; it became my daily work to obey the imperative to overcome myself. This appeal to my courage became absolute, and I recognized attack as the key. The repeated drain of their institutions demanded it of me; so did I tap into my death-dealing instinct.

Much of what I found embedded in his writings was a vicious and empty power, wholly temporal and polluted by commonplace sexual lust. But the efficacy of his methods, the orderliness of his realm, and the invigorating constant of the attainment of his desires I could not deny. If my end was not the same as his, could I not still use his means?

Once the weights and measures of Authority were in my hands, I would do with them as I pleased. The means would not determine the end! In the practice of certain physical manipulations, simple and subtle, ritualized and clear; by incorporating into my vocabulary the words and phrases I deemed intrinsic to an aristocracy of mind; by assuming the conviction that whatsoever I thought, spoke, or did was correct, I would prepare the ground for my future dominion, develop in myself the shell of Authority, and so become more like and thereby worthy of the Elect to whose company I aspired.

Thus I cultivated my sadism; I styled myself a Lucifer to attract the attention of God. It was only logical. His displeasure and punishment was preferable to the stagnant limbo where I now formlessly crept.

Criminal was this impulse, and I followed it, devoting myself to the practice of sadism as essential to my development. What was moral law to me? I recognized it as propaganda to weaken smaller minds and open them to my pincers. I needed at last obey nothing but my own conviction of grandeur.

Thus I entered into the sphere of the professional sadist. The orderliness of the business transaction seemed to excise moral consideration from my acts, and rewarded me besides with money enough to buy the luxuries I required. I was provided with a steady, willing stream of victims I could experiment upon any way I liked. The men were forced to present themselves as johns; that is, as pathetic beggars who had to pay to satisfy their perverted desires. I employed the persona of the prostitute as a further instrument of their degradation. The masochist has little physical contact with his "Mistress" but an abusive one, precluding all acts of intercourse, all kisses, all fond caresses. This was entirely agreeable, as I held the sexual act, particularly between man and woman, to be one of the more loathsome pastimes of humanity.

When I first embarked upon this vocation, I rejoiced in my freedom to indulge in a psychic orgy of narcissism and violence, without there being any question of a victim's revenge. My first act, when presented with a masochist, was to put him in bondage so that he could not escape me. As soon as I realized that he was helpless, I relaxed in a very peculiar way. My back straightened and my head poised floatingly upon my neck. My arms and legs moved slowly and with a dreamlike precision that seemed hydraulic; my torso was subject to hallucinations of being a kind of metallic pivot or hinge. These sensations that came on upon the masochist's forced submission were symptoms of my increasing conviction of the impersonality of my will, and so of my invulnerability. The exaltation in controlling another's every word and act, and in time, every thought, intoxicated me, and so evolved an addiction.

After the masochist's bondage began a vituperative monologue. The victim was first impressed with his physical repulsiveness, that this was evidence of his lowness of character. In this way, he was forced to accept the idea of his essential bondage to a more or less hideous physical shell. The monologue then evolved along the lines of the victim's particular theme: that he was a bad child, or dog, or a sinner; that he merited castration; that he was a sewer. The variations were numerous, but always he was a base creature. The finale of my diatribe was a sort of anthem I developed over the years, that I felt epitomized for the victim his place in life: that he was essentially a degenerate, a subhuman, and temperamentally incapable of rising above the muck where he gladly wallowed. Insults flooded out of me with all the ease of inspiration; I delivered myself of the most vile and twisted of ideas.

I occasionally looked on in amazement at the venomous force that came from her. But I told myself that she was the medium for this force, and not the force itself. I thrilled to use myself as the field for the strenuous battle of sadist contra masochist. I saw the operation of these opposing forces everywhere, and elicited it from every situation. In time, the effect of my power was no longer confined to the conscious few who admitted their sexual masochism. I came to be an inspiration to many to practice cruelty in a methodical fashion.

But one evening the intervention of this observant self who for long had witness the derangements "she" encouraged, the perversions "she" fostered and that "she" miraculously cured, now severely recalled me to the original task I had set myself: What was the true purpose of my sadism?

So remote had this end become, so involved was I with the intricate methods of control for the pleasure of control, that she could say without flinching: "No purpose! There is no meaning! What are you, a sophomore? Life is ugly and useless!" I had not quite forgotten my royal destiny, but I no longer worried about it. I expected nothing from the Elect, though I felt sure of prison. I found some pleasure, too, in the prospect of a cell. At last, to be like the hermits! I thought some about repentance; I backslid in a hundred other tiny ways, back to the vigilance of the nuns. I felt I was being watched as I tortured and abused my victims, many of whom were very attached to me and smiled radiantly as I spat in their faces.

By degrees all the influence I had acquired slipped away. I saw that I controlled only neurotic babies who deludedly adored me; and it was not even myself they adored, but an abstraction. I could not enforce my own ideas of obedience, for I was required to act as an ambassador for some greater power who unfailingly intruded itself and who by right exacted this obedience. That I too was at its disposal repelled me unspeakably, and incited me to more repulsive indulgences. To those of healthy character, my superiority was a species of psychosis.

Between the tantrums in the torture chamber, and the hauteur I affected in society, an impassable abyss widened. Within it, I was persecuted by an obscure and hateful Authority. My indulgence in certain forms of behavior—foul language, complaining, demands to be admired and catered to, relentless criticizing—had rendered me intolerant of a nonsubmissive personality. A world empty of the slavish soul would herald my extinction. Any discipline I had formerly possessed dissipated under the brutal ardor of my narcissism.

I could simulate self-control when in the presence of others, as the persona of the dominatrix demanded. But when alone, as I increasingly found myself, I did not bother to dissimulate. I no longer gazed at her violence astonished, nor did I warn or scold her. I attacked myself, tore at my heart with a ravenousness I could only term "appetite." I had an appetite for killing myself, and while crying or confessing brought some relief, more often did this hysterical victim's outburst degenerate into a masochistic display. Under the strain of the rule of the sadist, this animal part of me, uncontrollable, grew wilder and wilder. It seemed to the sadist that there was but one recourse contra the repeated outbreaks of self-pity, of longing for love, and that was to kill herself, and until she did, she was a worthless coward.

It was only proper that she kill herself now that she had discovered that she was one of the inferior persons. If she truly believed in the rule of the Elect, she would sacrifice herself to this idea, not dribble on, pretending to be alive.

But I was the correct sadist, and she was I; there was no distinction between us. She was my creation, and now all that was real—yet unreal, too, as I saw myself her slave. For she did hold in her hands the techniques to gain power, and naturally she first wielded them over me. As I considered this bondage, I observed a certain void had been fashioned in my heart by her presence, a void like a tiny, insistent maelstrom. It ate at the weak, it fed upon affliction, it possessed an appetite for carrion that would not be sated. So I did nothing to dissuade my slaves from their submission, for when I tormented them I no longer suffered from self-hatred.

Then I could elicit the obsessive notion that it was my right to receive their sickly veneration. I knew a morbid satisfaction in clinging to the idea that I possessed a special sensibility that penetrated and loved the secretive, the dark side of the moon I knew as my rightful province. As well I could not avoid remarking a real, preponderant slavishness in humanity, that had neither conception nor desire to conceive of a spiritual privilege. These persons were all particularly subject to a sadistic influence, and it was incumbent upon me to rule them. For as I am created in the image of cruelty, so they realize their victim nature in groveling before me. I become the reason for their vacancy, for their lack of control. You see I am no common vampire.

Why I came to the decision to describe in these pages the methods of controlling the tedious syndrome that is masochism is complex; primarily I wished to remember what I had learned. I considered very little an audience as I wrote. I hoped to be able to come to the end of the subject, and have done with sadomasochism altogether. For brief periods, I believed these methods, applied rigorously, would cure masochism. But there is no cure, only the alleviation of pressure. The idea that inferiority could be a delusion does not impress the masochist. For to lose control in the presence of a Greater is their religious pleasure. The door is opened gladly to a mortal wound, and romantically named nemesis. Against it one may wage an elaborate war, with rites of mortification, chases, attacks, battle losses, and crownings.

I may demonstrate again and again the use of the lock upon this door, but in my participation in the chronic breaking-in I myself go numb to the possibility of sealing the door.

That indeterminate sound from the house below: It's "her," unlatching the door to take a midnight stroll. She cannot stay put at night; the air is too thrilling . . .

I must maintain the integrity of my criminality—impossible now to retrace my steps. A sentimental idea! Let them lock me out all night. I will not repent, intolerable constriction: I have done more than ten persons in their lifetimes could pay for. I wonder often who will come to revenge themselves upon me . . . who will claim my head? To release me from myself and return me to my true home? I can say with conviction that I have made formidable enemies throughout my career. But I will stay deep in the entrails of the early hour where I remain unchallenged, for they are of the established strength, and they are very well organized. They would count it a great success to exterminate me. I fly in the face of their threats, their ranting, and I am not, I tell you, even mildly irritated by these puny restraints. For I cannot be destroyed.

AN EXCESS OF LOVE
by Jac Lenders

Michael, a novelist, and Hilda, his beautiful wife, share a home organized around the couple's day-to-day engagement in acts of sexual dominance and submission. A submissive and pliable spouse, Michael sees to Hilda's every need, even to the point of allowing for (and watching over) her dalliances outside the marriage. This passage, which culminates rather infamously in a "brown party" or "scat" scene, is an excerpt from Michael's diary, a daybook he has been ordered by Hilda to keep of their complicated relationship. Lenders's staccato, atonal prose lends an air of authenticity to this couple's "24/ 7" or "lifestyle" interaction, a common fantasy of those who play with power exchange and wonder what it would be like to live full-time under those conditions.

The house is large and stands on a quiet street. It is only about four hundred yards from the sea. It is a freehold property, three stories high, built in 1929. It is separated from the next house, on one side, by an alley leading to our garage. The other side of the house is built against the house next door.

Small front garden, fairly large garden at the back of the house. Third side of the garden formed by the blind wall of a house. Garden therefore very private and enclosed. Hilda loves gardening. She often potters around at the back of the house in the mornings.

Before we moved in, we had been living in a furnished flat

for several months. Bought the house, had it done up and had quite a few alterations made. But a previous owner had already installed oil-fired central heating with thermostats in most rooms. Almost unbelievable. Extremely pleasant.

Most of the furniture was bought before we moved into the house, all of it for some rooms in fact. The rest we have bought over the last few weeks. Hilda has, that is, because I am never allowed to leave the house.

There is a large basement, with a place for laundering at the back, the boiler room and two rooms with a small bathroom. Stairs outside leading into the garden, ending near the kitchen door. Another staircase ends in the hall.

The ground floor has two large reception rooms, a dining room with windows high up, looking onto the alley, and a kitchen leading into it. There is, of course, a toilet and a fairly large hall with the staircase.

On the first floor Hilda has chosen the back room for her bedroom, with a bathroom connected to it. The front room directly next to this bedroom is Hilda's sitting room. There are two spare bedrooms on this floor, one next to the bathroom and one in front of the house. In that room a shower has been installed, in a little cabinet.

The furnishing of Hilda's bedroom and sitting room is completely to her taste, and rather rich. Comfortable and at the same time somewhat impressive. The bedroom contains a very large bed, placed on a small stage, about eight inches above the rest of the floor. The placing and the size of this bed clearly demonstrate that it is the center of her life.

Her bathroom is very much her personal creation, luxurious without being vulgar, extremely comfortable in every way, without having lost style. The soft rubber flooring with the two fine rugs, the bath, very large and black, with again a "stage" round it, making it appear to be sunk into the floor a little, although it is not. All the fittings of course new and clever.

Basin for two people, with large mirrors with side panels which are movable, and the toilet rather low. Behind the bowl my master made me fit a ring into the wall, for me to be chained to on occasion.

These two rooms I only enter as the slave I am. This private domain of my master I only enter when ordered to. And then nearly always for the purpose of serving her, in various ways. The sitting room with the large TV set and radio, with the pick-up and the comfortable chairs and settee is very much her room, too. Even in here I am only allowed occasionally. And the bar is not for me to use.

The spare bedrooms are well-furnished, with two beds each. Light and pleasant, yet smart. It is all well done. It is done by Hilda.

There is an attic as well, low and dark, the beams now covered with layer upon layer of insulating material, the whole place never to be visited again.

The garage is large, room for one large and one very small car. Can be entered through door in the back, almost next to door of kitchen. Car can be driven straight into the street, people inside. It is all rather perfect.

It was very expensive. It is ours. It is even insured properly, Hilda has made sure of that.

It is the second floor, which I have not mentioned up till now. Leaving it to the last, for good reasons. It is the floor where I am now. Writing this.

Will continue tomorrow.

The second floor is my prison. It is a large and very comfortable prison. In parts. Four rooms. A large workroom or study. At the back of the house. Two large windows on the south, over-looking the garden. A balcony large enough to sit on in comfort.

Connecting with this room, at the front of the house, is an equally large room, combined bedroom and library. The wall between these two rooms has been partly removed, and an archway connects the two spaces and makes them practically into one.

A door leads from the workroom in the back into the other back room. Partly partitioned off, a kitchenette has been made in one corner. There is a workbench in the other corner and a rowing machine and a cycling machine largely take up the rest of the room. A door leads into the bathroom.

An enormous lavatory on the landing has been changed into a shower cabinet and a very small toilet space. I like a shower. Then there is the fourth room. At the front of the house. Not connected with any other room. With one door only, having a Yale lock and a heavy bolt. A bolt on the outside, that is.

This room is not very big. It contains a narrow, military type of metal bed, with a hard mattress, on which lie, neatly folded, three very rough brown blankets. Further, there is a "horse," originally designed for training purposes. A leather covered "body" on four wooden telescopically movable legs. There is a washbasin, without a mirror over it. And then there is the chair.

The chair is a formidable wooden construction, with flat armrests and a high straight back. Its seat consists of the wooden seat of a toilet. Under the seat and attached to it there is a white enameled bucket of the surgery type, but without a cover. On the armrests of this chair small wooden contraptions invite by their shape a man's wrists. To be placed on them. Then a similarly shaped piece of wood, connected to the first one by a strong hinge, can be placed over the wrist and locked shut. After that, the man cannot move his arms any more. For the legs, the same form of constriction has been made available. By me, of course. I have done all the work on this floor, which by its nature could not be executed by outsiders.

It was I who "altered" the chair to make it into a place of confinement in which Hilda could leave me for hours on end. It was I who fixed wooden paneling to one wall of this same room and put in all those hooks and rings. There are about twelve of them in that paneling. To tie me to. In every imaginable position. For all conceivable purposes.

The only other piece of furniture in the room is a small wooden chest, containing chains, ropes, leather belts, leather armcuffs, handcuffs, various locks, gags, and blindfolds. In the top drawer are a number of different whips. About ten. Different shapes, different sizes. The three most-used whips and the two canes rest on top of a small shelf against the wall.

This room is called my "bedroom." It is, of course, the place I am locked up in for a large part of my time. Nobody can get in without the Yale key. I can't get out because of the solid bolt on the outside. There is a heavy curtain on the inside of the door. The window is double-glazed.

But the room also contains a loudspeaker. The speaker of a well-known type of apparatus, which, when connected to the mains, amplifies all the sounds that occur in another part of the house, where a similar instrument is placed. We have instruments of this type, connected to the mains and broadcasting all sounds—to be listened to by me in my "bedroom"—we have instruments like that in two rooms. In my wife's bedroom and in the sitting room next to that bedroom.

My study is beautifully furnished and extremely comfortable. A magnificent black leather armchair of the airplane type, with a large leg-rest. A fine old chaise-lounge, with several cushions. A large, genuinely old desk, used as a writing table. A small, low typing table, and various chests and small tables. It is equipped with everything I could possibly need. Tape recorder, electric typewriter, ordinary typewriter, gramophone, radio. Not, of course, TV.

The library has space for a few thousand books. A very comfortable bed and couch. Good chairs. A washbasin and a large mirror. Everything, in fact, for comfortable living.

The kitchenette has a gas stove with an oven and a small refrigerator. And all the pots and pans required for breakfast and lunch.

This top floor is my prison. My "bedroom" is the prison cell. But I cannot leave the floor, either. A strong partition of latticework has been placed at the foot of the flight of stairs leading from my floor to the halfway landing. I can open the Yale lock, but I cannot open the bolt on the outside of the lattice door. I cannot reach it. Only someone outside my prison can undo the bolt. Again, nobody can enter my domain unless that person has the key to the Yale lock in the lattice door.

This then is my prison. This is where I live.

My floor has no telephone. But there is an intercom between my wife's sitting room and my study. She can speak to me without my having to use a switch. I can only speak to her if she has first spoken to me. The other end has been altered— by me, of course—so as not to make a noise, whatever I try.

Here I live. Every evening at six, I am allowed to go downstairs. In order to cook dinner for Hilda and me. Then we eat it together. Then I am sent upstairs again. At about half past seven. All the other hours of the day and night I spend in my prison. I take the air and the sun if there is any, on my balcony. I do my exercises on my cycling and rowing machines. Every day I must cycle six miles. And row one hundred and fifty strokes. The machines count them automatically and record the total on a counter. I must write down the daily figures on a sheet of paper on the wall. Hilda checks several times a week.

She visits me every evening, at about eleven. She enters and I get up. She stands and I kneel in front of her. I kiss her feet and wait. When she walks away, I may get up. She will sit down in a chair or on the chaise-lounge. We will talk. She will give me instructions. She will order me to come near. She will slap my face. A little later she will get up and I will stand waiting. She comes towards me. Strips down my slacks. She fondles my penis and my balls. Then she will take the cane, which is always lying ready on my writing table, and she will apply it to my buttocks. Three or four firm strokes. Then she will leave me. Often without a word.

Several times a week she will call me over the intercom half an hour later. I am ordered to her bedroom. She is lying in the large double bed. She orders me to undress and to enter the bed. Head first, my legs near her pillow. I wait till she tells me, then I kiss her. I lick and kiss her till she feels satiated. Usually after two, sometimes after three or even four orgasms. She dismisses me then, and I return to my floor. I know that she hardly ever forgets the bolt on that lattice door. After all, it is only a few yards from her bed.

I go to bed at twelve or a little later. In my comfortable bed, unless ordered otherwise. I get up at nine. I have breakfast and read for a while. Then I write in my diary. As I am doing now. It is half past ten now. It is sunny. The house is beautifully warm.

Later in the day, I work on my book. I have some form of lunch at about one or half past one. I do my exercises in the afternoon and sit on my balcony if possible. Then I work or read till six.

In my prison I always wear the same kind of thing: a track-suit. Slacks and blouse. Socks and sandals. Nothing else, ever, apart from the small pants, almost a support for balls and scrotum. This is my prison uniform. Only when we have guests will I be allowed to wear my other clothes. Up till now we haven't had a single guest.

But Hilda is doing her best. She goes out almost every evening. Sits in the kind of bar that may produce the friend she is looking for. She is dressed very smartly. She looks alright. And she can buy drinks for people and the bartender. It all helps. I expect her to achieve her aim soon.

Her aim is, of course, a tall, strong man of about twenty-seven or twenty-eight, a professional man preferably, of reasonably good looks, and keen to come and visit her twice or even three times a week.

She will lock me in that chair in my "bedroom" and I will listen to everything that happens in the sitting room and the bedroom of my wife.

That is her aim. She will succeed, in a while. I feel sure.

It began on Saturday evening. Hilda didn't come upstairs to see me. Instead she spoke to me over the intercom.

"Tomorrow I will spend my whole day with you. We will be all alone in the house. I want to find out if you are really my obedient slave. And I want to enjoy it. You'd better be prepared for a long, tiring day. Go to bed now. And stay in bed till I come and collect you. Don't move till I tell you. Good night, my darling."

I slept badly, of course. I spent hours imagining the happenings of the next day. I woke up at nine. I didn't stir. Hilda arrived at ten.

She was even dressed for the occasion. In riding boots and jodhpurs. And nothing else. She has not ridden a horse for years. She had pulled back her hair, straight, and put a tight ribbon around it. She was all set for the role of slave tester. If I hadn't been so anxious, I might have found it amusing. But not for long, anyway. Hilda in this kind of mood is no laughing matter.

She looked at me. And I sensed that things would be worse than I had imagined during the night. She was gay and felt fit.

I could tell from that one look. I have known her a long time.

"Get up," she said. As I don't wear pajamas, I stood naked next to the bed. "Kneel down." I did. "Head on the floor." I put my face against the rug.

"Stand up." I did. "Bend your knees." I squatted. "Stand straight." I straightened up.

"Kneel down." "Stand up." "Squat." "Stand straight." "Kneel down." The orders followed each other at a slow but steady pace. The voice was soft and calm. Hilda had sat down on the couch. Less than six feet away from me.

"Stand up." "Squat." "Stand straight." "Kneel down." I counted at first. Thirty times. Then I gave up. It was tiring. It went on without a break. I began sweating all over.

"Kneel down." "Stand up." "Squat." "Stand straight." "Kneel down." My erection was already as big as it would ever become. "Stand up." "Squat." "Stand straight." On it went. I desperately wanted to urinate.

"Kneel down." I nearly fell over. "Stand up." "Squat." "Stand straight." I think I swayed a little. "Straight," the voice cut in. I had to stand "straight" for some time, then. I began to feel the beginnings of exhaustion. "Kneel down." She must have gone on for half an hour. Or more.

Just when it would have become too much, the break came. It almost took me by surprise. I had got so much into the rhythm of things that I had become nearly automatic in my movements. I was kneeling down, and she kept me like that for a long time. It was like a rest.

Hilda walked over to my writing table and came back to me. Cane in hand. I looked without taking my head from near the floor. Her naked breasts shone in the little light there was. The curtains hadn't been drawn. From the shape of the *mammae* I gathered that she was enjoying herself. In other words, she felt randy already.

"Move," she said. I got up and steadied myself. We went downstairs. Into the bedroom, first. She made me stand in the corner, face to the wall. Arms high up in the air. She left the room for a while then. Back in the room I was to face her. She held a small plastic bucket. "Hold this, and pee in it."

I tried. My erection was enormous. "Be quick about it, or I'll get some ice cubes," my wife said.

Then she put her hand round my penis. "Go on, then," she said. It sounded like a terrible threat. She let go and grabbed the cane, which was lying on the bed. "Now pee," she whispered. I tried desperately. The sound of the cane on my skin almost surprised me. The pain took over. And the first drops appeared. She watched how it became a steady stream. There was an enormous quantity in the end.

She ordered me to the bathroom and made me kneel in the bath. Then she took the bucket from me and slowly, deliberately, poured the contents over my head. It ran all over me, of course. But immediately afterwards she made me lie down in it, with my arms at my side. And a little later a large plastic funnel was placed in my mouth, between my teeth.

"Breakfast," her calm voice said, matter of factly. Then I saw her bare buttocks appear over my head. Seconds later the funnel was filling up with my wife's urine. She must have stuck some cotton wool or something inside the spout, because only a trickle came into my mouth. But it went on coming.

"Don't spill a drop," I was told. I swallowed and went on swallowing. Hilda was standing next to the bath now and keeping a close watch. In the end I drank a lot. In slow motion.

When the funnel was removed, I had to sit on the wet surface of the tub, and my hands were handcuffed behind my back. Hilda left me and I didn't see her for more than two hours. By that time I was practically dry all over. Apart from my buttocks.

When she returned, she made me step out of the bath and

directed me downstairs, towards the kitchen. She was ready for lunch. I had to kneel down next to her chair. She had a tin of crab for lunch, soft rolls, three cups of tea, and a banana. She took her time over it. I didn't move.

She must have felt refreshed and strong after her meal. She ordered me up and we went to the second floor this time. To my "bedroom." I felt very tired, but without any hope for less than a long afternoon of pain and the rest. My wife had decided this was the day on which my slavery would be confirmed, in the most explicit manner. It was no use rebelling. After all, I am her slave.

Without any nonsense she put me on the bed, on my front. Arms and legs stretched out and wide apart. Securely and tightly fixed to the four corners of the metal frame. A pillow under my loins. My erection bedded in the fullness of it. My buttocks being the highest part of me in that position, rather sticking out and up.

"I am waiting," Hilda said.

I knew I had to beg. Plead, to be whipped. This was the most difficult test.

"Please, my master, whip me hard. Please punish me as much as you feel I deserve. Please make me feel that I am your slave."

She used a rather short and heavy whip. A riding crop. The first three strokes were almost unbearable. For a moment the pain went down into my groin. Then the very agony of the skin became more important. My body could not move much, but it tried to sway, against my better knowledge. She hit me about ten times. At the end of it, I couldn't stop myself from crying. I felt the tears running down and my nose became blocked.

"Ask for more," my master said softly. She would break me.

"Please," I snottered, "punish me more."

"Who are you speaking to?"

"Please, my master, whip me more."

She was hitting too hard. I couldn't bear it. I began to make noises. I probably yelled. Three strokes which were like burns.

"Ask for more." I couldn't do it. I could hardly control my tongue and lips. I was openly weeping by then.

"Ask for more. This is the second time that I order you."

"In a moment," I brought out at last.

"Now."

"Please, whip me more." But I knew that I would shriek.

She used all her strength, I believe. The leather burned my skin just below the buttocks. I did shriek. And a second time. My arms and legs moved, and my whole body tried to twist and turn. But all that happened was that I felt the leather round my wrists and ankles more than before. There was a short silence then. I knew we had reached the point at which the last remaining fragments of my will would go.

"Now tell me," she said simply.

"I will do anything you want. Whatever you want. Immediately when you order me to do it."

"I am listening."

"Anything at all."

"I think you need some more whipping."

"I will eat all of it."

That was my abdication. With that I bought the right to go on existing as my master's slave. And a temporary end to the whipping of that moment.

"Good," matter-of-factly. "Good, we will see about that, later."

It had never been forced upon me yet. It had always remained the ultimate threat. The ultimate horror. But never had I felt sure about her. One day, perhaps, she would go as far as that, even. I never stressed my willingness for it, unless I couldn't bear the pain any longer. As this time.

But it wasn't to be yet. I was left on the bed for some time.

Hilda went downstairs, I believe. She didn't return for about half an hour. The pain had slowly been converted into that hot glow of skin and tissue that is as tantalizing as a caress. As pleasurable as the weariness after a long embrace. The soft burning of whipped buttocks is like the aching of lips after hours of lovemaking with two partners. It is too much, but too lovely to regret.

When I was released by my wife, I had to sit down in "the chair." My wrists were locked, my legs left free.

"When I come back, you must be finished, unless you want me to cane you on your welts," my wife said. And she left me alone again. It was about half past two, I guess. My tiredness was becoming a pain. But I was glad to be able to relieve my bladder and my bowels. I defecated with all my might. Then I sat and waited. In my own stink. I was hungry. And afraid. Sometimes Hilda does frighten me. Although in the end it is always right. But I felt afraid, then. Perhaps because I was very tired and hungry, and because of the pain in my backside.

She opened the door, quickly freed my hands, and stepped out of the room again. From the corridor she said, "Take the bucket and come down."

I followed her. Holding the bucket in my arms. We went to her bathroom again. She made me step into the bath and stand upright in it. I was still holding the bucket. Hilda fetched a chair from the bedroom. She sat down on it in the door opening.

"Put it down," she said. I placed the bucket in front of me. "Now I am going to watch while you put your warpaint on. I will direct you. First get hold of all of it. Take it in your hands. Every little bit of it."

I bent down and fished out the three turds and one or two small bits. I made one lot of it in my hands.

"Let's see, we will use your chest as a palette. Stick it against your chest. Don't let anything drop off."

Well, all the instructions were followed as from then on. I know my wife. She will lose her temper at that stage, if not obeyed to the letter.

"First your beard. Not too much. All over. Then your hair on top. Now some on the nose and cheeks. And the moustache. Get some more. Under your arms. And the neck."

She sat, completely relaxed, directing my activities. She got up and went into the sitting room. She came back with a glass of Scotch and water. Sipping it.

"Now the penis and balls. A lot of it. More. A little brown stick, that's nice. Now that belly. Stripes. Good. That looks good. The rest goes all over the chest. And the hips. Wipe your hands all over the place. Now you look nice. My own brave in his very own private warpaint. I like that."

She was sitting there, still with her breasts naked and still wearing the boots and breeches. Sipping her drink and very gay.

"Only you stink." She looked me over carefully.

"Nothing left?" she asked. I looked and then shook my head. There wasn't.

"There isn't enough in your beard. What shall we do about that?" She got up and put her drink down on the chair. She stood inside the bedroom. Taking off her boots. Then the breeches. She was wearing small black panties. She took them off and entered the bathroom. She pushed the panties into my mouth and then sat down on the toilet. I watched her naked body relax. She looked at me and smiled. I smiled as well. We love each other so much.

We love each other so much. Oh, god, we love each other terribly.

With a total and almost amused calm, utterly relaxed, my

wife sat naked on the toilet and smiled at me, her love, dressed in "warpaint," standing naked in the bath.

My buttocks burned, my mouth was filled with the taste of her cunt, my body was aching with fatigue. But I smiled back, because we love each other so much, so much.

Strange are the ways of human endeavor. Deep are the secrets of human desire. There is no way out.

After a long while, Hilda lifted her right hand and slowly moved her forefinger in the way of telling me to come nearer. I stepped out of the bath. The same finger pointed down. I kneeled right in front of her. My head was near her belly. Over the open space between her thighs. I witnessed her act of defecation. I heard the dropping of the turds. I listened to the little squirt of peeing, a few moments later.

She placed her hands on my shoulders in a gesture of extreme relaxation. I rested my head between her thighs. My face against her skin.

We stayed like that for some time. Then my head was slowly pushed upwards. I remained on my knees, but straightened my body. I watched her right hand go up and wasn't surprised by the slap with which it hit my cheek. I was hit twice more. I felt the pain, but was not much bothered by it.

Hilda got up and stood next to me. She didn't speak. She kept the tension growing. Then she moved to the chair and took her drink in her hands. Sipped it. I was waiting, on my knees.

"Take them out," she said.

I repeated my fishing, only this time inside the lavatory bowl. I gathered together two pieces and then a third one, much smaller. I held them in my hands. Closing my hands together. Making one single substance of my charge.

Then Hilda stepped near and pulled the panties out of my mouth. A great warmth mounted in me. Fear. Or at least anxiety. My wife moved back to her chair. Sat down. Sipping her drink. I didn't dare look at her face. Gathered what she was doing from sounds and half-looks.

Oh, I remember the feeling well. Even though it was the day before yesterday. I sweated with anxiety. A deep, deep horror settled inside me. Never had I felt so much in the power of my wife.

"Now crawl this way," Hilda said after a long, long pause. I moved towards her, on my knees. My hands holding her ex-crement like treasure.

I was on my knees in front of her. Instinctively I placed my hands on the floor and bowed my head till it nearly touched them. Her legs were on both sides of my head. She remained silent. Sipping her drink. No doubt, looking down on me.

"Beg me," she said. Her voice was harsh. A sudden resolve.

My face was burning. Not with the pain, but with the sweaty anxiety that raged inside me. I swallowed several times.

"Please make me," I whispered.

"Make you what?" Callous, almost, but gay at the same time.

"Please make me eat it." I did not want to. I did not want to.

"Say: 'All of it.' "

"All of it."

"Nicely. Say it nicely."

"Please make me eat all of it, my master."

"Good." She got up. She moved away from me. She was standing at my side. She pushed me with her leg. Turning me. Then she stood in front of me. On the rubber floor.

"Put it down," she said. "On the floor.' I placed as much as would leave my hands on the shining floor.

"Now take it with your mouth." I looked at the wet, slimy, brown mass under my eyes. I bent over. When I placed my mouth over it, the smell hit me. I forced my head down. Touched it. Placed my lips round it. Got some of it inside my mouth. Then the revulsion conquered me. I couldn't stop it. I felt a strange pain inside my chest, then my mouth lost control and a stream of vomit burst out. And immediately afterwards, a second stream. Then there was only a short hacking pain in my midriff. I tried to master it. But a third short stream of yellow and green and brown was added to the foul mess on the floor. I rested my hands far forwards. Tried to calm down.

Hilda did not move. She did not speak, either. She was standing at my side. Not reacting at all.

A few minutes later she moved. She stepped into the bedroom and returned. I didn't look. I was still fighting my stomach. Then the end of the cane came under my eyes. Touching the small ball of excrement. Pushing it out of the mess. Towards a clean part of the floor.

"Take it," Hilda said. I took it with my right hand. Shuddering slightly.

"Put it in your mouth," she said, her voice steely. Determined. Leaving no hope. I obeyed. I placed the wet substance in my mouth and shut my lips over it.

"Get up." I got on my feet with difficulty. My diaphragm was pulsating. Hilda was standing in front of me. Cane in hand. Naked. But completely in command. Of herself and of me.

My tongue was without sensitivity, but the liquid filling my mouth became very nearly uncontrollable. I swallowed. I shuddered. But there was no further reaction.

Again Hilda took her drink and sipped from it. She looked at me all the time. Watching how much I could still take. I was becoming much calmer now. My stomach had stopped revolting against the inevitable.

"Sit down," Hilda said, pointing towards the toilet. I sat down and felt the pain in my buttocks anew. I had completely forgotten about it. Now it took command. But strangely it calmed me even further. I swallowed again. No reaction from my stomach.

Hilda moved the chair into the bathroom and sat down. She looked completely content. She finished her drink in one movement.

"Now you know what will happen to you if you ever dream of disobeying me. If ever. I think you will know better. I think you will remember this afternoon and never forget it.

"What I order my slave to do will be done. No matter what. It will be done, and it will be done immediately. And no exceptions. Nothing barred. Anything I say will be done. And that is final."

She felt happy. And I cannot deny that there was a great contentedness inside me. A deep feeling of having arrived home. A sense of finally being safe. Completely safe, in the hands of my wife. I swallowed several times. There was calm inside me.

I feel very tired now. I will continue later. Maybe even tomorrow. There is still much to tell.

ADAGIO

by Daniel Vian

Set in Italy in 1938, this novel was praised by Tino Roberto for "catching the final days of Capri's rampant sexuality and ultimate deception during its heyday of decadence and intrigue." Beautiful, spoiled, young Odile arrives to stay with Madeleine, her mother, an ethereal beauty and film actress. Also present is Madeleine's new lover, Umberto. When Odile and Umberto become lovers, Madeleine is overwhelmed with obsessive jealousy.

A party in the evening. Umberto has managed at last to find a case of champagne. He laughs as he moves from one guest to another with a bottle in each hand. Nearly twenty people have arrived at the house. The crowd is unexpected, a throng of Italians and Germans and Englishmen and Englishwomen and a man who claims to be a Hungarian count. Odile stands between the count and an English gentleman. The English gentleman is looking at the count. The count is looking at Odile. She has her head turned to the right, turned away from the count, avoiding his eyes, avoiding his attempt at a ridiculous flirtation. Behind them is a wall of the room, a candelabra, the framed drawing of the two women with their arms linked.

The old man is in his shack, in a half-crouch in a corner, his eyes on another old man no more than two meters away who appears to have just sat down on the floor with his back against the wall. The second old man is still supporting his weight with his right palm flat on the floor. His left hand is gripping something, either something attached to the lower part of the wall or something close to the lower part of the wall. His head is turned to his left as he stares at the first old man, a violent stare, fear in his eyes, his jacket lifted by his shoulders and almost covering the left side of his face. The first old man remains in a half-crouch in the corner, his hands on his knees, his eyes directed at the second old man, his mouth tightly closed as he looks at the second old man's face. The first old man says, "You need to be brave." The second old man nods, and he says, "Yes, I need to be brave, but I'm not brave. When will he come?" The first old man says, "Tomorrow." The second old man says, "I need to be brave, but I'm not brave."

Odile is unhappy. She feels surprise at her own unhappiness. She finds herself staring at Madeleine, gazing at her mother as she wonders about her unhappiness. "I don't want anything," Odile thinks. "There's nothing that I want." Sometimes she feels like a statue, a frozen relic of another life. Then she looks at Madeleine again, and she understands that what she feels is jealousy. How absurd, Odile thinks. How absurd to be jealous. She's more aware of her body these days. Is it the sun? Is it the sea air? Umberto is always looking at her body in the afternoon when she wears next to nothing on the terrace. My mother's lover. How sad it is. But she likes his eyes. She sees her beauty in Umberto's eyes. Yes, I'm desperate. I was always a desperate child, wasn't I? She tells herself that she wants happiness, that she has a need for happiness. She wants the eyes of men and she wants happiness. How stupid it is. You're such a stupid girl, aren't you? Then what remains for her? There's always a price to pay, isn't there? She has no idea what to expect. She finds Capri so tiresome. But then where would you go? You don't want to be in Paris now, do you? You're foolish, Odile. She can see the foolishness in her face when she looks in the mirror. How awful it is to see the foolishness in one's own face. Yes, Paris would be much better. It's not summer yet and all her friends are still there. They would think Italy so vulgar. Do I have a glow in my cheeks? Dear Nicole, I have definitely decided to cut my hair. She'll never write to me, of course. My best friend is a complete bitch. I'm sure they whisper about me. We all whisper about each other. What fun it is to do the whispering. They whisper about Madeleine, don't they? She always has someone in her bed. And of course in Paris it's much worse. The bitch Nicole laughs: "Odile, your mother is so elegant." Well, she's not that elegant when she has her clothes off. When she has her clothes off, you can see the way her breasts droop. Madeleine Fabre's tits. I wonder how she endures becoming old. It's not a comfort, is it? Odile, you're a bitch. Yes, I'm a useless bitch.

We see what is obviously the interior of a prison. There are two men in uniform. One man, in the foreground, has just opened an iron gate consisting of six vertical bars and one crossbar. The top of the gate is an arc that fits the arch above it. The other man in uniform is the lieutenant. He stands in the background. In front of the lieutenant is a young woman wearing a tailored suit, stockings, shoes. The collar of her white blouse is carefully outside the collar of her jacket. She stands with her hands at her sides, her feet together, as if she waits for an order to move. The lieutenant nudges the young woman and now she steps forward, moves forward under the arch and past the gate, past the guard who has opened the gate, the lieutenant remaining behind, standing there, watching the young woman and the guard as the guard now swings the gate closed with a loud clang of iron against iron.

Odile feels a wave of nausea as she drinks the champagne. She wonders where these people have come from, out of what obscure cave? Madeleine seems happy. These are Madeleine's people. These are the sort of people Madeleine knows in Paris. Madeleine enjoys these people. She desires them. She receives great pleasure from them.

Luco smiles at Odile. He asks her if she's happy. Are you happy, Odile? Yes, why not? It's a balmy night, the stars in the sky, the lights of scattered villas visible on the promontories. Capri is a mirage. This party is a mirage. This villa does not actually exist. Luco talks. He gazes at Odile's breasts as he talks. Odile remembers the feel of his penis in her hand, the feel of his hot blood throbbing beneath her fingers. She wonders what he does with his other women, his Italian girls.

The lieutenant is now in a large room with a number of other uniformed men. He sits at the right behind a table, leaning forward as he examines a sheet or a dossier or a message, his right hand raised to his chin, his head bent as he gives his attention to whatever it is that's on the table in front of him. Three other men in uniform can be seen seated around the table at the left. Two of them have their backs to the viewer and the third is half-turned in his seat so that his gaze is directed at the lieutenant. In the background are two more men, a civilian who stands with his eyes directed at the uniformed men around the table and a guard who stands behind the civilian with his eyes on the prisoner. No one moves. Then the lieutenant's hand moves as he slowly rubs his chin and the lower part of his face. He continues to stare at the paper in front of him, and then finally he pulls his hand away from his face and lifts his head and then turns it to gaze at the prisoner. This individual now lifts his right hand to his throat, grips his throat, and opens his mouth as wide as possible.

I have my memories. How many men has she known? My darling, you're such a child. You haven't known any men at all, have you? Sometimes she feels her life is impossible. Why does Madeleine want Umberto? It's absurd, isn't it? Why Umberto and not a minister in Paris. She had the Minister of Defense once, yes she did. Twice a week in a small apartment near the Place Vendome. The Minister of Defense and Madeleine Fabre. The Minister's wife appeared at the opera one evening wearing one of Madeleine's inventions. "And not looking her best," Madeleine said. "His wife has too much bust for that dress."

Luco leads Odile to a quiet part of the terrace. They watch the lights flickering along the Marina Piccola. Luco talks of his desire for Odile. Odile smiles at the fire in his words. He wants her to yield to him. He wants her to abandon her virginity. He kisses her hand. He presses against her body. Odile laughs, and she moves away. She moves further into the shadows of the terrace. Luco touches her again, his hands on her waist, her back. Odile suddenly feels so fragile in his hands. A shudder passes through her as Luco whispers in her ear again, "I can't wait." "Luco, don't be absurd." "Do you remember when we were together in Naples?" "Yes, of course, I remember." "Meet me tomorrow in the Piazza Umberto." "No, I won't." He kisses her neck again. Odile shivers as she feels his wet mouth rubbing against her skin.

The wet lips. May 1936. These are the wet lips of an Englishman pressing against Odile's skin, against the skin of her neck below her right ear. They stand in the shadows of a corridor, a light at the far end of the corridor, a door to somewhere. Odile stands erect, and the Englishman stands behind her with his lips pressed against her skin. "You're a tease," he says. Odile tells him she doesn't understand. "It doesn't matter," he says. "Come with me to a hotel," he adds. "No, never," she says. She pulls away from him, pulls herself free of his arms and moves forward, gliding in the shadows of the corridor, gliding towards the light at the end of the corridor.

We see a small group outside the house in the afternoon sunlight. The lieutenant has his back towards the viewer, and he stands at the left side, only the right side of his body visible. A few meters in front of him, two uniformed men are holding a third man, a civilian, between them. The prisoner is a small man, thin to the point of emaciation, his eyes bewildered, the white shirt that he wears under his dark suit showing a streak of fresh blood along the collar on the left side. The two uniformed men are much taller than the prisoner. The guard on the left is grinning as he looks at the lieutenant, as he leans toward the prisoner. The guard shows a distinct gap in his teeth, a missing upper front tooth. The other guard stands at attention, his expression vacant, his lips turned in a vacant smile. Behind the guards and the prisoner is the house, and we can see a young man leaning against the white wall of the house near one of the windows, relaxed as he watches the others, relaxed as he watches the uniformed men and the prisoner.

Alone in her bed, Madeleine considers her affair with Umberto. Does she want him? How grim it is. She has her whims, doesn't she? She's a woman of patterns. She has all these patterns in her life. Umberto is merely another pattern, a smaller pattern inside the larger pattern of these recent years. She's had too many lovers. And Umberto is not the best of them. Umberto is definitely not the best of them. It's too soon, isn't it? You can't pretend that it's not too soon. She thinks of his mouth. She imagines him talking. His lips are moving, but no sound comes out, no voice, nothing but a silent moving of his lips. All the stupid talk about Mussolini. I don't care about Mussolini. Darling, you're vicious, aren't you? Yes. All women like me are completely vicious.

The old man is inside his shack again, crouched in a corner now in the semi-darkness, his eyes turned sharply to the right as if he's looking at someone. A large burlap bag is leaning against his left shoulder, the bag having been deliberately moved there by the old man or else having just fallen on his body from somewhere. The old man's face is lit by candlelight, and now the candle flickers, throwing grotesque shadows on the wall near the old man. The view pulls back and for the first time we see the candle on a small crate and someone's hand in front of the flame, the fingers of the hand moving back and forth to create the shadows on the wall.

What Odile knows about her father: My father was an American soldier who impregnated my mother in the year 1917. That was a year after Verdun.

The man and the woman are either in the room or on the landing of the stairs. The man is behind the woman, leaning against her as if to comfort her, one of his hands visible as it cradles the left side of her chin. The woman has her head tilted to the side, her own hand clenched along the right side of her face, a wedding ring visible on the third finger. Her eyes are closed. She opens them a moment now, and then she closes them again. "When will he come?" she says. "Tomorrow," he says. "But I don't want you to die," she says. "I don't want you to die." He says, "Dying doesn't matter." She says, "Will you always love me?" He says, "I'll always love you."

In the midst of another night, Odile is again secretly on the terrace. She hungers to discover them. She stands at the balustrade in her nightgown, and she gazes at the sea. After a time, she moves along the terrace, gliding along the balustrade toward Madeleine's room, towards Madeleine and Umberto.

What do you want? She wants their intimacy. She feels compelled to witness their intimacy. Her mother's intimacy. Her mother and Umberto. How amusing it is that so many places here carry the same name: the Galleria Umberto in Naples, the Piazza Umberto in the town of Capri.

Odile is shocked when she finally stops at the balustrade outside Madeleine's room. Madeleine and Umberto are on the bed, and they are making love. Now for the first time Odile can watch it. What an enchantment it is. The two bodies are naked on the bed. Madeleine is on her back and Umberto is between her thighs, his hips between her thighs as he rhythmically thrusts his penis into the depths of her sex.

Never before, Odile thinks. She watches Umberto move. She watches as Madeleine now raises her legs to open herself even further to his thrusting. Madeleine's dark hair is in disarray about her face. Odile is amused. For the first time in her memory, her mother looks untidy.

Umberto continues his thrusting. Madeleine lifts a hand to his shoulder and now her rings are glinting in the lamplight. She's not young. Her mother is not at all young anymore. Umberto's penis is clearly visible, a thick bar of flesh sliding in and out of Madeleine's open sex. Odile can see the dark bag of his testicles swinging under his thrusting penis. And Madeleine's face? Odile wonders what her mother's mood is at this moment.

Madeleine's face is flushed, her eyes staring at the ceiling, her hands clutching at Umberto's shoulders, both hands, both hands clutching at his shoulders as he continues thrusting at her sex. Then he finishes. He calls out something in Italian as he gives the final lunge into Madeleine's body, the final thrusting, the spasm at last, his buttocks quivering in the ultimate spasm. Odile's head is swimming as she hurries away to find her room again.

The woman in the arcade has risen from the cafe table where she was sitting, and she now appears to be in the midst of a dance. A small crowd has gathered, a dozen or so people gathered around her, laughing at her, a man on the right leaning forward with his finger on his nose, a man on the left showing a gaping grin as he stares at her, a young man in the rear standing on something as he laughs at her. The crowd pushes in towards the woman. She dances. She wiggles her hips, shakes her arms, her head tilted to one side, her red lips parted in a gleeful smile. Someone says, "Who is she?" Someone else says, "They took her son." Someone says, "Then why does she dance?" Someone else says, "It's a dance of madness."

Now the jealousy is much worse. In the afternoon Odile complains of the heat. She swims with Xenia near the Punta Carena. When they return to the villa, Madeleine is amused by their wet hair. Odile goes to her room. She tells herself that she ought to have remained in Paris until August. There is nothing in Italy for her, nothing but a desperate emptiness, nothing but her stupid jealousies. Madeleine is too extravagant, isn't she? My mother is a blind woman. I don't understand why Umberto is so obsessed with her. But of course Umberto is a fool. What a surprise to see them together. What a hairy affair she has. She has never taken any sun and her body is so pale in the lamplight. And Umberto's organ. Odile quivers as she remembers Umberto's thrusting organ. In her room she gazes at herself in the mirror. Do my eyes look mournful? What an amusement to watch them. What a caprice. Madeleine would never understand it, would she? Or maybe she would understand it. I wonder if she's prepared to understand it. She can be sweet sometimes. When she has the men around her, she can be sweet. I must promise myself not to look at them again. But darling, you mustn't promise. If you promise that, you know you won't keep the promise. Does she have prettier legs? Are Madeleine's legs prettier than mine? She has her lovers, hasn't she? Odile wonders how long Umberto will last. Odile stands before the mirror and she holds her breasts in her hands and she wonders if her breasts will grow. A tremor passes through her as once again she thinks about Umberto's organ thrusting in Madeleine's open sex. It's a trouble, isn't it?

The lieutenant is in a street in front of an old church. He stands talking to a civilian wearing a slouch hat. The man holds a cigarette in his left hand, and his expression appears to be one of friendly amusement, as if he and the lieutenant are colleagues. Behind them, towards the left and near the old church, stand another civilian and another man in uniform. The lieutenant has his right hand in the pocket of his jacket. Now the lieutenant's left hand appears, his forefinger pointing upward, his head nodding. A dog runs out from somewhere, runs barking across the space that separates the two groups.

On the terrace in the afternoon, Odile teases Umberto with her body. She wears a pink halter-top and pink shorts. Her feet are bare, and as she lies on the chaise and opens her legs she knows that Umberto is looking at her. She can feel him. She remembers him with Madeleine. The image of them on the bed is never out of her mind now. She remembers Umberto's body between Madeleine's thighs, Umberto's waist gripped by Madeleine's legs, Umberto's buttocks twitching with each thrust of his penis. Odile wonders what Umberto thinks of her. Does he know that she's a virgin? She wonders what he thinks of chastity. She listens to him as he talks about Mussolini again. He talks of Mussolini, but his eyes are on Odile's breasts. Odile imagines him as a father. Will he marry Madeleine? Will Umberto marry a woman no longer in her first youth? Then the image of the lovemaking again. How strange to see Madeleine possessed like that, Madeleine with a flushed face and her legs thrown open to Umberto's organ. "We have clouds," Umberto says. "What?" she asks. "The clouds, darling. Look at the clouds in the east. The clouds over Vesuvius. Are you afraid of the volcano?" She says, "I'm not afraid." She thinks of his penis again. His organ looked so thick in Madeleine's sex. Odile wonders what it would be like to hold Umberto's penis in her hand. She glances at the front of his shorts, but she sees nothing. Everything is concealed. You're a silly girl, aren't you? You're a silly girl possessed by carnal thoughts. This is your mother's lover. Your mother is Umberto's mistress. Odile is motionless again. She sits with her legs apart, and she tries not to tremble as Umberto looks at her.

The old man is standing inside his shack with another old man. The first old man stands with his thumbs hooked in the waistband of his trousers. The second old man has his right hand raised to cover his eyes and the middle part of his face, his lips twisted in a grimace of despair, his body turned away from the first old man. Behind them is a shelf, and on the shelf is a half-empty bottle of red wine. We can see the dark opening of a doorway behind the second old man, but whether the doorway leads merely to another room or to the outside is not evident.

The second old man says, "Tomorrow?" The first old man says, "Yes, tomorrow." The second old man says, "Then it's hopeless." The first old man says, "No, it's not hopeless."

Madeleine is not trembling. Madeleine is with Luco in a villa in the Via Tiberio. Madeleine is naked and kneeling, bent over an ottoman as Luco kneels behind her with his organ in her anus. In her bottom. Luco holds her buttocks with her hands as he slowly thrusts his penis in and out of her stretched opening. Madeleine groans. Madeleine groans again. She turns her head, and she tries to look at his face over her right shoulder. But the angle is wrong, and all she can see is an old crucifix on one of the walls. She feels Luco's hands gripping her buttocks. She feels his long organ sliding in and out of her bowels. She turns her head to the front door again, and she rests her face on her folded arms.

The lieutenant is now inside a room, an office of some kind. He stands at the left, and we can see a series of small file cabinets in the background. There are three other people in the room, a woman and two men. The woman has turned away from the lieutenant's gaze, and one of the men has reached out to grab her left shoulder as if to make her look at the lieutenant again. The other man stands behind the first man, his head turned to look directly at the woman, his face twisted by an expression of scorn.

Umberto smiles at Odile. He says she's not at all like her mother. He says she's more delicate. Odile blushes. She sees the amusement in his eyes. She pretends not to understand him. Is he hiding something? Odile feels pleasure whenever he looks at her. He's wearing the black horn-rimmed eyeglasses again, and he reminds her so much of one of her teachers in

Paris. Once again she thinks of Umberto and Madeleine together, flesh against flesh, his organ thrusting at Madeleine's
hairy sex. It's complete. They make a complete couple.

Umberto smiles again. He says he thinks Odile has been
watching him and Madeleine at night. On the terrace, he says.
You watch us from the terrace. Odile is frozen, every muscle
frozen. A moment passes before she finds the will to speak. It's
not true. Umberto laughs. He says he doesn't mind. He says he
really doesn't mind it.

The two women have unlinked their arms, and now one
woman stands behind the other woman. The woman in the
rear has both arms around the woman in front of her. She has
her left hand placed just below the other woman's left breast.
Her right forearm is across the other woman's right hip, her
right hand covering most of the other woman's triangle, her
fingers pressing into the other woman's sex between her partly
open thighs. The woman in front has her right hand behind
her. Only part of the hand can be seen, but the viewer can
guess that the hand is pressing against the sex of the first
woman.

Odile is sitting in Umberto's lap. The first kiss is gentle. The
second kiss is more penetrating. Then Umberto lowers the pink
halter-top to expose her breasts. He kisses Odile's nipples one
after the other. Odile looks down and watches his mouth. Then
she turns her head to the side, and she closes her eyes.

SHADOW LANE

by Eve Howard

Eve Howard's Shadow Lane *series of spanking novels is an ongoing soap opera of the lives of a group of male and female spanking aficionados living in a small New England village. An articulate and popular spokesperson for women who enjoy spanking, Howard is particularly gifted at rendering the insights of experienced participants, as demonstrated by the following excerpt, which depicts the thoughts of a dominant woman as she switches, or submits to a spanking. As also seen here, Howard is faithful to the often-pansexual nature of many spanking communities, making her work a welcome departure from the strictly heterosexual texts of her more traditional predecessors.*

To infer that Marguerite Alexander was always on the make would be inaccurate, but if her victim was young, attractive, the slightest bit fetishistic, and within easy reach, no matter what the sex or erotic orientation of her chosen object, Marguerite would go after it and inevitably possess it. In this case, the morsel cast before the tall, voluptuous, Bennington-educated redhead was little Susan Ross, the eighteen-year-old sister of Marguerite's best friend, Laura.

Marguerite had come into Boston to shop and had decided to take Susan out to lunch. The little blonde was in her freshman year at art college and was living on her own in a loft in Back Bay. Marguerite came up with Susan after lunch.

436

A Boston January can be bleak, but Susan was living like a spoiled brat in a studio with hardwood floors and skylights. There was even a small fireplace with a mantelpiece above it. Susan set about starting a fire for Marguerite's pleasure with a log of absurdly expensive Georgia fatwood that Anthony Newton had sent her. Hard rain began to beat on the windows above the girls, and they could hear the wind whipping as well, but in here it couldn't have been cozier.

While waiting for coffee to brew, they lounged on Susan's bed, turning the pages of a photo album that Newton had begun filling with pictures of Susan in poses and outfits that appealed to his deviant tastes.

"Really, little girl," sighed Marguerite at last. "You can't show me pictures like that and not expect me to want to play with you!"

Marguerite was dressed in a purple heather tweed suit with a form-fitting peplum-waisted jacket and straight skirt. Her steep pumps with their four-inch heels displayed the sort of insteps that footslaves dream of worshipping. Underneath the stunning suit, she wore black silk-satin; her black-tinted stockings were breathtakingly sheer. As always, she wore her luxuriant auburn hair down to her shoulders, and vibrant lapis lazuli disks adorned her earlobes. In contrast to this portrait of a John Willie pinup girl, Susan looked like the schoolgirl that she was in a blue corduroy jumper, crisp white blouse, ribbed oatmeal-colored woolen thigh-high stockings, and shiny new Mary Janes. In spite of her appearance, Susan was not innocent, merely inexperienced; and even that was quickly being seen to.

"What do you mean?" Susan asked, leaning on an elbow to look at Marguerite.

"I mean I'd love to spank this pretty bottom," the redhead replied, meeting Susan's puzzled gaze with a mischievous smile.

"You?" Susan was amused. "But you're a girl."

"Haven't you ever played with a girl?" Marguerite practically purred, stroking Susan's compact, round bottom through the coarse fabric of the jumper. Susan pillowed her chin on her hands and thought for a moment, allowing Marguerite to continue to smooth her skirt.

"Yes, I have," replied Susan. "In junior high school I had a girlfriend I played spanking games with. This went on for about two years. But one of us would always take the male role. We never played those games without one of us taking the male role."

"I absolutely adore playing the male role!" Marguerite said with such vehemence that Susan turned to look at her. Then Susan boldly put her hand out to cup one of Marguerite's magnificent breasts, which the fine wool jacket outlined beautifully.

"You don't look or feel very masculine to me," Susan teased. "How are you going to convince me?"

"You won't have to look at me when you're over my knee, young lady," Marguerite pointed out, giving her flirtatious new plaything a sharp little smack on the seat of her skirt. Susan stretched out on her tummy again with her chin on her hands.

"Have you ever played with my sister?"

"Yes," Marguerite chortled. "But she's been too lesbophobic to enjoy it."

"That sounds like my sister," Susan commented, not resisting when Marguerite pushed her skirt up over her bottom to stroke her from her calves to her waist through her stockings and white petticoat.

"Mmm," said Marguerite, running her other hand through Susan's curly sandy-blonde hair. Then she pulled up the embroidered petticoat to reveal a pair of white eyelet briefs, upon which had been lavished eight rows of pink-edged frills. These delightful panties encased Susan's plump little bottom like expensive gift-wrapping.

"Another present from your admirer?" Marguerite patted Susan's firm behind.

"He wanted me to wear them today. He said he'd be in Boston tonight," Susan explained.

"Those really are irresistible," Marguerite commented. "Let's do this properly," she said, sitting up and swinging her long legs around, then easily pulling little Susan, who weighed about 100 pounds, into position across her tweed-skirted thighs.

Marguerite's movements were slow and deliberate, but tender. Since she had been in this particular position a number of times herself, she knew that certain factors were important to the comfort and pleasure of the submissive, such as being perfectly positioned and securely held.

Now that Susan's bottom was lusciously upturned across Marguerite's lap, the frilled present looked even more inviting. Susan's woolen stockings came to midthigh. Between her stocking tops and panties bottom her smooth white thighs were bare.

"So pretty!" Marguerite cooed, stroking Susan's bottom for a few moments more before spanking her. Marguerite intended to give Susan a "sex spanking," with a long warm-up, consisting of perhaps several hundred modest stingers; not enough to have the little girl kicking, but to have her feeling warm halfway through and soaking wet by the end. Unless a man was watching, Marguerite seldom had the impulse to be severe in disciplining other women. In this case, even more than at other times, she was interested in providing the most seductive experience possible for her pixie friend, because she longed for a little girl to spoil and call her own. Marguerite was very much like a man in that respect, even though she herself also enjoyed being spoiled.

Thus it came to pass that Anthony Newton was met, as he approached Susan's front door to knock upon it, by the muffled sound of a spanking from within the apartment.

When the imperious knock came on the door, the girls sprang apart and up like thieves. Since Susan's panties had stayed up, her clothes fell instantly to rights as she got to her feet. Marguerite went to check her hair in a mirror as Susan went to the door, flushing, as she hadn't done throughout the unremittingly erotic spanking she had just so dreamily received.

Susan looked at Marguerite before opening the door, and they wordlessly agreed that what had just happened, and what might happen between them in the future, would be their secret for the time being. Embarrassing Susan in front of her lover would have only provided a cheap thrill, whereas Marguerite was more interested in the long-term projection for herself and this uninhibited little moppet. To this end, Marguerite determined at that moment never to play with Susan for the jaded amusement of a man, but instead to keep her passion for this tiny treasure pure and exclusive. This resolve would enable her to gain Susan's trust.

"Anthony!" Susan cried, throwing open the door to admit the man, with all his crackling energy and demanding virility, into their warm, peaceful, playful girly world. "I didn't expect you until later."

"I told you I was coming in today," he replied grouchily, striding into the studio with every expectation of locking horns with a male rival. The wind was let out of his sails when he realized that his little girl had only been in the red-enameled clutches of the divine Marguerite Alexander.

"Well! What have you two been up to?" Newton was charmed by the notion of the gorgeous Marguerite dominating his new obsession, this submissive young girl.

"Nothing," said Susan, looking at her shoes.

"Not a thing," agreed Marguerite with a catlike grin.

"Oh, really?" Newton asked. He couldn't help but look cynical. Susan excused herself to get the coffee tray. He in turn seized the opportunity to enfold the tall redhead in his arms. They had been together only once, and that had been on Halloween, when he'd met her at the party in the house on Random Point, which he had subsequently bought.

"What sort of depraved mischief have you been up to here, young lady?" he demanded, holding both her hands in his. "Talk. I don't want to have to tie you up and beat the answers out of you." These last words of love, all but whispered in her ear, made her shiver.

On the night they'd spent together, she had brought him home to her house on the rocky beachfront on the very tip of the village. They'd gone up to her attic, where she had allowed him to dress her in a dainty riding costume, then pull her breeches down, crop and otherwise punish her satiny bottom, white shoulders, and back for hours before making love.

Marguerite remembered this as she let Newton take her in his arms and squeeze her lovely body to his own lean, athletic one, even permitting him to caress her mouthwatering buttocks through her slim wool skirt. Their scene had been good, but Newton craved a more juvenile-acting type of submission for everyday fare, and that was not Marguerite. Still, he reflected, breathing in her delightful perfume while she ground her immensely fruitful body against his, grown-up ladies had an allure that was equally intoxicating.

"Why were you spanking my little girl?" he asked.

"Is that what she is? Already?" Marguerite broke the embrace first. At that moment, Susan returned from the pantry with the coffee service.

"That's right," Newton replied. "And she'd better not forget it."

Susan, who hadn't blushed all the while Marguerite was playing with her, colored deeply as Newton watched her pouring coffee. Marguerite's own flat tummy felt a tiny flutter merely observing the effect that a hint of sternness in his tone instantly had upon Susan.

No sooner had Susan poured coffee for everyone and sat down on a futon beside Marguerite than Newton sent her back to the pantry for a bottle of whiskey to spike the coffee. The moment she was out of earshot, Newton was beside Marguerite.

"How can I tempt you to continue with what you were doing before I knocked?" he asked.

"Please," said Marguerite. "I can resist anything but temptation."

"Great! Name your price and you'll have it in Hong Kong gold by tomorrow, but I want to see that brat's panties down while she's over your lap."

"No, I don't think so," said Marguerite, breaking away from him without remembering how she had gotten in his arms so quickly again. "I don't think she's ready for that."

"Nonsense. A little embarrassment does a girl a world of good."

"No," Marguerite said, almost stamping her foot at him. "I don't think she deserves to be made a spectacle of."

"Is that so?" Newton contemplated thoughtfully. "But maybe you do."

"Oh, no!"

"Why not? Too proud to take a spanking?"

"You could say that," Marguerite agreed. So Newton took up the offensive. He had made this splendid creature whimper with every emotion before and was beginning to find the notion of doing again even more appealing than watching her spank Susan.

"I'll admit that spanking isn't very elegant for a lady like you. Even a whipping has a certain amount of dignity. And you do take a very good whipping. But there's nothing at all dignified about a grown-up lady getting a paddling, is there?" Newton cornered Marguerite as he finished this speech and was about to seize her when Susan re-entered with the brandy. So he gave it up and subsided into a chair, wearily allowing Susan to pour his drink.

"What I should really do is spank the both of you for keeping secrets and playing naughty games!" Newton wasn't serious, but Marguerite was inclined to indulge him. Perhaps it was because she found him charming and had not had her playful mood disturbed in the least by his entrance.

"To save my little darling embarrassment and give her something unusual to muse on the next time you take her in hand, I will bravely volunteer to take the spanking for us both, but only because it's coming from you, dear man," announced Marguerite on a whim. "And Susan can watch."

Newton could only approve of this generous gesture on Marguerite's part, although he couldn't understand why she should suggest such a thing. This was because, like most men, he was so preoccupied with her body that he never guessed at the subtleties of her mind, or the elaborate lengths to which she would sometimes go to seduce perfectly her chosen object. If Marguerite wanted to fix herself in Susan's thoughts, she could devise no better way than to submit to an over-the-knee spanking from the man Susan held above all others in regard.

Marguerite made Susan sit in a chair and she and Newton took center stage. A straight chair was placed in position. Newton cut his usual clowning when he saw that for some reason Marguerite had really decided to take a spanking in front of this little girl, rather than spanking the little girl in front of him. It seemed to Newton that the redhead must be out to enchant Susan rather than him, and he felt quite elevated by the romantic implications of her gesture.

In spite of the fact that Marguerite was the one who had decided on what the afternoon's entertainment would consist of, Susan was thrilled by the way Newton instantly took physical control of the tall, slim-waisted beauty, seizing her firmly by the arm and pulling her across his lap in one fluid motion. That he was practiced at placing women in this position was evident to his newest and most ardent young admirer. To Susan, Marguerite had seemed a goddess, with her long legs, improbably small waist, and gorgeous russet mane; in her four-inch ankle-strap purple high heels, she stood a full six foot one inch tall, but Newton, who was five foot ten inches and lithe, had no difficulty subduing her with the deftness that characterized his handling of women.

As Anthony's left hand curved around Marguerite's tightly corseted waist, his right hand smoothed down the mohair skirt over the breathtakingly voluptuous curves of her bottom. Arching and stretching across his knees to find the most comfortable position available to her in the stiff, constricting cinch, Marguerite asked prettily for mercy in advance to ensure a light and playful spanking from a man who'd been her lover for one night and who had given her a moving corporal punishment session, along with a sizable check.

"Why light?" Newton asked, barely patting her skirted behind. "Since you're here, we might as well give you what you deserve."

"I always deserve the best treatment because I'll accept no other!" declared Marguerite. "And besides, you have no reason to spank me hard," she added confidently.

"Please don't make me laugh. I can think of four irrefutable reasons right off the top of my head," Newton replied, winking at Susan, who was blushing to the eyes as she watched in wonder. "Would you like me to recount them?" he asked. When Marguerite assented, highly puzzled, as she could not remember being anything other than perfect with Newton every moment they were together, he began to list her errors, all the while continuing to pat and smooth over her skirt.

"First of all, let's talk about your insulting behavior towards me on the night we met," Newton began. "Remember Halloween?"

Susan herself could not think of that date without feeling somewhat wounded, even now. She had longed beyond all things to attend Hugo Sands' annual B&D party, but had not been invited. When she approached Hugo about this oversight, he informed her that this was an event for adults only. No amount of pleading would move him. This was because he had plans for seducing Susan's older sister, Laura, that night, and didn't want the younger woman, who had an obvious crush on him, to get in the way.

After being what she considered snubbed by her idol in October, Susan had brooded for the entire autumn, languishing with love for Hugo Sands. When Hugo saw Susan again at Christmas, he was inclined and had the time to take a renewed interest in her progress as a fledgling submissive. This was when he got the inspired idea of putting her together with Anthony Newton, the musical composer from New York with a preference for small girls. Susan instantly became Newton's favorite pampered pet, and they were together often, in spite of living in different cities. Even so, it still hurt Susan to have missed Halloween, particularly because of the exciting fistfight over Randy Price's sister that had ended the party.

"How did I insult you on Halloween? And what do you think you are doing? I won't have you pull up my skirt!" Marguerite tried to stop him from working the glove-tight skirt up her thighs and over her hips.

"I'm going to pull up your skirt," he told her firmly, giving her defending hand a sharp smack. "Stop struggling and lift up so I can do this," he added impatiently. "I'm not about to put up with any nonsense at this point."

"Oh!" cried Marguerite, realizing she had painted herself into a corner for what now seemed like no good reason.

The sight of the redhead's lower half revealed was spectacular, as her purple and black satin Victorian waist cinch laced to halfway down her hips, and a pair of black satin bikinis glamorously encased at least some portion of each large, luscious bottom cheek. Attached to the cinch were eight garter suspenders, which held up her sheer, seamed black stockings. Between the satin panties and the stocking tops gleamed the smooth, white, well-toned flesh of her exercised, cream-pampered thighs.

"How did you insult me on Halloween? Well, for one thing, you had the nerve to demand five thousand dollars to spend the night with you."

"Well, I can give it away to a poor man, can't I?" Marguerite pointed out. "Those who can afford to should spoil me."

"Have you ever heard such arrogance?" Newton asked Susan, while stroking Marguerite through the black satin panties in a way that made her arch to his touch like a stretching cat.

"Well," Newton continued, "believe it or not, I agreed to this bandit's demands and she took me to her house. And what do you think she did then?" When Susan merely stared back saucer-eyed, he answered his own question. "The spoiled rotten brat began to play the dom with me, suggesting that we begin the intimate part of our evening with me on my knees, renewing the shine on her stiletto boots with my tongue! I tell you, Susan, I was shocked and injured. Because I had been charming and considerate to her at the party, even discouraging others from subjecting her to a humiliating public spanking, she supposed I was submissive! Didn't you?" Newton demanded of Marguerite, applying a smart smack to her bottom.

"It was a reasonable mistake," Marguerite defended herself, reaching back to give herself a rub. "Dominant men are seldom charming or considerate, so how was I know that I'd met the exception?"

"You can see the way she's trying to flatter herself out of the damn good licking she has coming?" Newton gave Marguerite six or seven slaps, each of which fell on an alternate cheek and made her cry, "Oh!"

"What were the other two reasons you maintain you have for spanking me?" Marguerite asked, to distract him. This gentleman had a rather sharp hand.

"Well, just now when I came to the door and heard you spanking Susan, it gave me quite a start. I must admit that I lingered for a good five seconds before knocking as I tried to decide how I was going to deal with this interloper, the fiend who dared to lay his hand on my baby!"

"And what did you decide to do?" asked Marguerite, turning her head to look at Susan for the first time.

"I decided to wait and see how big he was. And now I do see . . ." Newton let this be the segue into lowering her panties.

"Tony, no!" Marguerite cried, twisting on his lap as well as she could in the stiff cinch as she tried to reach back and prevent him from baring her completely.

"Why not? Remember, this was all your idea! I was content to sit in Susan's only armchair and make idle threats to both you girls. Since this was all your doing, you're getting a real one now. Heaven knows you deserve it!"

"But what was the fourth reason?" Marguerite stalled, while reconciling herself to having her bottom bared.

"The fourth reason was your stubborn refusal to spank Susan for me. Whether you adopted this position out of sheer capriciousness or lesbian loyalty is immaterial. Either way you struck an attitude that cries out for correction. And here it comes."

Newton gripped her very firmly about her twenty-inch cinched waist and began to apply his palm to her amply padded bottom in a crisp, measured style. He was not a man to batter or pummel a woman with undue speed or force, or take a woman's breath away with the harsh crack of his hard hand delivered at full impact, although he had spanked one or two women rapid fire in his time. He normally preferred a more controlled pace, and if the girl was to be struck hard enough to make her pitch and kick, she should be a smaller girl than Marguerite.

Newton's objective was to warm the redhead's backside thoroughly, from the tops of her thighs to the crest of her womanly hips, without causing her to kick or scream or struggle in the slightest. Struggles were appropriate to grassy hills in June, when the victim was dressed in a halter and shorts, perhaps with her pretty feet bare. It wouldn't be fair to Marguerite to punish her cruelly enough to make her struggle without first unlacing her corset. Nor did he wish her to run her glamorous stockings in kicking.

Marguerite was absolutely correct: a woman who took pains to look so exceptionally provocative deserved the very best treatment. Therefore, even though Newton proceeded to spank her hard, even very hard towards the end, Marguerite scarcely noticed the severity of the spanking until the next evening, when her buttocks and upper thigh muscles began to ache. She had not experienced this characteristic aftermath of a really hard spanking for some time, and she had to think hard to remember who was responsible for making her feel stiff and sore.

"But it didn't seem as though he spanked me all that hard," thought Marguerite, remembering the awfully long time Newton had held her face down across his lap while his apparently tireless hand descended either to strike or caress her. He had rubbed her as much as he'd spanked her, and so sexily that she had almost ground her way to a climax while over his knee, a thing she'd never done before in her life. That Anthony Newton certainly put the romance back into discipline, Marguerite reflected, while giving her aching bottom a rub through her skirt.

SUNDANCER

by Briony Shelton

In this gripping novel of female masochism, Derek turns over his girlfriend, Sundancer, to a "Mr. Keiller" in order to pay back a very large debt. Keiller instantly makes Sundancer his powerless prisoner. In the following scene, as she gives her Master his birthday gift, a rigorous caning and whipping, Sundancer graduates from being a mere novice to an apprentice in the art of discipline. Through a final interior monologue, we are encouraged to climb with her, painful step by painful step, as she mounts the basement steps towards the room where her Master awaits her. N.B. The "Teddy" referred to in the excerpt is the protagonist's Teddy bear.

"Did you enjoy your meal, Sundancer?"

"Yes, very much, Master. Is it a special occasion?"

"My birthday."

"Many happy returns of the day, Master. I have nothing to give you, I'm afraid."

"Later, my dear, later. You will give me your body to punish. That will be present enough."

Hell. I thought I was getting a pain-free day. Mind, Teddy said nothing when I asked if it was a pain-free day. Wise Teddy: he knew, didn't he?

"Come, we will have coffee in the lounge, as usual, and then we will go to the pleasure room."

Still can't walk very well.

"I see you still move awkwardly, Sundancer. Oh, do sit down, I can't look up at you, it gives me neck ache."

Fire and cushions and comfort. So different from the pleasure room.

"Your leather straps don't creak any more. Are they comfortable?"

"Oh yes, Master. I don't know I'm wearing them."

But I did at first, when they chafed and rubbed and I was forced to shower and sleep in them.

"Do you remember the night you used my whip handle, Sundancer?"

"I can't forget, Master." Why mention it now? It's been days.

"You shouldn't have used my whip like that."

"I know, Master."

"I trust the lesson is learned."

"Oh yes, Master." Backwards over the stool watching as you took the strap and used it between my legs and on my inner thighs and I still don't know which mirror is the two-way one. How else would you have known?

Silence and stillness and no hint of why you mentioned that unless the memory is good for you.

Phone. Phone? Why haven't I heard it before?

"Mr. Keiller, it's for you. They said it's urgent."

"I'll be back in a moment, Sundancer. In the meantime, would you care to look at a newspaper?"

An honest-to-life paper. Feel rough paper, print of fingers, pictures made of dots not shiny pix of ladies with burning bottoms read something that does not talk of pain and lust and domination.

Save it, save it for when I can sit and read something that does not concern itself with pain. Will he let me take it to the pleasure room? Probably not.

All right, just look. At the date.

No.

Impossible.

Not impossible. Think about it.

I've been here ten days.

My job! My parents! What has Derek told them, that I'm ill?

"You've not opened the paper, Sundancer."

"I was surprised to see how long I've been here, Master."

"Yes, time goes by fast when you're enjoying yourself. Then let us go. Time I had my birthday gift."

Leave golden drapes and gold carpet and flames and warmth and go to harsh cord carpet and cold hall to cold pleasure room with cold mirrors. Twenty different Keillers and Sundancers. Keiller with birthday smile of pure glee at array of pain and promise of more to come.

"I think the cane tonight, Sundancer."

"As you wish, Master."

"The cane. The most perfect instrument of punishment ever devised. Formed of natural materials, thin enough to take up relatively little space, cheap enough that anyone can own a variety, and sharp and dangerous to inflict a good deal of pain. And with a willing submissive, what more could any man ask on his birthday? Kneel down. Arms on the floor. Head down. Don't move."

Don't move. I know better than to move. In the ten days that I have been here, I have learned that moving or evading your cane or strap usually means a lengthy session strapped down over the stool.

"Something different tonight, Sundancer. Tonight I will tell you what is to come, so you can count. Twelve, for now, just as you are."

Count and hurt and scream and count.

"Hands, I think, Sundancer."

No not my hands please not my hands please no no no.

"I'm waiting."

All right, if that's your birthday wish—

"Left hand, please, and keep your hand out for three."

See me in mirror see me shout out—

"Right hand, please, Sundancer."

Screaming hurts throat please please—

"Yes, Mrs. Heath?"

"Telephone, Mr. Keiller. They said it was very urgent, said I had to interrupt what you were doing."

"This is really intolerable, twice in one evening. Oh, all right. Sundancer, I'll be back. We're not done yet."

Oh Teddy Teddy my hands hurt he hurt me Teddy he hurt me hold me Teddy hold me.

No. No no no no. Go away go away no no no no oh look oh look so big so ugly so horrid look how it scurries listen to the legs clicking on the floors I hate spiders so big so—

Light gone darkness bulb gone can't move can't see hate dark now it's dark can't see anything scared where's the spider will I tread on it if I move is it touching me God is it touching me—

"Keiller!"

Touching me something touching me I know it is know it is Teddy hold on something touching my foot—

"Keiller! Help! Help me!"

Oh no wet trickling down he'll kill me he'll kill me I know he will where's the spider where is it will I walk on it hate them can't help it Master it just happened the door's just over there what if I step on the spider—

"Keiller! Help meeeeee! Keeiiilleeerrr!"

Nothing no sound where's Starchy she must have heard I screamed loud enough didn't I shriek loud enough even Teddy put his hands over his ears—

"Keiller! Get me out of here! Keiller I'm scared! Keiller it's dark! It's dark Keiller I'm scared of the dark! There's a huge spider in here! Get me out of here! Get me out of here! Get me out of here! Get me out of here!

"Get—me—out—of—here!"

Door. Light. Master has come to save me. Oh God where is it could I have moved could I—

"Stop this nonsense immediately!"

"Master the light went and there was a spider and I was scared and you left me and—"

"I said stop this nonsense immediately! Now what's the matter?"

"The light went out Master and just before it went out it showed me a huge spider and I was scared and I've—"

"Stop it! Stop—it!"

All right don't slap me again please!

"Now what's the matter with you?"

"I've got a phobia about spiders, and just before the light failed, I saw an enormous spider walking towards me."

"The door was just over there, Sundancer."

"There it is Master there it is please kill it or something please—"

"Oh yes, it is rather large, isn't it?"

Crushed. One movement of the foot, and it is gone. Menace gone. I could have made the door without stepping on it, but what if I had—

"I was so scared, Master. I couldn't see in the dark, and I didn't know where the spider was. I might have stepped on it."

"I see. And you consider that a good enough reason to make so much noise that my caller asked if I had a banshee in the house?"

"Sorry, Master."

"Sorry. You are not sorry. You completely lost your head. You gave me very awkward questions to answer to someone in very high authority. You have the rest of my birthday gift to give me, Sundancer, and we add to it atonement for your complete loss of self-control. I think the time has come for you to experience true pain, not the half-hearted stuff you have had up to now. Come over here."

Frozen to the spot.

"Sundancer, come."

Put Teddy down and walk. In the half-light, he doesn't know what I've done. Yet.

"Give me your wrists."

Clinks of steel through the rings cannot wrists chained together.

"Climb on this stool and link the chain over the hook."

So, help me!

"Did you wet yourself, Sundancer?"

"Yes, Master."

"Have you looped the chain over the hook?"

"Yes, Master."

"I'm going to take the stool away. If you are not securely looped over, you will fall. And I will whip you where you fall."

"I'm ready, Master."

"Right, you can hang there while I change the bulb."

Pulling my arms can't take the strain on my arms how slowly you move come back don't leave me in the dark oh what will he do to me please come back oh so slowly climb steps so slowly change bulb oh no not the whip please not the whip—

"Now, Sundancer, you will complete your birthday gift by learning what happens when you lose your head and shriek and carry on like that!"

Spin turn swing back and forward twenty Keillers in mirrors twenty Sundancers hurting everywhere pain in wrists pain in face throat raw Starchy must hear is she creaming on the sound of my screams stop it Keiller you'll kill me stop it Keiller I don't want to die don't hurt me any more—

*   *   *

Cold.
  Cold light.
  Dead crushed spider.
  Teddy's sad eyes.
  Teddy loves me if no one else does.
  Master will love me.
  Move.
  "No!"
  Must move.
  Must go to Master.
  Sundancer was wrong.
  Sundancer should not have disobeyed.
  Master is right.
  Must tell Master he is right.
  Wait for me Teddy I'll be back.
  Wrists chained.
  Why?
  Floor hard.
  Why am I on the floor?
  Stand up.
  Can't.
  Hurt.
  Everywhere.
  Must.
  Go.
  To.
  Master.
  Knees.
  All right.
  So move.
  All right!
  Moving.

Hurts.
Everywhere.
Slow.
Take.
It.
Slow.
Stairs.
One.
At.
A.
Time.
Cursed chain.
Remember.
Hook.
Ceiling.
Hanging.
Door—open?
Yes.
Knees and hands.
Hands and knees.
Cannot.
Stand.
Hurts.
Body.
Hurts.
Why?
Master.
Carpet.
Rough.
Tearing knees.
Tearing hands.
Remember.
Caned hands.

Remember.
Master with whip.
Teddy I'll be back.
Have to.
Tell Master.
He was right.
Sundancer.
Wrong.
Long.
Long.
Way.
Hands.
Hurt.
Carpet rough.
Tore hands.
Too dark.
Dark.
Spider in the dark.
Screamed.
Master right.
Sundancer wrong.
Mustn't scream.
More.
Stairs.
One.
At.
A.
Time.
Remember.
Master with whip.
Hanging from ceiling.
Stairs.
Steep.

Chain.
Clinking.
Pain.
Everywhere.
"Sundancer, what are you doing?"
"Master."
"Come here."
Arms.
Longing for arms to hold me.
Longing to feel arms around me.
"Master."
"Yes, Sundancer."
Bed.
Soft.
Sheets.
Soft.
"Master."
"Yes, Sundancer."
"Don't leave me."
"I won't leave you."
Hurt.
Everywhere.
"Master."
"Yes, Sundancer."
Close.
Master close.
Tell Master.
Sundancer was wrong.
To disobey.
Tell him.
"Master."
"I'm here, Sundancer."
"Fuck me."

"Yes, Sundancer, I will."

"Master."

"I'm here, Sundancer."

"Your slave, Master. Your slave."

"I know, Sundancer. Oh yes, I know."

WHAT LOVE

by Maria Madison

In this deliberate, thoughtful novel, Rosy is an unhappy, lonely, divorced college instructor until one night when a mysterious stranger slips into her life and initiates her into the realm of sadomasochistic sexuality. Under his tutelage, she proves an apt student, and for the first time experiences lust in its pure form. Madison's finest novel, What Love *is a thinking woman's exploration of female submission that is particularly valuable in its portrait of the way in which an "average" woman might reconcile masochistic desires with feminist politics.*

It's Wednesday morning and I'm alone in the sun. The walk is pleasant. I move quickly away from the poor areas to the large houses set well back from the road. They all have oval rose beds edged with silver-gray catmint and blue clumps of fading lobelia flanking their gravel driveways. It looks as though the same gardener has had his way with every frontage. I notice the burglar alarms, the anti-people alarms. All this wealth lying next door to inner city poverty is obscene.

It's further than I think to the maisonettes and I'm sweating by the time I reach their cool, shady frontage and the birches, which make a small inviting copse in front of them. A narrow path runs through the slender trunks and I follow it, glad to get away from the heat of the pavement. It's quiet here. Lovely. Everyone appears to be out at work. I walk past the front doors, seeing closed windows. The sudden shout of music cuts through the silence and makes me turn and go slowly back. The music dies away as a window slams shut. Then I notice that the front door in the end ground-floor maisonette is wide open. There's a man in the doorway. He shouts, "Hi." It's him. I feel I've been spying on him, chasing him like a schoolgirl with a crush. My innocent walk seems to be anything but innocent. The color rushes up my neck to my cheeks.

He walks toward me through a porch flanked by a wooden trellis. I stand still, stupid with surprise, my mouth open.

Today there's no suit. He wears jeans and a white sleeveless T-shirt. He's not big, but there's stealth in those muscles. He has nothing on his feet. I blink, looking at them. He seems different without his shoes.

"Hi," he says again. "Like the Indian summer?"

The stammer I lost when I was thirteen comes back. "It's a b-bit too hot to me."

Pause. "Really? The English always complain," he smiles a little, "don't we?"

I shrug. I suppose so.

His thumbs drag on the belt loops at the front of his trousers, pulling them down slightly so the dark curl of hair below his navel is visible. I feel a sudden panic and want to run away, but he is talking, persuading.

"Fancy a cold drink? It's cooler inside," he says.

"No, really. I'm on my way now. I've got to—" I step back as the thumbs slide out from the belt and he extends one arm towards me.

"Come on. Don't be silly."

Already his hand is in the small of my back, guiding me to the open front door. I ask myself why I am going with a complete stranger. I must be crazy. But it's the timber of his voice, a kind of do-as-you-will, do-as-you-won't quality about it. A soft voice, yet very clear, where emotions just scratch the surface. A voice from a man who doesn't care if I don't go with him because he's absolutely sure I will. He must read my subconscious, not listen to the rubbish coming from my mouth.

Inside, the cool white of the hallway stuns. I don't usually do this, I say. I don't go into strange men's houses. Never. He leaves me and shoots barefoot into the kitchen to go to the fridge. Okay, he'll leave the door open if I like, he shouts back. I know I should be more charitable, more trusting, but I can't take chances. "Thanks," I say, expecting him to be annoyed with me.

He returns with that smile and slaps a pink glass filled with clinking ice into my hand. "It's okay," he says, intentionally brushing my arm with his as he passes. "I don't blame you. I'm no gentleman."

We go into a white room with a white blind pulled halfway down over French windows. I sit on a white leather sofa with chrome legs. The carpet is off-white and spotless. In front of me is a low round glass table with a collection of paperweights in the center. One is a dandelion clock caught in round Perspex, arrested before it blew away. There are shelves along the entire length of one wall, holding books, junk, a TV, and a VCR. Behind me, level with my head, are pictures. Disturbing pictures. I don't like to stare too obviously, but they appear to be pen-and-ink cameos of women being sadistically treated by men.

He asks my name.

"Rosy, with a 'y,' " I say.

"Sad Rose." He laughs softly; it's more of a sigh than a laugh.

"Why do you say I am sad?" I ask, smiling tightly. I refuse to sit back in the squishiness of the sofa and stay bolt upright on the edge instead. The pink drink is Campari and soda, which has never been one of my likes. I gulp it down, wonder if he's put something in it.

"I saw you at the bus stop. So sad. You were crying. One of the most beautiful sad women I've seen." He cocks his head on one side and considers me for a moment. "No," he corrects himself, "the saddest."

"Oh, really," I protest.

He's sitting on the floor about four feet away from me, legs crossed like a Manx symbol, bits of dirt on the soles of his feet. His shaved skin is so smooth I'd like to reach out and touch it. He looks up, deep in thought. Then he lowers his head and looks at me from those shadowed eyes, and I feel an automatic response in parts of my body I'd like to think were hibernating. He's a fast mover. Too fast. Be careful I don't slip up.

"Listen," he says, and recites poetry to me:

O Rose, thou art sick!
The invisible worm
That flies in the night
In the howling storm,

Has found out thy bed
Of crimson joy
And his dark secret love
Does thy life destroy.

"Appropriate?" he asks. "I think so."

I try to ignore the reference and ask who is the poet. It's William Blake. Of course. Are you a lecturer, too, I ask? No, he's not. He's a lawyer and has taken the day off because the weather is nice. On the first day he saw me, his decree absolute arrived. A silence falls between us. I never felt like this with Zack as I do now—under pressure. Or threat, perhaps. I feel what I do from now on is preordained. The hollow thought strikes me: all resistance is merely a sin of pride, an act. Why can't I admit to myself that his looks alone turn me on?

"I want to talk to a woman," he is saying quietly, "without taking her to bed, but I want to be intimate. Do you know what I mean? Intimate."

The last words roll off his tongue and he nods his head at me. What does he mean? Am I the lucky charm he fancied the day his divorce came through? Interrupting my thoughts, he asks me questions about my life. Cautiously I tell him the bits I don't mind parting with, but I feel he knows what's between the lines. I tell him that Zack and I are good friends and watch his mouth twitch, aware of my lie. I tell him about my green house and wild garden, that there are no children. I tell him about Carol, and that I'm thirty.

"It's over," I say, and only then do I realize fully that it is. Zack and I were finished in my head before now, but not in my emotions. This man has managed to pry apart my armor and sink a knife into my weak spot so it cries out in pain. I choke back the tears and the drink jerks out of the glass. Pink Campari spills onto the white carpet. I jump up immediately, spilling more, and apologize as though I've cut off his arm or leg by mistake and not merely spilt liquor on his carpet. I make for the kitchen to find a cloth. Before I reach the doorway, he's up and has me by the arm. "Leave it," he says. I can't do that. It's a woman's instinct to try and rub out all the stains in the world, isn't it? For a moment it gets ridiculous—both of us jammed in the doorway, me trying to rush for a cloth, him pulling me back in the room. I can hear myself apologizing, all wound up.

Somehow he stops me and I calm down. "That was very undignified," he says matter-of-factly. He may not be angry—I wish he was—but I still feel foolish and clumsy. I look at the stain, hideously obvious. I want to lick it up. "And because of it I'm going to spank you," he says in the same even tone of voice, as if I've been looking forward to a spanking all my life. And he does.

Sunflowers always turn their massive heads to face the sun. It's called heliotropism. The second his arm moves around my waist, I find I have moved to where he wants me to be as though I've been drawn by the pull of some unseen force. I move there naturally until his hand is poised above the blue seat of my jeans. Then I feel the first male invasion of my body in six months. It's a shock. A delicious shock.

After several slaps, he lets me go and guides me gently back to the sofa, while he sits on the floor in front of me. I sink into the white leather softness and cry. He lets me cry for a while, then speaks.

"I didn't hurt you."

I shake my head. No, it isn't that kind of pain.

He sighs, touches my leg with his bare foot. "I know how it is to wall yourself up." He slides across the floor on his backside to reach up and get a box of tissues from the bookshelf. "I just took down a few bricks."

When I've recovered, I ask him if he's crazy. He smiles, shakes his head, turns the questions once more on me. Why do I think a stain on the carpet is more important than human suffering? Why do I look down self-consciously as though I was ashamed of my face? Yes, he's noticed my fingers covering my cheeks, mouth, always there checking, always fluttering. Yes, he can see I'm not wearing any makeup. But ordinarily I do, don't I? Yes, he thought so. Tugging at my bangs, tut, tut, trying to pull a shutter over my eyes. I mustn't wear anything on my face. No. My skin is perfect. My lips are soft, hesitant. My eyes hold a sparkle. I must promise not to paint my face any more, unless he tells me to.

He speaks slowly, softly, and I am totally unsure how to react. He tells me I have little confidence, I am paralyzed with hurt. I have stopped growing. I am frightened to find out who I really am. It will change, he says, but I must open myself to new experiences. I must move on.

He stops and it is like the end of a speech on a subject he has studied for years. I watch him stretch out and push his bare toes through the pile on the carpet. I am in a state of shock. "Your breakup . . ." I begin, but he cuts me off. Tells me he does not wish to talk about it, but adds with a grim smile that he thinks he has recovered from the hurt. I want to probe. He's so together and I'm just beginning to fall apart after it's all over. How does he cope?

"I ought to go," I say. I want to run from this man and think about everything that has happened in the dim privacy of the house. I want to make sense of it all.

He goes out of the room, leaving me sitting on the sofa. When he returns, he brings a small sandwich on a plate. "It's cheese," he says. He goes to hand me the plate, but before it reaches me, he pulls it back and puts it on the glass table next to the paperweights. He goes out of the room again and comes back with an old silver knife. Picking up the two triangles of bread, he begins to pare away the crusts in quick, neat movements. He cuts the sandwich in half, then in quarters, and lays the plate on my lap. He eats the crusts. One of his legs is stretched out towards me as he sits on the floor. The heel is resting in the wet patch of Campari, spreading it further. "You're very sweet," he says, talking while he is eating. "I like talking to you."

I tell him, trying to be impertinent, plucky, that I'm not in such a bad way as he thinks. I've never been smacked before

by a man. Never. He eyes me with a curious smile. "Spanked,"
he corrects me. "The word is 'spanked.' " I argue that children
get spanked, not grown women. "So what?" he says. "You are
little, aren't you?"

I don't want to leave with these words in the air. It would
look obvious. He'd know he'd hit a nerve. I know I was embarrassed, offended, know it was that last remark that made
me go. I look at my watch instead. He says, stay an hour and
he'll cook me lunch. Fresh linguini, how's that?

I'm surprised, but he has his own garden. He pulls up the blind
and opens the French windows wide. Outside is a small patio
with a brick-built barbecue and brick seating. Glossy-leafed
camellias grow in deliberate gaps between the patio stones, and
late summer flowers burst from every crack. There's no lawn
but a mass of large plants growing in gravel. A path leads to a
dense screen of bamboo. I'm curious to see what lies beyond.
Halfway down the path, I look back and understand why the
garden is filled with tall plants. The maisonettes above have
roof gardens that overlook his. The upstairs neighbor has a row
of big terracotta plants with little box trees in them, lined up
along the front of the balcony, equidistant from each other.
"Who's your neighbor?" I ask. He's behind me with a tray of
drinks. Two full glasses of soda with ice and ditto Campari. I
feel I want to tell him I'd prefer something else—gin, for instance. I'd also prefer to be asked what I'd like. He shrugs and
looks up. "A woman," he says simply. "Do the box trees say
anything?" I comment, trying to sound clever. He considers
their tall, clipped, upright form for a minute, frowns, and then
laughs to himself. "She might be short of a prick," he says.

Behind the bamboo, the garden tries to be Oriental. The
gravel has been raked into patterns. There are large white stones
in careful groups beside a pond. Stiff yucca and a fatsia bow

into the area form the boundary fence, which is high and private. There is a row of canes leading away from the pool. They are very close together, their tops cut at different lengths forming a gentle curve. More canes, uncut this time, break away from the first row at right angles. A thin rattan roof sits on the top, fixed to supporting poles. Half in the shade is a sun bed with a newspaper scattered underneath, the pages muddled up. "Sit down," he says. I do so, but gingerly. One of these beds collapsed on me once at Zack's mother's when I lay down on it.

He sits down a little way from me on a narrow path surrounding the pool. He tugs at his jeans, pulling them up to his knees. His legs are quite hairy. With a sigh, he sinks each foot into the water.

"There were fish," he laughs suddenly. "I guess I've killed them off."

The sun is surprisingly hot. I'm glad I'm wearing my hair in a plait. Coyly I wonder how he'd like it if I wore my hair down. He hasn't seen me like that.

I am sweating in my jeans. He tells me the next time I come I must bring a swimsuit. No, not a swimsuit: a bikini. I'd look delicious in one of those. He sits back, leaning on his arms for support. For a while we don't talk. When he calls the silence, I keep it.

I wonder to myself what he is going to do with me after the linguini, and whether I'm prepared to go along with it. When he coughs, I start to bluster. I'm a nice English girl, I say half-humorously, half in earnest. I don't know a thing about you, but I've never done this sort of thing before.

He opens his eyes straight into the sun and snorts. "I know," he says. "You don't want me to think you're a hungry little divorcée. I think you've played the good girl for too long."

He may be right. I don't seem to know who I am these days.

I tell him I feel different somehow since my divorce. "Of course you do," he says in the same matter-of-fact tone, with the same disarming pause before he speaks. I lower my eyes and ask in a disillusioned whisper how much longer before he says he wants to bed me. He winces, but the smile returns. He wags a finger at me.

"Rosy, you offend me," he says. "You're a naughty girl. Watch out I don't spank you again."

I fiddle with the ice in my glass. Ice in the shape of Christmas trees. He says we'll eat at about three. We sit in the sun for an hour. I pretend to have fallen asleep. Then he says he wants to massage me before he cooks the linguini. This time I say I'm going, and my lips pucker. I get up off the sun bed and he stands up in the pool. I've got him wrong, he says. He just wants to make me feel good. I need to relax. Look how my shoulders have risen. They're practically up to my chin. Really, he says, I should be more trusting. But—and he shrugs—I can go if I like; only he'd be much happier if I stayed.

When I drink something I'm not too fond of, I have this peculiar trait: I have to finish every drop. I always try to conquer my dislikes. It's my nature. I didn't like Zack at first. I thought he was pompous, but I gradually came round. Now, I see this old habit bringing me nothing but trouble again. Campari must be stronger than I think. When I say yes to his offer, I say it with the breath of Campari and Christmas trees. I don't know why I don't kick myself immediately.

He jumps out of the pond ripping up pondweed with his feet and stands there with it curling round his toes. "Great," he says, and his thumbs dig through the belt loops on his jeans.

I follow him into the house feeling apprehensive and excited. Since February, I haven't put a foot out of line.

Impulsively he takes my hand and leads me to a door in the hall. He finds it hard to open, as if there's a weight on the other side, and he gives it a little shove with his shoulder.

It's a small room, a white box. White walls, carpet, blinds, swivel chair—he gets really excited about white, I think—with a pile of album covers on the seat. The room is quite warm. On a low glass table, similar to the one in the back room, except that this one is rectangular, is a record deck and a mass of hi-fi paraphernalia. There are speakers fitted to the wall—two, three, maybe more. I can't tell because they don't look conventional like mine. No pictures.

On the carpet there are records, hundreds of them, in a long line against the wall. He tells me the room is specially sound-proofed—ceiling, walls, door (that's why it's hard to open) and triple-glazed. He likes music. He likes to make a noise when he wants to. I ask about the woman upstairs. She can't hear a thing, he says. In here, no one can hear you scream.

I put my hands on the wall, except it doesn't feel like a wall. I shiver. A padded cell. A torture chamber. I stand there and watch while he pulls down the blind and shoves the chair into a corner. He leaves me and returns with an armful of white towels. There are small objects sandwiched between them. Oil, talc, a small Chinese bowl.

"Did you shower before you came out?" he asks. I color. "I don't mean that you smell," he says, smiling, "although it might be nice if you did. Everyone has their own bouquet."

I look away from the glint in his eyes. I want to go—now. He thrusts a large towel at me and tells me to strip off while he gets a heater. I rush out of my clothes and wrap a towel tightly around me, over my bra and pants. I'm keeping them on.

He comes back humming and switches on a small fan heater. A smell that reminds me of newly mown hay circulates in the air. It's vetiver oil. He folds the remaining towels and lays them down neatly to make a plinth. He lights a candle and puts it in a small porcelain holder. Lie down and make yourself comfortable, he says. I kneel awkwardly on my towel and stretch out.

The towels on the floor are soft and warm, and my body sinks into them. "Relax," he says. "Don't be uptight. No one will hear you scream."

I laugh nervously into the towel. I lie still and wait for him to peel away the towel and lay his hands on my body. The hands of a man I don't know at all. I must be crazy or in a real state of shock, or I'd never allow this to happen. I hear him behind me, moving about, like a conductor preparing to conduct.

"I hope you like music," he says. "I'm sure you do. I'm going to put on something to help you relax."

I'm surprised at his choice, but I recognize the music instantly: "A Love Supreme," by John Coltrane. Zack had a copy loaned to him by a friend at college. It lay around for ages and he never played it, at least not while I was there. I never told him, but I listened to it a lot. Zack may be left-wing, but he still thinks jazz is dirty.

"Aha, I see you know it," he says, surprise, then pleasure in his voice. He must be observing every small, intimate reaction of mine to make such a comment without my telling him.

The towel slips from my body. I can feel his eyes staring. Three things happen at once. He shouts a "No!" of disbelief, slaps the tops of my thighs hard, and gets to his feet. What am I doing dressed? Don't I trust him? What's the matter with me? I listen for the anger in his voice but again it's oddly absent. Then he sighs and sinks to his knees beside me. I can keep the towel on if I'm so shy, he says, but he's not going one step further until I take off the rest of my clothes.

As it turns out, he helps me off with my bra and slides the panties down over my legs while I lie on my stomach. He starts the record.

The bass figure feels as though it's in the floor beneath me, throbbing up through my hips and thighs. I'd hardly call it a hypnotic piece, but it certainly demands concentration, so for a while I forget myself. That's right, he says, I have to listen. It's a very disciplined composition, like an Indian raga, limited notes and all that stuff. "Nevertheless," I say quietly, "it's an odd choice for a massage."

He throws the towel loosely back over my body and starts on my left calf as he kneels by my feet. "I won't say," he whispers, "your body could turn on a block of stone, or you'll jump up and spoil everything."

The music is soft and it draws me into the presence of the Great Man, Coltrane, so I begin to lose my self-consciousness. "Like it harder?" he asks. "Yes, please." As hard as you like. Hurt me with your fingers and thumbs and make up for all the starvation I've had since February. We're listening to "Resolution" now and he turns it down as Trane starts honking. But all throughout he still keeps one hand on my skin.

I can't fight these hands. They're wringing out every shred of resistance from my muscles. It now seems absurd to have been so churlish about undressing. He wants to make me feel good. Why can't I accept it? The truth is that I don't think you get something for nothing in life. And if a person inexplicably gives to me, I feel awkward, obligated. That it's wrong to take without reciprocating. But at the moment I don't care what he does as long as he doesn't take his hands away.

There's almost a religious intensity in the way he manipulates my flesh. He slides his hands up my back from my sacrum, his thumbs on either side of my spine. I realize he's squatting on my thighs, leaning forward on his knees. After ten minutes of this, I am delirious with pleasure.

He's sweating now, I can smell it, and pounding my buttocks with his fists, nice and hard. His breathing is slow and controlled. Then his hands suddenly fly away. I feel naked. I shiver for them to touch me again, and I edge on my stomach to where I think he's moved. I look round and see a face that's too dark, too quiet.

This is the moment to go. Now, come on. Grab your clothes and your dignity and run. You know what he expects. What he's going to do. I try to get to my feet, but something like thick leather, a belt maybe, or wider, lands across my buttocks, flattening me to the ground.

"No!" he says. "I haven't finished."

My bottom smarts more with surprise than pain. I swallow and press myself into the towel. What now? What next?

I turn and look at him in the silence. He feels, not sees, my nakedness, not aware of it until here, now. The black curls hang damply on his forehead, and his chin and neck shine with sweat. There is a wet stain spreading over the front of his T-shirt.

"I'm going to turn you over," he says to the apprehension in my eyes. "But just before I do . . ."

He smiles and smacks me hard. "Ow!" I say. "What are you doing?" He laughs and his voice purrs. The technique is known as percussion, don't I know? It stimulates the muscles. He will demonstrate. First we have clapping, as it's known. He hollows his palms and brings them down in a rapid succession on the tops of my thighs. And this: He's kneeling now, aiming sharp slaps on my bottom. They don't hurt to any degree, but I feel very embarrassed. Slap-spanks. Suddenly I feel hot. The room is a cell. I can't escape from this man and his strange, frightening compulsion.

His free hand is in the small of my back, steadying him, keeping me in position. "Nice?" he asks, through his teeth, as his fingers run away after the slap, lower down.

My legs begin to open like a book and his fingers open the

pages. The record is stuck on the last groove. Tick tick, tick tick. Apart from the sound, the room is quiet. The sound of his hand on my bare skin makes the silence in between almost solid.

He stops and rolls me over. This is it, I think. He's going to fuck me. It's technically rape, although he'll say well, I was naked at the time. I wait for the rasping sound of a descending zipper, but it doesn't come. Instead he kneels at my feet and lifts them until one ankle rests on each shoulder. He moves in closer and my legs are pushed further over until his head is between my thighs and his mouth inches from my sex. I squeeze my thighs involuntarily against his curls.

His tongue is hot and it makes me rise against the pressure of his hands holding down my thighs. He cups my buttocks and insinuates his tongue still further. I can feel my head in a kind of sick spin as he licks and sucks me into his mouth. It's obscene, but it's ecstasy. I look at the dark curls between my thighs, and I push out my hand to touch them. For a second he stops and looks at me. In that moment, his eyes run up the flushed length of my body. He slaps me again. And then his teeth close around me and shudder together on my clitoris. He bites gently, then harder, each time pausing to let his tongue flick over and around, making me tighten my thighs and try to stretch both legs. I am lost now, using him, and I don't care about the consequences. He stops, starts, stops until I am on the edge of coming. I begin to plead with him.

"What?" he says.

"I want . . . ooh!"

"Say it! Ask me! Louder!"

"Please."

"Please what?"

"Let me come!"

"Say it louder. Come on! Scream! Let it out!"

"Please. Please!"

I do as he says. I scream. He puts words into my mouth, and I repeat them.

"Say it! I want to come with your tongue in my cunt."

"Yes. Yes. I want to . . . come with . . ."

"Louder!"

". . . your tongue up my cunt."

And then his whole mouth takes me in like a glove, and I burst out of all the seams. The first wave rolls over, a tidal wave rushing for my womb. Then his fingers push, moving, moving, his nails dig into my buttock and the orgasms break away un-controlled.

When later I dress, I find that my jeans hurt me as I pull them over my hips . . .

Available now

The Captive
by Anonymous

When a wealthy Enlish man-about-town attempts to make advances to the beautiful twenty-year-old debutante Caroline Martin, she haughtily repels him. As revenge, he pays a white-slavery ring £30,000 to have Caroline abducted and spirited away to the remote Atlas Mountains of Morocco. There the mistress of the ring and her sinister assistant Jason begin Caroline's education—an abduction designed to break her will and prepare her for her mentor.

———

Available now

Captive II
by Richard Manton

Following the best-selling novel, *The Captive*, this sequel is set among the subtropical provinces of Cheluna, where white slavery remains an institution to this day. Brigid, with her dancing girl figure and sweeping tresses of red hair, has caused the prosecution of a rich admirer. As retribution, he employs the underground organization Rio 9 to abduct and transport her to Cambina Alta Plantation. Naked and bound before the Sadism of Col. Manrique and the perversities of the Comte de Zantra, Brigid endures an education in submission. Her training continues until she is ready to be the slave of the man who has chosen her.

———

Available now

Captive III: The Perfumed Trap
by Anonymous

The story of slavery and passionate training described first-hand in the spirited correspondence of two wealthy cousins, Alec and Miriam. The power wielded by them over the girls who cross their paths leads them beyond Cheluna to the remote settlement of Cambina Alta and a life of plantation discipline. On the way, Alec's passion for Julie, a golden-haired nymph, is rivaled by Miriam's disciplinary zeal for Jenny, a rebellious young woman under correction at a police barracks.

Forthcoming

Captive IV: The Eyes Behind the Mask
by Anonymous

The Captives of Cheluna feel a dread fascination for the boy whose duty it is to chastise. This narrative follows a masked apprentice who obeys his master's orders without pity or restraint. Emma Smith's birching would cause a reform school scandal. Secret additions to the frenzy of nineteen-year-old Karen and Noreen mingle the boy's fierce passion with lascivious punishment. Mature young women like Jenny Woodward pay dearly for defying their master, whose masked servant also prints the marks of slavery on Lesley Hollingsworth, following *Captive II*. The untrained and the self-assured alike learn to shiver, as they lie waiting, under the caress of the eyes behind the mask.

Available now

Captive V: The Soundproof Dream
by Richard Manton

Beauty lies in bondage everywhere in the tropical island of Cheluna. Joanne, a 19-year old rebel, is sent to detention on Krater Island where obedience and discipline occupy the secret hours of night. Like the dark beauty Shirley Wood and blond shopgirl Maggie Turnbull, Jo is subjected to unending punishment. When her Krater Island training is complete, Jo's fate is Metron, the palace home of the strange Colonel Mantrique.

❧ TITLES IN THE SHADOW LANE SERIES ❧ FROM BLUE MOON BOOKS

Available now

SHADOW LANE

In a small New England village, four spirited young women explore the romance of discipline with their lovers. Laura's husband is handsome but terribly strict, leaving her no choice but to rebel. Damaris is a very bad girl until detective Flagg takes her in hand. Susan simultaneously begins her freshman year at college and her odyssey in the scene with two charming older men. Marguerite can't decide whether to remain dreamily submissive or become a goddess.

————————

Available now

SHADOW LANE II
Return to Random Point

All Susan Ross ever wanted was a handsome and masterful lover who would turn her over his knee now and then without trying to control her life. She ends up with three of them in this second installment of the ongoing chronicle of romantic discipline, set in a village on Cape Cod.

————————

Available now

SHADOW LANE III
The Romance of Discipline

Mischievous Susan Ross, now at Vassar, continues to exasperate Anthony Newton, while pursuing other dominant men. Heroically proportioned Michael Flagg proves capable but bossy, while handsome Marcus Gower has one too many demands. Dominating her girlfriend Diana brings Susan unexpected satisfaction, but playing top is work and so she turns her submissive over to the boys. Susan then inspires her adoring servant Dennis to revolt against his own submissive nature and turn his young mistress over his knee.

SHADOW LANE IV
The Chronicles of Random Point

Ever since the fifties, spanking has been practiced for the pleasure of adults in Random Point. The present era finds Hugo Sands at the center of its scene. Formerly a stern and imperious dom, his persistent love for Laura has all but civilized him. But instead of enchanting his favorite submissive, Hugo's sudden tameness has the opposite effect on Laura, who breaks every rule of their relationship to get him to behave like the strict martinet she once knew and loved. Meanwhile ivy league brat Susan Ross selects Sherman Cooper as the proper dominant to give her naughty friend Diana Stratton to and all the girls of Random Point conspire to rescue a delightful submissive from a cruel master.

SHADOW LANE V
The Spanking Persuasion

When Patricia's addiction to luxury necessitates a rescue from Hugo Sands, repayment is exacted in the form of discipline from one of the world's most implacable masters. Carter compels Aurora to give up her professional B&D lifestyle, not wholly through the use of a hairbrush. Marguerite takes a no-nonsense young husband, with predictable results. Sloan finds the girl of his dreams is more like the brat of his nightmares. Portia pushes Monty quite beyond control in trying to prove he's a switch. The stories are interconnected and share a theme: bad girls get spanked!